I0545925

OUTSIDE THE WALLS OF INTRAMUROS

Wilfredo Garrido

Gondola Books
2008

Copyright © 2008 by Wilfredo Garrido

Front Cover: *"Battle of Quingua, April 23, 1899"*
Back Cover: *"Battle of Manila Bay, May 1, 1898"*
Source: U.S. Library of Congress

ISBN-10: 971-941622X
ISBN-13: 978-9719416227

All Rights Reserved.

This book is available at Amazon.com.

Gondola Books

2517 Herrera Tower, Rufino cor. Valero Streets
Salcedo Village, Makati City, Philippines 1227
Telephone (632) 8920896; Fax (632) 8920890

To General Antonio Luna,
"Success is a series of failures."

AUTHOR'S NOTE

"Outside the Walls of Intramuros" is the last of a series of three novels about three different topics that I published within the year. They were written in the past 20 years, but it is only recently that I have gained the liberty to share the same with the public.

The other novels in the series are entitled *"The Trail of the Chop-Chop Lady"* and *"Wild Roosters."*

All the books are available at Amazon.com.

1 October 2008.

WMG

Contents

Part One   **The Walled City**

Part Two   **The Insurrection**

PART ONE

The Walled City

"If old Dewey had just sailed away when he smashed the Spanish fleet, what a lot of trouble he would have saved us."

- *President William McKinley*

1

MANILA BAY

Everybody was eager to see the sea that day. The mood was light among the troops who were looking forward to the prospect of seeing the great white ships appear over the horizon. Everybody was upbeat, except, that is, Joaquin Calderon. He had braved the cold and the fog at the first break of sunlight to climb up a hill toward a promontory overlooking Manila Bay, only to run against a logjam of fallen trees knocked down by a recent typhoon. He was huffing and puffing as he struggled to keep up with his abler comrades who swept past him with reckless exuberance, kicking a cascade of stones and dirt that made the slope slippery for the laggards like him bringing up the rear. It was as if they were being prodded on by the horsewhip of a *Guardia Civil*, a fairly common experience that had incited a few of the men into joining this ragtag band. It didn't help that his teenage daughter Estrella was snickering astride a carabao as it carried her effortlessly up the slope. He was heavy. He was tired. And he had to make it to the edge of the cliff overlooking the sea or else all his exertions would be for naught, as he would miss seeing the opening shots of the struggle ahead that would end in his deliverance.

The spells of lassitude that punctuated the pace of life in the colony were going the way of the midsummer heat, replaced by the urgency of war preparations spurred by rumors of the coming of a Yankee navy.

At first, all he could see from the top of the promontory was the fog shrouding the waters over Manila Bay, streaked by the blur of diving sea eagles which patrolled the skies. When the fog eventually dissipated with the wind and the heat, his younger companions cheered as the dots over the horizon suddenly materialized into a column of ships. They waved and shouted and marveled at the puffs of smoke ejected by the distant ships, followed a few seconds later by the rolling thunder of gunfire which scattered the eagles away even as it shook the men watching on the cliff to the bones. They were all agog in jubilation over prayers answered and promises fulfilled.

Amidst all the bedlam, Joaquin could barely see the action through his pince-nez. "Give me my telescope, Caloy," he said.

"I left it in the cart."

"My *larga vista*?"

"Yes." Carlos shrugged at his older brother.

"What do you mean you left it in the cart? All this climbing and hiking, what's all this for – if you didn't bring me the telescope?"

"Over here, papa, you can see them clearly from here," his teenage daughter called out from her vantage point on a rocky ledge. "Look, papa, the warships are firing!" she added excitedly.

"With your eyepiece, I thought you didn't need the *larga vista*," said his brother Carlos.

Joaquin pocketed his pince-nez which he used only for reading but not seeing distant objects such as the warships that had stolen into the bay firing away at their targets. "*Dios mio*, didn't I tell you to bring my telescope? I had it all packed and ready this morning!"

"Don't be grouchy, papa. Come over here and enjoy the sight!" piped up Estrella above the cheers of the wiry men who followed the action with rapt attention from the cliff.

The young men waved their straw hats or shook their Mauser rifles in the air as they watched the unfolding battle, *"Mabuhay!"* they cheered after each volley. *"Mabuhay!"*

"I can't see anything," Joaquin complained. He looked different from the others. He was older, heftier, paler of complexion, and better dressed. The pince-nez which sat on his sun dial of a nose added to his distinguished looks. Although he carried not even a sidearm, it was clear that he was an officer of sorts to this ragtag band.

"That's because you're not wearing your eye-piece. Put on your monocle," said his brother.

"No, I still can't see that far!"

It was a most frustrating day for Joaquin. Somebody forgot to bring his telescope.

———————

The sun sets on Manila Bay at 5:30 p.m. during the summer month of May. In the days before the revolution put an end to normalcy inside the now-besieged city, the sunset was a welcome sight to civil servants not only because it ushered the cool winds but also because it marked the end of a working day spent in blissful indolence inside the colonial offices of the Walled City. It tolled the coming of the angelus and the start of vespers for the monks cloistered inside the walls of San Agustin church. In the fathomless dark that descended on this distant corner of the Spanish Empire after sundown, nothing flickered on the serene waters of the bay but the reflection of the lamplights of fishing boats, occasional *lanchas* and the flames of torches on the perimeter of the citadel, Fort Santiago.

In the wee hours of the morning of May 1, 1898 a squadron of warships stole into the waters of Manila Bay under cover of darkness. In the pitch-black night made darker by coal smoke, the flotilla steamed deeper into the bay in a convoy, guided only by the light on the stern of each ship which in the fog was visible only to the lagging vessel when it threatened to ram into another. Manila Bay's sheltered waters, although idyllic in normal times, was heavily guarded by fortified islets and ironclads belonging to the king of Spain. At the mouth of the bay were the islets of Corregidor, El Fraile and Caballo, each holding a battery of muzzle-loading cannons manned by Spanish sentinels. Deep in the bay off the Spanish naval base of Sangley Point, a dozen men-of-war loitered with anchors aweigh, lying in wait for the expected entry of the enemy. The time was midnight.

The flagship at the head of the column bore the heraldry of the United States of America consisting of stars and bars nailed to the prow. It was freshly painted with a camouflage of gray over the original color of white to disguise its crossing of the South China Sea. The flagship appeared eerily silent as it churned its way through the waves; gunners hunkered down behind shields, quietly eyeing the darkness for tell-tale lights.

Deep inside the hull, several decks below, there was a welter of activity. Blackened men were shoveling coal into a double row of furnaces, metal chambers glowing red hot with what seemed like lava. They were crew members tending to the engines of the flagship to keep it steaming at a steady clip toward the enemy. They worked without let-up scooping mounds of coal with shovels which they ladled into the mouths of the furnaces. Wrapped around the furnaces were webs of pipes connected to boiler tanks, whence the power that propelled the ship originated. Through the network of pipes ran steaming water, squirted at high temperatures to send turbines spinning and the twin screws whirling in the water. This chamber deep in the bowels abaft the ship was called the Black Room, and the sailors condemned to toil near the furnaces, "stokers." Heating the boilers was the toughest job in the warship and the least appreciated in battle.

The heat was infernal, the noise manic. When a stoker

reached the end of his endurance, he would step back to the middle of the aisle, between the rows of furnaces, where a shipmate poured water on his head to cool him. The bath soon got scalding as the water which pooled at his feet simmered to a boil on the heated iron floor, tenderizing his soles white. Like the slaves of ancient times who paddled Roman galleys into battle while shackled to oars, the stokers labored without complaint. They were red-blooded patriots. They might as well have been boiling Indians in a cistern. Hell, they wanted to settle old grudges against the Spaniards. Instead of skimping on their coal, the men threw heaps of it into the fire, heating the boilers into a storm and stewing themselves in the process.

Up on deck, all was well and cool. A man with a white moustache was looking out of the bridge of the leading vessel, the cruiser and flagship *Olympia*. Scanning the bay from his commanding view, the 61-year old man failed to detect any light on the islets of Caballo and El Fraile. It simply meant that the Spaniards manning the cannons on the sentinel islands had been forewarned of his coming. There were lighthouses on the islets to guide non-belligerent vessels into the bay but now their flames had been snuffed out. Neither could the old man see the torches of Filipino insurgents surrounding Manila, led by Gen. Emilio Aguinaldo whom he had earlier contacted in Hong Kong, sanctuary of Filipino exiles, to stir up trouble in the enemy's rear. No, at this hour, he couldn't even see the waters. He was a near-sighted old commodore, and the lenses of his binoculars were so badly ground that they were useless beyond a certain distance. A little hard of hearing (the result of exposure to gunfire in the Civil War which was aggravated by a recent target practice in the high seas), he had been dispatched to these unwanted islands so others could reap glory behind his back. For the more ambitious admirals of the U.S. Navy jostled for assignments in the Caribbean where a war was raging against the Spaniards centered on the island of Cuba which was under blockade by the Atlantic Squadron. That was where the action was. Covered closely by the tabloid press, every action in the Caribbean, no matter how trivial, was played up to fan the war fever back home. *Olympia*'s skipper was plying little known waters half-way around the globe. He wore on his epaulets the insignia of his rank: two anchors and one star. Ironically, he was the one who made waves. In less than a week, the shoulder straps would boast of two more stars each and he would be known throughout the world as a naval hero, Admiral George Dewey.

His flagship *Olympia* would acquire fleeting fame, too. To admiring congressmen it was a battleship; to his sailors the Flying Dutchman. In reality it was a second class cruiser, 340 feet in length and a lean 5,870 tons in weight, hardly suitable for the honors due a flagship of the Asiatic Squadron of the United States Navy. Although not the best in the American fleet, *Olympia's* armaments and equipment were the envy of declining naval powers such as Spain. It had two conning towers and twin screws to drive her at full steam. For weaponry, *Olympia* had two revolving turrets which each housed a pair of eight-inch cannons called breechloaders. Of late design, they loaded shells at the "breech" or butt of the cannon in contrast to the "muzzle-loaders" of ancient vintage which awaited the intruders inside the bay. In addition to its main armaments, the deck of the ship bristled with 40 other assorted guns, from five-inch quick-firing cannons to old reliable Gatling guns. The Yankees had reason to be confident.

To defend itself against similar guns of the enemy, the *Olympia* had matted its deck with steel plate, shielded its smaller guns, and wrapped its hull with a tough cellulose belt 33 inches thick. All of which didn't make the ship indestructible by any means; for a properly aimed shell would almost certainly punch a hole through a target. Launched in San Francisco in 1892, it was only six years old and thus better fit for battle than its commander.

The United States was then a rising power, having survived a cataclysmic Civil War intact and won the West from the Indians to enjoy full security on both sides of the continent. Itching for glory overseas, it was now eyeing the regal scalp of Spain and raring to take its place as a world power, somewhat in the manner of Great Britain, which rose to pree-minence at the expense of the Invincible Armada of Spanish King Philip II. The Pacific Fleet of Alfonso XIII which De-wey's Asiatic Squadron hoped to engage was not invincible. Obsolescence and the wear and tear of patrolling the colonies of an overstretched empire had caught up with it. But America could always trumpet to itself and the world, courtesy of the jingoistic newspapers of William Randolph Hearst, that the engagement was the greatest naval battle ever fought.

Nosing its way into the darkness of the bay, the *Olympia* led the six other ships into battle, all told the inferior half of the U.S. Navy which had deployed its best warships close to home. Meanwhile, the better half of the navy, the Atlantic Squadron, was sitting still in the waters off Santiago Bay, Cu-ba, blockading the bay but never daring to go in as Dewey was casually doing. Absent a storm that had greatly helped the British against King Philip's fleet, Dewey looked as if he were sailing mindlessly to his doom.

Having slipped into the bay at midnight, the fleet would soon find itself surrounded by hostile guns. Guarding the mouth of the bay were the sentinel islands of Corregidor, El Fraile and Caballo which sealed off westward flight to the South China Sea. Towards the east on the mainland shore loomed the walled city of Intramuros, the 16th-century citadel around which Manila had grown, its forts bristling with can-nons. To the south awaited the Spanish naval base at Sangley Point where Admiral Patricio Montojo had guns at the ready, both onshore and on board ships. Dewey was sailing towards certain death. But being old and at a dead-end in his career, he had no ambition left save to die in battle at sea. He was not even an admiral yet being only a commodore at age 61. Now, by doing what his counterparts in the Caribbean were ada-mantly refusing to do, he unwittingly thrust himself to the li-melight that he painstakingly shunned.

As the fleet skirted the islets guarding the mouth of the bay, a change in the ambient air told Dewey that he had arrived at his destination. The gale-force winds that had whipped the convoy during its crossing from Hong Kong had died down calming the waters. The anchor chains stopped scraping the bow. Water lilies and other flotsam extruded by the estuary of the Pasig River brushed past the hull of the flagship then drifted away unseen. Amidst the tranquility of the bay the throb of the ship's engines rose a bit louder.

The rest of the fleet consisted of the cruisers *Baltimore, Raleigh* and *Boston,* the gunboats *Concord* and *Petrel,* and the revenue cutter *McCulloch* – all built in American shipyards. The *Baltimore* (launched in Philadelphia in 1888) was more powerful than the flagship in one respect, having six turrets, each containing twin giant cannons to *Olympia's* two. The others were *Olympia's* inferior in every respect and seemed certain to end up as hulks in the bottom of the bay, given the Spaniard's superior defensive position.

Historians harp on the claim that Dewey entered Manila Bay "undetected." This was not the case at all. Events in the Caribbean had forewarned Spain's far-flung colony that the Yankees were coming. Spanish Admiral Patricio Montojo knew that war had become inevitable after the sinking of the battleship *Maine* off Havana, Cuba, a disaster blamed by the American tabloid press on Spain. Montojo had doubled the guards posted on the isles dotting the mouth of the bay and sent patrols to the South China Sea to look for enemy warships that informants in Hong Kong had espied being fitted for war. Just before midnight when Dewey's convoy slipped into the bay, a flare launched from the isle of El Fraile momentarily lit up the skies before sputtering out on the surface of the waters. Immediately thereafter, the battery on the islet opened fire.

The crisis was on. Dewey had to act. His squadron of seven ships was trapped like a school of fish that had blundered into a fish pen. Standing on the conning tower's lookout deck, Dewey did not even budge, his being hard of hearing no doubt beguiling him into complacency. His hair had turned white for lack of battles to fight since his first brush with death in the Mississippi River during the Civil War, and he wasn't about to pass up this last chance for glory. He rubbed his spectacles so that he could see the muzzle flashes through his binoculars but they were gone like will-o'-the-wisp.

Meanwhile, sprays of water rained on the deck, kicked up by the cannon fire that targeted the squadron but fell short on the waters harmlessly. The anchor clanked again. The ladders and ropes on the conning tower dangled, and chains clattered on the deck as the ship pitched to changed course. Dewey entangled himself on the sling of his binoculars. Okay, he had lost the advantage of surprise and the Spaniards were firing at him blindly in the dark. He was good at dodging fire.

There was a stir among the gunners on the deck who had been waiting tensely for the first shot. They were anxious as they had yet to prove their mettle under fire. A good display of pluck by the commander would inspire them into heroic deeds, but Dewey didn't even bother to stir them into action by delivering a fire-eating speech, or some other eloquent gesture, in the manner of Horatio Nelson. Among *Olympia's* crew, not a few thought that Dewey was a wavering, doddering, lackluster commander.

So thought Gunnery Sergeant Barton Bailey, 19, a native of Virginia, who counted himself among the less fortunate sailors pressed into service in the Pacific. Loath to die in an obscure conflict, he'd much rather be fighting in the Cuban front where scores of Yankees were reaping glory for their country. He considered himself especially unlucky to have been shanghaied to serve aboard *Olympia,* a second-class cruiser commanded by a sixtyish commodore who had spent the greater part of his career deskbound, skippering papers through offices. Old Dewey, he wasn't in Manila Bay to earn medals or reap honors. He was merely following orders from Washington like an obedient postman. No, glory was the last thing in his mind. The old numskull had no ambition left but to die wrapped in a sheet.

Bailey had just ended a three-hour shift shoveling coal into the furnaces of *Olympia's* Black Room and as he gasped for breath, his air passages rasped with coal dust which hung thick in the musty air below deck. What a way to avenge the *Maine*, my ass. He'd rather drown than be cooked alive in the infernal heat of the Black Room. His callused hands and par-boiled feet were numb as blood seemed to have deserted his extremities. Reassigned to the main deck to reinforce the gun-nery crew, he breathed a sigh of relief as the cool wind blew through the slit in the turret. Now, the wind carried the sound of gunfire from the distance. Huddled inside a bunker of steel, he knew he was in combat because a stray shrapnel pelted the turret and he could spot flashes through the slit, followed by a rumbling noise. My God, he was being fired at by the Spa-niards!

"The old man Dewey, he's worked us middling hard for hours. What's he gonna do now?" Bailey asked his partner.

"The old man's holding his fire. You know, he can't see much and is a little hard of hearing," his partner answered.

"Them *dagos* (as the Spaniards were called by vulgar Yankees) are shooting us from somewhere nearby! There must be islands out there in the fog. What's goin' on, Wolf?"

"Right, Bart. Shore battery. He won't fire until he has the enemy fleet in plain sight because that's the way it goes in naval battle, ships fight close quarter. Haven't you heard of Trafalgar or Salamis, Bart? This battle here is going to be no different," explained his partner, Wolfgang Messner, son of German immigrants.

"You think the old man knows what he's doing, Wolf?"

"Just sit tight, partner. He's ready. We're at battle sta-tions. But we ain't firing our guns anytime soon because na-vies don't fight in the dark. Never happened before and it's not gonna happen now."

"Wolf, I hope this doesn't get any worse than what you

read in them books."

"They just lobbed a few shells. The rest was the wind playing tricks on your ears."

"There's another! What are we waiting for? The old man's waiting till he sees the white in their eyes?"

The ship shook as if it had run aground on a sandbar.

"Ha-ha! Cannonballs," laughed Wolf. "They're just bouncing off like duds. If that's all they have, then we have won this fight. It's gonna be like shooting fish in the barrel, Gatling!"

But not quite. What they heard were actually pieces of their ship's superstructure falling on the deck and the roof of the turret with a clatter. They sustained a hit on the starboard side. Within the confines of the steel turret the sound resonated as if they were inside the belfry of a cathedral.

Bailey was itching to fire the *Olympia's* big guns. Little did he know that by the end of the day, he'd have fired not one or two shells but almost an entire magazine's worth in the time it took to sink the enemy fleet. But in the pre-dawn darkness, there was no telling how the *Olympia's* eight-inch guns would fare in a pitch battle. For like most of its crew, *Olympia* had yet to see action twenty years on after its launch. The flagship's main guns could glow red-hot after a dozen volleys or worse, crack under explosive pressure. These pre-combat jitters Barton Bailey now put aside. Being a patriot, a red-blooded Yankee to the core, he was willing to go through any trial to avenge the *Maine* and the 263 sailors that went down with her. Bailey's father would have recoiled at being called a Yankee for the family traced its roots south of the Mason-Dixon Line. But one generation after the Civil War the sons of the North and South stood as one again. They were all Yankees now.

Most ordinary Americans belonging to the generation who won and settled the West, as well as their descendants, were seekers of glory. Greatness was the ambition of every American whose fathers founded a nation on a wilderness belonging to the Indians. All aspired to some measure of success as a frontiersman, a lumberjack, an Indian hunter, or a plain old sailor like Barton Bailey. They were a patriotic, even chauvinistic, lot. And woe to the enemy who stood in the way! It's as if having tried to slaughter one another during the Civil War, and constrained to reconcile afterwards, they were waiting for a victim on which to vent their excess of belligerence. The American Indians were the first to suffer at the hands of a reunited and resurgent nation. And now, the sinking of the Maine with the loss of all hands presented a gung-ho generation with a worthy adversary upon whom to visit their wrath. If only he had a captain with more charisma than Dewey, that doddering numskull, he would even lay down his life just to get even with them dagos.

"My father lost an arm fighting them Injuns attacking Fort Belknap," Bailey told his partner as they waited and steeled themselves for the battle ahead. "He killed a hundred of them and they made him a hero back home in Virginia. Perhaps, Wolf, if we manage to sink just one Spanish ship, we'll also be wined and dined and paraded like heroes back home."

"I'm interested in no medals or commendations. I just want to get home in one piece, Bart," said Wolfgang. "But sinking some Spanish ships would give the folks back home something to cheer about. And keep my Daddy's printing press busy back home in New York."

As if on cue, they heard a volley of outgoing blasts that sounded shriller such as coming from smaller caliber guns. The gunfire issued from the other Yankee vessels trailing the *Olympia,* and Bailey itched at the prospect of firing the flagship's big guns.

"Hear that, Wolf? Looks like our gunboats are now in action! It should be our turn next. The old man's finally spunked up!" Bailey exclaimed.

But the order to fire was not forthcoming just yet.

"What are we waiting for, Wolf? Why are we sitting on our asses?"

20

"Easy, mate. Stop hollerin'. We've just begun to fight," said Wolfgang, mimicking some early American hero.

Bailey was getting impatient that Dewey had yet to bring their big guns to bear on the enemy. They had been discovered by the Spanish lookouts on El Fraile, and that pretty much took care of stealth. But Dewey didn't respond with overwhelming force. Instead, he ordered that the smaller guns of his lesser vessels return fire. That didn't seem to intimidate the enemy, or so Bailey thought. "This crazy, lowdown business..."

Wolfgang Messner was no veteran but he was learned beyond his years. Bailey's insatiable curiosity made him a perfect foil for Wolfgang who had an opinion on almost every subject in the world. He read everything he laid his hands on, including bits of newspaper and the Bible, and most especially books that dealt with sailing and naval warfare. Although he had little formal education beyond grammar school, he stood heads and shoulders above his comrades when it came to erudition. This earned him the moniker "scholar" among his shipmates.

Like his shipmates, Wolfgang Messner was far from awed by the unheroic exterior displayed by Commodore Dewey. But unlike the rest, he gave the old man credit for subtlety of actions that escaped the eye of the ordinary sailor. He was probably the only one among the crew members who had some inkling about what the captain was up to or who they were up against. The nervousness that assailed Barton Bailey was due to plain ignorance about their mission and the inscrutable naval tactics of their captain.

"Doggone it, Wolf. I never thought we'd actually be fighting a battle at sea. Three years in the Navy, and closest I've gone to war was when we rammed a Chinese junk in Hong Kong," remarked Bailey.

"Wait till the sun is up and we will be engaging the Spaniard in the greatest battle since Trafalgar," assured Wolfgang.

"How come you know it all, Wolf? Whereabouts do you learn these things?"

"I've been reading maps of the Philippine Islands. Here's what I think the old man's up to: he's sneakin' us into the middle of Manila Bay, where their shore guns can't hit us." Wolf drew a crescent in the air and planting his forefinger at its center continued: "He's gonna lure the Spanish navy out of their base to the middle of the bay and there engage them in battle. That way they don't get the advantage of their land guns."

"You really think Dewey can do that?"

"Have more faith in him, Gatling!" Wolf scolded Bailey, calling him by his nickname. "He's no doddering captain lost at sea. He's smart, I tell ya. Didn't you notice how he drew our convoy into a fine battle line during our drill in the high seas just by running up the colored pennants? He's got good admiral's instincts in his blood."

The two sailors talked mostly beyond the earshot of their officers and gunnery mates. They were members of a crew of eight officers and men that manned one of *Olympia's* two main gun turrets sporting twin eight-inch guns. The turrets consisted of two floors, the lower floor for the gunners and the upper for the officers, the latter being the cockpit bulging out to the air where officers jotted calculations on three chairs bolted to the floor.

Bailey's station as a gunner was a raised platform hard by the breeches of the twin eight-inch guns. Keeping him supplied with ammunition were three other sailors stationed on the deck two rungs below him. They manned the elevator which lifted the shells to the gun deck from deep within the hull as well as the conveyors which delivered the shells directly to the gun's open breeches. Packed with gigantic moving parts – gears, pulleys, racks, belts, pistons – not to mention explosives, the turret was a place more dangerous than any steel foundry in America.

Bailey had rehearsed his part of the operation during the

fleet's exercises conducted in the high seas a day after they left Hong Kong. The drill using live ammunition had gone well. Heretofore, they had trained mostly by simulation using hand signals without actually firing a shot. The live exercises had the added benefit of blowing away years' accumulation of rust and grime inside the gun barrels. Bailey relished his role in the gunnery crew. He was in charge of manually screwing shut the plug or "breechblock" of a loaded gun before firing away. The latter was accomplished either by knocking a hammer or switching a battery that burned the shell's primer with a bolt of electricity. He looked at himself as the triggerman.

He was only one cog in the gear. His teammates had their works cut out for them. The officers had to pick the target and hold it in their sights. With the aid of a "stadimeter" or range-finder, the officers in the cockpit calculated distance and trajectory with pen and paper and sliding rulers, all the while shouting instructions to Wolfgang, either to raise or dip the guns and whither to swivel the turret. Wolfgang, who was stationed beneath the massive guns, would accordingly manhandle a giant lever to raise or lower the guns. To keep the guns pointing in the direction of the target, he cranked a capstan which turned a series of interlocking gears like a giant clock's, thereby multiplying his muscle power mechanically.

Meanwhile, three sailors operated the elevator, a crude contrivance consisting of cables and pulleys, which fetched the shells each weighing hundreds of pounds from the magazine chamber below deck. They would then roll each shell into a trough that conveyed the shell into the open butt of either of the twin cannons. Only then could Bailey make the final move that sent a projectile hurtling inexorably towards the target. The rest was physics.

———————————

When Dewey returned fire at the Spanish lookouts on

the islet El Fraile who had discovered their intrusion into the bay, he did so using the small caliber guns of his rearmost ships rather than *Olympia's* big guns. He was not about to betray the strength of his fleet this early. The order to fire was relayed from ship to ship by Morse code, transmitted by means of flashes of light down the length of the convoy all the way to the cruiser *Boston* and the baggage carrier *McCulloch,* which brought up the rear. Both ships bombarded the islet with their six- and four-inch guns, a half-hearted response to the Spanish salvo, which served only to discharge the rust in their bores. The designated ships then ceased firing abruptly when the battery on the islet turned silent.

Commodore Dewey was pulling his punches. But he was also serving notice on Admiral Patricio Montojo, head of the Spanish Pacific squadron, that he had sprung the Spanish trap at the mouth of Manila Bay – or had he? It was obviously the strategy of the Spaniards to draw the American fleet into the bay, where they could be bombarded at leisure by a ring of guns arrayed on the islets and on the mainland. A bit like shooting fish in a barrel.

The brief exchange at the mouth of the bay occurred at midnight, too early to open a full-fledged battle. Thereafter, a five-hour silence ensued disturbed only by the chugging of engines and random cannon fire of undetermined origins. From the mouth of the bay to the shore of Manila was a distance of only 21 miles. Yet it would take Dewey all of five hours to cross the bay. For Dewey, steaming at 21 knots, chose to chart a roundabout course around the expanse of the bay. He was waiting for daybreak before closing in on his quarry. Yes, he had made the mistake of slipping into the bay too early. Accordingly, he idled in the darkness for hours surrounded by hostile guns.

At the southeastern tip of the bay waited the Spanish fleet, arrayed around Sangley Point, a base situated on a slender peninsula that jutted like a pier from the mainland, some seven south of Manila as the crow flies. Montojo didn't have to go hunting for the Yankee navy. All he had to do was wait for the darkness to lift, then bomb the hapless flotilla into flotsam under the full glare of the morning light. How many Dutch and Chinese ships had floundered in that bay after daring to challenge the Spanish hold on the islands? History will repeat itself at sunrise.

As he whiled away the dawn in the middle of Manila Bay, Dewey gave the base a wide berth, veering to the northernmost cove off Bataan, a preserve of jungle and mangrove swamps which posed no threat to his ships. There he spent the dead hours contemplating the foolhardiness of his timing, then he leisurely skirted the length of the coast until he came almost within reach of the shore batteries of Sangley Point. How could he have come in too soon? Simple calculation in the high seas should have told him to keep out of the bay till two o'clock in the morning at the earliest.

Dewey was Dewey. Recklessness had been part of his youth. As a navy lieutenant wearing a full crop of black hair and whiskers, he had steered a steamboat into Port Hudson upstream the Mississippi in the teeth of Confederate gunfire. His boat finally went aground on a sandbar and was blasted to smithereens like a sitting duck. In the end, he had to jump overboard ignominiously to save his hide. Now, a commodore, with white hair, white moustache and no whiskers, he was doing exactly the same thing. Dewey would never learn.

The darkness was lifting with the approach of sunrise. Dewey could no longer retreat to the high seas because the sentinel isles at the mouth of the bay, having been alerted, would gleefully blast his ships the moment he came within range again. Come broad daylight, all guns around Manila Bay – those in the base, in the Walled City, in the sentinel isles – would begin blowing up the stupid Yankees who were good only at piloting paddle-wheeled steamboats.

Montojo was not necessarily superior in weaponry such that he should be brimming with confidence. His fleet was made up of fourteen aging ships, some of them wooden sail

25

ships a little better than the galleons of yore, rigged up to carry cannons in their cargo holds. Montojo's fleet consisted of seven cruisers *(Reina Cristina, Don Juan de Austria, Castilla, Isla de Cuba, Isla de Luzon, Don Antonio de Ulloa, and Velasco);* five gunboats *(Márquez de Duero, General Lezo, El Correo, Quiros, Villalobos);* and two torpedo boats of antediluvian origins.

Most powerful among them was the *Reina Cristina,* launched in Ferrol in 1887, the flagship cruiser of the Spanish admiral. She had eight Hontorio breechloaders ranging in size from six inches to two inches, eleven rapid-fire cannons, two machineguns and five torpedo tubes. In a battle of maneuvers against the Americans in the high seas, however, the aging warship didn't stand a chance, having only a single screw and a top speed of 17 knots.

Notable for its defenselessness was the wooden cruiser *Castilla* – launched in Cadiz in 1881 – a "bark-rigged" galleon with masts and furled sails, weighed down by Krupp guns on 3,300 tons of flammable timber. Her rudder had been damaged in a collision with a Chinese sampan the year before, and she had to be towed into battle by another sampan, a measure of Montojo's war readiness.

But the Spanish admiral was not dependent on his fleet alone for firepower. He had other gun emplacements positioned around the arsenal buildings of his naval base in Cavite. Moreover, he was not planning to fight a battle of maneuver; not when he had the enemy trapped in the bay ready to be bombed at leisure. If the Yankees didn't beat a hasty retreat under the cover of darkness, Montojo had a gaggle of sitting ducks before him by daybreak.

History had unfairly condemned him for sleeping on his job that fateful May Day. In fact, he had been busy making preparations for days if not weeks prior to the expected Yankee attack. His decisions regarding the deployment of his guns were informed by careful calculations with which any admiral worth his salt would concur, given the hand he was dealt. So conscientious was he that the week before the battle, he had sent patrols out to the South China Sea to look for Yankee warships hiding in the outer coves of the colony. Admiral Patricio Montojo was not quite so reckless as Dewey.

For five anxious hours after El Fraile fired its cannons, both protagonists kept vigil on each other in the pre-dawn darkness. With no other means of finding a ship than by the naked eye, the Spaniards and the Americans could only wait for sunrise. Dewey cooled his hulls in the safety of the Bataan anchorage at the northern expanse of the bay, whence they steamed towards Sangley Point at a carefully measured speed, hoping to reach the Spanish battle lines at daybreak.

Petty Officers Bailey and Messner saw the lightening sky through the gaps in the turret's gun ports. As the turret swiveled to train its guns landward in a precautionary move, they beheld the tropical landscape gliding past them. Palm trees dotted the sea shore while behind it beckoned forested hills, its lush foliage tinged in various shades of green. Farther inland, mountains loomed blue in the distance. The expanse of greenery was broken only by settlements of brown huts, with wisps of white smoke from cooking fires floating above thatched roofs. Occasionally, outrigger canoes, some with sails, rode the waves toward the horizon.

Midway through their foray south, they sailed past Manila. What caught Bailey's attention in particular was Intramuros, otherwise called the Walled City. Built on the estuary of the Pasig River, it had giant walls of masonry, seemingly erected as solid ramparts along the full length of the shore. Even from afar they looked formidable and, as he would soon discover, on some parts thicker than they were tall. Accretions of grass bristled on their tops and in their niches, growing as tenaciously as barnacles and giving the walls a forbidding appearance. Between breaches on the wall facing the sea jutted ancient muzzle-loading cannons taken off sail ships to reinforce the fort, their bores naturally camouflaged by the grass that had grown on the stones over the centuries.

Bailey could make out the domes of Spanish churches rising above the walls, ribbed orbs that resembled helmets of old conquistadors. Crosses topped some of the domes like covers of chalices lending the view the august aura of a medieval Vatican. Guarding the mouth of the river was a 16th-century fort, occupying one whole corner of the Walled City, on whose emplacements Bailey, on a reconnaissance mission, would later find modern Krupp artillery transported from Germany at great cost. This was Fort Santiago, the citadel of the old city of Manila.

"Remember the *Maine,*" Bailey uttered the battle cry to himself, awed by the prospect of battle in so strange a land. No one in the turret responded.

He was on his toes. Since four o'clock in the morning, he had quaffed three cups of coffee served by the stokers.

"So, this is the Philippines," he remarked.

"Yeah, a colony of Spain. That's Manila yonder there, the capital and that's where the Spaniards rule the islands from their palaces behind the walls," Wolfgang Messner commented.

"What's a colony, Wolf?"

"That's a territory owned by your country but not part of it, I mean a distant land where you send soldiers and governors to civilize the folks and find spices and goods that you can't produce back home. Sort of like Alaska, but not Alaska," Wolf tried to explain.

"Alaska but not Alaska?"

"Because Alaska ain't got no people, you muggins. A colony's got people to governize."

Bailey thought he understood. "You've got Spaniards all over Cuba and South America and the Pacific and hereabouts. They sure got colonies aplenty."

"They got there ahead of everybody. They had ships sailing the oceans when we were just a poor colony of England. They got the good places before others got into the game."

Wolfgang Messner had more to say about the islands, gathered from a history book on Manila which he had obtained during a port call in Hong Kong, plus six-month old newspapers from the ship's library. A blond German-Jew who gained his love of reading by helping his father run a printing press, he related to his comrades that Manila was founded by conquistador Miguel Lopez de Legazpi in 1571, that it was built upon the remains of a Muslim village at the mouth of the Pasig River, that it started out as a small fort surrounded by palisades just like the Cavalry outposts in Indian territory, that it was easily overrun by a Chinese pirate name Lim Ah-Hong in 1574 who blew into town with 5,500 men in 62 war junks, that the Spaniards were forced to build stone walls between 1600 and 1648 to withstand subsequent assaults by the Dutch who held a rival colony in the nearby Spice Islands. In 1762, the British, aiming to widen the Seven Years' War to Spain's colonies, took the Walled City after a siege and occupied the capital for 18 months. They had to give up their conquest for lack of native support, returning the islands to another century of Spanish rule. The name Intramuros referred to the walled citadel within Manila, taken from the phrase "there are Moors inside" which echoed the city's Islamic beginnings.

The place Bailey and Messner were seeing for the first time was many times larger than the original outpost built by the conquistador Legazpi, its population having spilled over the walls to form communities straddling both banks of the Pasig River and along the shores of Manila Bay. The part of the city inside the walls resembled Europe with its domed buildings, a similarity that stopped where the shantytowns stood in the suburbs.

The history lesson was interrupted when they heard their officer bark the command: "Go to battle stations!" It was now five o'clock in the morning.

At exactly 5:06 a.m., the *Olympia* shuddered as the shockwaves of an underwater explosion traveled through her hull, jolting Bailey out of his reverie. The Spaniards had strung out rudimentary mines offshore to fence off the city and their naval yard at Sangley Point. The Yankees, expecting to draw fire from shore batteries since enemy ships were nowhere in sight, were totally caught by surprise by the muffled explosion underwater. The moment of reckoning was now at hand.

Bailey was nervous but also pumped up at the prospect of seeing action for the first time. He was about to fight an enemy whom he knew only from the yellow tabloids, the villain of the Caribbean, the treacherous dago who sank the *Maine*. This was how Daddy must have felt when he defended Fort Belknap from a horde of Indians, he mused.

At 5:15, the batteries inside the Walled City opened fire on Manila Bay's latest intruder, its Latin gunners determined to see the Yankees go the way of the Dutch and the British. The sea around the attacking fleet threw geysers into the air, splashing seawater upon the targeted ships' deck and superstructure.

Dewey's fleet sustained no damage from the defenders' initial salvo. A direct hit would have been of no effect as the cannonballs would have simply glanced off the armored plating of his warships. Naval warfare was on the cusp of a revolution that saw sail ships giving way to ironclads. The winds of change had not quite reached the faraway outpost of Intramuros which clung to its muzzle-loading cannons dating back to the age of the galleons. Having smooth bores – without the interior grooves that made projectiles spin in the air – the guns of Intramuros spat out balls of iron, which traveled erratically in the wind without any steadying spin, all in the manner of boulders thrown off Roman catapults.

In contrast, *Olympia's* cannons were forged of a far more advanced technology dating back only to the middle of the 19th century. Made of hardened steel, the typical American cannon had two openings, one at the bore and the other at its butt or breech, where the shell was loaded – hence, the term "breech-loading." Airtight, it fired an elongated cylindrical shell that fit snugly inside the bore, a much better shape than a spherical cannonball, thereby sealing tightly the firing chamber. Its bore was grooved on the inside or "rifled," thus making the shell screw its way through the wind and travel straight. Most notably, its destructive force was not derived from the raw kinetic power alone of a hurtling cannonball. It carried a warhead filled with gunpowder which exploded upon impact, hurling shrapnel and mayhem around.

The cannonading by the defenders of Intramuros continued for about fifteen minutes. It had no effect on the invading fleet, except to shake the nerves of its raw sailors.

Then, surprisingly, if belatedly, the Spaniards unveiled its modern artillery – Krupp, Hontorio and Ordoñez breech-loaders mounted on specially built emplacements inside Fort Santiago. They were just as good as the American guns. Acquired during the last ten years by farsighted Spanish governors who feared the encroachment of rival Western powers into the Pacific, the guns posed the greatest danger to the attacking American fleet. The defenders unleashed a probing barrage then paused to see how the Yankees were taking the fire. Would the Yankees turn around and run?

Commodore Dewey did run. But he didn't turn tail. He ran the gauntlet without even returning fire, steaming past the Walled City towards the Spanish fleet which awaited them off the peninsula of Sangley Point.

The column of Yankee warships was now fully exposed in the light of day, billowing coal smoke in the air as it snaked past Manila southbound. The gray paint that Dewey applied on his ships in Hong Kong was useless as a camouflage; on the contrary, it only advertised their belligerent intentions. But in spite of the steady bombardment, the fleet set off no retaliatory fire, to the considerable anxiety of the sailors aboard. Maybe the old man, who was hard of hearing, was unaware of the intensity of the cannonading? Or, doggone it, maybe he'd fallen asleep on the bridge! Bailey thought irreverently.

Dewey had set his sights elsewhere. His mission was not to besiege a city. His mission was to destroy the enemy fleet at its stronghold in Sangley Point, which was way down south. So he left the Walled City in his wake, its defenders' hostility unrequited, sailing on to his rendezvous with history.

Dewey had so arranged his ships such that the weaker craft was deployed in the middle. At the head was his flagship *Olympia,* with the cruisers *Baltimore* and *Raleigh* following close behind; staking the middle were the gunboats *Concord* and *Petrel*; bringing up the rear was the old cruiser *Boston.* Wholly left out of the convoy was the baggage carrier *McCulloch,* which was ordered to wallow in the middle of the bay, just out of range of the guns on Corregidor Island.

In the days before the radio, a fleet commander communicated with his captains by means of colored pennants strung up the mast of his flagship. Thus did Dewey issue his orders, by means of a sequence of color-coded flags strung along a halyard and hoisted up the mast by a signalman, to be interpreted by his captains peering through telescopes. So it was on that fateful May Day morning in Manila Bay that the masts of the Yankee fleet bloomed with colorful pennants, their festive appearance belying the menacing messages they contained. To *Olympia's* skipper, Captain Charles Gridley, who was standing by his side, Dewey communicated in a cool monotonous voice, almost languorous for its matter-of-fact tone, totally out of tune with so dramatic a moment.

At 5:41 a.m., Dewey joined the Battle of Manila Bay with the eminently practical words: *"You may fire when you're ready, Gridley."*

———————

2

A MESSAGE IN AN OIL LAMP

The outcome of the naval battle that the Filipino rebels witnessed from a bluff overlooking Manila Bay was a signal event in the lives of brothers Joaquin and Carlos Calderon. The defeat of the Spaniards was their gain, and they gained in a way that promoted the prestige of the family in the revolutionary movement Katipunan. The collapse of the Spanish authority meant the rise of the Filipino elite to positions of power. Joaquin Calderon was a physician educated in Spain. Carlos, his younger brother, was a munitions expert. Both had become indispensable to the revolutionary leader General Emilio Aguinaldo. Joaquin was valued for the information he had about the goings-on behind the forbidden walls of Intramuros, the seat of the Spanish government, which Joaquin was privileged to enter by virtue of his social status. On the other hand, the skilled artisan but unschooled Carlos owned a foundry that made everything from cannons to bolos, implements that were in short supply in General Aguinaldo's army.

It was Joaquin who stood taller in the eyes of the revolutionary leader, for he belonged to the ranks of the Filipino aristocracy – the ilustrados – to which one gained entry not by birth but by education. Even Joaquin's half-brother Carlos was an outsider to his class. Not even Aguinaldo (who was schooled only in the rudiments of reading and writing in a barrio school at Cavite Viejo) could qualify as an ilustrado, not having any of Joaquin's sterling credentials: preparatory school at the Ateneo de Manila, a medical degree at the Universidad de Santo Tomas, a diploma in surgery in Spain. Many an ilustrado who was thrust to positions of power by fate or merit would influence the course of Filipino history, for better or for worse.

High as they were in the totem pole of Filipino society, the brothers recognized that there was one Filipino who stood heads and shoulders above all else: Jose Rizal. Doctor, linguist, novelist, poet, naturalist, sportsman and, above all, patriot, Rizal was a shining example of what a Filipino could achieve, given only a fair shake in life. Unfortunately, he was also dead, executed by the Spaniards two years earlier on suspicion of aiding a rebellion that had broken out in August 1896.

The rise of the Calderon brothers began during a failed attempt to spring Jose Rizal from his jail cell in Fort Santiago, in early December 1896. It was a plan born of the imperative to fill a gaping hole in the patriotic movement: its lack of an inspirational figure. The 27-year old Aguinaldo, a mayor of the small town of Kawit (a.k.a. Cavite Viejo), was too young and too raw to be a credible voice of revolution. He needed a well-educated propagandist to air the objectives of the revolution. Aware of his own shortcomings, Aguinaldo could think of no better mouthpiece than Dr. Jose Rizal, the foremost intellectual of his time, a physician, polymath, and the author of two anti-clerical novels *Noli Mi Tangere* and *El Filibusterismo*.

Ironically, Rizal had been jailed the previous month on charges of leading the rebellion, which was patently untrue, because Rizal was a pacifist who favored reform over revolution. Aguinaldo was the rebel leader guilty of the sins the Spaniards ascribed to Rizal. The rebels hatched a plan to rescue Rizal from a certain death sentence, the fate that awaited those charged with treason, but because of its dangerous nature, they had to get Rizal's concurrence to the audacious plan. Reaching him was a problem because he was being held incommu-

34

nicado. Accordingly, they decided to smuggle a message to him by means of an oil lamp with a secret chamber. The rebel leader turned to Joaquin who in turn chose Carlos to make the lamp to order. In his Manila foundry, Carlos crafted an oil lamp made of brass with a false bottom so ingenious that not even the most eagle-eyed Guardia Civíl would find it as anything other than an ordinary appliance. It took the skilled craftsman two days to fashion the double-hulled *lamparilla*, the hidden compartment inside being extremely difficult to render waterproof absent a perfect soldering method. So he made a pouch out of fine linen fabric which he soaked in varnish and left to dry to render it impermeable. The final product, shaped like a horned Viking helmet, was openly delivered to Jose Rizal by one of his sisters. The lamp passed muster after a cursory inspection.

The rescue plan was doomed from the start. Rizal flatly rejected the daring mission and promptly relayed his veto to a rebel sympathizer who visited him a day after he received the message. He told him that the plan was militarily impossible, if not suicidal, since it would take an army with siege weapons to break through the walls of Intramuros, not to mention the well-guarded inner wall of Fort Santiago, before the rescuers could reach his cell. Dozens of brave lives would be lost in an operation guaranteed to fail. In the end, the rescue operation became a death watch.

The revolution seemed to be losing steam, five months on after its outbreak. Although the Spaniards had been driven out of key towns, particularly from the rebels' bailiwicks in Southern Tagalog, the colonial regime still held the capital Manila in their stranglehold. As if to prove their point, the Spaniards were now poised to execute their leading light with impunity. While the revolutionary movement had its fair share of ilustrado intellectuals among its ranks, none of them shone as brightly as Jose Rizal. It was precisely for the purpose of dispiriting the movement that the regime railroaded his execution. For in the absence of a philosopher who could articulate the objectives of a revolution in the manner of a Jefferson, the Spaniards hoped that the rebellion would go the way of previous revolts – starting with a violent flare-up then flickering out slowly from infighting or lack of resources.

The Katipunan revolutionaries could only wring their hands in frustration as the colonial government swiftly moved against Rizal. In a summary trial lasting a little over two weeks, Rizal was charged, convicted and sentenced to die by musketry. His counsel *de oficio* Lt. Taviel de Andrade appealed the verdict to the governor-general Camilo de Polavieja who affirmed the death sentence, then still undeterred, to the Archbishop who turned down his entreaty with a yawn and a wave of a bejeweled hand. The Church was not about to lift a finger to save a professed mason who in earlier times would have burned at the stake. When the sentence became final on December 28, 1896, the Guardia Civil was given only 48 hours to carry out the execution.

Now, it appeared that the rebellion was quickly to lose steam with the loss of its reluctant muse. But then, a strange twist of fate turned tragedy into triumph. When it became obvious that his death was a foregone conclusion, Rizal did something that was to guarantee that his voice would be heard beyond his grave: he slipped word that he wanted to send a message to the Filipino people. Knowing Rizal, a man of letters and a romantic figure, Joaquin was sure that the message was bound to be electrifying. Nothing could move a man to eloquence more than the imminence of death, especially in the case of a poet in the same situation, challenged to compose his own epitaph. Rizal's plan was relayed to Aguinaldo by his sister Trinidad who did not dare act on the request alone lest so momentous a message be compromised. How to smuggle the message out of his cell?

Joaquin answered the poser: Why, in the same manner the abortive rescue plan was smuggled inside! And so, the doctor became the instrument by which Rizal's last words would survive his death. He was tasked to escort Rizal's sisters to visit their brother on the eve of his execution.

In the meantime, news of the death sentence was heating up passions in the countryside. The Spanish overlords had so estranged themselves from the people they had colonized for 300 years that they failed to appreciate the effect that the verdict wrought on the collective psyche of a repressed populace. To friars and magistrates who lorded it over the colony, condemning an eloquent patriot to death was the swiftest way to smother the revolution in its cradle. To the ordinary people who saw in Rizal the embodiment of their own aspirations for their children, it was murder most foul. Not well-versed in the writings of Rizal, if they could read at all, they could identify with him as fellow victims of a despotic regime.

To the common man, the utter injustice of Jose Rizal's fate can be evoked by a brief recitation of his background: He brought himself up by sheer talent and ambition from the ranks of the underclass to the heights of privilege. He was born of a middle class family living in the small farming community of Calamba, Laguna, with no pedigree, no patrons, no positions in the colonial government; the beneficiary of no special dispensations from the clergy. He attended the Ateneo de Manila and the Universidad de Santo Tomas literally by the sweat of his parents' labor. The family had to sell parts of their landholdings to support his education in which he reaped honors after honors from a tender age. In an effort to raise a prodigy of a son to his full potential, the family invested a lifetime's savings to minister to his needs, at the expense of his ten siblings consisting of an older brother who was content to be a farmer and nine sisters who aspired to nothing more than a life lived in domestic tranquility. Scraping the bottom of their limited resources, the family managed to send him to Spain to become a doctor, an extraordinary accomplishment in a backward land where a man seldom set foot on another island in his lifetime. Shortly after coming home from Europe, he was arrested. At age 35, before he could realize the fullness of his promise, he was condemned to die for denouncing the oppression of his countrymen and for advocating their freedom and dignity. What an injustice! What a cruel blow to such an exemplary Filipino family!

Reduced to the scale of the ordinary, it was like having to raise a baby born of excellent health, nurturing it with mother's milk and porridge so he would grow up to be a strong farm boy, able to plow the field behind a carabao from dusk to dawn, only to have him killed by a neighborhood bully. Now, magnify that to the scale of a man who had achieved great things that would make an entire race proud, and one could begin to share the feeling of the rabble over the imminent execution of Jose Rizal.

In the late afternoon of December 29, 1896, the women in Rizal's life paid their last respects to their beloved one. The party consisted of his mother Teodora, sisters Lucia, Josefa, Trinidad, Maria and Narcisa, and his companion and lover Josephine. The womenfolk were escorted by Dr. Joaquin Calderon, his brother Carlos and a Jesuit priest. The doctor had the added role of seeing to it that Rizal was in good health so that, whatever happened on the morrow, the young man could not be said to have died of natural causes. Torches illuminated the way for the shadowy figures striding through the narrow hall of the prison which echoed with the footfalls of the women visitors shod with wooden clogs and the booted Spanish jail guards who preceded them. In nervous anticipation, Joaquin fumbled for the monocle which he kept in his breast pocket to make sure that he could later read whatever message Rizal wanted to deliver to his people – and to his annoyance, found it missing. With heart thumping and the mood in the air sodden with grief, he assumed as normal a countenance as he could muster, knowing that he was to act as the sisters' comforter and confidante and not least, the final interlocutor of the leading light of his generation.

What could the message contain? To Dr. Calderon, steeped in the ideas of Rizal as expressed in his novels *Noli Mi Tangere* and *El Filibusterismo*, it had to be a political essay in

38

the vein of the Communist Manifesto of Karl Marx with its ringing exhortation: "Workers of the world unite! You have nothing to lose but your chains. You have a world to gain." To the less lettered Aguinaldo, it had to be an unequivocal call to arms of the kind that the man had refused to endorse in life.

The Spanish jail keeper stopped by the metal door barring Rizal's jail cell and whipped out a sheaf of keys which clashed like a tambourine. His warden addressed the women: "Señoras, I give you an extra *quince minutos*, since this is your –" he paused, theatrically, "last visit."

Carlos, who tagged along behind the women ostensibly as a chaperone, fixed a gaze at the vaguely familiar officer's face in the dim light of the torch. Capitan Esteban Zaragoza! This was the man who had once hit him with a horse whip for no reason at all while astride a white stallion ambling along Escolta.

To the menfolk, Captain Zaragoza barked: "Take off your dirty sandals and shoes, the man keeps a clean room, I don't want him upset."

As if we didn't know, thought Joaquin, taking off not only his shoes but his European-made derby hat as well which he handed to the Spanish sentry rather impudently.

As they filed into the anteroom, ducking under a low brick arch, someone stirred in the main chamber and stood up to greet them. He was a short, medium-built figure, barely above five feet tall, unkempt, unwashed, with stubbles on his face but he exuded an air of serene authority as if he were convening a meeting in his office. Jose Rizal.

"Mother, how is father doing?" he asked.

"He wanted to come but his health wouldn't permit it."

"How are you, Sisa?" Rizal turned to one of his sisters.

"We've brought some books ... but..."

The sisters, provincial, naturally reticent, had none of the self-possession that came along with formal schooling. They tried to speak, but were incoherent as sobs and sniffles punctuated their speech. They beheld for the last time their illustrious brother, for whom they sacrificed so much and who in return made them ever so proud with his lofty achievements, now brought so low, in a way they never would have imagined in their worst nightmares. "Pepe...tomorrow, we can't bear to think of tomorrow...if only we could trade places with you...."

Rizal didn't want to dwell on his impending death. He hushed them up, and turning his attention to his other visitors brightened. "Hello, how are you, doctor?" Rizal spotted his colleague Joaquin. "Last time I saw you was in Madrid. Or was it Paris?"

Joaquin was flattered at being recognized by his fellow doctor who was his junior in age if not in station, and whom he preceded to Spain by six years. "It was, uh, um ... Manila."

"Oh, yes, at the printing shop of Del Pilar. Writing was simple business then. But no longer. That's why I'm in trouble." The prisoner was almost self-deprecating, incongruously courtly in his bearing as if oblivious of his fate. "Tell me, how are things outside? How are the people reacting to my case?"

"In Manila, in Cavite, people are talking of nothing else."

"I hope I didn't let them down. I made it clear to my colleagues in the Propaganda Movement that I was not for armed revolution, like what they are doing in Cuba. I'm after peaceful reforms. Reforms without bloodshed."

"Differences of opinion are now moot. We are all behind you now."

There was nothing wrong with his health, observed the doctor. The man was keen and vibrant as ever.

The women tried to engage Rizal in meaningful, if tearful, conversation. "Pepe, we brought along a priest."

Joaquin wondered what Rizal's reaction would be to the entrance of the priest who accompanied them, but who stayed in the shadows of the anteroom until bidden. From what he knew of Rizal, the caped figure might as well be the

Grim Reaper. Joaquin knew that Rizal, a professed atheist, had famously quarreled with the friars. But this one was a Jesuit who, being a proponent of progressive thought since the Age of Enlightenment, couldn't be lumped together with men of the cloth at large.

Rizal stopped the priest on his track. "Just a minute, father. *Un momento.* I'll be done with this first."

"Can you at least do this for mother?" said Trinidad. "Let him hear your confession?"

Rizal made for his desk that was illumined by the flickering light of a lamparilla. He blew out the light making the gloomy cell even darker. "Here, Trining" he addressed his sister by her diminutive, then in a whisper added: "I have something for you."

Joaquin watched intently as Rizal gave Trinidad the brass lamp which Carlos had ingeniously crafted to contain secret messages. Trinidad, who was privy to the lamp's secret contents, took the lamp proffered by her brother. She handled the lamp gingerly, as if it was a heavy burden she could scarcely bear, looking at her brother then at Joaquin with uncertainty. Joaquin took his cue. He quickly divested Trinidad of her precious gift, afraid that she might drop it thereby soaking the piece of paper hidden inside, rendering it unreadable.

"There is something inside," Rizal told his two co-conspirators in an undertone.

The following day, at 6:30 a.m., two columns of Guardia Civil riflemen marched out of Fort Santiago over a bridge across the moat that separated the Fort from the rest of Intramuros. Between the columns of soldiers was a man dressed in European fashion wearing a derby hat and a heavy woolen suit, his arms tied by the elbows behind his back, his feet shackled at the ankles. The procession was preceded by a band of drummers, who beat a funereal cadence, with which the shackled prisoner had difficulty keeping pace. Their destination was the grassy field of Bagumbayan located outside Intramuros a short distance from the foreshore of Manila Bay.

Brothers Joaquin and Carlos, standing at the far side of the field close to the shore, could scarcely see the short figure between the columns except for the pot-shaped derby hat bobbing up and down. But they knew that the condemned prisoner was none other than Jose Rizal. The event was devoid of the hysteria that attended executions of criminals in the past, with people crying out for blood and creating a hubbub. The crowd watched in stunned silence, except for a few Spanish ladies attired in hooped skirts and white parasols who having wandered onto the scene by accident stayed and watched in fascination, chattering among themselves.

The squads of soldiers were unhurried but watchful, marching to the pace of the drumbeats, uncertain of the reaction of the vast majority of the crowd composed of untrustworthy *indios*. Joaquin watched with a growing sense of foreboding as the prisoner took his last few steps toward a clear spot between two lampposts, where he would be stood up to be shot. Carlos Calderon gnashed his teeth at the cheery expressions of the Spanish ladies which were in stark contrast to the funereal mood of the rest of the crowd. He was mollified when one of the Spanish civilian officials bearing witness to the execution walked up to drive them away with a wave of his swagger stick.

Carlos was even more enraged to recognize the head of the contingent, Captain Esteban Zaragoza, the mustachioed Guardia Civil officer who was Rizal's jailer and who had once struck him with a horsewhip. *"Kuya,* do you see what I see?"

Joaquin was too focused on Rizal to notice anything else.

"Esteban Zaragoza."

"Uh-huh," grunted the doctor.

Having reached the place of execution, the Guardia Civil riflemen redeployed. One column broke away to picket the perimeter of the killing field. It was then that the now isolated prisoner was revealed for all to see. From his vantage point, Joaquin saw that Rizal was now clean-shaven and immaculately dressed recalling the beau who had held court before Filipino expatriates in European salons. The arms that once fenced ambidextrously with the foil were tied behind his back with hemp lashed at the elbows. Standing beside him was his lawyer Lt. Andrade who had defended his client with an excess of zeal that was unexpected of a court-appointed attorney. Also nearby stood two priests, who alternately looked up at the skies, then their prayer books, and then at their condemned ward who had long since strayed from the flock. They were Jesuits, Fr. Jose Villaclara and Fr. Estanislao March, who were specially chosen by Rizal to be part of his cortege, not having been tarred with the sins of the clergy whose vices Rizal had denounced in his books. Joaquin, who this time had brought his binoculars, peered at the condemned man in order to take the measure of the man at the brink of death. Rizal's eyes were steady but distant, being focused on the infinity of the hereafter, and he hardly seemed to notice the crowd gathered around him.

The drummers beat a final roll that eerily lapsed into silence, broken by the sound of shuffling of feet and the claps of rifles shifting position. The second column had split into several squads that formed a platoon in the foreground of the execution area. The first squad faced the prisoner being tasked to do the firing. The others, their backs to the firing squad, faced the crowd, rifles held at port, ready for any trouble.

Then Captain Zaragoza walked stiffly to Rizal who now stood alone and asked him a question, doubtless for his last words. Rizal shook his head. Unbeknownst to the Spaniard, his last words had already been written and at that very moment was in transit to the rebel headquarters at Kawit. Next, a friar approached and whispered in Rizal's ear ostensibly to ask if he was now ready to confess as he had steadfastly refused to do at his cell. (Historians offer conflicting accounts in this regard. Some claim that he confessed on the eve of his execution thereby reconciling himself with his faith, a version others criticize as a sop to sentimentalists who were uncomfortable with his Masonic background). Whatever did happen, Joaquin Calderon could say with the unimpeachable authority of an eyewitness to history that he never saw a Spanish friar, not even the friendly Jesuits, extract a confession from Rizal, a lá Joan of Arc, either in his jail cell on the eve of his execution, or in the grass field where he was shot. In the latter instance, he saw that Rizal merely shook his head in response to the friar's obvious query as he stood between the lamp posts.

As if to spite him for his last-minute show of defiance, Captain Zaragoza returned to his prisoner and holding him by the shoulders pivoted him around, so that Rizal's back was now turned toward the firing squad. Even ordinary criminals were allowed the dignity of facing their executioner. Not Jose Rizal. He was to be shot like a fleeing coward.

The Guardia Civil captain marched back to his position adjacent to the firing squad. For a moment he stood at attention, and then reached for his saber with a flourish, unsheathing the long blade with a clink heard over the bated breath of the crowd. *"Listos!"* At which command the firing squad cocked their Mauser rifles held at the ready. *"Apunten!"* They aimed. *"Fuego!"*

A burst of gunfire broke the stillness of the killing field, reverberating through the morning air, its shock wave impacting the crowd at their collective chest, who gasped as one as if they were the ones hit. The shots found their marks on different parts of Rizal's back which was drenched with a fountain of his blood. His hat flew into the air; his body was flung forward onto the dirt; blood and a tooth dislodged by the force of the impact sprayed out of one side of his mouth. Otherwise, his youthful profile was unmarked. The bound hands on his back unclenched and went pale as the life streamed out of his body.

It was said later that Rizal, to right the apparent humiliation of being shot in the back, turned around as he fell to face his executioners. But this was physically impossible as the sheer impact of a volley of shots hitting his back would have thrown him instantly forward, like being hit by a runaway locomotive. Moreover, being bound and shackled, he could not have steered his body in any direction, as a person with free use of his limbs conceivably can. In any case, Joaquin could declare ex-cathedra, being an eyewitness, that Rizal was tossed unceremoniously forward. But this was by no means an undignified death as Rizal comported himself calmly to the very end.

There was silence. Joaquin was too stunned to react. The eerie stillness was punctured by shouts of *"Viva España!"* mostly coming from the soldiers.

The Spaniards thought they had silenced once and for all a dangerous man. But, no. History was more fickle than fiction, with surprising twists and turns.

From the grave, Jose Rizal was able to speak his last words. At the town of Kawit, before a huddled crowd of partisans, Joaquin Calderon arrived breathless from Bagumbayan and broke open the base of the double-hulled lamp with one swipe of the blunt edge of a bolo and out spilled a wad of paper carefully folded inside a pouch of white fabric that glistened with oil. The unmistakable sinuous handwriting of Jose Rizal in quill pen came into view as the paper was carefully extricated from its protective wrap and gently unfolded as if by the surgeon's hands. Was it a last will? Was it a political essay – a defense of his moderate views in the Propaganda Movement? No, as it turned out, it was nothing more inflammatory than a poem, an ode to his land and a young life cut down in full bloom.

"It's a poem," observed the doctor. "In the Spanish language."

"Basahin mo," said Aguinaldo in his native Tagalog, leaning over his shoulder, propped by a sword. "Read it. Nobody here can translate Spanish better than you."

"It has no title but the first line ..." the doctor first read it to himself as he worked to translate it in his head, "says it all: *'Adiós patria adorada...'*"

"Aloud!" barked Aguinaldo, thumping his sword.

In front of a crowd composed almost totally of the rabble, Dr. Calderon read out the first lines of a 14-stanza poem which bore no title but which was later to be known the world over as *Mi Último Adiós*. My Last Farewell.

> *Adiós, Patria adorada, región del sol querida,*
> *Perla del Mar de oriente, ¡nuestro perdido Edén!*
> *A darte voy alegre la triste mustia vida,*
> *Y fuera más brillante, más fresca, más florida,*
> *También por ti la diera, la diera por tu bien.*

The sonorous poem was to inspire a revolution in a way that Jose Rizal would not have approved.

Calderon, at first, missed its political significance. He was carried away by the elegance of the poetry, expressive of all that was beautiful in the Spanish language and the Old World culture it embodied, in which he was raised and by which he was delivered from the ranks of the underclass to the society of the learned and privileged. As he observed the faces of the common people who listened in rapt silence at his rendition of the poem, Joaquin had no doubt about its power to inspire.

The body of Rizal was buried in an unmarked grave in a cemetery at Paco, without ceremony, without a coffin, just a cadaver in bloodstained clothing. At the time, even common criminals executed with the garrote were buried in plain wooden boxes, with a cursory prayer and perfunctory blessing from a Catholic priest. The firing squad leader, Captain Esteban Zaragoza, was in a hurry to get rid of the body lest it attract crowds. And so he unloaded the body from a cart wrapped in a sheet and, together with two soldiers, dumped the body into a pit and covered it with dirt and quickly left to pick up their routines of keeping the peace in the city.

———————————

46

The Calderon brothers' role in ferreting out Rizal's last words made them folk heroes back home and cemented their reputation as leaders of the patriotic movement. They gained the undying gratitude of Aguinaldo who was credited for masterminding the poem's retrieval. Aguinaldo was to be amply rewarded with an army of recruits who would heed his call to arms in due time.

The revolution of 1896 was launched simultaneously in two places, the north and south of Manila. In the north, a proletarian by the name of Andres Bonifacio organized a patriotic secret society in the slums of Tondo, and when their existence was betrayed to the Spaniards, they armed themselves and skirmished with the Spaniards in the hinterland of Caloocan. In the south, the gentleman farmer Aguinaldo who was then the mayor of Kawit armed his constituency of farmers with bolos and a few Mauser rifles as he began the popular task of evicting the friars from their vast landholdings that had reduced entire towns into serfdom. Both leaders called their movement the Katipunan and claimed to draw their inspiration from Rizal. But while Bonifacio met only with defeat at the hands of the Spanish Army, Aguinaldo took town after town following a strategy of attacking Guardia Civil detachments and sacking the convents of the friars, appropriating the captured firearms for his growing army, and distributing the looted grain to the locals afterwards. His audacity gained him more recruits or otherwise inspired the populace to revolt. In just over a year of fighting, Aguinaldo found himself at the outskirts of Manila. He was surprised that a 300-year old regime would crumble so quickly.

Then, the uprising literally ran into a brick wall when it could not breach the walls of Intramuros which had protected Manila over the centuries against attacks by pirates and rival European navies. Even the cannons that they had seized from the provinces could not make a dent on the capital's defenses.

Meanwhile, the Spaniards now found themselves outnumbered, the rebel army having swelled in size and still growing with each passing day, even as the regime's pool of local conscripts had long since dried up and reinforcements from Spain reduced to a trickle over which their embattled compatriots in Cuba had prior claim. The fire of revolution that started out in Latin America was now eating at the Spanish empire's eastern fringes.

In the ensuing stalemate the Spaniards sued for peace, enticing Aguinaldo to sign on to an armistice. Bribed to the tune of $850,000 in gold in exchange for laying down their arms, Aguinaldo agreed to go into exile in Hong Kong on Christmas Day of 1897 pursuant to a settlement called the Pact of Biak Na Bato (broken stone). But the pact proved true to its name because both parties broke it as soon as they awoke from their bad dreams. While in the British colony, Aguinaldo used his money (only half of which was paid) not to enrich himself as the Spaniards had hoped, but to buy more and better weapons for his standing army.

It was in this context that Commodore George Dewey waded into the troubled waters of Manila Bay.

———————————

3

THE SUN SETS ON AN EMPIRE

Commodore Dewey saw that the enemy was dead in the water to his port side as his Asiatic Squadron approached Sangley Point. The Spanish fleet was arrayed in the manner of a picket line, consisting of two parallel rows running the length of the coast, with an outer row made up of the cruisers and other ships of the line and an inner row hewing close to the shore composed of the smaller gunboats. The outer line extended from Sangley Point naval base in the south to the port of Manila seven miles north. The inner line was concentrated midway in the waters of Bacoor Bay, ready to rush to the aid of either end of the battle formation. Dewey could distinguish the flagship *Reina Cristina* by its gaudy ensign fluttering on top of its mast signaling the presence on board of Admiral Patricio Montojo. He thereafter made the ensign his reference point as he bore down on the backbone of the enemy line off Sangley Point. At a distance of 5,000 yards, his Asiatic Squadron had crested the horizon and lowered down on the enemy, an intimidating chain of silhouettes closing in fast at flank speed.

Montojo's handicap was not so much the age of his fleet as his defeatist siege mentality that belonged to a surrounded army. He chose to fight at a standstill, using his ships as stationary platforms from which to lob shells at a moving target. Waiting to be attacked, he thought that his position off the shoreline of Manila Bay was impregnable, being within the protective range of his land artillery. Like the walled city of Intramuros and the sentinel isles, his fleet never moved except, that is, to sink.

Going into Manila Bay, Dewey did not know the exact state of the Spanish navy. Although he had been informed that Montojo's capital ships were at least 20 years old, he was not aware that the rest of the Spanish fleet were refurbished merchant ships, stolid ironclads, which could not have survived a trip across the ocean. Nor did he care. They might not be able to maneuver in the open sea but they had guns, and a well-aimed volley could sink one of his own.

Dewey had spent a lifetime waiting for a break. Nearly half a century of peacetime had reduced his career to that of a merchant marine captain prowling well-traveled sea lanes. Now was the chance to redeem the humiliation that had scarred him early in his career when he was forced to abandon his crippled boat in the shadow of Fort Hudson under weathering Confederate fire. Sixty-one, but not necessarily the wiser, he was grabbing at this last chance for naval glory.

It was 5:41 in the morning when Dewey languidly asked his skipper Captain Gridley to fire "when you're ready."

His men sprang to action. Inside his turret, a revolving bunker of steel, gunner Barton Bailey went flailing after the humongous mechanisms that were the tools of his trade. Hours of fidgeting had stirred up the volcanic energy inside him to the point of explosion. Now that he could unleash it, he vented his pent-up energy with alacrity to punish the dagos whose treacherous compatriots sank the *Maine*. Well, now buster, it's your turn... he thought.

"Open the breeches. Load!" ordered Lt. James Cocker who was in command of *Olympia's* forward turret.

A tubular shell weighing 250 pounds slid down a trough and aligned itself with the butt of one eight-inch cannon. Bailey unscrewed the thick cap sealing the butt (the breechblock), swung it open around the hinge as he would a furnace door in the boiler room and stepped out of the way. A steam-powered piston plunger shoved the shell into the open butt. Packed densely with explosives, the shell was too heavy to be man-handled like the cannonball of yore. He screwed the breech-block back into place to seal the butt, locking the shell in the firing chamber. He repeated the process with the other gun of the pair, then waited for Wolfgang to train the guns at a target. This Wolfgang did by cranking a wheel under the twin barrels – click, click, click – ratcheting up the twin guns notch by notch to keep the target within range. He then pulled at a lever that engaged the steam-powered machinery which swiveled the whole turret around almost a full circle, alternately push-ing or pulling at the lever as one would with a joystick, to keep the twin guns pointed at the target whichever way it moved.

Lt. Cocker coordinated the team effort assisted by two junior officers. From the cockpit on the upper floor of the tur-ret, separated from the battery by a platform of iron grating and rails, he could see the target and also be heard by his crew. He kept the target in his sights by means of a stadimeter, his telescopic gun sight, an optical rangefinder that looked and worked like a surveyor's transit. He dictated aloud the stadi-meter reading, from which one junior officer calculated the trajectory, while the other fixed the target's bearing with the aid of a compass. Their calculations were then translated forthwith into intelligible orders shouted to the gunners.

When Captain Gridley gave the order to fire at will Lt. Cocker already had a target in his sights. He was amazed to see that the enemy fleet was dead in the water, like sitting ducks! It made his job a lot easier because he only had to com-pensate for the *Olympia's* speed. This is going to be a turkey shoot, he thought to himself. Cocker trained his sights on the ship with the tallest mast upon which flew a distinctive stan-dard, resplendent even in the distance. He didn't know for sure then that he was aiming at the *Reina Cristina*, Admiral Monto-jo's flagship. His reading indicated that the range to the target was 5,030 yards. "Steady...Hold! Fire!" His commands were repeated by his subordinates who bellowed out the orders in turn to the waiting gunners below. "FIRE!"

Bailey switched on a battery which set off a primer detonating the shell in the firing chamber. The blast sent the turret ringing. The floor quaked, the platform creaked, and the gun barrel recoiled with the force of battering rams breaking down a castle's gate. Then, Bailey fired the other gun. Once again it thundered inside the steel bunker. His eardrums rang as though a pair of cymbals had caught his head in the middle. The vibration shook his skeleton like a tuning fork, making him feel as if his nails were flaking loose and his scalp sloughing off his skull. He shook his head. He couldn't cover his ears because his hands were busy. He could only flinch.

This was not a drill. During the exercises in the high seas while en route to Manila, he had fired only half-charges that went off somewhat feebly. Now, the shells he was firing were full-charges that exploded with unstinting force, lobbing their deadly projectiles at Spanish ships thousands of yards beyond. He could not say precisely where they were falling, because he couldn't see anything outside the turret.

After a pause that allowed the officers to pick which target to hit next, Bailey unscrewed the breechblocks of the twin guns in turn. Smoke billowed out of the open breeches, which coughed out a spent shell the size of a bucket. The warheads – huge bullets of steel designed to pierce armored hulls – were gone, lodged hopefully in the bowels of an unfortunate enemy ship. He allowed the empty shells to fall down to his feet and roll away, being too hot for him to handle.

No sooner had he collected his breath than another batch of shells began sliding down the trough, to be rammed mechanically into the twin guns' open breeches. Bailey quickly shut the guns' loaded butts screwing the breechblocks as far as they would go to obtain a tight seal like plugging a bottle with a piece of cork. "Fire!" A bolt of electricity ignited the primers detonating the charges one after the other to send another round of warheads hurtling towards the enemy fleet. Bailey fired his guns as quickly as they could be loaded and aimed. The automated parts worked well sparing him dangerous labor. But after six rounds, the guns became dangerously hot. He recoiled at the thought of touching the stubby rear of the smoldering guns as they reeked of burning metal.

"Gimme the flannel, Wolf!" he shouted to his friend.

"It ain't hot enough, touch it again."

"It's burning hot!"

"Here, take my cap." Wolf tossed him a grimy cap.

Bailey used the cap like a potholder, wrapping it around the wheel-like handle of the breechblock so he could twist it open without touching bare metal. "If this goes on, I'm afeard the shells will explode short of the water."

"Nah, they won't," assured Wolf. "We must keep firing until we're told to stop."

After firing six rounds on each barrel, Bailey felt utterly wasted and fagged out. He could hardly breathe inside the smoked-filled turret, thick with sooty gunpowder residue which coated even the lenses of the gun sights. The heat trapped in the turret recalled the infernal conditions of the boiler room. His eardrums threatened to rupture in the din. His teeth had been shaken loose too; at least that's how it felt inside his mouth.

The *Olympia* steamed past Sangley Point which lay toward the southernmost point of the Spanish fleet's picket line, then it wheeled around to make another pass at the stationary enemy fleet. Bailey sensed the ship's turnaround as Wolfgang swiveled the turret around so that the guns pointed towards their targets now located at *Olympia*'s starboard side. Soon after, the order to commence firing was given and Bailey resumed his gunner's duties. He was too focused on the demands of his job that he didn't keep tabs on the number of times *Olympia* wheeled around to make another pass at the enemy fleet.

Then, amidst a spray of sparks the battery-powered electrical firing mechanism of the eight-inch guns went awry.

Now, he had to resort to percussion primers. To Bailey's chagrin, he was no longer just pulling the trigger; he was going to do the hammering itself. The substitute primer had to be exploded manually, with a blow of a hammer, instead of being ignited by electric current supplied by the battery that was now dead. Bailey risked being blown apart as he worked the percussion primer by hand. I'd forgotten how to do this... I'll blow myself to kingdom come, or so he thought. They had not used percussion primers during target practice and Bailey had to trawl the depth of his memory for practical lessons that he had long forgotten as an apprentice. Now, he was real scared. But his troubles weren't over.

"The gas pads are swelling, Wolf!" he shouted to his partner as he inspected the gun's open butt after the latest round. "It's leakin' gas."

Gas leaking out of the firing chamber reduced the pressure within causing the warheads to fall short of the target. Some shells, loosened from accessory parts by rough handling, fizzled out altogether. He had to dislodge the worthless duds by inserting an iron rod into the butt and ramming them out of the bore. Heretofore, most of the shells that he handled went off without a hitch such that the ensuing recoils threatened to burst open the breech of his guns or loosen the barrels from its stand, but overheating was starting to stifle the battery.

The outgoing barrage of the eight-inch guns was by no means the only din of battle heard inside the turret. There was incoming fire, too. Shrapnel, grapeshot, and debris – pieces of *Olympia* torn off by hostile fire – rained intermittently on the turret. Once Bailey thought a cannonball had struck the turret because he heard a deafening clangor. It was only a matter of time before a lucky shot sent them underwater in the next hour to mingle with the fish.

There was romance in dying for one's own country but abstract patriotism was not the motivating force that drove him on during the battle. He had a job to do, and that was that. Whether it was an act of heroism was for others to say. It was no big deal. He was caught up in the maelstrom of activity, an operation of calculated mayhem in which one man performed a tiny bit of a gargantuan task in concert with hundreds of others and, in so doing, must perforce synchronize his movements with that of the rest of the team. All the time he loaded and fired the twin guns, others kept up with him calibrating the range, cranking wheels, shoveling coal or hoisting ammunition. There was a measure of compulsion to the whole effort that was opposed to the idea of heroism.

To mingle with the fish was his ultimate destiny because as a sailor he dreamed only of being buried one way. That is, to be wrapped in sailcloth like a Bedouin Arab, sewn up from head to foot, with the last stitch of the needle being through the nose, then sent sliding down a board into the sea, all in accordance with ancient maritime custom. That was how a sailor was supposed to meet his end, unless slain by the glorious fire of battle and never recovered at sea. But then, from the way things were going, he wondered if ever he would be sent to the bottom with any ceremony at all. If somebody had told him then that not one American sailor would die in action, or that all hands aboard the Yankee fleet would survive the course of the entire battle virtually unscathed, he wouldn't have believed it.

Meanwhile, other Yankee sailors performed their individual tasks with the reckless courage of the condemned, there being no chance of deserting their posts. Among the gunners, those manning the rapid-firing small caliber guns were particularly busy. The ammo handlers hoisted shells for the lesser guns through a manhole as though fetching water from a well. In the magazine chamber located below the waterline, other mates worked like gnomes in a subterranean mine doling out clusters of shells which they stacked on baskets and hoisted by hand to the gun deck.

They, too, like the stokers who manned the furnaces in the boiler room, didn't know what was going on. These unheralded wretches who worked below the waterline were the most vulnerable in case of a mishap. There were few means of egress from the bowels of a steamship that had little elbow room, being crowded by a tangle of pipes leading to the boilers and coal bunkers. Moreover, at the sound of general quarters the night before, all hatches were battened down with only the ventilation ducts remaining open. It was through the ventilation funnels that considerate shipmates stationed above deck, who had the hottest view of the fighting, shouted down details of the battle to keep their morale up. "One sunk! There's another burning!" These snippets were invariably met with cheers even as they cringed at the near-misses that splashed water on the hull, or swayed with motion sickness as the ship suddenly veered to change course, not to mention the pain of unrelenting labor that left them bone weary. But they took the beating through clenched teeth. Dying was hardly a fate worse than what they were going through now.

Unlike the crew of the five-inch guns who had a clear view of the battle through their gun ports, Bailey couldn't see what was going on. But he was one curious soul who couldn't stand the idea of being kept in the dark, firing his pair of eight-inch guns blindly. As far as his officers were concerned, he had no need to know what was going on outside the confines of the turret. But he wasn't a horse that wore blinkers at work either, allowing itself to be reined in or prodded on by whiplash. If only he could step out of the turret to watch the action with his own two eyes....

———————

Even to an ordinary sailor like Bailey who was by no means well-versed in the intricacies of naval tactics, it was obvious that Montojo's deployment of his fleet was a mistake because it made sitting ducks out of his ships instead of Dewey's. The Spanish were easier to hit. On the other hand, the Americans being mobile were elusive targets. Given that Montojo had so arranged his ships to stake out a small sector of the bay,

Dewey's attacking column had to approach the defender's picket line at an oblique angle closing in at 2,000 yards then wheeling away as far back as 5,600 yards so that its wake drew an elongated ellipse on the bay's surface, parallel to the defender's line. In other words, Dewey was running circles in front of, if not around, the Spanish fleet.

Admiral Montojo commanded the Spanish fleet aboard his flagship the *Reina Cristina* which sat in the middle of the picket line. Montojo cut a dashing figure on the bridge, arrayed in full-dress uniform adorned with colorful epaulets, braid, medals and other raiment befitting his rank as commander of the Spanish Pacific fleet. His flagship was no less conspicuous on account of its hulking presence and not least, the admiral's standard which fluttered atop the mast resplendent with the heraldry of Spain's royal navy and a magnet to Yankee shells.

During the first pass of Dewey's attacking column, with *Olympia* at the spearhead followed by the cruisers *Baltimore* and *Raleigh*, the opening salvo of the trio found its mark on the opposing fleet's flagship. The *Cristina* took a hit on her forecastle which housed her captain and navigation equipment. Another hit tore a chunk of timber from the mainmast, causing the structure to break and topple over the bridge with a crash. Still another shell from an eight-inch gun carted off the smokestack, scattering a trail of coal dirt across the deck. Collapsing walls, splintering planks, exploding shells massacred the crew manning the Hontorio rapid-fire cannon on the foredeck, greatly reducing the flagship's firepower. Hurtling pipes and shrapnel pelted the bridge where Montojo oversaw the battle, doggedly determined to defend the colony where the sun rose on the Spanish empire.

Notwithstanding the carnage, Montojo stood stretched to his full height, a white-haired figure with graying moustache – a spitting image of Dewey of whom he caught glimpses while peering through the smoke with his binoculars. Flying debris mortally wounded his skipper, Captain Cadarso, who continued to execute his commands with unflagging resolve to the very end. A piece of shrapnel tore into Lt. Jose Nuñez, the helmsman, who kept steering the wheel that had become slippery with his blood. "Nuñez took the wheel with coolness worthy of the greatest commendation, steering until the end of the fight," Montojo later reported to the king.

Montojo spiritedly fought back the attack of the lead American cruisers which by then were steaming away even as the gunboats *Petrel* and *Concord* in the middle of the column took up the slack raking the Spanish ships with small caliber fire from six-pounders and Gatling guns. "The Americans fired most rapidly," he wrote of the attack. "There came upon us numberless projectiles, as the three cruisers at the head of the line devoted themselves almost entirely to fight *Cristina*, my flagship." Montojo staggered back as all kinds of projectiles chewed up the wooden deck of his flagship and ripped to shreds the chain-link netting that screened the bridge as well as the rigging of the masts that remained standing. A direct hit dislodged the anchor which plumbed the water like a huge fishing hook dangling from its chain. Six-pound and three-pound shells raked the shields of his Hontorio breechloaders till they became useless. Through it all Montojo stood his ground on the bridge of his embattled flagship.

At 7:30 disaster struck when shells hit the vital parts of *Reina Cristina*. One shell burst crippled the steering mechanism of the ship when it tore into the rear assembly shearing off the rudder. "I ordered to steer by hand while the rudder was out of action," he reported to his superiors in Madrid. "In the meanwhile another shell exploded on the poop, and put out of action nine men." He also reported that a warhead penetrated *Cristina*'s sick bay riddling the wounded sailors who took refuge therein, hastening their death. At the end of the second hour of fighting a fusillade of shells ignited a fire in the ammunition room. "I had to flood the magazine when the cartridges were beginning to explode," he said.

In due time, the admiral gave the order to abandon

ship. But the proud Spaniard would not abandon his standard, a noble piece of heraldry adorned with fancy embroidery, which was partly to blame for drawing so many shells in his direction. The proud ensign no longer flew in the sky, he discovered. It was lying crumpled on the deck, still tied to the tip of the fallen mast. After ordering a wounded sailor to gather the symbol, he reluctantly disembarked to a waiting whaleboat and transferred his command to another ship.

Unwilling to concede defeat yet, Montojo clambered aboard *Isla de Cuba,* a doddering cruiser weighed down by dozens of spent Yankee warheads. "And with great sorrow, I hoisted my flag on the cruiser," he reported.

The one-sided contest had little to offer by way of affirmative lessons that would enrich naval tactics. Neither protagonist made complex maneuvers such as those undertaken by the opposing British and Spanish fleets at the Battle of Trafalgar where Admiral Nelson outwitted his rivals in so spectacular a fashion, bearing down in two columns against a cluster of Spanish and French vessels, which he proceeded to tear, disband, and eventually encircle. Dewey's passing maneuvers against a stationary enemy was an unavoidable move dictated by geographic necessity. What the Battle of Manila Bay did teach other captains was that one should never fight a naval battle at a standstill as did the hapless Montojo aboard the *Cristina,* who gathered his ships tightly around him like a mother goose protecting her brood, fending off aggression at the periphery.

Faced with an immobile enemy, Dewey merely passed the formation of Spanish ships as a mounted officer might review a company of troops standing at attention. His attacking column blasted the principal target *Cristina*, even as they took potshots at the other vessels coming in and going away. The wooden man-of-war *Castilla* (which was already a cripple before the battle even began), the *Don Antonio de Ulloa, Velasco, Isla de Luzon,* all inert cruisers trying to hold the line suffered the same fate as the *Cristina* for they presented themselves as targets of opportunity difficult to miss. The only Spanish vessels that broke ranks to give the Yankees a fight were the agile gunboats which kept darting out from behind their burning capital ships like wolves to harass the attackers.

Having reached a placid corner of Manila Bay in the first each pass, Dewey's squadron wheeled around to "counter-march," past the Spanish fleet for more of the same, this time headed in the opposite direction. In his second pass under the noses of the Spaniards, Dewey again reviewed the line, firing "twenty-one gun salutes" of live shells that sent down *El Correo, Villalobos,* and *Quiros* to the realm of Neptune. When Dewey passed the enemy flagship he found it already in flames, with ammunition exploding like firecrackers in its holds, and dragon breaths of flames shooting out of its portholes. He was surprised to see Montojo's ensign flying on the mast of another ship, barely visible through the smoke, but his trained eye recognized the vessel as a third-class cruiser weighing just over a thousand tons, discounting the tons of American warheads lodged in it.

Dewey decided to let his adversary off the hook, so that he may be able to view the completeness of his disaster, and courteously ordered Captain Gridley to point his guns in another direction, "if you don't mind."

The problem with the eight-inch guns that bedeviled the crew of *Olympia's* forward turret was life-threatening not only to Bailey but also to everyone else inside the turret. After protracted use, the butt of each gun expanded in the crucible from repeated explosions, wreaking havoc on its firing mechanism. When Bailey tried to screw the plug securely into the breech he was appalled to see that it fitted loosely and shook in its socket. The thread of the breechblock's screw barely mated with the grooves on the inside of the breech which had expanded on account of the heat generated by repeated firing. Pretty soon, Bailey feared the gun will explode in two places, at the muzzle and the butt!

That was not his only problem. "Hey, somebody get me a gas pad!"

"Stop hollerin' for goodness sake," answered Wolf, who went about his tasks uncomplainingly. "Just set your teeth hard and do your job, Bart," he added.

"Can't do my job without it."

The gas pad, which Bailey desperately needed, was an internal seal inside the breech that was vital to maintain pressure in the firing chamber. An airtight bag made of neoprene rubber, it was fitted inside two split rings shaped like horseshoes. When the gun recoiled the bag was squeezed and expanded laterally like a compressed balloon, pushing against the split rings, which pressed on the walls of the chamber, sealing it. In a sustained battle, the gas pad was eventually reduced to a pulp by the pounding of countless recoils and had to be replaced. This was the part of his duties that Bailey least liked because not only did his hands get burnt as he groped inside the smoldering firing chamber but his face also got singed by the leaking hot gases.

Bailey's problems with the guns caused him to redouble his efforts just to keep up with the rest of the crew. His shipmates in the turret and elsewhere on the ship soldiered on at their posts performing their respective tasks apparently without stint. Rest be damned! He could stop only if everybody else stopped, or else his comrades would cowhide him till he was black and blue. Eventually, the incessant firing took its toll not only on the crew but also on the guns they were manning. The twin guns began to balk, spewing out shells that only fizzled, forcing Bailey to ram their remnants out of the barrel with an iron rod. What a waste of energy for his bone-weary body. Sometimes he had to reload two or three times before a shell would go off. So he resorted to inspecting every shell before loading to make sure it wasn't a dud by seeing to it that its warhead was securely mated to its casing. As troubles piled up one after the other – e.g., shells misfiring, the gas pad frayed, the breeches swollen and leaking gas – it looked like the eight-inch guns were just about to go kaput. With the gun crew doing in three steps what formerly took one, the whole business broke down.

"Confound it, might as well stoke coal," complained Bailey.

"If you can't make it go off, Bart, leave it be," advised the giant German who had stripped down to his pants, baring a muscle-bound body awash in sweat.

"Let's not waste ammunition," concurred the mates handling the elevator. "Tell the lieutenant they don't go off no more."

"I don't want to sit on my ass while there's fighting outside, but, darn it, what's there to do?" lamented Bailey. "Where's the shavetail Cocker?"'

"He's up there with Cap'n Gridley," said Scott Preston, one of their crew mates.

"If you ask me, I would say cease firing and let the guns cool down," Bailey suggested. "I got a feeling they're about to blow up in our faces."

"Look for Cocker!" growled Wolf. "Before we blow ourselves up."

"I'll go get him," volunteered Scott Preston.

The misfires didn't go unnoticed on the bridge. Alerted by the breakdown in order below deck, Captain Gridley himself bounded down the ladder, followed by Lt. Cocker who had to slide down the hand rails.

"What's the problem?" Cocker asked aloud.

"The guns are misfiring, sir. The breechblock won't close. It's loose and a-leakin' gas," Bailey answered, pulling at the handle of a closed breechblock which appeared no longer air-tight.

"Begging the Lieutenant's pardon," Bailey continued, "perhaps if I just piss on it..."

The other gunners laughed.

"Sir, some shells are duds, aren't screwed tight," Scott Preston butted in. "The no-good stuff from the bottom of the stockpile."

Cocker and Gridley mulled the situation together. They confirmed the crew's findings. The skipper Gridley then ordered the crew to cease firing and leave the shooting to *Olympia*'s lesser guns. In a report he would later submit to the Navy Department, he wrote that: "The ammunition hoist was temporarily out of commission on account of blowing of the fuse... Had three misfires with battery of right gun... In renewing the fuses they were immediately blown out... shifted to percussion primers with good results. In left gun one shell jammed, after which used half-full and half-reduced charge... Many shells became detached from the cases on loading and had to be rammed out from the muzzle."

Bailey welcomed the unscheduled respite for he was completely fagged out and worn to a frazzle. What the hell, he had been firing the guns for more than an hour without letup and he deserved a break like everybody else in his team if only to catch a breath of fresh air. He was looking forward to being able to decamp the hellish confines of the turret without being taken to task for deserting his post. As soon as the order to stand down was given, everybody in the turret made a beeline for the exit.

As he stepped out of the turret, Bailey's eyes were drawn towards the navigation bridge above the conning tower where Dewey was directing the battle. He was rewarded with the sight of the old captain peering through his binoculars at the enemy fleet all the while mouthing inaudible instructions to the signalman at his side. The signalman was stringing ensigns and color-coded pennants with a halyard and then hoisting them up the foremast, which was how Dewey communicated his orders to the rest of the fleet. Oh, he was a beaut! His white hair and moustache as well as his white uniform – for he was probably the only man aboard *Olympia* who remained completely clothed – were smudged with soot. He stood on steady sea legs on the open deck in front of the wheelhouse protected only by a netting of wire mesh and chain-link, which was stretched taut over his head by cables to form a canopy. The sight of him standing nonchalant made Bailey mighty proud. Whatever doubts he harbored about old man's guts – expressed by the names the crew called him such as "numskull" and "dunderhead" – vanished in an instant. He had mistaken Dewey's reserve for timidity.

"He's just like Stonewall Jackson, standing his ground!"

Then, eager to see what damage they had wrought on the enemy ships, Bailey went to the port side railing to join a gaggle of his shipmates who had preceded him there. They were a sweaty and dirty bunch, in various states of undress, and to a man relieved to be out in the open air and able to see with their own eyes the unfolding battle. What they beheld did not disappoint. The Spanish fleet had absorbed severe punishment. It was in disarray with ships burning, belly-up, mangled, wallowing low in the water, or all of the above. The wooden cruiser *Castilla* was now a funeral pyre. The flagship *Cristina* was a tangled mess of broken masts and rigging, her smoke stacks sheared off and the whole superstructure afire in several places. Only the bow jutting out of the water was what remained of the iron cruiser *Austria*.

"Lo and behold! We've tanned them, and tanned them good!" exulted Bailey, who punctuated his observation with a rebel yell: "Hip...hip...hooray!"

Thereupon, his shipmates joined in with: "Hooray for Ole Dewey!"

The *Olympia* was then cruising the placid waters in the middle of Manila Bay beyond the range of enemy guns but with a clear view of the battle. Dewey had withdrawn *Olympia* from the frontline signaling the fleet that he was breaking off for "breakfast." It was the only naval battle in history where a captain had the luxury of time to serve breakfast in the middle of the fighting. At 7:35 in the morning, while Bailey was taking a breather behind his faltering guns, a strange call came from Lt. Cocker. "Okay, boys, take a break, food will be served." To all the ships in the line, the signal sent up by the colored pennants spelled somewhat thus: "Withdraw and take breakfast." What, eat breakfast while bombs were falling everywhere? Was the commodore crazy – behaving like an old numskull again?

Bailey was stumped for words. Low as he was in the totem pole, he knew that it was wrong to take a break in the middle of a battle. Even if they had the edge, they should press the advantage instead of resting on their oars, as it were. The battle at this hour was only half-won.

Dewey was Dewey. He had determined that his sailors, after two hours of battle, were getting hungry – as Barton Bailey in fact was – and lest any of his men perish of starvation, breakfast must be served while shells were falling around his ears. His men only had to die a brave death.

"At 7:35 a.m. I ceased firing and withdraw squadron for breakfast," Dewey himself recorded in his log book.

The entry was corroborated by the skipper of the gunboat *Petrel,* Lt. Commander George P. Colvocoresses, whose chronology of the battle was later submitted to the Department of the Navy.

Lest he demoralize his captains or embolden the enemy, Dewey didn't let on the real reason behind his flagship's withdrawal: *Olympia's* main armaments were out of commission from overheating, thereby compelling a break to give them time to cool down; moreover, ammunition for her five-inch guns was running low. (Dewey's serving meal to his crew would later be seized upon by the American press as yet another manifestation of Dewey's coolness under fire.)

The flagship saw little action after it broke off engagement. Suddenly idle, her gunners were assigned less deadly, if unfulfilling menial chores, or else set at liberty to prowl the deck as interested spectators of the battle. A quick inspection of the guns and armory revealed that the report about the

Olympia's dwindling supply of ammunition was erroneous, for there was enough of it sitting in unopened crates that was missed by the fog of war. The mistake was not necessarily a bad thing. For the crew needed a respite.

Bailey assigned himself to the quarterdeck together with Wolfgang Messner, Scotty Preston and the rest of the crew of the forward turret. They cleared debris from the deck which included the detritus of eight-inch shells that had misfired from his guns. They also repaired the rigging of the foremast of which several cables had been severed by hostile fire. Otherwise, the *Olympia* was unscathed, which could not be said of one of its whaleboats that had been shot through like a sieve. It was hanging upended from one of its davits and had to be jettisoned overboard.

From time to time Bailey and his crew mates would drop what they were doing to watch the action or ogle Dewey at his command post, especially when the signalman hoisted a new set of pennants up the foremast. They had come to recognize the ensigns identifying the other ships in the squadron by their distinguishing colors. But that was as far as their knowledge of naval code went. Bailey or Wolf would sidle up to their shavetail, Lt. Cocker, to ask him to interpret the signals going up in quick succession. Cocker happily obliged. For example, when the ensign of the cruiser *Baltimore* fluttered atop a string of colors, Cocker read: "Designated vessel will lead." That was the order for its skipper, Captain Nehemiah McDyer, to take the lead and resume the attack while Dewey watched from a safe distance munching on an apple.

The commodore had chosen well in designating the *Baltimore* as the squadron's lead combat ship. It had more big guns than the flagship, with six hull-mounted gun turrets containing eight- and six-inch cannons compared to *Olympia's* two. Early in the battle, the *Baltimore* had broken away from the column to give chase to the British warship *Esmeralda*, which had followed the squadron across the South China Sea to espy on the operations by the Americans who had given away their intentions by painting their warships gray at the Hong Kong harbor. After shooing off the nosy British, the *Baltimore* turned around to join the battle as the freshest Yankee vessel in the line.

To the sailors watching from their vantage point on the *Olympia*, it seemed certain that victory was near at hand. The Spanish cruisers that remained afloat were either burning or listing badly. None was returning fire. The Yankee gunboats *Petrel* and *Concord* were darting about the burning hulks and occasionally would disappear behind the smoke into Bacoor Bay itself. Only the shore batteries in Sangley Point offered token resistance. And that was soon to end. A new set of colored pennants was hoisted up *Olympia*'s foremast signaling: "Attack the enemy batteries, earthenworks." Forthwith, *Baltimore*, *Raleigh* and *Boston* turned their attentions to the shore batteries in the Sangley naval station as well as the gun emplacements along the foreshore of Manila Bay between Sangley peninsula and the Walled City, most of which guns had not dared fire at Dewey's squadron. The flagship *Olympia* rejoined the action to the cheers of the men on her deck. She lobbed two well-aimed eight-inch shells at a corner of Intramuros where the Pasig River emptied into the bay.

It was this last shot that proved decisive. Whereas Montojo's ability to take a beating was just about limitless, the Spanish army had far less fortitude. The bombardment of the Spanish army's artillery positions unnerved the defenders more than they wrought actual damage. The effect was immediate.

At 12:30 past noon, Bailey heard spontaneous cheering at the sight of a white flag flying atop a building inside the Walled City. What could have the shells hit to prompt such a reaction?

"Look yonder! They've run up the white flag!" the eagle-eyed Scott Preston shouted.

"But it's the Spanish flag... it's been there all morning," said an unbelieving Bailey.

"That's not the Spanish flag. The Spanish flag's yellow," corrected the scholarly Wolf.

"It's white... it's white!" chorused the other sailors as the smoke lifted.

And so it was. At that very moment other unmistakably white flags were being hoisted along the length of the peninsula of the Sangley Point naval base. Bailey's imagination flew as his attention turned past the enemy combatants to the inhabitants under the domes and gables of the Walled City. What could be inside those palaces? Princes and monks praying for a miracle from the sky? Beautiful ladies in hooped skirts scurrying for cover inside monasteries? It would take him a little while to get better acquainted with the inhabitants of the old city.

In his post-mortem report to the secretary of the navy, Commodore Dewey wrote: "[T]hree batteries at Manila had kept up a continuous fire from the beginning of the engagement, which fire was not returned by this squadron... [A] message [sent] to the Governor-General to the effect that if the batteries did not cease firing the city would be shelled. This had the effect of silencing them." Barton Bailey's observation that the flag had been there all morning might have been correct after all. The sailors aboard *Olympia* had spotted the white flag, belatedly.

"We've licked 'em, Gatling, and what a bang-up job it was," crowed Wolf.

"Yeah, we sure did," Bailey could only agree as patriotism welled up to warm the cockles of his heart. "Listen up, I got no doubt that the old man is the greatest captain in the world."

"What do you think happened to the dago admiral?" Scotty Preston asked.

"Probably skeddadled back to his mama," gloated Bailey, uncharitably. "No match to the commodore."

At 1:20 p.m. Dewey signaled to his scattered ships: "Prepare to anchor."

Lt. Cocker was now reading the pennants aloud without any prompting, to the cheers of the sailors crowding the foredeck. The rest of the squadron queued up behind *Olympia* which by then had skirted dangerously close to the Walled City.

At 1:30 p.m., another signal went up. Bailey and his shipmates watched adoringly as the old man himself assumed the duties of a signalman, running up a streamer of pennants with his own hands. It read simply: "Anchor at discretion."

Dewey's utter lack of airs in performing humble chores waxed ironic and made for dramatic effect on his men, more than outright exultation.

Victory was complete. All seven Yankee ships were still afloat and all of their crews accounted for, with only eight men slightly wounded. In contrast, all seven Spanish cruisers were sunk, to hinder shipping to and from Bacoor Bay for decades to come. A few of the smaller gunboats were salvaged to serve the occupation force. A total of 167 Spanish sailors died and 214 were wounded that day.

To wind up what became known as the Battle of Manila Bay, Dewey applied the finishing touch that set him apart from the other admirals who were at that very moment staking out the harbor of Santiago Bay, Cuba, waiting for the enemy to break out and give them battle in the open sea. He mustered out the musical band which was the least noticed part of the crew and whose members made themselves useful during battle performing sundry tasks including stints as coal passers and ammunition handlers. On the quarterdeck of his flagship which was then not totally cleared of debris, they lugged their brass instruments and serenaded themselves and the crew for a job well done. The band's repertoire consisted of American hymns and martial tunes, waltzes, and a Spanish dance beat that the crew lapped up for its backhanded compliment to the defeated enemy. The Americans had gained a foothold on the Philippine Islands.

4

UNCHARTED WATERS

The Spanish-American War which sent Dewey's Asiatic Squadron to Manila Bay was fanned by war fever that swept the United States over the sinking of the American battleship *Maine*. Sent to protect American citizens stranded in the Spanish colony during Cuba's revolution against Spain, the battleship blew up under mysterious circumstances in Havana harbor on the night of February 15, 1898, with the loss of 263 lives – the worst disaster in American naval history up to then. Though the cause of the tragedy was never ascertained, the so-called Yellow Press dredged up all sorts of evidence from the Havana harbor to prove that Spain was the culprit. "War! Sure!" cried a headline in the New York *Journal,* a tabloid owned by William Hearst. "Maine destroyed by the Spanish: this proved absolutely [by] the existence of a TORPEDO HOLE."

In fact, no one ever had the opportunity to examine the *Maine's* wreck for the existence of a torpedo hole as she had immediately sunk to the bottom of the bay half-buried in mud beyond reach of even the most intrepid tabloid journalist. Nevertheless, the editors of the *Journal* allowed themselves the license to embellish the wire reports. They even illustrated the tragedy with a sketch of the *Maine,* floundering in the water as it burned, with the heads presumably of her sailors bobbing in the surrounding waters. A picture to stir horror and fury across the land.

President William McKinley refused to heed the cries for vengeance that reverberated across the United States in the days immediately following the tragedy. He was too punctilious to rush to judgment and pronounce harsh punishment for the alleged culprit. But being a good politician, he also realized that he could not afford to lag far behind public opinion, especially when it came to redressing an outrage against the flag by foreign kings – long the nation's pet peeve. In the end, McKinley had no choice but to pronounce the Spanish guilty.

It took him two months to convince himself of Spanish culpability. On April 20, he finally gained enough moral certainty to issue an ultimatum to the Spanish king demanding that he "relinquish his authority and government in the island of Cuba" within three days, an indirect judgment of guilt against Spain. He meant that, by way of punishment for its crime, Spain had to suffer the loss of its Caribbean colony.

Its imperial pride stung, Spain refused to bow down to demands of an upstart power, a republic at that. Already, it had lost most of its New World possessions in the course of a revolutionary upheaval that had swept through South America. Of all its colonies, Cuba held a special place in the Spanish empire. It was in the Caribbean after all where Columbus landed prefiguring 500 years of imperial glory for Spain as the mightiest colonial power in the Americas. Spain could not be seen as having been driven out of the island by a former British colony which had previously expelled them from California and Florida and now styled itself as champion of Cuban independence. The symbolism of the cross and the sword of Columbus being flung back across the ocean was too much.

Angered by what it saw as imperial arrogance, the United States declared war on Spain, calling on its teeming masses of tired, poor and hungry immigrants as well as homegrown patriots to rally around the Statue of Liberty and fight for the cause of freedom. There was no better cause to galvanize a nation that had freed itself from the British imperial yoke and become a haven for oppressed people everywhere. Americans volunteered for service in droves, making the war the most popular ever fought by the United States.

It was in light of these events that Commodore Dewey set sail for Hong Kong on February 26 from the Japanese port of Nagasaki. Informed by diplomatic sources of the presence of a Filipino rebel general by the name of Emilio Aguinaldo who had exiled himself to Hong Kong, Dewey had the entire island searched for the rebel leader but Aguinaldo was nowhere to be found having already set sail for Singapore. The commodore promptly telegraphed Consul E. Spencer Pratt in Singapore to seek out the elusive leader.

In Singapore, the Americans cut a deal with Aguinaldo that was to bedevil Dewey throughout his stay in the Pacific. The U.S. consuls were in favor of arming the Filipino insurgents. For less than idealistic motives, they suddenly saw the benefits of raising a Filipino Indian army to harass the Spaniards. They saw Aguinaldo less as a patriot than as an Asian Geronimo, one with the potential for tying up much of the Spanish army in the Far East. Consul E. Spencer Pratt found out for himself that the revolutionary leader who spoke Spanish was hardly the stereotype of an Indian he had in mind. Aided by a British interpreter named William Bray, he urged the Filipino revolutionary to return to Manila immediately and wage war on the Spaniards. "I've heard that you wanted to meet with Commodore Dewey in Hong Kong. We reiterate our willingness to help in your struggle against Spanish rule. We'll help you bring your men to Manila aboard one of our ships."

"Help us go back to our country? We're going there all right, with or without your help, but there's no sense going home before we get the weapons we need to arm our men. We've been fighting the Spaniards for more than a year with little more than bolos, and I tell you, you can't win a revolution with knives," reasoned the Filipino general, who, at the age of 29, carried the authority of a leader of a revolution.

"How soon do you wish to return to your country?"

"There is no time to waste. We have to resume our struggle now. *El tiempo perdido no se recupera jamás.* Lost time can never be recovered."

"How many guns do you need?"

"Up to 20,000 bolt-action rifles. The latest stuff like the kind you're using in Cuba," replied Aguinaldo.

"Well … we will have to consult with Washington. That's an awful lot of guns you are talking about." Pratt hesitated, faced with a demand that exceeded his brief. "We're engaged in the Caribbean, as you very well know. I'm not sure we have that many guns to spare in our armories. But I assure you, in your struggle against Spain, America is right behind you as a friend and ally."

The American consul made no hard offer to ship tons of arms to General Aguinaldo, a commitment only the highest officials in Washington could make. The only tangible assistance Pratt could readily offer was transportation to the Philippines. "I'll arrange for one of our boats to take you back to Manila."

Aguinaldo was not in a hurry to be repatriated by his putative ally. He was also confused, if not altogether suspicious, about the Americans' motive for engaging in war against Spain. "Tell me, *amigo,* why are you fighting the Spaniards?" he asked.

Pratt was caught off-guard. He was hard put to describe America's reason for waging war in a language that would impress a clueless foreigner. *Because the Spaniards blew up the* Maine … No, that didn't sound right, either. Something more sublime was needed. Something…well, Jeffersonian.

"To liberate the people of Cuba, and your people, too. That you may enjoy the blessings of democracy… We are fighting the Spaniards today for the same reasons our Founding Fathers fought the British – to bring freedom to an oppressed people. America will fight for your liberation. So that you and your children's children may live in freedom and partake of the benefits of democracy."

Aguinaldo believed every word he heard. He may have been impressionable. But he was inclined to trust the words of an American high official. Never in his life had he heard democracy being spoken of by the Spanish, not even by the learned friars in the universities. It was a merely a rallying cry of the ilustrados, the Spanish-educated Filipinos who were the propagandists of the revolution. The statement of an American official, backed up by a boatload of weapons, was far more inspiring to the practical Aguinaldo than the exhortations of fellow patriots.

"Are you saying that if we fight the Spaniards side by side with you, you will allow us to gain our independence?"

"Absolutely. That's what our Founding Fathers shed their blood for."

Aguinaldo broke into a grin of wonderment. He was amazed at the nonchalant way the American purveyed the ideal of freedom, as if the same were a commodity, and the Filipino was just as eager to buy into it. "In that case, you can consider us your brothers in arms." He seized Pratt's hand with both of his and shook it vigorously. "I am glad to hear what you have just said. I'm going to Manila."

Aguinaldo took Pratt's word as an official statement of American policy. He was convinced that the American government had authorized the consul to declare its support for Philippine independence. And he was dead wrong.

The young revolutionary general agreed to be transported back to the Philippines aboard an American vessel. But the designated boat had left Singapore harbor without him. Instead, Aguinaldo boarded the Hong Kong bound British packet launch *Malacca* which was ferrying a boat load of rebellious Chinese coolies expelled from Malayan mines. With his closely cropped hair, he stood out like a sore thumb among the pigtails on deck, a lonely figure homeward bound to fight for his people's freedom.

In Hong Kong, he caught up with Dewey's fleet. He noted that the American warships were being painted gray, obviously in preparation for battle. Elated, he began rounding up his exiled officers in preparation for their return to the Philippines.

Washington, D.C.

On May 7, 1898, Colonel Oliver Travis of the Coast Guard and Geodetic Survey jogged up the steps of the White House carrying a rolled map tucked under one arm. He was received by J. Addison Porter, personal secretary to the president, who ushered him into the executive office. There, the visiting Coast Guard officer was introduced to President William McKinley, 55, a portly figure who was also known as the Great White Father to the American Indians. An even-tempered man of Methodist upbringing, he was a deeply religious leader who was slow to anger and paused at great length to commune with the Almighty on the eve of a fateful decision. As such, McKinley had to be stampeded by a wrathful Congress and even more furious press into declaring war on Spain. And now, before he could fully adjust to his role as a war time commander-in-chief, President McKinley had been handed by Commodore Dewey an unexpected prize, a group of islands halfway across the globe, the exact location of which he could not quite ascertain, which was why he had sent for Colonel Travis. The president was examining a globe beside his desk, turning it round and round, unable to find the cluster of specks inconspicuously tucked away in a remote corner of the globe.

The Coast Guard surveyor helped him out. "There you are, sir," said Colonel Travis, stopping the globe as the president's hand hovered above the archipelago, "the Philippine Islands." To give McKinley a better perspective of the location of the islands, he unrolled the map he brought along for the purpose, which he spread on the president's uncluttered desk.

"That's Hong Kong... the South China Sea... the island of Luzon ... *Manila Bay*. That's where our Navy is," he said, tracing Dewey's journey with his forefinger.

McKinley scrutinized the islands and remarked self-deprecatingly: "It is evident that I must learn a good deal of geography in this war."

McKinley could be forgiven for his ignorance of geography. In fact, hardly anybody in America knew where in the world the Philippine Islands were, an uncharted territory in geography classes.

After news broke out of Dewey's triumph, the press reported comments by their readers. From Mr. Alfred Dooley: "Most Americans didn't know whether they were islands or canned goods."

From Brig. Gen. Thomas Anderson who would later sail with the first contingent of expeditionary troops to support Dewey: "I couldn't tell a Filipino from a Hottentot."

The news, however, was electric. Hitherto preoccupied with the war in Cuba, the American public turned their interest to even more engaging happenings in the exotic Far East.

It wasn't easy for the news to reach home, though. Dewey, in an uncharacteristic act of rashness, had cut the submarine cable connecting Manila to the outside world after his request to use it to send a telegram home was turned down by the Spaniards. Now, he was effectively isolated in the remotest frontier of the Spanish Empire. It took his cutter *McCulloch* three days to reach Hong Kong to find a telegraph office. From there, his communiqué ran a circuitous route around the world's relay stations before reaching the secret communications room of the Navy Department. For without a Trans-Pacific cable, the telegram had to be dispatched to India first, then to England, whence it ran along the Trans-Atlantic cable to New York, finally to be relayed to Washington, D.C., a Magellanic journey for so terse a message.

The first official to receive Dewey's communiqué was Secretary of the Navy John D. Long. Ever since Dewey departed Hong Kong on April 24 en route to Manila on a mission to find and destroy the Spanish fleet, the Navy had lost contact with its Asiatic squadron, which had strayed to a port in mainland China to take on coal before crossing the South China Sea. At that time before radio, there was no means of ship-to-ship let alone ship-to-shore communication, save for visual signals sent by light or pennant. At the approximate time Dewey was expected to be in Manila, the atmosphere in the Navy Department was tense. Secretary Long had laid cots on the floor of his office so that his assistants could keep an unbroken vigil on the telegraph equipment.

Competing for information about Dewey's fate was the Yellow Press. It was engaged in a circulation war that was even fiercer than the shooting war itself, with its evenly matched protagonists fighting for the credit of breaking the most dramatic stories of the war first. Its leading rivals each had an Asiatic bureau of sorts. With Dewey in Manila were Joseph L. Stickney of the New York *Herald* and Editor Edward W. Harden of the New York *World* whose publisher was Joseph Pulitzer, Hearst's arch-competitor in the business. Trying to one-up each other for Dewey's graces, they volunteered for useful chores aboard the flagship, such as serving meals. Stickney, who had once served as a naval officer, managed to wangle a juicy posting as Dewey's factotum during the battle, to the utter dismay of Harden (who would later claim to have fired a gun at Montojo's fleet). To the taciturn commander, they were an intolerable nuisance and he sought ways to be rid of them. The loss of the South China Sea cable put the correspondents in the same predicament as Dewey and created the situation for their hasty departure. Accordingly, they fought for the last available bunk on the *McCulloch* – which was being sent back to Hong Kong so that Dewey could telegram Washington, D.C. of his victory – and Dewey was only too happy to see them go.

It was a mistake. The correspondents were licking their chops at the opportunity to scoop each other and the Navy. As Hong Kong harbor loomed into view the correspondents gripped at the railings, willing the *McCulloch* to reach dry land in a hurry. The ship made it to the harbor on May 7, 1898, bearing news already a week stale. As soon as their ship dropped anchor, Stickney and Harden raced down the gangplank, seized two rickshaws waiting for passengers on the pier, and raced for the nearest telegraph station. They drove their stolid rickshaws like charioteers, waving their notes in the air as they tried to make way through the crowd, past a line of stalls in the marketplace, along the narrow and winding streets of the British colony. They jumped down at the same time in front of the nearest telegraph office, located below lines of drying laundry. With a bump and a shove, the older Harden won the foot race.

The same day, at the Bureau of Navigation located in the Navy building in Washington D.C., the telegraph device, which looked like a rat trap, tapped out the cryptic message: "Hong Kong McCulloch Wildman." It was an advance notice that a message from Dewey was coming in shortly. Third Asst. Secretary Thomas Cridler seized it and sprinted down the corridor calling out to the cryptographers to stand by for the long-awaited message from Manila.

In the meantime, the scoop hit the streets. Extras from the tabloid press trumpeted the eyewitness accounts of correspondents who had been to the battle in Manila Bay, transporting the public into paroxysms of joy. The account of navy veteran Stickney of the *Herald* captured the imagination of the reading public the most. He immortalized the famous quote from Dewey – "You may fire when you're ready, Gridley" – having ably served beside the commodore as his shoe-shine boy during the naval battle.

Upon receiving the full text of Dewey's dispatch, Secretary John D. Long faced the public and a full-court press at the lobby of the Navy building. The extras hitting the streets had taken the wind out of the message. But knowing the exaggeration to which the tabloids were prone, the public now wanted official confirmation of the story, and there was no better source than Dewey's own communiqué. Long didn't even have to read the piece of paper in his hand to reassure the audience. His smile betrayed it all. He read:

> On May 1, the squadron met and vanquished the enemy. I have taken possession of the naval station at Cavite, Philippine Islands. I control Manila Bay completely and can take city anytime... but have not sufficient men to hold it."

Even before he finished, the building resounded with clapping and cheering. The audience paid no attention at all to the caveat in the communiqué speaking of the need for troops to maintain Dewey's precarious foothold in Cavite, a problem that was to gather urgency in the next few days. It was enough for them to know that he had thoroughly vanquished the Spanish fleet, a result that greatly assuaged the anxiety of families whose loved ones served aboard Dewey's ships. Dewey's victory propelled the United States to the rank of a world power. He was the outstanding national hero in what was to become known as the Splendid Little War.

The cheering had also something to do with the appearance of Theodore Roosevelt who stole the show from his superior, Secretary Long. The assistant secretary of the Navy, who had personally ordered the Asiatic fleet to leave Nagasaki for Hong Kong the month before, waded into the crowd to announce that he was resigning his post in the Navy Department to volunteer for service in the Caribbean. He was to lead a mounted corps of Rough Riders to fame on the hills of Cuba, upon which exploits he would build a political career.

The Congress wasn't behind in its applause. Caught by

the news in one of its fractious moods, it temporarily put an end to partisan squabbles on the floor and joined the nation to express its congratulations in one voice. With rare unanimity, it voted to grant awards to the improbable war heroes. It appropriated $10,000 to buy a sword for Dewey and brass buttons for his men. When it learned that the president had promoted him to the next rank of rear admiral, the Congress, not to be outdone, confirmed him to the next higher rank of admiral, then still dissatisfied, changed its mind and kicked him further upstairs to the top of the totem pole as Admiral of the Navy, the ultimate rank. Dewey's epaulets changed insignias in quick succession from a one-star, two-anchor ornament to a four-star, two-anchor decoration. Not since General Ulysses Grant, the man who led the Union Army to victory in the Civil War, had a military man received so many honors from a grateful nation.

Dewey's naval feat of arms stood in stark contrast to the performance of the far superior Atlantic fleet in Santiago Bay, Cuba. There, Admiral William Sampson, who had at his disposal not one but two huge battleships, was determined *not* to enter the bay. Admittedly, it was a body of water that unlike Manila Bay was unsuitable for naval warfare being not much wider than the estuary of a river. But it was the notoriously inept tactics that Admiral Sampson employed with such commitment that stood him poorly next to the cool and daring Dewey. In an effort to keep Santiago Bay closed and the Spanish navy trapped inside, he sent a suicide mission under Lt. Richard P. Hobson aboard the explosive-laden coal ship *Merrimac*. His mission: to bottle-up the blockaded Spanish fleet by deliberately sinking the *Merrimac* at the narrows. The Spaniards were only too happy to oblige. As Hobson steered his coal ship along the narrows under cover of darkness, Spanish shore guns blasted the vessel to kingdom come, sinking it short of the chosen place, thereby leaving the narrows still clear to outbound traffic. The Yankee press even put a brave face on the ignominious incident by reporting that Hobson was pulled

80

out of the water by the Spanish commander himself, Admiral Pascual Cervera "who congratulated him on his bravery" – i.e., failure.

With the Atlantic fleet content to patrol the mouth of the bay, Admiral Cervera, who was feeling the heat from the American land forces closing in on Santiago, made a run for it – while the Americans had relaxed their guard to lay siege on yet another Cuban port – and almost succeeded. Turning back in time, a force under Commodore Winfield Scott Schley intercepted the Spanish column as they were filing out of the bay. "Poor Spain!" cried the captain of the flagship *Maria Teresa* as his ship was spotted. "This is her last bid for glory..."

A forced battle ensued. Once again, the Spanish squadron went belly up but the battle failed to fire the interest of the Yellow Press and, as a consequence, didn't capture the imagination of the American public. It wasn't won right.

After the war, a disgraceful affair broke out among the commanders of the Atlantic fleet in which they disparaged each other's role in the accidental victory at Santiago Bay. Admiral Sampson tried to win credit for the victory at the expense of Schley. The papers made public the spectacle of the admirals scrambling for crumbs of glory, of which Dewey had the cake all to himself. Supporters of Admiral Sampson condemned the conduct of the recently promoted Schley, second-in-command at Santiago Bay, for nearly allowing the Spanish fleet to escape. Backers of Admiral Schley lashed back at Sampson by accusing him of deserting his post on the eve of the battle. To resolve the fray, Dewey lent his respectability to the Navy by heading the Schley Board of Inquiry to determine which party deserved the credit, or discredit, for the outcome of the battle in Santiago Bay.

Meanwhile, at Sangley Point, the stranded heroes of the Asiatic Squadron heard little of the applause that greeted their victory, not even in the form of reinforcements or relief. For if Uncle Sam was lavish with his praises, he was sparing with his supplies. Deployments were bound only in one direction: Cuba. The build-up of forces at the railhead in Tampa, Florida turned a reclaimed swampland into tent a city of 25,000 men which was successively deluged with ammunition, clothing, fodder, guns and medicine. Turned into an extensive supply dump without proper infrastructure to alleviate its swampy conditions, the tent city became a breeding ground for diseases. Thousands of soldiers became casualties to the camps' unsanitary conditions even before they set sail for Cuba, the most prominent being William Jennings Bryan, soon to be McKinley's tormentor.

President McKinley decided to divert some men and matériél to the Philippine theater thereby offering some relief to the congested dump in Tampa, not to mention Dewey's fleet which was languishing an ocean away. He was able to muster a spare contingent of 2,500 men under Brig. Gen. Thomas Anderson to make up the expeditionary force to the islands. In overall command of what came to be known as the Eighth Corps was Maj. Gen. Wesley Merritt who knew nothing of the country that Dewey had made famous only recently. Admitting his ignorance of the land he was about to conquer, he couldn't decide whether to take along a Cavalry brigade, because he wasn't sure whether he could find horses on the islands. So he settled for infantry.

"Am I to seize the entire Philippine Archipelago or only Manila?" he asked McKinley.

The president replied cryptically. "All islands will be given order and security while in the possession of the United States."

With no clear mission in hand, Brig. Gen. Anderson set sail for Manila from San Francisco Bay on May 25, 1898. For the first time in its history, the United States was sending an invading force across the ocean.

5

A DAY IN THE LIFE OF A DOCTOR

The demands of his profession had Joaquin Calderon rushing back to Manila. His stint with the rebels in the province of Cavite was a disappointment because the rebels did not pay him the proper respect befitting his high opinion of himself. Neither did they feel any need for his services as they would rather be treated by a barrio quack. In Manila, he was one esteemed fellow patronized by Chinese traders and friars and even a few Spanish civilians. The sinking of the Spanish fleet in the shallow waters of Bacoor Bay meant there was greater need for his services in the capital than in the rebel-held territories, and that was where he gravitated. In the immediate aftermath of the disaster, the situation in the walled city of Intramuros, now besieged from the sea as well as from land, was desperate judging from the bedlam in the streets, with the Guardia Civil running about like headless chicken, and residents preparing to evacuate ahead of the expected invading forces. The only hospital within the enclave was the San Juan De Dios infirmary, an adjunct of the Universidad de Santos Tomas, and it was overwhelmed with casualties who began trickling in the afternoon and throughout the night following the battle. It was to the hospital that Joaquin proceeded, spurred as much by the call of duty as the tug of loyalty to his Alma Mater, where he as well as Jose Rizal after him studied medicine.

The floor of the hospital was slick with blood, body fluids and tissue. Given the state of 19th century medicine, the hospital was by its nature dirty. Lack of scientific understanding of the causes of infection condemned many people to die in its wards while seeking a chance to live. For all its reputation as a house of horrors, as all hospitals were known in those days, the San Juan de Dios infirmary held a special place in Calderon's heart, a 200-year institution that straddled the colonial era. It was there where he was born and it was there where his wife died giving birth. Poor hygiene was the order of the day. It was considered as nothing but the unavoidable aggravation of hospital work and filth its natural by-product, as manure was in a cattle farm. The doctors donned soiled aprons and the nuns who served as their nurses wore smeared habits as badges of hard work, seldom changing in the course of their duties and looking no better than butchers. The exception was Joaquin Calderon. He was reasonably abreast of Victorian medicine that trickled down to a scholarly few doctors who had had a modicum of European education. He had learned to scrub his hands before as well as after performing surgery. He wore only clean aprons. He did not subscribe to the view of his older colleagues that frequent washing or bathing removed the natural oils in the skin that kept away germs. The recent discovery of microscopic life in the form of bacteria tended to vindicate his obsession with cleanliness, but it was mostly ignored by doctors who refused to accept their existence or significance to medicine. His style of practice was considered sissified by his colleagues who regarded themselves as part naturalists and part adventurers, in the same guise as alchemists and navigators of yore, imbued with esoteric powers that bordered on the occult.

The number of wounded soldiers that were arriving at the hospital by the wagon load was more than the staff could handle. Joaquin made his rounds of the hospital wards and corridors which were crowded with patients lying on cots or on mats on the floor. He was assisted by nuns who had minds of their own and who operated by the power of prayer. Inside the main hall lit by sunlight streaming through the open windows, he grappled with the main task at hand: performing surgery. His operating table was nothing more than wooden planks placed on top of two sawhorses, with an upright barrel on the side covered by a towel on whose top he laid out his surgical equipment and in whose hollow interior he stored his other tools of trade – a portable contraption that could be easily carried to the field on emergencies. Joaquin took pride in such tidy inventions by which he succeeded in saving countless lives.

His most common operation was amputation. With ingenuity born of need, he had found exotic cures to enrich his apothecary, ranging from the ground tusk of a wild boar to dried herbs prospected from the countryside where they grew wild and plentiful. In the case of amputation, he was particularly proud of a solution he had to the biggest challenge faced by a surgeon: deadening a patient's pain. Ordinarily, an operation was undertaken by brute force, requiring the aid of four burly attendants who had to hold down each of the patient's limbs while the doctor cut open a screaming patient. Chloroform and laughing gas, newly discovered anesthetics, were not locally available. Joaquin had to rely on quickness, because pain was a function of speed. On this score, his colleagues couldn't care less about pain because it was considered a necessary, if unwelcome, cost of physical rehabilitation. The standard equipment was a carpenter's saw. The problem with this tool was that it wreaked too much damage to the tissues, being more suited for cutting lumber for which job it was originally invented in the first place. Using a saw to cut a limb was unimaginably tricky, given that the patient was alive and often kicking and screaming, causing the saw to shift positions several times, thereby carving out more flesh and bone than advisable, and the five to ten strokes it took to cut through the limb was an eternity in terms of the excruciating pain it inflicted on the patient. Joaquin was proudest of a tool he had specially made by Carlos: a bolo that was nearly as broad as it was long, looking somewhat like a scaled-down guillotine with a handle. While the old method took as long as a minute and left a gruesome mess, his new technique was over in a second. With one hack of the surgical bolo to the gangrenous limb – which had to be positioned squarely on a thick board of timber, a chopping block, as it were – flesh and bone cleaved cleanly, and the patient felt nothing but a nip. It was not entirely painless, however, because there was no way to benumb the next step. In order to stop the bleeding, Joaquin had to cauterize the wound, that is, burn the open veins with a red-hot iron to the sound and smell of sizzling flesh. He had yet to invent a better tool for this follow-on procedure.

The doctor had long been inured to the slaughterhouse horror of the hospital, but one patient who was unfortunate enough to book a ticket to his chopping block drew conflicting emotions from his person. The man was smeared with his own blood, his face bruised and scratched as if he had fallen off a horse, one bloody leg askew. One look at his face recalled to him the worst atrocity committed against his people. For this man was none other than Esteban Zaragoza, the captain of the firing squad that had shot Jose Rizal dead.

"This isn't a navy man," Joaquin said, having seen that almost all of the casualties taken to the hospital were sailors of the Spanish fleet now resting at the bottom of the bay. "What happened?"

"The shells that landed at Fort Santiago. One hit the courtyard while he was standing there and he was blown off his horse. Unlucky man, he," said a Guardia Civil sergeant who had carried the man to the hospital with two other soldiers.

"What's his name?"

"Esteban Zaragoza. Captain."

"Zaragoza..." The name rolled bitterly from Joaquin's lips.

"Yes, do you know him?" asked the sergeant.

"No. I heard the nurse noting down his name."

"Look at his leg."

"It's pretty bad." Joaquin noted the broken shin bone sticking out of the flesh. "It has to be amputated."

"N-No." The patient was listening, though half-delirious. "Don't cut my leg, *por favor.*"

"He's lost a lot of blood. I don't think he can stand an amputation right away. Let's wait until tomorrow."

The sergeant drew Joaquin close. "He can't stay here long," he whispered. "He fears for his life. If not for this accident, he wouldn't have dared go out of Fort Santiago."

Joaquin knew very well the reason why. "He will be attended to, at the time of my choosing. Either he loses his leg or he loses his life," he said curtly.

When he reported the identity of his last patient to his brother Carlos, the latter was staggered by the news that he was rendered momentarily speechless. Then quivering with rage Carlos stared balefully at his older brother and blurted out, "Kill him, *Kuya*. Kill him!"

Joaquin was taken aback. "I'm a doctor, Caloy. I can't do that."

"Two years... I've thought of nothing but... Revenge!" Carlos seethed.

"The Hippocratic Oath... haven't you ever heard of that?"

Carlos Calderon, a blacksmith, seized a hammer and pounded it hard against the anvil with an explosive bang. "KILL HIM!" he blared.

There was no way Joaquin could argue with his brother who articulated his feelings in terms of gestures or epithets rather than coherent statements. So scared was the doctor that he fled the shop toward his adjacent clinic.

Carlos ran after him. "I'll kill him myself if you won't

dare do it!"

It was then with a sense of urgency that he operated on Esteban Zaragoza the following morning. The only concession that he was willing to give to his older brother was to refrain from using the surgical cleaver that Carlos had fashioned for him, for it was discomfiting for him to have to wield the blade, knowing that its creator wanted to use it differently. The patient being six-foot tall and heavy-set, the doctor needed to adopt precautions to overcome any reflex resistance from him. To deaden the pain, the patient was first intoxicated with the native liquor *lambanog*, and then his wound was dabbed with an opium-based tincture.

"Listos, apunten, fuego!" He couldn't help recalling Captain Zaragoza's words as he rolled up his sleeves to commence the delicate surgery.

As to the main part of the job, the standard procedure was to cut the flesh first with a scalpel, then the bone with the saw, but experience taught Joaquin that this only lengthened the agony of the patient as the scalpel worked far more slowly than the saw. Therefore, Joaquin used only the saw. With three soldiers and two nuns assisting him (two soldiers to hold the leg that was going to be amputated, and the others the arms), Joaquin picked up a carpenter's saw that had seen better days, having been handed down from generations of friars (who used to do the job of surgeons) to a succession of doctors, and prepared to sever the leg an inch above the fracture. The swollen flesh had become so sensitive to touch that the opiate did not seem to have any effect. Upon contact with cold steel, the leg jerked and the patient groaned. Joaquin had never gotten used to the scene, and he had to work quickly to get it over with. The howl that escaped the man's mouth as he performed the procedure was so indescribable that his five assistants were terrified into loosening their grips, vicariously feeling the pain that seemed to flow like electricity from the patient's limbs and into their hands as the jagged blade sawed at the flesh, then the bundled muscles, then at the tendons, then at the bone and then more flesh until the leg finally separated, revealing a bloody stump with the white core of the bone within dribbling bone marrow fluid. If pulling a tooth sans anesthesia was bad enough, one could imagine having a root canal with a hand drill. "God-have-mercy-on-your-soul, Esteban Zaragoza," Joaquin sputtered, one syllable per stroke, his only expression of ill will against his patient whom his brother would rather see dead.

That was not the end. In order to stop the bleeding, pursuant to the Victorian techniques that he had learned in his studies abroad, Joaquin now prepared to cauterize the wound by singeing the veins and arteries so as to cause them to swell and thereby stanch the bleeding. In less serious injuries, applying hot oil to the wound was enough to do the trick but in the case of amputations, with the entire cross-section of a limb exposed as a bleeding stump, he had to apply stronger techniques. Thus, he took out a branding iron that glowed red hot having been stuck inside the furnace for cremating body parts, which he pressed all over the stump to singe the veins and arteries close, to a seething sound like fat extinguishing charcoal embers and the smell of broiling meat. The patient ululated until he mercifully lost strength and passed out.

"That should stop the bleeding," the doctor dropped the branding iron.

"El Señor Capitan," asked the sergeant. "Is he..."

"He's just sleeping," one of the nuns interjected, anticipating the question.

The soldiers who had not seen such gory mess even in warfare were shaking at the experience while the trained nuns casually dressed the stump and disposed of the detritus.

"He'll come to in about an hour," said Joaquin, scrubbing his bloody hands in a wooden pail filled with water. "Whew! My hardest operation so far. His calves are almost as thick as my thigh."

"What now, doctor?" asked the sergeant.

"You have to leave."

"What? But he needs further care."

"No, you have no time to waste."

"El Capitan needs to rest."

"His life is in danger." Lest he be misunderstood, he quickly added: "No, not from the operation. Some people are after him as you yourself said. There are certain people who want him dead."

Joaquin was then expecting Carlos to come barging into the hospital with a dagger hidden in his clothes to finish off his patient. He was not merely being paranoid because Joaquin knew his brother was perfectly capable of murder, especially in this case, recalling his vow of revenge uttered on the field of Bagumbayan. Without further ado, Joaquin and the sergeant bundled the patient into a hammock borne by the soldiers and saw them out of the courtyard into an alley leading to a gate that opened into the safety of the inner walls of Fort Santiago. "Go! Hurry! Don't stop!" he shooed them off as if he could hear the footfalls of Carlos hot on his heels.

Joaquin, like his brother, had the memory of Jose Rizal's execution seared to his brain. He also shared Carlos's anger at the atrocity that was crying out for redress. But to visit vengeance upon the culprit while he was a patient under his care revolted against common ethics. The doctor in him was relieved to have saved the life of a wounded man, but the rebel in him was guilt-stricken at having to let go of the man who owed a blood debt to his people, this man being the personification of Spanish injustice.

Carlos arrived at the hospital shortly after his intended victim had left. He was carrying a basket filled with provisions supposedly intended for a sick relative he had come to visit. He was with two male companions who were similarly disguised. Carlos proceeded to his brother's station peering at the faces of the wounded soldiers he passed by.

"This is a Spanish hospital." Joaquin accosted his brother as soon as he saw him. "You can be arrested here."

"Where is he?" Carlos asked.

90

"It's too dangerous here, Caloy." Joaquin edged him away, speaking in a hushed tone. "Don't you know this place is crawling with soldiers?"

"I am prepared to kill and to die. Where's the *capitan*?" Carlos was fearless.

"He's gone. The Guardia Civil took him away," answered Joaquin truthfully.

"Is that..." Carlos pointed at the doctor's apron. "Blood?"

Joaquin shrugged. "You know what I do."

"Whose...?"

"Oh, please, Caloy. It doesn't matter. To have blood in my hands means nothing, it's just a job."

Carlos inspected the corridors and checked out some wards looking for a certain patient. When his discreet search of the premises failed to turn up the Guardia Civil captain, Carlos returned to where his brother was standing.

"He must have been here. Your patients, mostly Spaniards."

"You better leave," Joaquin steered his younger brother toward a door. "Sooner or later they'll find out you're not relatives of any of the patients here."

Carlos had to wait another time to exact his revenge.

———————

6

OUTSIDE THE WALLS OF INTRAMUROS

"Looky yonder, what are those buildings?" Bailey wondered aloud.

"Why, they're churches you're looking at," said Wolf.

"How do you know they're churches?"

"Because they have domes on their rooftops, like the Capitol and our statehouses back home."

"Ain't they statehouses then?"

"They got no statehouses. This is a kingdom, you muggins, not a republic like ours. It has no Congress, no statehouses, no nuthin'. What they got here beside churches are the palaces of nobles who run the place."

"What else can you find in this place, Wolf? Come on, learn me more."

"Here, they have nobles and lords who rule for life without getting elected. The people they rule are mostly poor and ignorant. In the end the poor people revolt and overthrow the nobles so they can set up a republic like ours based on the principles of liberty, equality and ...uh... eternity."

Nobody in the ship could launch himself so confidently on any subject matter under the sun as Wolf Messner who had educated himself reading books and six-month old newspapers in the ship's library. He was looked up to as a scholar by the unlettered former stowaway Bailey.

The two sailors were sitting on the bow of the patrol boat *Petrel* spying on the goings-on around the Walled City of Intramuros from their anchorage three miles offshore. They boondoggled their time fantasizing about the land and the people of the colony they had never seen before except as specks on the map. The past three weeks had been an unmitigated ordeal for the stranded sailors as they had been unable to make a landing on the main island of Luzon. They suffered one minor setback after another in the hands of the unyielding Spaniards which threatened to deflate their morale.

The Americans had eyed Intramuros as their next trophy, the key to the conquest of the colony. Initially, Dewey had hoped to overawe the Spaniards into submission by parading his ships within sight of the Walled City, but his bully tactics – so unbecoming of his character – had the opposite effect. The Spaniards simply watched, entrenched behind walls. In a waiting game, they were going to come out the winners.

Then, Dewey wanted to borrow the city's telegraph lines, which ran underneath the South China Sea toward the British colony of Hong Kong, so that he could send dispatches to Washington. For this purpose, he designated an embassy composed of Lt. Cocker and four escorts, among them the intrepid pair of Bailey and Wolf, to visit the Spanish lines and request – or rather, demand – access to their telegraph facilities. Waving a white flag of truce, the unusual delegation strutted down the cobblestoned streets of Manila with the airs of marching conquerors, gawked at by ordinary Filipinos every step of the way. When they declared their purpose at the gate called the Postigo, separated by a moat filled with running water, the Spaniards simply thumbed their noses at what they regarded as an insolent demand. They were not about to help the *yanquis* trumpet to the rest of the world the defeat of Spanish arms.

Hurt and humiliated, Lt. Cocker's party sailed back aboard the gunboat *Concord* to Sangley Point, Cavite, seven miles away, where the Americans had made their camp in the abandoned base of Montojo. They reported to Dewey that the Spaniards had already grown more arrogant and defiant in their defeat. "They cussed and bullyragged us," Bailey put it coarsely. "They treated us like we were the ones who got licked."

"Let's teach Montojo another lesson," recommended Cocker.

Montojo was not to blame for their humiliation. He didn't control Manila and its civil works. The one in charge of the city and the colony at large was the governor-general, Basilio Agustin, who had 17,000 men holed up in Intramuros, driven out from the countryside by an insurrection waged by a young revolutionary named Emilio Aguinaldo. It was the governor-general who refused to recognize the American victory over Spanish arms as his army remained intact.

Such distinctions were lost on the Americans who spoke of the Spanish as one enemy cut out of the same cloth. For once losing his temper, Dewey armed his sailors with dredging poles and ran his flagship along the length of the bay to fish out the submerged Manila-to-Hong Kong cable. After his men hooked it up, he rashly ordered it cut – to the cheers of Bailey who thought he had gotten even.

Then, he sat down to gloat. As days passed and the Spaniards made no attempt to reconnect the line, Bailey realized that his commander had followed the wrong advice. They were isolated! Only by dispatching a boat to Hong Kong could they inform Washington of their predicament. Unless Washington shipped in infantry from San Francisco – reinforcement that would take at least a month to arrive – he had no hope of ever avenging the personal insult he had suffered at the gate of Intramuros.

At a strategic level, Dewey despaired of ever taking the Walled City. He might be able to bomb the capital, but the only way he could seize it was by storming the walls. And this was the Army's job. The difficulty of the matter was demonstrated by the fact that while the Filipino insurgents had seized the hinterlands of Manila, they were unable to breach the walls of Intramuros as in previous rebellions over centuries of Spanish rule. Without land troops from the mainland, Dewey could only blockade the enemy from the sea, while the badly armed Filipinos held a precarious hold on the land. Under these circumstances, the beleaguered Spaniards could very well sit out the stalemate until Dewey's ships rusted to junk and the Filipinos reconciled with their masters.

The old captain was reduced to patrolling the waters off the Walled City, with Bailey being assigned to the gunboat *Petrel*. The realization that the Spaniards had got the better out of the standoff gnawed at his sailors' morale. As Bailey mused over the humped rooftops of Intramuros, he actually envied the enemy ensconced in their luxurious mansions. He imagined Montojo being treated for his wounds inside a palace, attended by uniformed *muchachos* singing his praises and being fed *liempo* and ox tongue while the Americans subsisted on canned food. Ah, what a reversal of fortunes for the poor Yankees!

"How long do you think we're gonna stay here, this godforsaken place?" he asked Wolf as they sat side by side on the bow of the *Petrel*.

"I dunno. One month, two months, who the hell knows?"

"I don't give a fig about politics, this great game of colonies like what these politicians are playing, Wolf. I just wanna go home," Bailey sighed. The idea of staying in the distant land, and possibly fighting a land war there such as his Daddy had fought in the Indian Wars, held no particular allure to him. This land was even more alien than the wilderness beyond the Rockies or the badlands of Northern Texas which his Daddy spoke about with dread. True, white men had already conquered the place, and they needed only to pick up where they left off. But he had no heart for fighting a war of conquest against the natives of a remote group of islands that had no apparent value.

Bailey's father William came from rural America and his knowledge of the world was limited. He was born somewhere in the James River that ran through Richmond, Virginia, the precise date and location of which event his grandpa could not pinpoint for reasons undisclosed. At any rate, the year was 1878, give or take away one winter. One thing certain about his origins was that he was a red-blooded American unlike Wolfgang Messner who was smuggled as a three-year old into New York Harbor by his parents, persecuted Jews from Prussia. His earliest known ancestor, Thomas Barton Bailey, founded the first iron and brick foundry in America at Richmond in the late 17th century. He later bought land on both sides of the James River and cultivated tobacco to become a man of wealth in his eighties. As Richmond expanded and his descendants multiplied, the estate split into parcels of individual farms and changed hands until by 1855 William Barton Bailey, Bailey's grandpa owned only 80 acres of tobacco land tilled by 47 slaves.

Bailey's father never enjoyed the fruits of his family's riches. He never worked in it, in fact. As a young man, he left the land in the care of his mother to join the U.S. Cavalry in northern Texas, which in the 1850's was actively engaged in driving the Plains Indians from its territory. Originally from the Midwest, the Plains Indians were drifting ever southward into white man's territory in search of fertile land and the vanishing buffalo. In 1858, Barton's father figured in the Battle of the Wichita Village when a mounted corps under Captain Earl Van Darn sallied out of their stronghold in Fort Belknap, Texas, to destroy a Wichita encampment in the early hours of the morning. Instead, it was the white man's force that almost got annihilated. In five hours of fighting, Captain Van Darn got badly wounded, bristling like a porcupine, with arrows. Several of his officers and men were killed in hand-to-hand combat around wigwam huts. William Bailey himself suffered injuries inflicted by a tomahawk that left his right arm lame. Had the Wichita Indians not fled in fear of what might happen next, they could have massacred the whole company, and Barton would have never been born.

Barton used to listen awestruck to his father's yarns about his exploits as a young man. His heart bled, however, when his stories turned to William's tragic experiences during the Civil War which broke out two years after the Battle of the Wichita Village. Because of his crippled arm, his Daddy didn't serve in Lee's army and sat out the war as an invalid in the family farm outside Richmond, the Confederate capital. It was five years of privation during which his family had to keep a tight watch on their 47 slaves who were itching to flee to freedom in the north. Barton wept when his Daddy told him about how Richmond was sacked by its own hungry citizens on the night of its fall to the Unionists, how neighbors trembled in fear when Grant marched through the city at the head of a conquering army and how, in the first week of April, 1865 Abe Lincoln rode through the streets of Richmond in a grim parade past humiliated southerners. Barton wished he'd heard only Indian stories.

After the Civil War, the Baileys never recovered. While the family's 47 freed slaves flocked north, carpetbaggers flocked south; and the Baileys sank deeper into poverty. Young Barton swore never to fritter away his life in the farm and to seek prosperity in the north. After his father died a broken man at the early age of 56, he set out from his home to try his luck in the shipyards of Philadelphia. But he never did find prosperity there. So, in 1895, the young man falsified his age to enter the fledgling U.S. Navy as an 18 year-old recruit although he was one year short of the required age. He was attracted by the shiny Monitors slipping out of American shipyards to realize Washington's strategic plan for building a world-class Navy that was begun with an appropriation from Congress in 1890. There, Bailey would find his calling.

He began his naval service as a stoker. Bailey toiled with devilish vigor shoveling coal into the furnaces of *USS Miantonomoh*, a Monitor-class warship that was the pride of the Atlantic fleet. He was promoted to other parts of the warship but repeatedly fell back to the Black Room for repeated breaches of discipline. After a year of infernal menial labor, Bailey jumped ship during a port call on the British colony of Hong Kong and became a castaway in Asia for seven months. Then, in December 1897, he was caught stealing peaches in the port city of Shanghai by the Japanese who maintained an enclave there. He was turned over to the U.S. Navy forthwith. Mercifully, he was not hanged as a deserter (the Navy was short of men at the time). Instead, he was condemned to the Black Room for six months, retrained and handed the use of a Gatling gun – thus, his nickname "Gatling" – and soon he earned his first stripe as a gunnery mate, which position he held down to the fateful battle at Manila Bay. Bailey had come a long way since fleeing rural life in Richmond.

Now, he was in the Philippine Islands in the far side of the Pacific. Never in his wildest dreams did he expect that he would taste battle as a navyman since it was always the Cavalry that got into hostilities. It was only the beginning of a life of adventure that was to overshadow his father's experiences in the West.

The origins of the U.S. Navy were just as humble as Bailey's. When the 13 colonies broke away from Britain to form the Union, they had no navy to speak of. Their merchant ships were easy prey to pirates, especially in the Mediterranean where the Barbary Powers ruled by Arabs made a living seizing American ships and men for ransom. In 1784, Thomas Jefferson wrote his colleague James Monroe: "We ought to be a naval power, if we mean to carry our own commerce.... I am of the opinion that Paul Jones with half a dozen frigates would totally destroy this business of Arab piracy." But the 13 states, then governed by the Articles of Confederation, were too poor to buy even a dozen frigates. Instead, they began sending feelers to their former colonial master, Britain, which had a navy powerful enough to protect American shipping. The mercantilist Britain wisely deemed it better for its commercial interests to see American ships being raided, thereby ridding the sea of a competitor. Benjamin Franklin lamented that he had "heard in London, that if there were no Algiers, it would be worth England's while to build one." Piracy and kidnapping for ransom became an abiding threat to American prosperity. So, the fledgling republic degraded itself for the greater interest of its commerce and paid through its nose for a treaty with Morocco, one of the Barbary States, for $10,000, about the price of the next ransom.

Even as the United States grew in wealth and power, it remained averse to spending money on a standing navy. It preferred to arm privateers whenever the need arose for the republic to fight at sea. Meanwhile, its merchant fleet steadily expanded in size and reach, plying the world's oceans in floating caravans that provided temptation to other kinds of enemies.

Insults to the American flag – derided as "striped bunting" – became the order of the day. The prime offender was the greatest naval power in the world, Britain. During the Napoleonic Wars, for instance, British warships, starved for sailors, hijacked American vessels at sea and dragged out Yankees kicking and screaming for service in His Majesty's navy. The practice was formally called "impressment," a tradition held dear by labor-short Britain. Apart from monarchy, Americans never found a tradition so objectionable.

Such outrages to American honor provoked cries for retaliation. Patriots were in high dudgeon denouncing the brazen seizure of American nationals for slavery, turning a blind eye to similar practices in the south. Ironically, the Americans most offended by impressment were farmers in the landlocked Western states who seldom saw the sea or rode ships, if ever. On June 4, 1812, the United States Congress boldly voted to declare war on Britain, 79-49, the decisive votes being cast by Western delegates who didn't take British insults lightly. They finally got even the following year. American Commodore Oliver Hazard Perry routed a fleet of British brigs under Captain Robert H. Barclay in the Battle of Lake Erie. In addition to humiliating the mistress of the seas, Perry took away several British brigs as trophies.

The United States also learned lessons during the Civil War. The South ordered warships from England which proceeded to build them in a headlong rush despite dire warnings from the North. When English authorities showed signs of heeding Unionist warnings, one vessel slipped out of a Liverpool dockyard under cover of darkness and another followed suit half-finished to find their way to Confederate hands. Christened *Alabama* and *Florida,* the two smuggled warships, together with the *Shenandoah,* proceeded to prey on Union shipping with impunity, claiming 60 victims. Clearly, a navy was essential in war.

The other power guilty of bullying the United States at sea was Spain. And Spain was imprudent enough to commit a string of offenses when it was declining and the United States was rising. On February 28, 1854, Spanish troops searching for criminals boarded the American ship *Black Warrior* in Havana and arrested its crew, only to release them later. Yankees raised Cain. The next affront proved far more explosive. In October 1873, the Spanish gunboat *Tornado* hunting for Cuban insurgents gave chase to the *Virginius,* an American paddlewheel steamer engaged in gunrunning in the Florida Straits. The steamer managed to throw its cargo of weapons overboard before being captured. Found guilty of smuggling guns into Cuba, its skipper was condemned to die by firing squad despite appeals for clemency to General Juan Burriel, the local Spanish satrap. On November 4, a firing squad stood up the skipper against the wall, along with a motley group of Cubans and British captives, and shot them all. Four days later, Burriel executed another dozen prisoners, three of them Americans.

Across the Florida Straits, the Yankee press cried murder and urged revenge. "We Demand an Eye for an Eye," said the New York *Journal.* President Ulysses Grant ordered a punitive expedition to set sail for Cuba but backed down when he could muster only a flotilla of paddlewheelers. In crisis, Uncle

Sam chafed at his naval weakness. The lesson sank deep when Britain, having the wherewithal to enforce its will, sent a warship to Cuba and threatened to bomb Santiago if General Burriel didn't release his English captives. Burriel promptly complied. It was an example the Americans never forgot; but it would take them till the turn of the century to enshrine "gunboat diplomacy" in their foreign policy. Meanwhile, they had to keep swallowing the unending affronts to their national pride.

Then, on February 15, 1898, the *Maine* sank in Havana with the loss of 263 lives, a disaster blamed on Spain in the absence of credible suspects. By this time, the United States, who already had a navy worthy of the name, knew what to do.

Now, Barton Bailey was watching the fruits of that navy's initial accomplishment – the destruction of the Spanish fleet. And on the ruins of the Spanish navy the United States staked its claim to a place in the select club of the world's great powers, right on the heels of upstart Japan. The significance of the victory in Manila Bay was lost on Bailey who didn't grasp the strategies of leaders nor cared about the business of imperialism.

———————————

Bailey craved for relief from the drudgery of pointless patrols. Life ashore the toehold of Sangley Point was a little better. A peninsula, it was ideally suited to be a naval base but it was an island unto itself in the completeness of its isolation. There was nothing to see but the sea on all three sides, plus a stretch of dry land that led to a sleepy fishing village. In his idleness, the young sailor tried to relieve the irritating spell of boredom by getting to know the locals. He learned to converse with Filipinos at the naval base in broken Spanish complemented by sign language to ferret out tidbits of information about the situation in the city. He interrogated Manila-based European merchants who gravitated towards Sangley either to do business with the U.S. Navy or out of sheer curiosity. He thought that the Spaniards inside their palaces in Intramuros were better off. From the grapevine, it turned out that Intramuros was not a sentinel standing proud at the mouth of the bay, but it was in a hell of a lot of trouble.

Within the walls were refugee officials, bishops and traders driven from the provinces by the irresistible tide of revolution, just like in Cuba. They had chosen to take refuge in the capital rather than wait for the beleaguered Spanish Army to quell the uprising. The insurgents had still not gathered for the final push on Manila because they were still waiting for the arrival of their leader from Hong Kong; but instead of holding on till the Spanish army came to their rescue, the Spanish civilians and clergy conceded the countryside to the natives. It was only in Intramuros, the old city within a city, where they could breathe easily. Although the Spanish civilians were largely spared the gun and the bolo of insurgents, they hesitated to leave the safety of the walls, because they hated the smell of the *indios* (as they called the natives) more than revolution.

The more Bailey learned of the Spaniards the better he understood the precariousness of their state. Now, he no longer wanted Dewey to bomb the Walled City in retaliation for the shabby treatment they got at its gates. They were suffering, too. He didn't wish to bomb the priests and the nuns crowded in the churches and monasteries. Neither did he want to waste ammunition on the Guardia Civil who were camped in tents in the square, hungry and war weary after having been run out of the provinces by their colonial subjects. Or the friars evicted from their rich plantations in the countryside subsisting on porridge and lard. Or the governor-general and his court who still lived in luxury in his palace. More crafty, more merciful, methods of conquest were called for, something becoming of a "respectable, well brung up" commander such as Dewey.

7
RETURN OF AN EXILE

The doldrums of inactivity brought Bailey into contact with the natives of the islands. He had expected them to be wild, savage, and backward, but his first brush with their leaders gave him his first impression of the quality of the Filipino revolutionary.

Early in the morning of May 19, 1898, Dewey roused the crew of his flagship from their quarters in Sangley Point to finish repainting the *Olympia*. He was going to see Emilio Aguinaldo that day – more than two weeks after the battle.

Bailey climbed down the side of the ship to clean its hull while hanging from a webbing of manila hemp. Armed with a steel brush and suspended in the air, he scrubbed what remained of the gray war paint that had camouflaged the ship so that its original whitewash, its regulation color, would show through. It was still dawn. The sun had not risen over the steeples of Intramuros yet Dewey was driving them hard as if they were out to fight another battle. And for what purpose? To honor an obscure Filipino general whom Bailey had heard vaguely about while in Hong Kong. Could there be a general among the natives who had no army in sight?

He was down and ornery, idleness having put a damper on his spirits. What in blazes were they cooking up in the captain's quarters? Dewey's rambling explanation about the reason for their prolonged stay, delivered at the mess hall yesterday – "we are fighting an extension of the Spanish-American War" – was neither morale-boosting nor enlightening.

As far as Bailey could see, hanging from a rope, none of Dewey's ships came out of the battle unscathed, contrary to legend. *Olympia* was a mess. Three planks were torn up from the deck, the work of cannonballs that shook lumber loose from nails. The whaleboats, hung from the bridge by nets, were crushed to a pulp and had to be jettisoned accordingly. The rails of its parapets were ripped in sections, with several stanchions blown away. The cranes that hoisted the boats and cargo were broken down.

Most spectacularly, the hull was pitted all over from the pummeling it received from shells and debris, scarred with dents, holes, gashes, burns. It was this ship that Bailey and other crewmen were trying to primp up early in the morning so that it would look presentable to a visiting dignitary.

Bailey took a bath by jumping into the bay, then scrubbing himself while holding on to a line; then he rinsed himself with a bucket of fresh water at the navy building. Dewey had ordered everyone to look as trim as his ships. In his cabin, he "put on the frills" by changing into a sailor dress, with a scarf knotted at the neck and a flap draped on his back. He could not change his shoes because he had only a pair and it took effort to mop off the coal dust that clung to the leather. When he climbed out of the wooden barracks that once housed Spanish sailors, he looked spic and span as a piece of linen fresh from a steam laundry.

The rebels were massing in a field just outside the Sangley Point yard. The naval base was part of the province of Cavite, the home ground of their guest of honor General Emilio Aguinaldo. It was in Cavite where the young revolutionary, then a little-known mayor of the nearby town of Kawit, had thrown the gauntlet at 300 years of Spanish rule. Like the Indians in Thomas Bailey's stories, the early morning encounter unfolded with the sight of Aguinaldo's troops streaming out of the palm groves to mass in the field, growing in number by the second, until they formed two ragtag battalions which marched with notable lack of military bearing, each man shuffling out of step with the other. Bailey was not so impressed with their uniform – straw hats with the front brim folded up, loose tunics and baggy pants. He was, however, struck by the weapons each of them carried – a bolo and a rifle – which made them look very dangerous indeed. From a distance he couldn't recognize their rifles which particularly seized his interest but he guessed that they were Mauser rifles which were just as good as the Yankee's Krag.

"Surely, they don't look nothin' like the Spaniards," said Bailey.

"And we are putting on the frills for these folks?" commented Wolf. "They're gooks."

"What?"

"They ain't niggers and they ain't dagos, so I call 'em gooks."

"Ha-ha," Bailey burst out laughing. "That's how we call them stokers when they get smeared up with coal and you can't tell one from the other." So it happened that the Filipinos rebels came to be known to the Yankees as gooks, as distinguished from the Spaniards' dagos. The Yankees would later dub themselves the even less flattering name "goddams."

The soldiers' language waxed with inventiveness. With a friendly attitude toward the natives, Bailey refrained from calling them pejorative names until, that is, much later when the going got tough. He was surprised, however, to discover that the locals were just as adept at name-calling – i.e., discriminating themselves into classes of *"indios"* (pure-blooded natives), *"mestizos"* (mixed-blood locals), "ilustrados" (the educated class), and *"Kastila"* (the pure Spanish).

Gathered on the deck of the *Olympia,* the uniformed sailors stood at ease along the parapets buzzing animatedly in keeping with Dewey's directive to "all hands to line the port but not to stand in salute." The commodore merely wanted to put on a show to impress upon Aguinaldo the power and discipline of American arms but not to give him honors, hence, the casual reception.

History records the reception as having occurred on a bright morning of May 19. By receiving the revolutionary general, Dewey did not mean to honor him as a head of a revolutionary government or an organized army. On the contrary, he meant to overawe the visitor with the magnificence of the American arms in order to win over his allegiance. For this purpose, he held the meeting on board the flagship instead of onshore in the captured naval base of Sangley Point and, for more dramatic effect, he anchored the ship a hundred yards offshore so that Aguinaldo would have to approach it by riding a launch. They explained that the *Olympia* was unable to dock by the pier because of obstacles posed by the wreckage of Spanish warships a few feet underwater.

As Bailey watched from the side of the ship, Aguinaldo's party consisting of five officers made its way toward the *Olympia* on board a tugboat. One rebel holding a bamboo pole cleared the vessel's way by poking aside drifting flotsam.

Bailey sized up the delegation of revolutionaries and compared them to the bunch of Indians whom his father had fought in the Battle of Wichita Village. For all their ferocious looks, they could not win a battle against superior arms of the U.S. Navy or even the Spanish army. They wouldn't last a day. They'd be blown over the creek by the Spanish cannons as soon as they approached Intramuros. Why, they even had trouble climbing the ship! To get aboard the *Olympia* the visitors had to stand precariously on the bow of the tugboat so that they could reach the flagship's ladder, not an easy operation while the tugboat was being tossed about by the waves. They scrambled up the ladder one by one. Bailey helpfully extended a hand to the lead man of the boarding party, a slight officer with a braided cap, and heaved him aboard. He pulled over the second man and almost fell overboard, overpowered by the latter's weight. This was a rather portly fellow, nearly twice his size, a dapper and fair-skinned native whose courtly demeanor set him apart from his mean-looking companions. They were followed by a retinue of officials who soon crowded the starboard side of the bridge.

Bailey later identified the first man as General Emilio Aguinaldo. He was rather unimposing for a head of an army but a far cry from the gooks that shoveled coal in the boiler room of the flagship. Slender, brush-haired, barely over five feet in height, he wore a trim uniform with brass buttons, frilly epaulets and a sword that almost touched the floor as it was too long for his height. He was barely thirty years old but on his shoulders rested the burden of freeing his people. In his hands was the blood not only of Spaniards but of fellow patriots who had crossed him. He would make a good ally for Dewey.

"He's ours," Wolf pointed out to Bailey. "He's gonna be our ally and if McKinley doesn't send us enough troops, we'll probably rely on his army of gooks for ground support."

As they watched condescendingly, the revolutionary leader shook hands with the squadron's lesser captains in their ceremonial dress white, and then was ushered to the commodore's quarters to hold a private one-on-one talk with Dewey. It was part of the plan to keep the meeting informal without the official blessings of Uncle Sam.

With their leader cloistered with the host, the other Filipinos fidgeted on the deck stared at by crewmen.

Bailey managed to loosen up the guests by striking up a conversation with one of them, the portly aide who put on airs. "Howdy, gentleman."

Wolf nudged him. "He doesn't speak English."

"I'm Bart Bailey. *Como esta usted. Hablas English, si?*" Bailey had learned a smattering of Spanish from his Daddy.

"Yes, I do speak English, sir," the portly gentleman spoke. "How do you do?"

"How de-do. So, you are a Philip – what do they call

'em, Filipino."

"Yes, a Filipino. I'm Joaquin Calderon. The general's physician."

"Doctor, huh."

The man nodded. "Yes. I studied at the Universidad de Santo Tomas and I traveled to Europe and that's where I learned your language."

"Spain?"

"Uh-huh."

"You studied in Europe?" Bailey was amazed.

"I studied my preparatory course in Manila, but I took special courses in medicine in Madrid."

"Oh, I see."

Bailey was bowled over. He could not believe that a man of such refinements could be a native, or educated locally, or that so backward-looking a place could have a university at all. Standing next to him, Bailey felt decidedly inferior, not having gone past grammar school in his native Virginia. So impressed was he that he scanned this unusual native species from head to foot. Unlike the other insurgents, he had a fair skin and projected elegance. He was dressed to the nines in a derby hat, an overcoat with a chain watch, and buttoned boots. His most striking features, however, were a monocle sitting on his nose and an upturned moustache whose wings curled up to trace the contours of his chubby cheeks, a style that gave him an expression of perpetual smile. He was so different from the others that Bailey couldn't understand how the muggins he could have belonged to the same race.

Joaquin Calderon was what the locals called a *"mestizo"* and an *"ilustrado"* – distinctions that rarely converged on a single man. A mestizo was a native of mixed blood, most likely sired by a Spanish soldier or a friar; whereas an *ilustrado* was an educated or "lettered" Filipino who studied either in a local university or in Europe. Calderon belonged to that aristocracy of the learned entitled to privileges in the Spanish colony that no brown-skinned ignorant Filipino could ever hope to

108

achieve. It was his class who had agitated the rabble into rebellion two years before, an heroic act of self-sacrifice. Several of them had been thrown to prison and executed as a result, the most prominent being Jose Rizal, a physician who studied in Madrid, traveled across Europe preaching the cause of his people and written books denouncing the abuses of the friars. Now, they had been overshadowed by their less lettered countrymen who had been inspired by their literature to take up arms against Spain, most of whom belonged to the rabble or, like Aguinaldo, the landed gentry.

"You must have seen how we clobbered the Spanish fleet." Bailey tried to cover-up his feeling of inferiority by impressing upon Calderon the power of American arms.

"In fact I did, sir, I was watching from the shore," answered Calderon in an ever courtly, even patronizing, manner.

"We tarred and feathered them."

"Pardon?"

"We licked 'em."

"What?"

There was an audible difference between the King's English taught in college and the slang spoken by Americans, especially southerners. A trifle embarrassed, Bailey switched to standard English which he used only when speaking to superior officers. He said: "I mean to say we engaged the Spanish in battle and sent all their ships to the bottom of the sea."

"You did. You most certainly did!" the dapper doctor laughed uproariously.

"We found the enemy and we had them," butted in Wolf.

"I understand you're also fightin' them Spaniards," Bailey addressed Calderon.

"Yes, but what we're fighting for principles – like what our Latin American brethren are doing, fighting for self-determination."

"As happening in Cuba, I reckon. The people there grew tired of being taken for slaves by them Spaniards and so they decide to take up arms in pursuit of liberty, equality and.... How is that again, Wolf?"

Wolf said nothing.

"Yes, yes, and if you remember your own history, too, you also fought a war of independence against Britain."

"Bet your hat you're George Washington," Wolf rudely interjected.

Bailey changed the subject. "Say, doc, you're a native of this place. If you could just tell me what's inside the Walled City and what are those buildings and domes which you could see from miles away... I have been very curious about your country."

Calderon adjusted his monocle and peered distantly across Manila Bay in the hope of catching a glimpse of the Walled City. It was not visible. "Intramuros," he said wistfully, smiling under his upturned moustache, "that's the seat of our government, where you can find our finest churches, our palaces and universities. There is much to see there. We dream of the day when we can have that city and call it the capital of a free Philippines."

"Intermoors, that's a fine name. Whereabouts do you live?"

"Not inside, but I studied there. I do have a clinic outside the walls where I conduct my practice. You are welcome to visit us someday."

"You bet your ass we'll march into that place at the head of an army," Wolf interrupted.

"And if you could visit us, I and my daughter will entertain you."

The mention of a daughter intrigued Bailey but he skirted the subject. "You will, doc? I'll shove right to town when I get the chance."

The two stopped talking when they noted a stir among the Navy officers and uniformed rebels gathered in the quarterdeck, a clear space on the ship reserved for ceremonies. The white-haired Dewey had reappeared along with the youthful

Aguinaldo who looked even darker in his gloom. As both Americans and Filipinos cheered, Dewey patted Aguinaldo on the shoulder in a comradely, if patronizing, manner, a gesture that the latter reciprocated with a glum smile.

What did they talk about? To begin with, they must have discussed the promise given by Consul Pratt in Singapore to support Aguinaldo's fight for independence in exchange for help in tying up the Spaniards in the Philippines while the war in the Caribbean was in progress. They must have also talked about the possibility of launching a concerted assault on Intramuros if no American troops came on time.

The two sides exchanged handshakes, which the Filipinos did clumsily, it being a Western custom they did not practice. They then disembarked in disorder, trying not to slip.

Bailey again assisted the heavy doctor down the ladder, this time exuding goodwill for a new-found friend. He waved over the top of the ladder as the Filipino plopped on the tugboat. "Bye-bye, Whacky Doc," he invented a nickname for the doctor taken from the pronunciation of the name Joaquin ('Whackín'). "See ya." Then he turned around and jabbed Wolf on the ribs for being so rude to the Filipino.

"That was shameful thing you did, Wolf. How could you be so rude?"

"Don't care much for them gooks."

"You should hear yourself talk. That gentleman was a respectable, well-brung up fella." Bailey was perplexed that the German, who prided himself in his erudition, could be so intolerant.

The meeting with Aguinaldo proved inconclusive. Nothing happened after that. The only feedback the Americans got from the meeting was a long letter from Joaquin Calderon in broken English and elegant Spanish, inviting Bailey to visit him at his clinic in Manila, enclosing a map of Intramuros and its environs.

———————

8

A MISSION IN FORT SANTIAGO

On June 10, 1898, Barton Bailey received an urgent summons. He was recalled from his patrol boat *Petrel* to report to Captain Charles Gridley who, next to Dewey, was the most famous man in the Asiatic Squadron.

"Gunnery Sergeant Bailey, you are going into Intermoors," said Gridley.

"Beg your pardon, sir?"

"You are going to enter the Walled City secretly, gather information about its guns and fortifications, then come back," explained his shavetail, Lt. James Cocker.

Bailey stood silent. He was not sure whether this was a punishment or a distinct honor being served up to him. "Ah, um...."

Gridley, a squat man with a fleshy face and dense crop of moustache, seemed to have spotted a trait in Bailey which made him uniquely qualified for the job, something that Bailey himself wasn't aware of. "This is a hush-hush operation known to only a few, do you understand? And we chose you because you have a knack for befriending the natives. Find out what is the best way to take Intramuros without an army to back us up."

That was a tall order. It was not written in the books how a navy might lay siege on a fort or take it by storm, like asking the Cavalry to intercept the Spanish Armada in the high seas. The plan to infiltrate Intramuros, as Bailey very well understood, was born out of the navymen's impatience over the delayed arrival of reinforcements. They had the morale of exiles. Three weeks passed since the naval battle and still no Army troops. Once in a while the cutter *McCulloch* would sail for Hong Kong to communicate with Washington through the closest available telegraph line and to take on supplies. When the cutter reappeared a week later, Bailey's restless comrades would all be agog with anticipation; but Dewey was always vague about the tidings it brought, if any. They did not believe his assurances that American troops were on their way. Otherwise, why wouldn't he cite the precise number of troops and their units? If there were troops being deployed at all, they were headed for Cuba, the main theater of war, and none were bound for this godforsaken place. The darned McKinley had forgotten his men in the Pacific.

The first month's anniversary of the battle came and went and still no American convoy appeared on Manila Bay. The first five days of June passed at thirty knots of anticipation and only the *McCulloch* turned up in its weekly run across the South China Sea. The delay bore out Bailey's suspicions about McKinley's priorities.

Dewey himself maintained an uneasy grip on the panhandle of Sangley Point peninsula where he was in constant danger of being attacked. He felt so insecure in fact that he kept a skeleton force to man each of his warships lest the Spaniards sally out of their citadel and trap them in their beachhead, without hope of escape by sea. Having cut the undersea cable in a flash of anger, he could not even keep in constant touch with Washington to monitor the coming of the promised reinforcements. As the weeks drifted by without good news for the Squadron, Dewey's hold on his men got shaky, with breaches of discipline becoming a daily occurrence.

Just feeding them was a problem. The ravenous appetite of the likes of Barton Bailey in the tropical climate was that of famished Crusaders breaking a 40-day penance. The *Olympia* alone counted 466 crew members; the *Baltimore* 395; the *Boston* 272; the gunboats *Petrel* and *Concord* 100 and 150 men respectively; and the baggage carrier *McCulloch* 130. Altogether, Dewey had to keep full and battle-ready 1,808 voracious men at Sangley Point who were getting restive by the day.

If there were too many mouths to feed in his contingent, there were too few hands available to wage a land war. The enemy had at least 17,000 troops inside Intramuros, who were by no means starved or demoralized. They were able to supply themselves with provisions from the provinces, not being completely surrounded by the Filipino rebels who had no capacity to lay siege on the city, and through various gates in Intramuros, gobbled up the produce of church-owned farms sprawling across hundreds of thousands of hectares, that is to say, the bulk of the agricultural land in the colony. No wonder the soldiers, sustained by their patrons in the Church, had the stomach for a drawn-out war. Had they chosen to sally out of Intramuros, they could have clobbered the Yankees at Sangley Point and driven them back to the sea and left them to patrol the bay aimlessly. Fortunately for Dewey, they were beset by their own problems.

The German strategist Wolfgang Messner summed up their situation in this wise: "Just because we won one battle doesn't mean we've won the war. The Spanish are in control of the land, and there are 20,000 of them here, plus probably thousands more in the other islands. How do you go about conquering an entire archipelago with the ships of the Navy alone? These are things old Dewey didn't consider. And I don't think this is part of his plan either. We should start thinking of going home."

"Then, why doesn't Dewey decide to break camp and go home?"

"Because Washington has other ideas. Why do you think the *McCulloch* keeps going back and forth between Manila and Hong Kong? Because the politicians in Washington are giving him new orders that go beyond the original objective of sinking the Spanish fleet."

"Can he do that? Can *we*?" asked Bailey skeptically, unable to fathom the strategy of the war.

"That is the problem. We can't take this country with our Navy alone. We gotta bring the Army to this place."

Bailey was better able to relieve the monotony than his comrades. Often he stole away from the sentries at Sangley Point to roam the nearby towns, then came back at night with strange stories.

"Guess where I went yesterday," he would tell his gang.

"Why, what you been doin', Gatling?" they would ask.

"Like goin' courtin' in town where Spanish señoritas live."

Wolf's eyes bulged: "You did!"

"Just kidding." Bailey was not telling. He showed a lock of hair that he kept hidden in his pocket and grinned sheepishly.

"That's horse hair," said Scott Preston.

"Smell it. Doesn't it smell just like a newly bathed squaw?"

"I haven't smelt a newly bathed squaw. But I have smelt a newly scalped Indian," retorted Wolf. "And it smelt like rotten flesh."

After one of his forays out of town, he was caught by a sentry clambering over the fence and he was promptly thrown in the stockade. It wasn't as bad an offense as jumping ship in Shanghai and he was detained for a total of ten days, after which he was brought face to face with Gridley.

Apparently, the captain had investigated the case and decided that he could put to good use Bailey's restlessness.

That was how Bailey came to learn of Captain Gridley's plans for him. What Gridley told him confirmed Wolfgang Messner's analysis of the situation.

"The Army is on its way here," said Gridley. "And we have to provide them with the necessary intelligence about the lay of the land."

"Are we gonna occupy the islands?"

"I don't want to dwell on that. The most I can tell you is that we are clearing the way for the Army to come in and take over the theater of operations."

"So, that's it – that's what my comrade Wolf has been telling me all along."

"Whether we are going to seize this colony and make it our own is for the politicians to decide."

Bailey could not turn down a direct order from his superiors who were in turn implementing some inscrutable strategy from Washington.

The clincher came when Gridley ended the briefing with: "This is the last important thing for us to do. When the Army arrives, it's going to be their show."

To be chosen to cap the Navy's mission in the Philippines was an honor he could not decline. He wanted to do it most of all to please the old man, who despite his promotion to Admiral of the Navy, was to be relegated to a supporting role as baggage carrier to the Army.

"If there's going to be any fighting, I need at least Wolf Messner, a big man and a darn good fighter, too."

"No, there's not going to be any fighting. You can't bring anyone with you that will give your mission away. Perhaps a native companion will do."

"A native. Someone to guide me around the place."

"Yes," concurred Gridley. "But not a Yankee."

"I know one local," Bailey said, thinking of someone.

When Bailey told Wolfgang Messner about the mission at the barracks, the German blew his top.

"What do you mean you can take a gook but not a Yank?" Wolf felt insulted.

"Nothing personal. Two Yanks on a reconnaissance mission will easily give us away. I can take a native who can cover up for me."

"Who do you have in mind?"

"There's Whacky Doc Calderon. He gave me a sketch of his address when he was aboard the *Olympia*."

"The big fat one with the curly moustache who liked to put on airs? Ain't he Spanish?"

"He's a native."

"So, where are you gonna go?"

"We'll mosey around Intermoors a li'l bit."

"Go looking for friends and allies?

"What the top brass are up to, I dunno, I don't have the foggiest idea," Bailey professed ignorance about Washington's objectives. "I'll check out the guns, the fortifications, the camps."

"When will the brass come to their senses? Haven't they realized that they can take the city only by a ruse and not by brute force? Just like Troy!" Wolf hooted pompously.

"I don't care the shucks what they're up to. It's better than sitting on our butts here, swatting flies."

"Wish you luck, Bart, you're going to the lion's den. Don't trust anybody out there, not even that Spanish fella."

Bailey paused for a moment to think and added: "Whacky Doc, he told me he's got a cute little señorita in his place," he grinned, eager to start his adventure.

Outfitting himself for the mission, he took nothing but a Bowie knife, a pistol, a compass, and a sketch of the streets of Manila leading to Doctor Calderon's clinic. Bailey boarded a gunboat and rode in silence along the coast of the bay toward the Walled City at the mouth of the Pasig River. One wall of the Spanish bastion faced the bay and another wall bordered on the river. Under the ruddy illumination of a setting sun which glowed like a lighthouse at the mouth of the bay, Bailey scanned the outline of the wall covered with grass and lichen through the ages. Repeated patrols during the past few weeks had etched on his mind the features of the wall. It was a pile of boulders and masonry plastered together by mortar, as though hastily built to forestall an invasion. The upper half was more evenly constructed, being composed of firebricks neatly arranged in tiers. Topping it were guardhouses of stone, shaped into domes in the style of churches with windows cut into the sides – and there was not a shadow of a man in any of them, Bailey noted. Dewey could very well take the walls by surprise if only he had enough men and equipment. And tons of luck.

At the mouth of the Pasig River, he came within sight of Fort Santiago which occupied a corner of Intramuros offering a commanding view of the bay and the estuary of the river. It had steep 30-foot walls that leveled to a plateau, partly submerged in the river like an iceberg. There, standing on a gun emplacement on top of the wall was a cluster of Spanish soldiers who maintained a tight watch on the breadth of the bay, particularly in the direction of Corregidor Island at its entrance and the captured Sangley Point naval base farther east. And therein lay the danger, Bailey thought. The battery of the fort was capable of wreaking havoc on an approaching enemy by reason of its strategic location at the estuary of the Pasig River. No way could an invading force barge its way through the estuary in the teeth of gunfire coming from the guns mounted on the fort.

"Ready when you are, Gunny. Just say when you wanna go," said the skipper of the gunboat who gave Bailey all the leeway to choose his jumping-off point.

"If you could drop me off the wall, I won't mind," joked the passenger.

"Oh, no. They'd blow us out the water."

"I'd mole in at night when no one's a-looking and come out of some lady's bedroom."

"Bring us some undies and knickers then."

They exchanged pleasantries in the early night with Bailey hardly showing any sign of nervousness. "Brave lad, this!" the skipper said to his men.

"Okay, we're getting near. We're getting ready to go," said the pilot with his hands on the rudder.

At the port area half a mile away from the northern wall, crowded with outrigger boats and sampans, Bailey disembarked. Far from being an object of curiosity, he simply melted into the mass of fishermen and merchants bringing their goods to the marketplace. Hell, he could have been a Spanish civilian buying supplies for the refugees behind the walls, or an English trader checking on the arrival of a steamship from Europe. Taking Calderon's letter from his pocket, he tried to locate the man's place in the strange territory with nothing to guide him but his hand-drawn map streaked with arbitrary twists and turns. In his confusion, he feared unwittingly straying into the den of insurgents in the slums of Manila and being taken prisoner. He had even more difficulty understanding Calderon's instructions written in a curly, calligraphic style, filled with strange words and phrases. Lost in the maze of alleys and canals, he decided to forgo his search that night and resume it in the light of day, spending the evening inside an empty church.

The following morning, he continued his search in the commercial district of Escolta, an area outside the walls abutting on the Pasig River, paved by cobblestones. The shops consisted of two-storey structures with gabled roofs, balusters lining their balconies and windows covered with latticed panels made of flattened shell and wood. At street level, the sides of the buildings were lined with awnings of canvas propped up by stilts to provide shade and cover to the stalls crowding the sidewalks. Horse-drawn carriages rambled down the street past merchants selling fruits, religious icons and trinkets. Bailey wended his way along the sidewalk hedged by rickety stalls, fast on the heels of pigtailed Chinese traders, women lugging rattan baskets and half-naked laborers driving pushcarts. This was a place quite unlike Virginia, he thought, and more like Shanghai.

He came across a rail track embedded into the street pavement which conveyed passenger trams called *tranvias* to unknown stations. Once again, he felt lost in this sprawling, unplanned, disorderly city, which could not have been more chaotic had it been swept up by the tide of rebellion. His only clue to the exact location of Calderon's place was a statement in his letter that his clinic was "situationed in the middle of the position of two blacksmith's shops far apart between each other in Calle Real." Well, he was in Calle Real now.

At a corner marked by a post topped by a lantern burning oil at daytime, he bumped into his first Spaniard. It was a horseman sporting a fedora making his way past a nondescript crowd of civilians with the air of proud unconcern as if the colonial regime of which he was a privileged retainer was not under attack. Upon sighting another group of Spaniards riding a carriage, wearing military uniform, he began to wonder whether the report that the colonial regime was under siege by the rebels was true. For surely, these Spaniards were not behaving as if they were caught up in a revolution, strolling around idly without any care in the world.

He came upon a typical shop with a canvas awning whose sign froze him on his feet. It said *"Joaquin Calderon y Paras, medico y cirujano."* Finally, his destination. The place stood next to a busy blacksmith's shop from which issued sounds of hammering. Whatever the Spanish words meant, Bailey sure could read the name of the mestizo fop on the sign. Convinced that he was in the right place, at the right time, he knocked on the door.

A girl with an ornate comb on her hair looked out from the window. "Ah, señor...?" She was hanging lengths of yarn soaked in a red dye from a pole extending out of the window.

"Buenos dias, Señor Calderon, donde esta? Um, I'm an American sailor from a merchant ship offshore. "

The girl stared at him transfixed.

Bailey stared back and repeated his introduction.

"Papa! Papa!"

"Don't be scared, sweetie. I'm a friend of your Dad."

Must be the doctor's daughter, thought Bailey, a comely sweet señorita.

From the adjacent shop booming with the sound of pounding, a burly man appeared holding a hammer and a pair of tongs. He shouted something in Tagalog that sounded aggressive.

"Buenos dias, sir, I'm looking for a doctor, Señor Calderon."

"Yo soy Señor Calderon. Como te llamas? I'm Señor Calderon, what is your name?" said the thick-set man, dripping sweat. "Estrella, go inside."

This was the wrong Calderon. The Yankee visitor hesitated. "I'm Bart Bailey. An American."

Presently, a ponderous man wearing a pair of suspenders appeared in the door of the clinic. "Ah, Señor Bailey, *mi amigo!* Come in! *Como esta usted?"* he greeted, his upturned moustache a bit ruffled.

"Howdy, doc?"

"Glad to have you here. My clinic is closed today, it's Sunday, but you're welcome, come in, come in. Did you receive my letter?"

"I did, and just about at the right time. I wanted to see you regarding some business."

"I didn't expect you to honor my invitation, *sarhento,* I didn't know you will be coming. As you can see, it's all a mess and dirty, this little flat of mine."

"It's all right, sir. We can talk outside."

"No, no, come inside." Joaquin ushered the visitor inside his clinic which doubled up as his residence. "Estrella, clear up the sala."

Bailey walked into a cramped room dominated by a dentist's drill powered by pedals and a chain. Glass jars containing wilted herbs and seeds sat on a shelf. His eyes, however, kept straying toward the girl of about sixteen who heeded her father's call to pick up the loose strings and swatches of cloth on the floor.

"You've got a pretty gal here..."

"Go upstairs, Estrella." The man was not so generous with the attention of his daughter as the American had hoped. "This is my brother Carlos, he operates a foundry next to my shop, so pardon the noise." Joaquin pointed at the half-naked artisan who had followed from the adjacent workshop. "Caloy, this is my friend Barton Bailey, from the fleet of Admiral George Dewey. Remember the ships we saw firing at the Spanish in Manila Bay? He was on one of them!"

Carlos muttered something, then disappeared back into his workshop.

Joaquin tried to make Bailey feel at ease. "Sit down. *Habéis desayunado ya?* Have you taken your breakfast already?"

"Yup, thanks."

"So your commander finally let you out?"

"Well, yes and no. He sent me here but not on shore leave. Official business. There is something I would like to talk to you about."

"Oh, so, your commander has a message for El Jefe, Señor Aguinaldo?"

As Bailey fumbled for words in an attempt to explain his secret mission in a discreet manner, Joaquin noted his discomfort and stopped him on his track and instead invited him to dine with them first, explaining that it was a tradition among Filipinos to prepare a sumptuous meal on Sundays. Over a hearty meal of roast chicken and *tanguigue* fish marinated in coconut milk, Bailey gradually unwound himself and disclosed the purpose of his visit. He had to find a way to get behind the walls of Intramuros and examine the layout of the citadel, with a little help from a local familiar with the territory. He bragged that an army was coming to make mincemeat of the enemy and capture the whole city. Nothing stood in the way of American conquest. He promised to wield his influence with Dewey (of which he had actually none) to make Joaquin Calderon governor of Manila if only the good doctor would assist him in his mission.

Calderon nodded attentively. "The security at the gates is quite tight...guards posted at every entrance, gate passes, but we can find a way."

"The last time we went there, they cussed and kicked us out. That is why we have to resort to some disguise to get inside, with a little help from your side."

"Me, I have a gate pass that I can use whenever I want to visit the hospital. You, I can make you look like a Spaniard, or a doctor. You need to speak some Spanish."

"No great shakes to me, *habla Español,*" blurted out the ebullient Bailey.

"Very well then, we can give it a try. You will improve along the way."

All the while the Yankee guest could hear the sound of hammering next door which progressively irritated him. "How can you stand that racket all day?"

"I can't complain. It's owned by my brother." Joaquin walked away from the table and pounded on the door, shouting in Tagalog. Presently, the muscle-bound blacksmith appeared through a door connecting the two adjacent shops. "Caloy, Gunnery Sergeant Barton Bailey wants to help the revolution and get inside Intramuros. El Jefe Aguinaldo will be interested to hear the news."

Carlos softened his manners toward Bailey, then grunted, but he did not say a word.

"You know, my younger brother makes all sorts of blades – bolos, knives, daggers – which you might need in case the fighting gets rough. The Spaniards are expert swordsmen," added Joaquin.

Just as Bailey attempted to strike up a conversation with Carlos, the man disappeared back to his shop. Either he was reticent or he was one rude sonofabitch. From his seat in the dining table, Bailey kept throwing sidelong glances at the beauteous Estrella who was standing demurely in the kitchen, waiting to serve the guest more food. He was attracted by her coyness which accentuated her unadorned beauty, being gifted by nature with a tan skin of silken softness, fin-shaped nose on a delicate face and a contoured figure, which showed under her simple house dress. Like Joaquin, she was a *mestiza* but with a lesser proportion of Spanish blood, having a pure-blooded native for a mother – thus, her tanned complexion. For Bailey, she was an exotic beauty of the Orient sea, the sweet señorita of his dreams whom he likened to the Princess Pocahontas of Indian stories, and whom he would later look upon as an inspiration to his Pacific adventure.

"Her mother should be proud to have such a pretty gal who knows how to cook."

"You can now watch the clinic, *hija,*" the father again tried to keep her away.

"It's closed for siesta," she answered impassively in Tagalog.

"This clinic, this is also your home, this li'l flat."

"We have a house in the farm, but most of the time we're here. This is where I make my living."

"She lives with you."

"When I'm around, otherwise she lives in the province. When do you plan to go inside Intramuros to do the reconnaissance?" Joaquin tried to keep the talk from jumping off track. "We have to time it right."

"As soon as possible."

"Let's see if we can have it tonight. But if you don't mind, I will have to report this to El Jefe General Aguinaldo so there would be no suspicions I'm dealing with you without his knowledge."

"No problem."

In the night they got ready to slip into the Walled City, with Bailey wearing an overcoat and a fedora ordinarily donned by the typical Spanish official. Being oversized, the hem of the overcoat reached almost down to his knees, and when he dropped his Bowie knife and compass into its pockets, they settled somewhere beyond the reach of his fingers. He was too embarrassed to ask the portly doctor for a smaller size, disinclined to admit for the record that he was smaller than the doctor.

Calderon groomed himself. *"Ella, yo necesito un abrigo, un sombrero y un a par de guantes.* I need an overcoat, a hat and a pair of gloves."

If Bailey was uncomfortable with his garb, he was rather amazed at the fastidiousness with which Joaquin Calderon primped himself up. It was as if the man was going to a party, not embarking on a dangerous adventure. Over his suspenders he put on a swallow-tail coat with capacious collars, duly stuffed with a cravat that he knotted on his neck. He greased his hair with Macassar oil in front of the mirror, then fussily preened his upturned moustache, curling its ends like ribbons and twisting some unruly strands into place. Helping him get dressed, Estrella polished his boots with a horsehair brush, waxed them all over with a candlestick, then buffed the wrinkled hide again till they glowed in the night. He then carefully put on his pince-nez by clipping it on his nose, which eyepiece bestowed on him an aura of eminence and gravity – so magical was its effect that Bailey watched him awestruck. He stood mesmerized as the doctor practiced strutting about in his attire, clicking his boots and stretching ramrod straight. Grooming was everything to a *mestizo* and an *ilustrado*. It opened doors that couldn't be entered by an uncultivated Filipino. It ushered him to the society of the privileged. Before leaving he put on his derby hat and stumbled on Barton Bailey. "Ha-ha, I almost forgot you. Wait, you must carry a cane so you'll pass for an Englishman. No, no, that will not do. You're supposed to look Spaniard," Joaquin fussed over the American. "Give me a swagger stick, Ella, there on the wall."

Almost suffocated by the collar of his coat, Bailey shrugged meekly, still too embarrassed to complain. He wasn't used to "putting on the frills."

Joaquin sprayed him with perfume, then pronounced him ready to visit Intramuros. *"Que hora es?"*

"Eight o'clock or thereabouts."

Calderon closed the door of the clinic, looked to the darkened street, and called someone: "Pssst!"

A light carriage pulled over. It was driven by a lowborn Filipino who was wearing nothing but rags over a skeletal body. The contrast between him and Calderon gave Bailey an idea of the breadth of the social divide that separated not only the colonizer from the governed, but also the natives from each other.

"Why did you have to park so far, *Dios mio.*" Calderon treated the driver hardly any better than a Spaniard would. The man belonged to the *indio* masses who composed the bulk of Aguinaldo's army but who were not represented in the delegation that showed up in the general's visit to the *Olympia.* It was a paradox of the Filipino character that these people would cooperate in a national struggle for self-government without sympathy let alone respect for one another.

The light carriage was a two-wheeled affair, called a *calesa,* hardly bigger than a rickshaw, driven by a single horse and good enough for only two passengers. It had a bare seat of hard wood and a single board for a roof. Bailey doubted whether the carriage was strong enough to carry both of them, but when Calderon plopped inside and it merely creaked, he followed on board.

With a shake of his reins, the driver took them along the rambling alleys of the Escolta commercial district, their way illumined by two lanterns hanging on both sides of the carriage and light coming from surrounding buildings. Bailey had an eerie feeling of being driven through a village of colonial America trod by outlaws such as Ben Franklin.

Calderon softened toward the driver. "Señor Bailey," he introduced his fellow passenger.

"He isn't a Spaniard, is he?" the man asked in Tagalog.

"No, Berto, *esta yanqui.*"

Bailey grunted, pulling his oversized coat around him.

"You may not know it, but Berto is a member of the underground. Most people here are with Aguinaldo." Calderon tried to put the American at ease.

Bailey stayed quiet.

"Our friend." Calderon patted him. *"Nuestra amigo."*

At the bank of the Pasig River, which served as a moat between Intramuros and the rest of Manila, Bailey found himself approaching a bridge brightly lit by torches. It was lined with parapets of crossed bars and was floored with planks of wood that made passage by thin-wheeled carts tricky. Gingerly, the driver steered his carriage across the bridge to keep either wheel from slipping off the edge of a plank and thus capsizing it along with its distinguished passengers. Bailey had other concerns in mind. He realized that he was nearing the gate of Intramuros whose walls were faintly visible behind the torches. Pursuant to his intelligence mission, he took note of the surroundings with eagle eyes. Under the bridge a convoy of outrigger boats paddled their way towards the mouth of the river in the night. The river was about 200 hundred yards across, too wide to be spanned by the Army's pontoon bridge, and the low banks partly supported by dikes seemed prone to flooding. In any battle, access to this bridge was crucial, he keenly observed.

After the carriage crossed the bridge, the Yankee spy was startled off his wits by the tolling of massive bells.

"What the hell is that?" he quavered, sinking into the collar of his coat. "Are we caught?"

"It's eight o'clock. The churches ring their bells at eight o'clock for vespers."

They soon faced an imposing gate at the northern wall of Intramuros which was tightly guarded by the uniformed Guardia Civil, reflecting the abnormal situation in the colony. One of several entrances into the citadel, it was called Parian Gate because it opened up to a district populated by Chinese, dubbed "Parians." There were gates of all kinds in the Walled

City that stood as the seat of the colonial government: a gate for high officials; gates for ordinary inhabitants; a gate for the clergy; and one gate for the exclusive use of the Archbishop and the governor-general (neither of whom liked the other) called the Postigo. Protected by a drawbridge over a moat, the Postigo was the backdoor to Intramuros jealously guarded by armed sentries even during peacetime, trespassing on which was punishable by death. It was this last gate that Bailey tried to enter with Lt. James Cocker, meeting a humiliating rebuff that still rankled in their memory. Quickly passing over the Postigo for the Parian Gate near the Chinese quarter, the visitors prepared to enter the forbidding City.

"Let me do the talking," said Calderon, nudging his companion with his knee.

Bailey reached for the pistol which he had tucked under the overcoat.

"Stop! Your passes, please, señores," a voice halted them on their tracks.

Bailey observed three sentries posted outside the gate and an undetermined number hidden in the shadows behind the wall. From the way the wall was constructed, it was next to impossible to force the gate without the use of heavy artillery. Apart from the timber doors braced with steel, the heavy arches and massive stones could withstand ordinary cannon fire. The gate followed a classic design reinforced by military necessity to a ponderous excess, topped by a triangular pediment and flanked by colonnaded walls. The ersatz columns were embedded in the walls with convex humps projecting. The walls and pediment were decorated with bas-reliefs of conquistadors and priests intertwined in a tangled frieze that symbolized their common role in the country's colonization. In the faint light emitted by a row of torches, Bailey had trouble distinguishing the guards from the statues, which seemed to come alive in the night to take their places among the living.

A Guardia Civil sentry brandishing a Mauser rifle came over to inspect their identification. He checked Calderon's *cedula* or certificate of residence, then, for good measure, examined him from head to foot. The perfectly tailored clothes, the pale skin, the upturned moustache – all badges of privilege, especially the last – invited an approving nod from the sentry. Then, he set his eyes on Bailey.

"*A donde vas?* Where are you going? What is your business inside?" he demanded in Spanish.

Bailey groped for a fitting response but the language suddenly deserted his tongue.

"I'm accompanying the British consul to his residence," Calderon jumped to his rescue. "He just came off a ship at the port and is quite new to the place. *No muy bien, esta cansado.* He's not well, very tired."

"*Esta anglo?*"

"That is correct, sir. If you please, gentlemen, we have an overdue appointment with Admiral Montojo."

"Who?"

"Er... the admiral.."

"Why so late in the night? *Por que tan tarde?*"

"He got held up by the Americans in the Bay. It is a matter of extreme importance, señor."

"Is he bringing some news about the *yanqui?*"

"The Englishman needs to advise him on some matters which we are, unfortunately, not at liberty to disclose."

"Aha, the Englishman will teach the admiral a lesson in seamanship?" The guard asked mockingly of the disgraced admiral, within the earshot of another sentry, who also laughed. They all belonged to the Guardia Civil, a service unit of the army, which held a poor opinion of the defeated admiral.

After an exchange of banter that considerably eased the guards' mistrust, the two visitors passed muster. They entered the gate forthwith whose timber doors swung to accommodate them. Bailey was dripping cold sweat at the close shave, deeming himself lucky to have picked up the self-assured Calderon as his companion.

"Why did I ever make you look like a Spaniard? You could pass perfectly for an English gentlemen, eh, Your Excellency?" Calderon ribbed him, tittering in the calesa.

Bailey sighed. It was not time for jokes.

He got down to business. After the gate closed behind him, he was able to measure the width of the wall and was intimidated by its dimensions. It was about 40 feet thick at the base and only 25 feet in height, thus wider than it was tall. As the wall rose, however, it tapered so that it measured only six feet across at the top. Solid as a pyramid, it was massive enough to withstand bombardment from the American's heavy guns, especially that portion on top made of firebrick, harder than rock and durable enough to last for ages. There were gun ports in the wall at 30-yard intervals, breaches wide enough for a man to squeeze through, each guarded by a vintage cannon dating back to the 16th- or 17th century. And herein lay the weakness, Bailey judged. He doubted if the muzzle-loading cannon, cast solid and drilled hollow through the bore, could still fire effectively, being apparently fit only for ornamental purposes. It belched with enough force only to propel the load a couple of hundred yards, a tenth the range of *Olympia's* guns. On the basis of the gun's antiquity, he judged the defenses weak.

As for the buildings, Bailey felt less than capable of assessing their military value. They were in fact useful only as shelter for U.S. Army troops or headquarters for civil administrators, he thought. To estimate the number of civilian casualties that a full-scale attack would cause, Bailey kept asking Calderon about the inhabitants as well as the functions of certain buildings. Some of the grand edifices clearly had religious functions, with stained-glass windows, statues and crosses on their façades. They had to be spared damage. Likewise, the train of buildings that walled off whole blocks of the city had to be preserved, being parts of monasteries and convents, or colonial offices suitable for conversion into military headquarters. Looking wistfully at the windows of more palatial buildings emitting soft rays of candlelight, he could only imagine the luxurious appointments that surrounded their privileged residents, definitely more cozy than the cabins of his ship. He looked forward to the day when he could live in one of them.

"That one is Santa Lucia church," Calderon pointed out landmarks. "This is the Palacio de Alcalde, which is where the governor-general is living temporarily."

"Gives me an idea where to house our big shots," Bailey thought.

They passed by an endless wall of red stone, reinforced by buttresses and embedded columns, topped by framed windows that ventilated the upper storey of the building. "This is the San Agustin monastery, the largest in the entire city. You can find offices of high-ranking officials here and the apartment of your amigo, Admiral Montojo."

"Ah, Ol' Monty, we'll finish him off if he ain't dead yet," said Bailey, less charitable now.

If the concrete structures of the city were open to his inspection, its politics was not. The serene façade of the buildings was deceptive, masking the turmoil and crisis that afflicted its residents. More than the architecture of its edifices, the Byzantine politics of the city was revealing of the colony's true character.

For here, within the walled premises of the citadel, lived the quarrelling factions of the Spanish colonial hierarchy, blood enemies forced to share one bed. The rivals carried out their never-ending power struggle on the eve of the fall of a 300-year regime. The Archbishop tried to undermine the power of the governor-general, Basilio Agustin, by making unflattering comments about the army's capabilities in secret messages sent directly to the Spanish Cortes in the homeland. In this challenge to the commander-in-chief, the Archbishop had the support of Admiral Patricio Montojo, the army's traditional rival, who condemned the army for failing to support the navy during the Battle of Manila Bay. And Montojo's skill at infighting was considerably better than his skill in leading a navy. His machinations with the Archbishop would succeed in overthrowing Agustin and installing a puppet to head the army whom they would treat no better.

In the lower ranks, there were internecine conflicts, too, especially in the fractious clergy. The Augustinian friars closed their convent to the Dominican friars, both of whom competed for control of the colony's arable lands – the former having title to 65,000 hectares and the latter 60,000 hectares on Luzon island alone. Both ganged up on the Jesuits, considered straight-laced politicians who owned no land but who caused sedition to sprout wherever they pitched their mission. All of them prayed to the Lord to rain lightning and plagues on the ungrateful Filipinos whom they had redeemed from paganism and ignorance only to see them rebel in the end.

If the clergy was fractious, it was united when it came to resisting reform to better the lots of the natives. Friars of every order stubbornly fought off attempts to distribute their estates to the peasantry. Instead, they badgered the government into cracking down on the natives, even if it meant burning down whole villages and executing captured rebel leaders. It was the clergy that was instrumental in the execution of Dr. Jose Rizal, who satirized the abuses and degenerate lifestyles of the friars in his novels. Finally, it was a friar, Padre Emilio de la Rea, who had spilled the beans on the existence of an underground revolutionary movement the Katipunan by sharing with the authorities his knowledge thereof acquired from the confession of a guilt-stricken member, nevermind that he was breaking the sanctity of a sacrament, thereby forcing the Katipunan to launch their rebellion prematurely in 1896 to avoid a crackdown, from which uprising Aguinaldo emerged as the most powerful leader.

The colony was more valuable to the clergy than to the Spanish government, which could wring out only so much taxes from the peasant population. It was not an economic jewel on the Spanish crown as much as India was to the British Raj, being poor, undeveloped and of late rebellious. Instead, it existed more for the aggrandizement of the Church than enrichment of the home country.

The hatred harbored by the natives against the clergy, born out of centuries of oppression, was deep-seated and bordered on the irrational, contradicting their Christian upbringing.

As the head of the local clergy, the Archbishop commanded the loyalty of a formidable political group. It was the alternative government, in fact. In the olden times, whenever the governor-general died, it was the Archbishop who temporarily filled his shoes while word of the death was borne over the waves of the ocean by ship to mother Spain half a world away. Now, strengthened by Montojo, the Archbishop was on the brink of capturing power from the hands of a living governor in the last days of Spanish rule. The Church had no intention of being run out of the colony.

Headquarters for the army was Fort Santiago, a corner of the Walled City guarding the mouth of the Pasig River. Governor-General Basilio Agustin governed the colony from his Spartan headquarters in the barracks of the old fort.

Though his hold on the army remained tight, General Agustin had lost considerable political power. For he was influential only for as long as he controlled the provinces in the archipelago, where colonial authority lay in tatters, except in a few isolated southern islands. Now that his army had been expelled from the rebellious provinces in the main island of Luzon and thrown into a cramped enclave within Intramuros, General Agustin was beleaguered from within and without. To make matters worse, he had lost whatever support he had from the navy, his traditional rival. He had contracted the ire of Admiral Montojo for pulling his punches during the Battle of Manila Bay. He had refused to unleash the full force of his shore guns on Dewey's fleet for fear of drawing retaliatory fire that would have caused the destruction of palaces and churches. He preferred to see ancient Intramuros intact to the Royal Navy afloat.

As far as Admiral Patricio Montojo was concerned, he made the wrong choice. After swimming away from the burning hulk of *Isla de Cuba,* he headed straight for the San Agustin church in the Walled City, limping from a leg wound, and there complained to the Archbishop about the army's inaction during the battle. He believed that the army had deliberately allowed the fleet to sink to strip him of power – what a way to defend the most precious eastern jewel on the Spanish crown! White hair rumpled, his tunic spotted with tatters of seaweeds and his boots filled with broken bits of coral, he denounced General Agustin bitterly before the Archbishop who, taken aback, advised him to say the Hail Mary five times and come back sober. He had spent more years in the colony than Agustin and had completely mastered the art of infighting. He easily won over the support of the Church. Partly because of their joint efforts, the Spanish Cortes replaced Agustin with General Fermin Jaudenes three months after the battle – too late to turn back the tide.

"That is Fort Santiago, you can't get in there, it's closely guarded," warned Calderon as he tried to steer the calesa away from the army headquarters.

"Just gotta take a peek."

"That's where the army has its headquarters. Let's go somewhere else."

Bailey could not be restrained. This was the highlight of his intelligence mission, an inquiry into the capability of the Spanish army. From an elevated ground outside the wall of the fort he climbed atop an aqueduct so that he could get a vantage view of the fort spread out beneath him. He immediately caught sight of the guns pointed at the bay, illuminated by gas lamps and torches in the night. They sat on the gun emplacement called Baluarte de Santa Barbara which guarded the mouth of the Pasig River. Through his old binoculars imprinted with Montojo's ensign, he was surprised to notice that

134

the battery was not composed of old cannons as he had expected but modern rapid-fire guns such as those possessed by the U.S. Army. From their outline he determined that they were Ordoñez and Krupp breech-loaders. Their loading mechanisms consisted of the so-called sliding-wedge breechblock which allowed fast firing. Its main part was a wedge that was simply inserted into a socket in the manner of a drawer when closing the gun. In contrast, the *Olympia's* eight-inch gun had a grooved plug that was screwed into the breech to withstand recoil of a greater force but it was slower to operate since the plug had to be turned repeatedly into the groove, unlike the retractable block of the Krupp gun. He had to pass this important intelligence to Captain Gridley who had confidence in his knowledge of weapons.

Transfixed by curiosity, carried away by his mission, he stood too long on the aqueduct and as a result attracted the attention of a Spanish guard who marched from the gate to apprehend him. "Freeze! Hold it right there!"

"Oh, my God," trembled Bailey.

"No, *señor capitan,*" Joaquin Calderon interceded for him. "He's just a sightseer."

"Hands up."

"Forgive him, *capitan.* He's just a British tourist interested..." The doctor bit his tongue, realizing he had made a mistake.

"A spy! Halt, turn around, both of you!"

The two of them were arrested on the spot. The guard prodded them with the bore of his rifle toward the gate of the fort, but Calderon, overwhelmed by the thought of rotting in prison to the forfeiture of a lifetime of hard work, resisted as best he could. He sat on the ground, weeping like a child, and refused to move any farther. Consequently, he was beaten by the guard with his rifle butt. "Fat *indio!*" As Calderon bawled and rolled in pain, Bailey flared with uncontrollable rage. He hailed from a place in the south where honor was inviolable, even that of a lowly trapper to whom it was an inalienable

135

right beyond compromise. And here he was watching a distinguished doctor being pummeled like the worst outlaw. Without thinking, he pounced on the guard blazing with fury, wrestled away his rifle and tried to knock him unconscious.

"Go away, Whacky Doc, run, let me deal with this dago. Go! Shove off!"

The commotion drew the attention of more guards, five of whom came running from the fort. As Bailey pounded the senses out of the sentry, he felt blows raining on him from behind and hands grappling him to the ground. He collapsed and stopped resisting. Sad as he was at being captured, he was satisfied that he had saved the honor of a man.

The flash of a carriage vanishing behind a corner was the last image he remembered of the scene. Joaquin lit out to safety, he thought with satisfaction, knowing that the man wouldn't be able to stand torture.

He was shackled. Clasps were nailed around his ankles linked together by a chain. His arms were manacled in the same manner. He was subjected to greater humiliation than that from which he had tried to spare the doctor.

What would they do to him? What dire punishment awaited him in the hands of the vengeful dagos? He was at a moment of crisis in life where he had to measure the time by the second, in pace with the beating of his heart, expecting an abrupt turn in one's destiny at any moment. The only uncertainty that faced him was the kind of punishment that would be meted out to him by his captors. Either he would be imprisoned or he would be shot – that was the fate that awaited him before the end of the day. The glowering face of doom did not hold any promise of salvation.

True enough, the cruelty refined over three centuries of despotism, perpetuated with the solemn dispensation of the clergy, was visited upon the hapless Yankee. How he wished he had sunk to the bottom of the bay where conditions were more merciful, more agreeable to human dignity. Quizzed by an army captain, stripped to his bare skin, he was found to be an American from the distinctive tattoos on his biceps: an anchor and a snake with the incongruous words "U.S.A. Forever." The officer observed: *"Esta yanqui,"* words that sealed his doom.

"Shall we call on the general?" asked the bruised soldier who had captured him, an army lieutenant.

"Let's keep this secret for a while. We don't know how the navy would react, or the Archbishop. This thing has to be handled with velvet gloves."

Bailey listened with cocked ears.

"You just gave us a problem, *yanqui,* you should never have fallen into our hands," said the captain.

"If we keep him here, sooner or later, the navy is going to find out and Montojo is going to move heaven and earth to get him, and doubtless he will make things difficult for the army. Let's keep him somewhere else where nobody's going to notice him."

The two army officers argued inside an office building about where to keep their prize catch.

"Okay, then, there's only one place," said the captain.

"I know what you mean," nodded the lieutenant.

The two officers agreed on an obvious place to detain him. They brought him to the notorious dungeon of Fort Santiago, an age-old prison located right under the bunker housing the battery of Krupp guns. Built in 1592 on a station called the Baluarte de Santa Barbara, it was the same battery that he had espied the night before. It held a subterranean prison that inhabited the nightmares of the few Filipinos who had survived its diabolic conditions. For a time it served as an ammunition depot but since it was periodically flooded, it was converted into a prison for captives whom the regime considered particularly dangerous – such as those convicted of rebellion – and expanded to contain a network of tunnels. Rizal was considered too high-profile a captive to warrant imprisonment here but for the foot soldiers of Aguinaldo's army whom the world had never heard of (such as Joaquin Calderon or his brother

Carlos, for that matter), the dungeon beckoned as their ultimate destination.

As soon as Bailey stepped into the narrow entrance, tight as a mine shaft, he smelt the dankness of the dungeon. The stone walls were moist, spotted by a growth of mushrooms that flourished in the dark, and the blocks of stone were matted with the roots of trees that had wormed their way between crevices from the garden above ground. The stink of human refuse became suffocating as he groped deep into the interior. In the gloom, Bailey almost slipped on the floor slick with mud and detritus. He knocked his head on the roots of trees that dangled from above and the overhanging beams that held up the roof. His shadow being a step ahead of him, he groped his way inside and noticed that the floor steadily grew wetter as he wormed deeper. The reason was that the dungeon was located below the bed of the Pasig River. During floods water seeped through crevices in the walls and settled on the floor of the dungeon where it stagnated for months on end. To keep the prisoners' feet dry, platforms were laid on the ground inches clear of the water. Cells were built as niches on the wall penned in by wooden bars.

Bailey was pushed into one such cell barely wide enough to stretch in, to the sound of snapping padlock. It was the ultimate humiliation for a proud southerner like him to be entombed in so infernal a prison, worse treatment than that experienced by a runaway nigger recaptured by his master in the bad old days before the Civil War. It was better for him to die fighting than waste away his life in this manner. But whom would he fight now? Not his shadow, not the rats or cockroaches, not even the figures of prisoners stirring in nearby cells.

As soon as he sat still on the wooden platform which elevated him from the stagnant water pooling on the floor, he sensed the cold feet of rats creeping across his legs, then nibbling at his toes. He sprang to his feet and kicked the vermin away in reflex, only to knock his head on the planks above

138

him. The tails of rats slithered under his folded knees to vanish into the dark. Equally disgusting but more numerous were the mosquitoes that swarmed all over him, not to mention the cockroaches that crawled on his hair and face. He killed dozens of the insects but more emerged from the tomblike darkness to torment him.

This was the end of his mission or his serviceable life, for that matter. His comrades would never know what became of him. Unfortunately for them, they would never be able to make use of the valuable intelligence he had gathered with reckless disregard for his personal safety – too reckless, in fact. As days passed by without any news of him, Captain Gridley would write him off for dead and recommend him for posthumous recognition. They would honor him as one of the heroes of America's quest for greatness, and all the while he was growing beard and claws and wattles in this Earthly purgatory. Poor Bailey was as good as buried. To the rest of the world, he might as well be a drifting soul.

These were the thoughts that ran through his mind as he squatted on the wooden platform, unable to stretch. He could do nothing but grieve. He enjoyed no peace of mind even in his loneliness. His slightest motion sent his chains rustling on the floor and his prison rags grazing against his skin.

From other cells in the dungeon, he heard the moaning and cursing of other prisoners. He felt no sympathy for their plight. They could be plain criminals mingling with equally miserable patriots, between whom it was hard to distinguish. The more they made noise the more wretched he felt. He hated the sounds of pain. He hated the snoring of the ones asleep. He wanted nothing more than to return to his ship even if he were to toil in the Black Room every other day of his life, for there, at least, he had freedom.

After a few hours, he screamed. He cursed in a voice that reverberated through the length of the tunnel and exited as wails in the wind. "You goddamned Spaniards. Get me out of here! This is not the way to treat a prisoner of war!"

"*Hoy*," said a voice in Tagalog. "*Sino ang ulol na ito.*" Who's that fool?

"*Isang Kano,*" another answered. An American.

"I'm no criminal, I deserve better treatment! Let me outta here, you miserable idiots!"

"Shut up!"

Bailey spent days, weeks, months in the dungeon, he couldn't be sure. After losing track of time in the unchanging darkness, he heard the jangle of distant chains being loosened at the mouth of the tunnel, followed by the shuffle of approaching feet. Just as he began to feel drowsy, partly induced by the noxious odor emitted by the stagnant water, a couple of guards bearing torches appeared and hustled him out of the tunnel by his manacles. Groggy, he thought it was just a nightmare unfolding in the abyss of his mind, for he was convinced that he was beyond the reach of possible redemption, having neither friend nor countryman in this purgatory. Outside the dungeon, he was stunned back to life by the blinding rays of the sun beaming on his face, a sight that revived his flagging hopes. He no longer took any interest in the Krupp and Hontorio guns guarding the fort. The same had ceased to have any significance to him.

All that he cared about now was being able to enjoy the rays of the sun, to bask in the luxury of unbounded space and fresh air of the outer world, which meant so much to a prisoner. His endless incarceration had impressed on him the value of walking under clear skies.

"Leave me be," he muttered to his guards when the latter made an attempt to move him. He planted his feet firmly on the ground while his guards pried open the shackles that hobbled his movements. "*Yanqui*, you follow we, no talk, no fight," said his captors in broken English. "Or you dead."

They were tall Spaniards with fedoras, jackboots and holstered pistols. Their tan uniform was unadorned, completely bare of the trappings of royal accouterments that distinguished the uniform of officers. They were of his race, he noted.

In no mood to resist, Bailey obeyed their orders in a trance even as they asked him to wash, cut his claws and trim his beard. Doubtless, they were preparing to execute him and deliver his body as a warning to the Americans, which fate did not exactly faze him in his miserable state. He had lost his enthusiasm for war, demoralized by the failure of his mission and consequent imprisonment. His spirits began to perk up when he was brought to the Palacio del Alcalde, which used to be the residence of the governor-general but now inhabited by the man who wielded the real political power in the colony. It was next to the monastery of the Augustinian friars, a complex of buildings interlinked by walkways and arcades, the secular repository of clerical wealth.

Bailey was kept in suspense of what lay in wait inside the luxurious palace. When liveried servants showed up to feed him a rather spicy meal of exotic concoction, which he wolfed down to the last morsel, he was even more mystified. Was he being served his last meal? Knighted? The mind of the Spaniard was beyond his grasp.

Then, Admiral Montojo himself showed up in full regalia, decidedly dandier than Calderon in his deadliest outfit, with trimmings and medals and buttons glittering on his tunic. Bailey was taken aback. Still wearing his prisoner's rags, but without his manacles, he was at once flattered and alarmed. What did he do to deserve this treatment?

"Buenos dias, yanqui," growled Montojo in a voice devoid of hospitality.

"How do you do, sir," the long-haired Bailey muttered back politely.

"How were you treated by my soldiers?"

Bailey felt his two escorts stirring behind him. "Oh, well, nothing I wouldn't expect."

"You shouldn't expect any mercy from us. You shot even noncombatant ships, you fired at sailors jumping into the

141

water, you burned our ships even after they had been abandoned and captured."

The loquacious Yankee deemed it impertinent to talk back.

"I brought you here not because I want to be lenient with you but because I want to make a proposition" – Montojo paused – "to your admiral...."

Bailey felt his hopes rising.

He owed Montojo a debt of gratitude for taking him out of the dungeon. Unknown to him, the Spanish admiral had moved heaven and earth to get him out of the army's turf and into his own hands. The scramble for his custody broke out as soon as news leaked out concerning the only positive development in this war, first picked up by the friars, then inevitably by the navy. Admiral Montojo immediately laid claim to the prisoner as the commander most aggrieved by the destruction of the Spanish navy. He wanted to wring out valuable intelligence on the armaments and composition of the U.S. Navy. On the other hand, General Agustin hanged on to the prisoner as a hostage with immeasurable intrinsic value, who could be swapped for future military concessions from the Gringo invader. Besides, he wanted to win credit for the first concrete achievement of Spanish arms. He had taken the only American prisoner in this war! In the event the King launched an inquiry into the conduct of his forces in the Pacific, Agustin could present Bailey as living proof that he had accomplished something whereas Montojo could show only hulks.

Montojo again showed his skill at infighting. Supported by the friars who practically bankrolled the army with the proceeds of their vast landholdings, he cut off all supplies to Fort Santiago. After days spent in ever tightening scarcity which they tried to alleviate by rationing their declining food stock, the proud governor capitulated. He agreed to surrender Bailey in exchange for 1,000 tons of grain and 100 barrels of salted pork – not necessarily a bad price for a single Yankee prisoner.

Facing the admiral, Bailey did not know that he had become Montojo's trophy. Nor was he grateful. He was gaining in confidence as he plumbed the depth of desperation behind the admiral's façade of arrogance.

Montojo continued: "I brought you here to ask you to act as an intermediary between us and the admiral. Here's my proposal: ask the admiral to withdraw his ships beyond Corregidor, back to the South China Sea, and we will leave Manila as an open city and withdraw to the town of Caloocan, five miles away. All we want is that we be given a free hand to deal with the *indios* and pacify the colony."

Even before the interpreter finished, Bailey bristled: he was not interested. His dander was up.

Montojo continued: "I know that your situation is getting critical at my base in Sangley. You don't have enough men to go on the offensive, your navy is in poor shape, you are in no position to take Intramuros."

"It ain't so." Bailey protested.

"In fact, we can launch an attack against you anytime and drive you back to the sea."

The more the admiral disparaged the American strength, the more Bailey's patriotism was aroused. "Oh, no, the goddams will be happy to give you a rematch," he sneered.

Montojo toned down his voice. He changed tack. "I see. Tell the admiral that we know you are getting your supplies from the local market. We will prohibit every merchant and every fisherman from supplying you with food. You will starve to death!"

Bailey rose to the challenge. "And we can bomb your positions on land. We're ready to take the field to face your army anytime you felt like testing our strength. There's no doubt in my mind that if ever your army attacked our positions, the goddams will make short work of you."

"Oh, no. Dewey will not bomb our churches and monasteries. He is not the Hun."

Bailey stood his ground.

"Look at it this way, *yanqui*. Sooner or later, the *indios* will be your enemies, too. Your interests are in conflict with theirs. They want independence, you want their land – there's no way you can get along with each other. Now, if you leave my flank free and allow us to vanquish them, then we can face the negotiating table without any distraction from third parties."

"You send an envoy to take it up directly with the commodore."

"All you have to do is bring our message to your superiors."

"I can't cooperate with the enemy."

Montojo fumed and gripped the corner of the table, aghast at the *yanqui's* effrontery. "Very well. Let us see." He paced around.

Matched against Bailey, the Spanish admiral ran into a reef. He was a study in frustration as he realized that he could not even whip a lowly gunnery sergeant, a prisoner at that, right in his own palace. It was a personal affront that derogated the majesty of his rank as reflected by the extravagance of his uniform. Epaulets trimmed with frilly locks nested on his shoulders to give heft to his torso. A festoon of cords, called aiguillette, was strung loosely from the right side of his collar to the tip of his left shoulder so that it sagged to his breast like a chain-watch. Embroideries of silk and gold adorned the breadth of his tunic, accentuated by the glint of brass buttons. It was this richly packaged commander that the lowly Yankee had rebuffed at every turn, and he was not about to let the insult pass unredressed.

As the naval commander paced the marble floor, his interpreter followed closely at his heels, ears cocked, straining to catch the admiral's grumbles.

"Your history this century" – he stretched himself to his full height to deliver a tirade – "is a long list of affronts against our country and our possessions in the New World," he said in a steadily rising voice. "You took away Florida in 1821 and

144

Oregon after that. When Mexico became independent you took away Texas and other Spanish possessions all the way up to the Rio Grande. Now, you have designs on Cuba, Puerto Rico, the Marianas and, God forbid, the Philippines next, which is 10,000 miles away from your shore! When will your aggrandizement of land belonging to my country end? Cite one instance in which Spain has done the same to you."

Bailey was not quite so well-versed in history as his comrade Wolf. He was stumped for words. "All I can say is that I can't be seen to be giving aid and comfort to the enemy. I'll get shot for that."

"Take him away. Damn *yanqui*, they're all the same, from their commander down to the lowest rank, so full of hot air!"

Bailey was overtaken with fright at the thought of being hauled back to the dungeon of Fort Santiago. He regretted the way he had goaded the admiral into losing his temper – no way for a prisoner to treat his captor, especially a colonial high official used to commanding the subservience of an entire race. When he emerged from the palace, he made a run for it. He simply broke away from his escorts and headed straight for the nearest gate – or what he thought was a gate. He didn't ever want to be returned to the dungeon, even if he were to be shot like a dog, in which event he would have caught his last breath a free man, if only for one fleeting moment. Unable to find his way in the Byzantine maze that was the network of alleys of Intramuros, and chased by bullets that ricocheted from wall to wall of the surrounding buildings, he blundered into the near-by Santa Lucia church with its heavy doors that looked as if they were constructed to withstand a siege, held together by iron braces and thick iron nails like those of a medieval castle. The doors opened up to another maze of corridors that led in-to the courtyards and blind alleys of an adjacent complex of buildings and a monastery. To cut off his pursuers, he doubled back and closed the twin doors of the church, one heavy wing at a time as they were too wide to be spanned by both arms. Determined to play a deadly game of cat-and-mouse with his pursuers, he lost himself in the thicket of pillars, and then sneaked into the midst of statuaries that were more populous and more forbidding than those found in fog-filled cemeteries of English horror novels. He finally exited into the sunlight of a courtyard located in the heart of the monastery filled with a flower garden where he lost himself behind the hedges. As he looked for a way out, a monk peeked out from behind a pillar and signaled him furtively to follow. He was so wrought up with fear of the consequences of recapture that he placed himself in the hands of a total stranger, who pointed him toward a dark corridor that led into the cloisters of a monastery.

"Don't say a word, you'll be safe here," said the monk, looking gentle and non-threatening in his habit. "Don't mind my brothers." He pointed at the other monks puttering about in a trance, absorbed in their prayers. "They can't hear you."

The hooded Samaritan introduced himself as Padre Cerezo, the friar in charge of the Santa Lucia church and who was the monastery's only access to the outside world. "I know there's a war going on outside but you can find peace and sanctuary in our monastery. Nobody will harm you here. You can stay until you find it safe to venture outside" so said the good friar.

Very well. Bailey whiled away the next few days playing with two novices in the safety of the courtyard, fencing with them using foils taken from Padre Cerezo's sword collection. He was securely insulated from the Guardia Civil by thick walls of masonry and maze-like network of passages, not to mention the air of inviolability exuded by a monastery. Even the long arm of Montojo dared not breach such sacred barriers on pain of excommunication. In his idleness he reminisced of the childhood that he had left behind in Virginia in his rush to make a living as a runaway. He developed a healthy appetite for food that the friars hoarded in bountiful amounts, including wafers of unleavened bread that was intended to be served during Communion but not yet blessed. And when he tired of playing with the kid friars, he retired to the top of the church steeple, a tower accessible by a winding ladder, where he discovered an interesting pastime of the Father Cerezo: astronomy.

He studied the constellations in the night and learned to identify them by their Greek appellations, although there was no way he could associate the clusters of blinking dots with the heroic figures the names suggested.

"I've discovered two comets already, and one was named after myself by the British Royal Society of Astronomy. Comet Padre Cerezo. Isn't that beautiful?"

"It's out there?"

"It comes around every 62 years and its next coming is when I'm 120 years old," the priest added with a dash of humor.

"What's there in the stars that interests you?" the prisoner asked a profound question.

"It's by seeing the stars that you become aware of the power of God and the vastness of his Creation. In the Bible, you read only terrestrial matters which make you self-centered. Up there, you see a world without mankind, unknown and as yet unrevealed."

"Ain't they merely points of light?"

"Each point of light is a world – a planet, a sun, a separate universe."

"How do you know when they're merely blinking lights? Even through the telescope, they're nothing but lights."

"You know because they never change positions, even as our Earth travels the vast distance around the sun. If they were just as small as fireflies in the night, they would move against the background of darkness, just as an island recedes as a ship passes by."

"Hmmm, I never thought so before."

Bailey was stumped. He had never before ventured into the field of the abstruse. To him, the world was confined to the immediate vicinity bordered by his senses, no farther than the horizon of common sense. He had seen actions played out under his nose, of hurricanes slamming the coast, of navies battling, but not the strategy of leaders, the tide of history, the politics of rebellion.

The lessons taught by the Agustinian friar in cosmic thinking inspired him into adventurous explorations in the night. Driven by curiosity, he put the telescope mounted atop the church steeple to greater use than the priest could ever have imagined. Alone in the night, with the bells silent all around him, he lowered the telescope to terrestrial levels and proceeded to scan the apartments of the San Agustin monastery, sections of which were occupied by Spanish officialdom. He managed to espy on earthly gods more exquisite in beauty than the Greek figures he had seen only in drawings, such as the wives and mistresses of colonial officials who had the habit of stripping their layered garments by the candlelight. There, he was able to spend many a night afloat in dreamy world of erotica, such that his right eye became redder than the priest's. His knowledge of astronomy never improved, much to the cleric's bafflement. However, from the way the priest locked himself up in the tower at odd hours of the night, even when overcast clouds covered up the stars in the skies, Bailey wondered whether the old cleric was not engaged in similar exploration. "Padre, why is it that you're up in the belfry even when there ain't no stars in the sky?" he asked as soon as Father Cerezo descended. The priest look embarrassed. "You see, son, the study of astronomy is not about stars alone. It is about man's place in the universe, the insignificance of his existence compared to the infinity of space. It makes you feel humbler," he said grandiloquently. Bailey heard no mention of the study of anatomy.

One time, he was forced to climb the steeple in the full light of day. Church bells were ringing all over the Walled City. The sound of hoof beats and carriage wheels echoed in the street. The fire of emergency seemed to sweep the air, and it originated from somewhere beyond the walls.

With a mass going on in the church and chants of Latin prayers echoing all over the courtyard, he ascended the steeple even though its bells were ringing. He was used to the noise. He had been inside a turret clanging under the impact of debris and cannonballs, and that was worse. The sound of gunfire broke through the din to peter out as echoes. Had the Guardia Civil overcome its hesitation and decided to bomb the church in order to smoke him out of his sanctuary, in this case using excessive force to flush a rat from its hole? The Spaniards seemed more willing to destroy the city's landmarks than Dewey himself!

As the rolling booms from apparently distant guns continued to reverberate for no reason at all, he crept toward the notches of windows on the steeple and slowly, warily, raised himself to take a peek outside, first poking his nose in the air like a periscope to sniff for danger, then, finding none, finally taking courage to scan the surroundings with his eyes. He could see not only the citadel of Fort Santiago but past the giant walls of Intramuros all the way up to Manila Bay.

And guess what he saw in the horizon? A convoy of alien ships. The closer he scrutinized the convoy the less alien it became. The Americans had arrived! Yes, he was sure of himself. It was headed by a warship leading a retinue of four transports, with smokestacks and masts but no conning towers. Bringing up the rear was a smaller warship that must have caught up with them from a nearby base. They all steamed past the sentinel isle of Corregidor across the whole breadth of Manila Bay on their way to join forces with the naval contingent at the captured base of Sangley Point. Bailey was filled with pride for the same reason that Spaniards were seized with terror. He whooped it up in the belfry waving frantically in the air. "The Yanks, the Yanks are coming!" he hollered as the bells clangored around his ears.

The convoy carried the 2,500-man Army contingent headed by Gen. Thomas Anderson which had set sail from San Francisco Bay on May 25. It was just the initial batch of an American expeditionary force that would eventually number more than 40,000. It began disembarking the troops on July 1 at Sangley Point naval base, quickly crowding its barracks and spilling over to the fields.

Even as the landing of the advance party struck terror in the hearts of the Spaniards, other convoys were crossing the Pacific to continue the troop build-up in the islands. On June 15, three weeks after General Anderson left San Francisco, another contingent followed hot on his wake, consisting of 3,500 volunteers led by Gen. Francis V. Greene, a New York militia officer. He was followed by the overall commander of the Eighth Corps (as the entire expeditionary force came to be known), Maj. Gen. Wesley Merritt, who brought with him an additional 5,000 troops.

The invading army began arriving piecemeal in the months of July and August, 1898, bringing the total strength of the Eighth Corps to 11,000 men, a sizeable force that betrayed aggressive intentions against the entire colony. The improbable victory at the Battle of Manila Bay had given birth to a new foreign policy in Washington.

At the end of July, General Merritt landed at the head of a regiment of 5,000 men supported by artillery which he deployed some 15 miles from Sangley Point in an open field outside Intramuros, within sight of its defenders but outside the effective range of its guns. Their presence was intended to cow the Spaniards into a more tractable behavior. It had its intended effect as far as Bailey was concerned. By this time the Spaniards were so caught up preparing for the next round of battle that they had forgotten about their lone Yankee captive. There were thousands of other Yankees to keep watch on now – fresh, better armed, and trained to fight a land war. They would have their hands full.

Bailey observed them as they made a bivouac three miles away from Intramuros, digging trenches behind ramparts of stone and pitching their tents in a circle, with their artillery deployed at the perimeter. The mere knowledge of their presence boosted Bailey's morale as much as it dampened the spirits of his hosts, a reversal of fortunes that served him just fine. He could now do anything he liked in the convent with the self-assurance of a man of the house. With the hour of his deliverance, he waved at the Guardia Civil below to catch their attention.

"Heyya! I'm here! Are you looking for me?" he taunted.

It was an impetuous gesture that in different circumstances could have cost him his life.

Sure enough, two soldiers entered the Santa Lucia church to drag him out of the sanctuary, nevermind the threat of excommunication. Desperate times called for desperate measures. They brought him to Admiral Montojo, not as a trophy but as some sort of a pawn for diplomacy, one who could help negotiate a way out of this fix, sort of like a peace dove freed from its cage to bring an olive branch to the Yankees, with which strategy Bailey was happy to go along. He found himself again face to face with the Spanish admiral who had lost his air of arrogance. In fact, the man looked humbled. For his part, Bailey suppressed his pleasure at the turn of events. He acknowledged the crushing responsibility of the admiral who was confronted with another potentially career-ending disaster in the space of just three months.

Montojo said: "One can see that the Americans have expanded their objectives in this colony. They won't stop at neutralizing our navy, they also want our colony." Addressing Bailey directly, he continued: "You have too many men and too many heavy weapons, enough to fight a full-scale land war. Your mobile artillery, they're offensive weapons, not just siege guns. To a military eye it is plain that the objective of your government now is to get the whole of the Philippine Islands but I must warn you, there's a long and hard fight ahead against the *indios*. Out there is a mountainous country with a vast wilderness, not fit for conventional war."

Bailey bucked up. He tried to defend his country's obscure intentions in the islands. "Whatever the top brass in Washington order us to do, we as soldiers can only follow."

"Acquiring a colony is not just winning wars, like your Indian Wars, it is winning over people's hearts and minds because you can't kill them all," Montojo lectured the cocky Yankee, who did not appear to him very bright. "That is why, Señor Bailey, I want to reiterate to you my offer to open up negotiations with Admiral Dewey over how to end this conflict. I can teach him how to fight the *indios,* even join forces with him to pacify the islands so we can share in our common effort to spread civilization and Christianity to all the peoples of the world."

"I'll think about it."

"You don't have much time to decide. I'm practically giving you your freedom."

"Let me go, and I'll see what I can do."

"I have one word of advice to Dewey: learn to live with the *indios* and give them the gifts of Western civilization, but deal with them with an iron hand. We gave them Christianity, the best the Spanish culture could offer but in the 330 years we've been running their affairs for them, they've repeatedly risen against us and this is the worst outbreak in our entire rule, the height of their ingratitude."

Bailey had little patience with history and stuck to his simple demands. "Just lemme go and I'll relate what you said to the commodore." He still had to get used to calling Dewey admiral. "I can't tell my superiors how to run the war."

Bailey was dismissed. Suddenly, as if waking up from a dream, he found himself being thrown back in the dungeon of Fort Santiago.

———————

9

IN THE LAIR OF INSURGENTS

Kawit, Cavite, June 12, 1898

There was something ironic in the character of the American soldiers who were landing on the shores of Manila Bay. Dispatched from America to show the flag of an emerging world power, they were mostly farm boys from the cattle ranches and homesteads of the West, or working class men from the grimy factories of the East; coarse, uncouth and uneducated; the sons of the tired, poor and hungry immigrants who were flooding the shores of the United States from Europe. They had none of the social graces or Latin sophistication of the Spanish colonists. They could not even hold a candle to the ilustrados of the Propaganda Movement. Yet, the same poor, ignorant soldiers had at their disposal a modern military machine that had brought an empire to heel.

What was the secret of their success? What were their designs on the islands? What kind of future did their arrival portend? Joaquin Calderon resolved to bring his observations to the attention of the revolutionary council.

After escaping the Spanish sentries by the skin of his

teeth, Calderon fled Manila for the safety of Cavite which was firmly in rebel hands, save for the tiny peninsula at Sangley Point held by the Americans. Not only was he genuinely fearful of being incarcerated by the Spaniards, he was also anxious to report to Aguinaldo the intentions of the Americans. *Jesus mio,* he must tell El Jefe that the Americans were spying on the Walled City preparatory to an attack, that an invading force was sailing across the ocean to reinforce Dewey, and that the revolutionary council had better study the problem of dealing with two enemies, the Spaniards and the Americans, two white powers with a history of fighting Indians. The islands were the ultimate prize of the war. Rather than fight them both at the same time, Calderon wished to advise Aguinaldo to join hands with the Americans to vanquish the hated Spaniards, then deal with the newcomers at an opportune time.

Despite smarting from all the bruises inflicted on him by the Spanish sentry, he was in greater awe of the power of the Yankee invaders than that of the colonial master. Dewey was the man to beat, the new conquistador. They might not be the cultural superiors of the Spaniards, as exemplified by the coarse Bailey, but they were masters of brute force.

Calderon was one of those lettered Filipinos who were ambivalent about their loyalty to the revolution. They maintained close ties to Mother Spain who had nurtured their language and culture. Like the ilustrado members of the Propaganda Movement that preceded the revolution, Calderon originally preferred reform to revolution until, that is, overtaken by the martyrdom of Jose Rizal. They were stampeded into joining the revolutionary cause by the utter injustice of Rizal's execution that served to nullify the regime's moral ascendancy and abrogated its right to govern. If passions were to cool down, there was no doubt that the ilustrados were to prefer an enlightened rule by the Spaniards to mob rule by the hoi polloi. The arrival of the Americans brought a new element to the political equation and further beclouded the prospects of the revolution and with it Calderon's future. He must meet Aguinaldo in order to draw out a plan on how to deal with the newcomer.

For their part, the unlettered *indios* were neither doubtful nor irresolute about their aims. They wanted to overthrow the Spanish regime. They wanted to do away with all vestiges of colonialism, give every peasant and worker political rights, run the Church out of politics, and confiscate the landholdings of the friars. If Calderon loved the friars for giving him education, the peasantry hated the hooded clerics who owned most of the arable land in the country and kept them in permanent serfdom. Comprising the majority of the population, they had long chafed under centuries of exploitation and discrimination. It was time to declare the country's independence and assert their right to majority rule.

Joaquin Calderon hurried to bring the latest tidings to Aguinaldo. He rode the same carriage that had taken him to Intramuros in escaping toward General Aguinaldo's headquarters in Kawit, Cavite, 20 miles south of Manila and 5 miles from the American beachhead at Sangley Point. The bucking of the hard seat as the calesa negotiated the rough road aggravated the pains all over his body, the lingering result of the beating he had suffered in the hands of the Spanish sentry. From time to time, he urged the coachman to prod his calesa a little bit faster, to whip the horse a trifle harder, because besides meeting with Aguinaldo, he did not want to miss an important ceremony: *La Declaracion de Independencia* to be proclaimed that day at the balcony of the general's house. His thoughts kept deserting their focus as he tried to shield himself with his derby hat from the muck splattering his way, kicked up by the carriage wheels. He pulled out a pocket watch from his coat: seven o'clock! Santa Maria, he'd never reach Kawit in time for the great event, the symbolic declaration of freedom that was within the grasp of eight million Filipinos.

It took some effort to salve the bruises on his body, even for a doctor like himself, more so the psychological trauma. *Maria y Josef,* he felt like a stray cat set upon by a pack of dogs.

Never before had anybody roughed him up the way the soldiers had done in Intramuros. The flog from the horsewhip of the Guardia Civil was a pinprick compared to the blow from the rifle butts. Upon reaching his clinic groaning and panting that tragic night, he immediately set about treating his own injuries, assisted by his daughter Estrella. First, he boiled a wad of herb from his apothecary and drank its slag as analgesic. Then, he crushed fresh leaves of the guava tree in a grindstone and pressed the juicy pulp to the cut on his brow. That was herbal medicine practiced in combination with Western science taught in the venerable medical college of Santo Tomas. His upturned moustache, thanks Lord Almighty, was untouched, with not a hair broken or plucked.

Scared of the prospect of arrest, he left his clinic at dawn the following day and immediately hied off towards Cavite. He left Estrella in the care of his younger brother Carlos, promising to be back as soon as the situation stabilized.

Nearing the town of Kawit, the finicky doctor fixed his appearance so that he would look dandy at La Declaracíon. By looking the part of a well-bred mestizo, he expected to impress General Aguinaldo's low-born underlings into giving him a choice place in the ceremony. He had to upstage other ilustrado officials in the revolutionary council with whom he would be competing for space at the General's countryside mansion which, albeit imposing, was not capacious enough. And dressing well was the best way to get a leg up on his colleagues.

"Have you gone to Kawit, Alberto?" he asked the coachman.

"I used to go every Saturday to buy candles for the altar of Padre Cerezo," said the coachman, "but haven't done so since the Americans came to town. Until now."

"Why, what have you to fear from the Americans?"

"Padre Cerezo don't trust them, he has known them in Mexico. They love to pick on things Spanish."

"So, that's what you think of my friend, Barton Bailey?"

"Ah, him, I rather like the guy. He gave himself up to save another."

"It makes me rather sad to think of what might have happened to him."

"The dungeon of Fort Santiago, that's where he must be."

"Don't say that, Alberto!"

"I pray to God he meets his fate bravely... and doesn't mind eating the rats."

The dapper doctor crossed himself at the thought of his friend being condemned to rot in the squalid dungeon of the fort. *"Maria y Josef!"* He banished the thought of Bailey from his mind, too revolted to rue his plight while all along busy fending off the spray of mud with his hat, squirming at the filth that spotted his pants. It was nothing compared to the sewer that was the underground prison of Fort Santiago.

As they came within sight of the church tower of Kawit, guerrillas appeared along the road, posted in front of every thatched house on the road leading to the residence of Aguinaldo. Most of them men were armed with nothing more deadly than the bolo, a broad-bladed machete used for chopping canes or firewood. A few carried ancient flint-lock rifles undoubtedly taken from captured Spanish outposts in isolated coastal areas. They were quick to recognize a Spaniard from a mestizo and an ilustrado one at that. Traces of Filipino blood stood out on the features of a mestizo which even good breeding could not totally obliterate. In the case of Calderon, not even his tail coat, his monocled right eye and, yes, his upturned moustache, would fool the guards into thinking he was a Spaniard. Accordingly, he wasn't stopped and was promptly waved through and saluted as befitted a Filipino dignitary. The doctor was flattered at the respect they accorded his eminence.

Apart from the guerrillas, he found hardly any inhabitants around. There were none inside the thatched huts lining the road. There were none on the rice paddies except for the scarecrows standing forlorn on the dikes. The inhabitants of the barrios had gone elsewhere, perhaps to the town center of Kawit to attend the same momentous event that had drawn Calderon.

In the town proper, they ran into a roadblock. The guerrillas hereabouts were not only better armed but stricter as well. Toting Mauser rifles and glowering under their wide-brimmed hats, they flagged down the one-horse calesa carrying Calderon. They took a look at his coat, his monocle and winged moustache – and held him up for questioning. Calderon was outraged.

"Just a minute," a pistol-packing officer said without showing the least deference to the ilustrado passenger. "Your pass, please."

"Pass! What pass? I'm General Aguinaldo's physician."

"I'm sorry, but no one without a pass is allowed to enter."

"Then, why is almost everybody in town?"

"We know every inhabitant of Kawit, but not…"

"You mean you don't know me? Dr. Joaquin Calderon, *circujano y medico?* The only doctor in the supreme council?"

The officer took a second look at Calderon's Western attire and still was unimpressed. "Your cedula then."

Choking with indignation at being cavalierly treated by an *indio* officer, Calderon pulled out from his wallet a cedula or residence certificate, the same that the Spanish guard had demanded from him at the gate of Intramuros. Levied by the colonial government as a way of collecting poll tax, the cedula functioned also as an identification card.

The rebels themselves had already repudiated any obligation to paying such taxes. At the outbreak of the revolution in 1896, the first hostile act of the rebels was to tear up their cedulas. The officer likewise rent Calderon's document to tatters. "You don't need this now, Señor. Pass on."

The doctor went rigid with indignation, his plump cheeks becoming as red as his lips. How dare this ill-bred sol-

158

dier teach him the proper way to conduct himself as an insurgent! These followers of Aguinaldo were decidedly more boorish than the low-born Gringo pirates.

He rode away muttering a string of Spanish expletives that scared his coachman as well as the horse. *"Peste, leche, que barbaridad!"* He recovered his good humor only when he saw the joyous expressions of the people parading along the road headed for the ceremony: women, farmers, artisans who had answered Aguinaldo's call for support. People from all walks of life were curious to see the sideshows to the event – a folk dance, a cockfight, a band playing, in addition to fiery speeches denouncing the Spanish abuses.

Scene of La Declaracíon was Aguinaldo's home. The rebel leader belonged to a landed family who could have sent him to the Universidad if he didn't prefer cockfighting to reading. His mansion was an ornate building of wood and stone, with a gallery on the second floor overlooking the street. Elaborately carved balusters lined the whole length of the gallery, and the ubiquitous translucent scallop shells filled the latticed windows. To mark the occasion, fronds of yellow palm leaves, studded with red hibiscus and bougainvillea flowers, decorated the walls. Girdling the façade of the mansion was a huge streamer of red, white and blue stripes, the colors of the nascent republic.

Below, on the paved street, a huge crowd was gathered. Soldiers wearing hats with folded brims formed a phalanx along the street to block the front of the house, their Mauser rifles sticking in the air. Men and women of all ages gathered under the balcony of the Aguinaldo residence, the women taking up most space with their voluminous gowns and open parasols.

Calderon arrived just in time for the historic event, after giving due allowance to the Spanish *mañana* habit. His carriage could not make much headway in the narrow streets made narrower still by the overflow crowd. He had to alight at the heels of the procession surging towards Aguinaldo's house but his rotund body could not burrow itself through the crowd with any more ease. Heavens help him if he failed to get a choice seat that his position deserved. Managing to reach the General's mansion, he was distressed to see that a bunch of ilustrados who looked more splendid than he had already arrived ahead of him. It was an extraordinary site: dozens of ilustrados, the cream of the educated elite, gathered in one place. Borne by four luxurious couches (much bigger than his calesa), they looked more distinguished; for they were decked out in top hats, scarves of braided silk and gold chain watches adorning the vests of their swallow-tail coats. They strutted about with inlaid canes that were used more as swagger sticks than walking aids, for they were all young and strode briskly into the mansion with their coattails swinging like the tail feathers of strutting fighting cocks.

Members of Aguinaldo's advisory council, the ilustrados, lent an air of respectability to the revolutionary movement which had so far advanced on the back of its low-born foot soldiers recruited from the rabble. They were doctors, playwrights, editors, painters and seminarians. They composed propaganda for the movement, explained its objectives in the language of Jefferson and Rousseau, and presented the face of the revolution to the outside world. It was rare for such a stellar group of intellectuals to be gathered in one place. A single bomb exploding in their midst would set back the literacy level of the archipelago to the Stone Age.

Calderon felt left out. Waving his cane to make way for his ample body, he pushed through the crowd. He must not be left behind! To be excluded from the company of his peers – and forced to mingle with the rabble – was a disgrace he could never live down. So determined was he to join his peers that he rammed his portly body through the phalanx of revolutionary soldiers, only to see their rifles barring the door.

"No señor," said a guard. "But the General's house is too small to accommodate everyone."

"I'm one of them, I'm the General's doctor."

160

"You may wait till the ceremonies are over."

"Impossible, that's the only reason I came here, to attend the ceremony. And I have an urgent message for Aguinaldo from the Americans." The doctor came up with all sorts of excuses.

"Surely you're not so in a hurry as to risk the General's life. His residence is a small place. If we admit one more man upstairs, this house might collapse!"

"He needs medical attention."

"I'm sorry, doctor, but that's the way it is."

Calderon could only poke his head through the door – in time to see the last coattail flapping its way up the staircase. He swallowed his pride and retreated to the crowd. It was unbecoming of a gentleman to quarrel with a coarse peasant.

Thus, Calderon became the only ilustrado to watch La Declaracíon from the street, in the thick of the common herd. He felt humiliated to be standing out in the crowd like an unhorsed knight, but there was nothing he could do.

Buffeted by the crowd that was applauding the rousing speeches delivered by Tagalog officers seeking their minute of glory, Calderon was consoled to note that he could actually see more of the ceremony from the ground than from the balcony. He was positively buoyed to hear a band strike up a martial tune, a rare treat in the countryside. By and by, he found himself applauding along with the folks.

The crowd was not moved by the Declaration itself – delivered by a stripling named Rianzares Bautista who read the text in monotone – but by the appearance of Emilio Aguinaldo on the balcony. The spare general with a close-cropped hair stepped into view, gripping the handle of his sword that almost scratched the floor and flashing a uniform weighed down by epaulets. He waved at his people who waved back with their hats, umbrellas and bare hands. As a result, Calderon had trouble seeing the hero of the occasion who delivered a speech that galvanized the listeners.

"My fellow Filipinos! The rule of Spain is at an end. We

have taken control of the provinces, the southern islands, the friar lands and now we are about to take control of the City of Manila. After more than three centuries of trying and dreaming and hoping, we have won back our country!"

"Viva! Mabuhay!" the crowd cheered.

"We thank Spain for uniting our archipelago," continued Aguinaldo. "We thank Spain for turning Manila into a city of learning that has produced some of our greatest patriots and for teaching us her fertile language that we have used to express our ideas on freedom.

"Most of all, we thank Spain for giving us the Catholic faith that has united us in a common belief amid our ethnic differences and transformed us from a group of warring tribes to an intensely God-fearing nation. But where the Cross has been firmly planted in our soil, the sword has not ceased to make inroads into our lives and into our souls. This has been the cause of so much resentment against Spanish rule and the cause of our rebellion. Three hundred years has managed to unite us under one God but in the end united us against Spain. For while the Spaniards have been content to be our shepherds, we refuse to continue being the sheep. Our rulers have tried to mold us in the image of Spaniards, yet they refuse to consider us their equals. This is the cause of our rising. This is the fire that drives our quest for freedom.

"In sending back our rulers on their ships whence they came, we hope to live independently as a nation, to raise our sons as free men, and to share with them what we have learned from Spain that we treasure. That is the purpose of our revolution; and that is our concession to Mother Spain. *Viva La Independencia! Mabuhay ang Bansang Pilipinas!*"

Calderon was swept up by the roar of the crowd and he found himself applauding and cheering along with it. He was moved by the lyrical language of the speech that matched the inspiring eloquence of *Mi Último Adiós*, Jose Rizal's paean to his country sung from the grave. He gave credit for its composition to an ilustrado in the revolutionary council, for it was well known that Aguinaldo neither had the gift of gab nor flair for the written word. The speech demonstrated the influence of the lettered men in his cabinet.

Before the doctor could breathe his second wind after cheering his heart out, the leader unveiled a surprise that he had reserved for this historic occasion: he unfurled the flag of his free country on a pole extending out of the balcony. Designed in Hong Kong by exiled Filipino patriots, it was a tricolor consisting of a white triangle and two bands of red and blue. Inside each corner of the triangle was a star and at the center was an image of the sun with eight pointed rays. All sorts of occult meanings were attributed to the colors, the red signifying the blood of martyrdom and the blue, peace. The three stars represented the three major island groups of the archipelago and the eight rays of the sun stood for the eight rebellious provinces in the island of Luzon placed under Martial Law by Governor-General Ramon Blanco in 1896. When the country was in a state of peace, the flag was supposed to be raised with the blue stripe over the red stripe. In times of war, the flag was turned upside down. Thus, a banner with which to goad the Spanish bull and make it see red.

As Aquinaldo ran the flag up the pole, with his generals helping him pull the cords to share the honors, the band struck up a martial tune. It was the new national anthem, a fast-paced marching song in the vein of the Marseillaise. Calderon listened to the Spanish lyrics being sung over the rumble of the band and even as his heart swelled up with patriotism, he couldn't help noticing that the music sounded terrible. Blame it on the band, he said to himself, ashamed of the unworthy thought.

Calderon finally got an appointment with Aguinaldo in the afternoon, after the crowd had retired to watch a cockfighting match and the ilustrados had taken to their siesta.

The upper floor of the mansion was deserted, save for two maids sweeping the litter of flowers and leftovers. The guerrilla officers had gone to neighboring houses to partake of

163

hearty dinners prepared in keeping with the fiesta mood of the day. Good riddance, Calderon thought. The flag hung limp at the balcony.

He found Aguinaldo in the company of an officer in a private room dominated by a rack of swords. Away from the admiring crowd, the man looked utterly insignificant. Short, slight, he had no striking features that would inspire instant respect such as a curled moustache or a tattoo. He was young at 29 but old in experience. Proud of his own provincial up-bringing, he took such a stern dislike to ilustrado foppery that he wore only military clothes and cropped his hair close so that his bristles stood stiff as the fibers of a coconut husk – seemingly to spite the fashion of the elite.

The sight of the other visitor in the office made Calderon doubly happy. It was Gen. Antonio Luna, an old buddy whom Calderon had met in ilustrado circles. Educated in Spain, self-taught in military science, he possessed the rare distinction of being the only ilustrado in command of a fighting unit. He was an expert swordsman as well as a *pistolero*. He certainly had the looks of a military man – tall, rugged and brawny – wearing a resplendent general officer's uniform that set him apart from his lettered peers. The only features that he shared with the ilustrado gentleman were a winged moustache and an exquisite command of the Spanish language.

Having known him since when he was a student, Joaquin looked up to Antonio Luna as a big brother and idolized him for his martial skills that other ilustrados could only envy. As soon as he entered the room, he gave the surprised Luna a warm embrace.

"My compadre, my dear general."

"Ho-ho-ho," howled the rugged Luna who had a booming voice. "It's my old buddy from Barcelona."

"I didn't expect to see the two of you together."

"And where have you been, Señor Calderon?" Aguinaldo asked reproachfully. "Didn't you consider La Declaracíon important enough to deserve the honor of your presence?"

"I was here, I was *there*, my general, on the street. It was your guards who prevented me from entering your home," Calderon vigorously defended himself.

Looking at the doctor's plump body, Aguinaldo broke into a smile. "Just as well. My poor house was creaking under the weight of visitors. Joaquin would have been the last straw."

"My compadre eats too much tortilla – that's why he's so fat!" bellowed Luna.

Joaquin took the ribbing good-naturedly. "I don't eat much. But I keep putting on weight, anyway."

"And what's that bandage, Joaquin, may I see? What on Earth happened to your eye?"

"Ran into a Guardia Civil. I got beaten. My fault."

"What?" Luna blustered and nudged him with a fist. "The cowardly puñetas dared to strike you? Well, give me a few days, and I will run those bastards to the ground. We'll teach them a lesson that they can no longer treat the *indio*s like trash."

"What brought you here so late?" The cooler Aguinaldo changed the subject.

"It's like this…" Calderon began as he took a seat and related to the two men his experiences during the past few days. At the end of his narration, he opined gravely: "It's my conclusion that the Americans are here for the long haul, that they have greater designs on our country than we first thought. That *yanqui* Barton Bailey, he boasted that a large force is coming from San Francisco to reinforce the small contingent in Sangley Point."

"And why are you going around town with a *yanqui*?" Luna frowned.

"First, he befriended me on the warship, then he sought me out," he said looking at Aguinaldo. "Then, I took him around town so he could have familiarity with our common enemy."

"Señor doctor, I don't want you risking your neck for

an alien, certainly not a *yanqui*. There aren't enough men like you in my organization to risk losing one," Aguinaldo admonished.

"They way they are acting," Luna mused, "they must be after our country."

"No, no, General Luna," Aguinaldo allayed his fears. "They assured me in Singapore through this Consult Pratt that they are here to open up a second front to tie up the Spaniards. So the Spaniards cannot send reinforcements to Cuba. He specifically promised us independence in exchange for our support."

"So, why did they treat you shabbily during your meeting on that big ship? Dewey made you exert extra effort to see him aboard his ship instead of receiving you on dry land as if he wanted you to pay tribute. You were made to look like the Cebu chieftain who bowed down to Magellan. You should never have done that." Luna was the only general who could afford to speak bluntly to the leader.

"I don't think that was lousy treatment," Calderon sided with Aguinaldo. "They were very hospitable there, they didn't treat us shabbily."

"It's the symbolism that rankles."

Joaquin defended the chief from criticisms that he was being too acquiescent toward the Americans. The visit to Dewey on board the *Olympia* was now regarded by most members of the revolutionary council as an indignity; they had been carried away by their boyish glee in wanting to set foot on one of the warships that had brought down the Spanish navy. The council members had since concluded that Consul Pratt's promise of independence in exchange for help in fighting the Spaniards was just a ploy to inveigle the Filipinos to keep the enemy preoccupied on land while the Yankee maneuvered at the backyard. The ilustrados privately blamed Aguinaldo for his naiveté. Despite the skepticism of his advisers, Aguinaldo had fulfilled his side of the bargain by mobilizing his forces to bottle up the Spanish army inside the Walled City which was now surrounded. That made the war simple for the Americans. Now, all that was left was for them to do was bring down the walls of the city with their big guns – which they were preparing to do without voicing support for the Filipinos' quest for independence. Aguinaldo was denounced for playing into the hands of the Americans, most notably by the warlike Luna.

"I can't sacrifice the lives of my men by throwing them ill-armed at the walls of Intramuros," Aguinaldo responded to Luna's criticisms. "That will not do. We will have to rely on the big guns of the *yanqui*."

"And once he gets in his big guns, he'll turn them on us. That's the whole trouble. We are letting in a wolf to drive a fox out of the house."

"Let's not pass judgment on them at this point," Calderon said in support of Aguinaldo. "Holy Almighty, they haven't done anything yet."

"Your friend, what's his name?" asked Luna.

"Bailey. Barton – or maybe Martin."

"You heard him say there's an army crossing the sea right now?"

"Well, maybe he was just bragging. I noticed those uncouth white men brag too much."

The ilustrado general sank into contemplation, breathing down his bushy moustache. "I'm afraid history is going to repeat itself. In the 1500's the conquistadors came from Mexico and they were able to colonize us because we received them with open arms. And it gets me into my hanging mood to see the same thing happening now."

"You're going to hang me, compadre?" Calderon said to Luna, defensively.

"No, compadre, I don't mean it that way. But I'll be damned if after having beaten the Spaniards, we succumb yet again to another colonizer. That cannot pass, not without a fight," said Luna gravely.

"You tend to be paranoid about them, Americans,"

Aguinaldo gently reproved his commander. "Perhaps you need to take a siesta."

Joaquin Calderon was not altogether guileless in his support of Aguinaldo who, for all his deference to the ilustrados, took his own counsel on military matters. In spite of his apparent weakness in dealing with the Americans, Aguinaldo was a quietly ruthless man. No better episode illustrated this dark side to the leader's character than what had happened to a revolutionary rival, Andres Bonifacio. Two years before, when waging a revolution was the only business around absent political alternatives, he quelled all challenges to his leadership. In a quarrel over turf with Bonifacio who led a rival faction of the Katipunan, Aguinaldo turned on his ally with the same viciousness he employed against the Spaniards. He arranged Bonifacio's arrest and execution on trumped-up charges of committing "treason" against the movement, i.e., competing against Aguinaldo for leadership. So much for the charge of Aguinaldo's softness.

Now the undisputed leader of the movement, he threw himself to the task of forming an enlightened leadership as if to atone for his sins. He made it a point to pack his cabinet with ilustrados who lent the movement their prestige, but he reserved the officer corps of the army for men of his class, the sons of the soil, save for the one post given to Antonio Luna, an ilustrado who had the temper of a peasant. Within the two groups were conflicting opinions as to how to deal with the Americans.

"As of now," Aguinaldo weighed in his view, "we can't afford to misread the intentions of the Americans and risk a war with two enemies. It's better to let them take a crack at the Spanish army and we'll see if they'll leave content with a victory over Spain."

"What else did he tell you, that *yanqui*?" Luna asked Calderon.

"He was vague about their intentions, Sergeant Bailey. I didn't pry but paid close attention to how he went about his business," the doctor continued to report on his experience.

"Like what?"

"Like studying the fortifications, the guns, the walls of Intramuros."

"He came alone?"

"It was supposed to be a spying mission."

"And *you* helped him do it?"

"Well," shrugged Calderon, looking at Aguinaldo for help in fending off Luna's persistent interrogation, "I heard it from El Jefe that they were our allies. We were fighting against a common enemy. Don't look at me like that, Antonio."

"I have to give you credit for bravery." Luna relented. "And that's when you were accosted by the Guardia Civil?"

"They gave us a chase, I fought them off and knocked down one of them, but Señor Bailey was left behind."

"In that case ... he was captured. Ah-ha-ha, he's in the dungeon!" Luna inexplicably burst out laughing.

Calderon was offended by Luna's morbid sense of humor. "Do you think it's funny knowing that you have comrades languishing there, too?" he remarked with biting sarcasm. "We could end up there someday, you know."

"Ha-ha-ha, what a foolish *yanqui*!"

"Pipe down, there are people sleeping," the host Aguinaldo said, referring to the guests taking their siesta in the next room.

The ill-bred ilustrado who was also fond of ribald jokes was irrepressible, an oxymoron in his contrast to the stereotype. He leaned back on the rack of swords as he continued to laugh uproariously, sending the blades rattling. Aguinaldo had to break up the meeting when some officers grumbled in the next room, awakened from their siesta.

The two military men were to dominate Calderon's life in the months ahead. While his relationship with Aguinaldo was stiff and formal, his friendship with Antonio Luna was more personal and intimate, dating back to their boyhood days. Calderon might look up to Luna as a big brother, but he was the wiser one who frequently had to intercede to keep the impulsive Luna out of trouble, particularly in Spain where both of them studied medicine. There, while Calderon concentrated on his schooling, Luna frequented the bars of Barcelona. He figured in a number of drunken brawls in the seedy bars of the Basque capital which landed him repeatedly in the police station of the Guardia Civil. He escaped a jail term only because the police was far more lenient in the mother country than in the colonies. When he did return to his studies, he buried his nose into studying the military treatises of Clausewitz, an easy read for Luna who was enamored of guns, the épée, and occasional duels. As a result he was able to finish college with only a degree in pharmacy. Beefy, mustachioed and irascible, he had a temper that suited him for Aguinaldo's general staff rather than his advisory council where the most lettered Filipinos sat in the service of the revolution.

Calderon put himself between the two classes of revolutionaries, striking a balance between accommodation and resistance.

———————

10

THE SWORD OF THE CONQUISTADOR IS PASSED

On a bleak moonless night at a beach in Sangley Point, a dirty young man stepped out of an outrigger canoe and headed straight for the Navy barracks.

"Is that you, Bart?" Wolfgang Messner stared at him, transfixed on the dark. "Hey..."

Bailey did not say a word.

Wolf stepped back in dread. "Honest Injun, you ain't a ghost?"

"Put that gun away, buster."

"It's him, it's him!" Wolf rejoiced, recognizing the unmistakable voice. "He's back!"

"Why are you lookin' at me like that?"

"I can't believe it, I thought you was dead."

"I just done my mission and I gotta see the captain."

"Where have you been, Gatling? What have you been doin' all this time in Spanish territory?" asked Scott Preston.

"Sorry, but I gotta see Captain Gridley first."

"Come on, we've been dying to hear from you. What's going on there behind those walls? Are the Spanish preparing to attack us?"

"First thing to do ... is have a hot bath." Bailey remained tight-lipped, much to the disappointment of his comrades who found in him a changed man.

Six weeks after he disappeared into the darkness of Intramuros, his comrades gave him up for dead. The superstitious sailors touched him, patted him, turned him around, prodded his body – it was Ol' Gatling in flesh and blood, all right. He appeared ghostly only because his face was smeared with dried muck the color of ash; otherwise, he was healthy from overindulgence in Spanish food.

Finding him unusually taciturn, they forced him to imbibe a swig of whiskey in order to loosen him up and get him talking. Bailey wasn't his normal talkative self. He just sat on his bunk and asked to be left alone, promising to talk later. "I'll tell you when it's all over, folks, but please leave me be." He gave the impression that he had failed in his mission and that he was lucky to have been spat out of the jaws of death alive.

Bailey didn't fail. For the past three days, he had been acting the part of a messenger between the Eighth Corps and the Spanish Army, exchanging messages concerning the surrender of the Walled City of Intramuros. It was a measure of the Spanish demoralization that Montojo relied on a Yankee emissary instead of a neutral third party. Released from captivity in the first week of July 1898, he crossed the American lines at the advance Navy outpost in San Cristobal, just half a mile away from the Walled City, carrying a sealed envelope from Admiral Montojo and immediately reported to Captain Gridley.

There he observed the decline in the Navy's influence and the consequent ascendancy of the Johnny-come-lately U.S. Army, a reversal of roles apparent in the way his superiors treated the letter from Montojo. Although it was addressed to "His Excellency, Admiral George Dewey," the admiral declined to open it and passed it straight to General Wesley Merritt, in deference to the latter's status as commander of the expeditionary force, which relegated the Navy to a subordinate role. Whatever its contents only General Merritt was privileged to answer in behalf of the Americans. Bailey was never informed of the tidings it brought.

Well, it didn't really matter. Acting like the good soldier, Bailey meekly submitted to a debriefing in the hands of Captain Gridley that was almost as bad as the interrogation by his Spanish captors. He tried to arouse some humanity out of the Navy martinet by describing the suffering he had undergone in the clutches of the darned dagos, but Gridley was interested only in the nuts and bolts of Spanish gunnery. He'd say: "They tortured me till I was black and blue, then dumped me in a dungeon like you've heard of only in story books, the worst hoosegow ever made by human hands, smelled like the muggins, then they jammed me into an old trap of a cell, no bigger than an old lady's closet, hang it, I thought I'd never get out of the place alive." Then, when it was Gridley's turn to speak, he'd ask: "How about their Krupp guns, did they have sliding-wedge breechblocks?"

"Looks like it, I could see the butt, rapid-firing, rifled, the works. And then, they closed the whole damn place, they fed me to the rats, you could feel them nippin' at your toes..."

"How many of the Krupps are facing the bay?"

"Five, six or thereabouts, couldn't tell. I saw only those on top of the dungeon. Oh, it was terrible underground. There were roaches and worms – and the odor, oh my God..."

"And the Hontorios, are they just as good?"

So frustrated was Bailey with Gridley's indifference to the sordid details of his imprisonment that he lost interest in retelling the same stories to Wolf and his fellow gunners, the people who were most interested in hearing his yarns. It was in that condition Bailey turned away from his comrades.

As soon as General Merritt had prepared a reply to Montojo's letter, Bailey hastened back to Intramuros aboard the gunboat *Concord.* Although anticipated by the Spaniards, his return required the same clandestine arrangements as his previous visit. The reason was that the Spanish camp was divided into two factions: Montojo and the Archbishop on the one hand, and the governor-general and the Spanish Army, on the other. While Montojo and the Catholic hierarchy favored honorable surrender, the Spanish Army – which had yet to taste defeat in arms in the hands of the Yankees – was girding itself for all-out resistance. In his tightrope diplomacy, Montojo had the resolute backing of the Archbishop who didn't want his churches to come under bombardment from the same guns that had sent the navy to bottom of the bay. But Governor-General Basilio Agustin who headed the other faction was equally adamant in his belligerent policy, eager to draw blood and redeem the honor of Spanish arms, even if his army's rank and file weren't so keen on picking a fight. Against this backdrop of intrigue, Bailey landed in the dead of the night within sight of the Walled City, 100 yards from the gate called the Postigo, which was the chosen rendezvous. It was an indication of the disarray in the Spanish camp that the Postigo was no longer being devoted for the exclusive passage of the Archbishop and the governor-general but was being employed for clandestine exchanges of a Byzantine nature. Before proceeding to the gate, the *Concord* exchanged signals with the Postigo in the pitch-dark night. The gunboat flashed the signal "Viva" in Morse Code, and a navy sentry on the gate flashed back the word "España." His way clear, Bailey climbed a rugged dike of boulders on the edge of the bay, groped his way around the periphery of the wall, then waded across the moat to come under the raised drawbridge of the Postigo. He whistled a dissonant tune that was supposed to mimic a songbird but that fizzled in his nervous lips. The obviously human squeak served its purpose, getting the sentries' attention, who threw him a rope instead of lowering the drawbridge.

Bailey clambered up the face of the wall kicking and pulling until he came level to a sally point, a breach in the wall from which troops came out to launch surprise attacks at besieging forces during olden times. As he paused to catch his breath, two burly arms suddenly poked out of the breach and yanked him inside.

He was whisked inside a dingy apartment at one end of the San Agustin monastery where he handed over the sealed letter to a low-ranking navy officer. He never got to see Admiral Montojo. He spent the whole night and the following day cooling his heels, waiting for a written reply. The next evening, he retraced the punishing route back to the waiting *Concord.*

And so it went for the next three exchanges over a period of one week. He never did see the contents of the letters, which were sealed with wax, and he wasn't privy to the discussions that took place at either camp during the drafting of the letters. With his unfailing instincts, he could more or less deduce the contents of the letters from the expressions on the faces of the men who handed over, or took delivery of, the letters. The Spaniards were invariably nervous, the Yankees immodestly pleased.

The exchanges came to an unceremonious end one night when Bailey was almost dragged back into the hellhole of Fort Santiago. In the evening of July 14, he approached the moat which was fully illumined by torches and to his surprise found that the drawbridge was lowered spanning the chasm of the moat when it was supposed to be raised at night to keep out intruders. Suspicious, he hesitated before crossing the open span which appeared too inviting for comfort. He first examined the faces of the sentries under the faint illumination of the torches and noted that they looked different from the previous ones: some of the guards wore army uniform instead of sailor's clothes – meaning, no doubt, that the army had seized control of Intramuros from Montojo's navy. Alarmed, he turned around and ran for his life. He dropped the envelope on the drawbridge in panic and he scrambled over the rocks that blocked the shoreline just as gunfire crackled behind him. He skulked away with bullets zinging past his ears.

In the meantime, the *Concord* reappeared from the dark and skirted the breakwaters of the walls until it got close enough to him to throw him a line. Bailey looked behind him to see a mad scramble on the drawbridge between Montojo's sailors and the army troopers. It was an amazing sight. He didn't realize that he had dropped his letter until he was safely aboard the gunboat.

The scramble for the letter was another indication that all was not well in the Spanish camp. Montojo did not seem to carry enough authority to commit the whole of the Spanish forces to an agreement.

Bailey was sure he had failed in his mission.

Reporting to the brick-hearted Gridley aboard the *Olympia,* he tried to downplay his close call with death. He was not going to get any commendation for it anyway, or sympathetic ears, for that matter. "I moseyed along a bit toward the bridge but when I saw the guards, I kinda hesitated. They were different from the ones I saw the previous nights. So, I made a dash for it," he narrated in the captain's private quarters.

"The bridge was lighted?"

"Yeah, unlike the previous nights."

"You dropped the letter?"

"That was the sorry part, sir," Bailey said, fidgeting apologetically. "I panicked, I mean, you know…"

"You should have tucked it in your pocket, goddammit," Gridley snapped.

Bailey was taken aback. "I botched it, sir, and I'm real sorry."

Gridley brushed aside his answer. "Some wore navy uniform and the others army uniforms?"

"Yeah, they didn't shoot each other but they went crazy over it, shoving and a-wrestling on the bridge. Lt. Cocker, he saw it from the boat, too."

Gridley mused over the last part of the story as if trying to plumb its implications. He didn't share his thoughts with the fidgety Bailey who found him completely wooden, devoid of feeling, in stark contrast to his own display of guileless emotion.

With a wave of his hand, Gridley stood up and said: "Come here, I want you to meet some people."

Affrighted, Bailey followed the captain to the map room on the upper deck. With a man like Gridley, nobody quite knew what was going to happen next. Was he going to be court-martialed for losing that letter and compromising the whole operation? To his surprise, he found himself face to face with the top brass of the expeditionary force, Maj. Gen. Merritt of the Eighth Corps and Admiral Dewey of the Asiatic Squadron. He immediately stiffened into a salute.

"So, this is the man I've been wanting to meet!" Merritt greeted him exuberantly. "Gunnery Sergeant Barton Bailey, for the past two months, you have been engaged in a dangerous mission which had an important bearing on the fate of the entire expeditionary force in these islands. You have shown great courage and perseverance in undertaking a dangerous task, over and above the call of duty. Your gallantry in action has been duly noted and appreciated by the high command. As a result, we are awarding you this Certificate of Merit Medal."

Bailey stood frozen in rigid attention as he heard the unstinting praise pouring forth from the highest-ranking officer in the Pacific front. To have heard it from Captain Gridley would have blown him away. To hear it now from Maj. Gen. Merritt was way beyond his most feverish hallucination. It was overwhelming!

Bailey executed a rigid salute as the general pinned the medal on his uniform, stamped with the image of an eagle and held by a ribbon. "Th-ank you, sir," he stammered. He had trouble steadying himself at so unexpected an honor.

It was beyond comprehension that his string of misadventures would amount to heroism, much less deserve a commendation. The undeniable reality of the moment took a while to overcome his disbelief.

Gridley allowed a faint smile.

Dewey watched smilingly, nodding at the proceedings. "You made me proud, young man. You did the Navy honor."

The simple praise from the gentle admiral of the Orient Seas broke the last remaining prop to his fragile reserve. He burst into tears. It was raw Gatling Bailey.

When he returned to his bunk at the Sangley Point barracks for a well-deserved rest from his extended journey, he was still dazed by the whole experience that his usual loquacity deserted him. He simply collapsed on his cot ignoring Wolf's pestering.

The following days, he felt completely idle. There was nothing left for him to do at Sangley Point, and nothing for the Navy, for that matter. The lapse of the Navy to a secondary, supporting role became obvious as soon as the build-up of U.S. Army forces was complete. Although Admiral of the Fleet Dewey was the highest-ranking officer in the theater (or in any theater for that matter), it was General Merritt who ran the show as commanding general of the Eighth Corps. The Navy acted out the role of a baggage-carrier, storekeeper, ferry, and coast guard. Knowledge of the Navy's diminished role made Bailey pity the admiral who carried out his reduced responsibility with dignity, always deferring to the imperious Merritt on matters of military planning.

As his verve returned, Bailey chafed at his idleness. He wanted part of the action that was increasingly being carried out by the Army, especially as he anticipated a military offensive in the next few days. He knew that the negotiations with the Spanish colonial forces had been a failure, the scuffle at the Postigo drawbridge revealing a power-struggle in the Spanish camp that was likely to paralyze decision-making. The U.S. Army needed simply to sneak behind the quarrelling factions to take the city by the back door.

Unknown to him, the situation in the Spanish camp, while confused, was by no means chaotic. Montojo gained the upper hand in the political infighting and was able to dictate the terms of settlement in behalf of the Spanish side. He had struck up a deal with General Merritt, allowing a negotiated end to the war without further bloodshed. The terms were so ingenious that they allowed the Spanish forces in the beleaguered Walled City to capitulate without humiliation. As agreed upon, in the second week of August 1898, the U.S. 4th Infantry Brigade under General Thomas Anderson would deploy 5,000 infantrymen around the walls. The Asiatic Squadron meanwhile would sail from its moorings at Sangley Point to the mouth of the Pasig River to bombard the outskirts of the city. On the other hand, the Spaniards would put up a show of resistance firing their Krupp and Hontorio cannons at empty space. Then, the Americans would enter the Walled City to accept the Spanish surrender.

The settlement was reached without the knowledge of Governor-General Agustin who still commanded an army of 17,000 men. But Montojo, supported by the clergy, decisively dealt with the recalcitrant commander. On August 5, after the scuffle on the Postigo drawbridge between navy and army sentries, Montojo determined that he had had enough and threw down the gauntlet. He sent a company of troops to arrest Agustin as soon as the latter emerged from his morning mass at the San Agustin church. He was quickly bundled on a merchant ship and, with the Americans' blessings, was sent on a Magellanic voyage into the sunset, reappearing in Spain to hear the King's page read the news of his retirement. Into his shoes stepped General Fermin Jaudenes who became a puppet not only of Montojo but also of the Archbishop.

On August 13, an ill-numbered day, the Americans put the plan into action. They drew the wagons of war around Intramuros, and even more ominously, deployed the Asiatic Squadron bristling with guns in a battle line outside the Manila harbor in full view of the city. This saber-rattling put terror into the hearts of the Spanish army and civilians who became amenable to Montojo's leadership, precisely the effect the Americans wanted.

Only a few officers in either camp were fully informed of the plan, the better to protect the honor of Spain, or what remained of it. The Spaniards must appear to have put up a brave resistance, succumbing inexorably to superior force.

It was a rainy day. The wind roiled the waters of Manila Bay rocking the warships of the squadron which had sailed through more hospitable climes when they first crossed the sea a good three months ago. The ominous weather added to the war jitters of the battle-tested crewmen including gunner Bailey who was always ill at ease at the prospect of battle, even one so lopsided. Bailey was manning a six-inch battery of the gunboat *Petrel* which was given the honor of leading the Asiatic Squadron into battle.

He was destined not to fire his gun. His skipper, Commander E. P. Wood poured cold water on Bailey's anticipation of combat. "Only the cruisers will fire. This is the Army's show, folks," he said under the driving rain.

Sure enough, from a distance, the flagship *Olympia* roared from its months-long slumber with a volley of cannon fire, followed by the three other cruisers in the squadron. Then ... wait a minute, Bailey wondered, something was terribly wrong.

The gunnery sergeant in him noticed something suspicious. The guns were hitting nothing, that is, nothing of value. The shells landed on the Chinese quarter, on the slums, on the edge of the commercial district, all of which were civilian targets not worthy of the gunpowder spent. The Walled City was spared the cannonade with nary a dud landing in the midst of the domes and gabled roofs. "Gee, something tricky's going on here." He checked the angles of the guns firing through the rain and noted that they were aimed far too high. He put two and two together and then realized that the Yankee top brass, perhaps in cahoots with the Spaniards, had arranged to fight a mock battle.

His itching hands fell to his sides. "The goddams are a lot smarter than I thought," he laughed at the whole charade.

"They could sweet-talk a victory from the devil himself. If it ain't the darnedest thing I've ever seen."

With nothing to do, he climbed up the rigging to the *Petrel's* foremast poop to get a commanding view of the unfolding mock battle. From there, he caught sight of the infantry marching on Intramuros in orderly lines, the stripes on their trousers swinging in mass synchrony like the legs of a centipede. Teams of horses pulled the mounted artillery across a muddy field which they had trouble negotiating in the rain, their handlers stopping every so often to dig up the wheels of the gun carriages that kept getting mired.

Within sight of the walls, they formed battle lines. The artillerymen detached the guns from their limbers (two-wheeled carts containing spare parts attached to the gun carriages), swung the barrels around to face the target and aimed in the direction of Fort Santiago. The troops continued to maneuver in the field, their Springfields and Krags loaded with live bullets. They exchanged fire with the Spanish guards on top of the walls and at that point the battle became real, resulting in casualties on both sides. "What in the Devil's name is going on?" Bailey shouted at the surprise twist, noting that the bloodshed was not consistent with a mock attack. Now hidden from his view, the two sides skirmished in the rain, with the Americans dropping to one knee to fire, then marching to another position to take a potshot at the enemy, a quaint kind of maneuver that conformed to the tactics of the time. Covered by fortifications and unscathed by the shelling, the Spanish soldiers sniped at the enemy with intent to kill – all against the orders of Admiral Montojo whom they didn't recognize as the leader.

From the top of the gunboat, Bailey noticed another commotion inside the city. Amid the cracks of rifle fire and the booms of artillery, he could hear the eerie tolling of the church bells trilling faintly through the rainfall. The city was sounding its alarm. Now, he was really edgy. What if a crazy dago gunners let loose a salvo from those Krupp guns at the *Petrel* which was sailing well within range of Intramuros' walls? he shuddered.

"All right, men, we're moving in, too!" ordered his skipper, Commander Wood. "Get ready to land at the harbor!"

"What the hell's going on?" Bailey was confused. This was getting out of hand.

"Admiral Dewey gave orders that all hands and officers form companies and secure the ports," said a gunner whose name he didn't know. "Might as well since we can't fire our guns anyway."

"But this is supposed to be the Army's show," Bailey protested.

"We can't be sitting on our butts while there's a shooting war outside. The goddams are treating us like poor cousins."

The mock battle was just as susceptible to the fog of war. Soldiers on either side were carried away by their impulse to kill. According to Filipino historians, several Americans were killed or wounded during the staged battle, which did not speak well of General Merritt's tactical – or rather, theatric – skills.

At noon, a white flag rose over the roof of the San Agustin complex. Because of the smoke and rain-induced mist, the Americans did not see the flag of surrender until 1:00 o'clock p.m.

There was disorder at the Manila harbor, a mile away from the Walled City where the fleet converged after raining bombs on the suburbs. Bailey jumped to the pier uncertain as to which unit he belonged while his comrades disembarked from the larger ships plodding down the gangplanks. All Navy hands were instructed to form companies, and his homing instinct, reinforced by his sense of camaraderie, drove him back to his mother unit in the *Olympia*. Together with Wolf Messner and Scott Preston, his unit formed a battalion-size contingent. Armed with Lee rifles, the Navy column was smartly dressed in caps, knotted scarves and white summer suits, which provided a striking contrast to the Army's suntans.

"Hey you, Wolf, Scott, how you doin'?" Bailey greeted his comrades cheerfully.

"You've been doin' your own thing for way too long," remarked Wolf. "Will ya join us this time?"

"Hey, they're surrendering," exclaimed Scott Preston. "They'll be turning over the city to us and we're gonna live in them castles!"

"Gatling's in on this. Only that he won't tell. He's gone over to the goddams, he ain't one of us no more," said Wolf.

"Doggone it, Wolf, I'm still one of the gang."

"Why don't you share with us your stories?"

"They're nothing to brag about," shrugged Bailey.

"See, look at him, so puffed up, so full of shoot!"

As the skies opened up to let in the sunlight and the sound of cannonade died down, the Navy contingent marched towards the Postigo in two companies, watched in awe by natives along the streets of the outer city. They discovered that the U.S. Army infantrymen had already secured the walls, with wheeled cannons facing the gates and mounted officers signaling directions. They could go no farther as the drawbridge was raised, leaving a moat block the entrance to the Walled City.

Lest the Yankee cannons blow the gate into smithereens, the Spaniards voluntarily lowered the drawbridge on the Postigo. The trampling of dirty shoes desecrated the span that once allowed only the passage of the two highest officials of the colony. With a collective nudge and a surge of bodies, the U.S. infantrymen swung open the interior gate, there to be greeted by Spanish army officers in stiff attention. They looked defeated but dignified.

Bailey's company of Navy crewmen marched behind the main horde of U.S. Army troops which paraded through the streets of Intramuros, herded by a cavalcade of officers resplendent in their glittering swords and starched tunics. It was almost a parody of the annual Marian parade, in which the ivory statue of the Virgin Mary alongside the icons of other saints were borne on top of silver *carrozas* to be carried along the streets of Intramuros, accompanied by Franciscans and Dominican monks in a show of holy fraternity, the whole procession being headed by a soldier of the Spanish Army in honor of St. Ignatius of Loyola who was a military officer and a saint and who symbolized the clerico-secular regime that governed the colony. Goodbye to all that.

Having secretly visited the place a number of times before and enjoyed the hospitality of its resident monks, Bailey didn't share the feeling of triumph and vainglory that puffed up his comrades as they trooped past the crestfallen residents. He had learned to sympathize with their plight, with the indignities and deprivation wrought upon the residents of a city under siege; and now this.

The surrender ceremonies took place in Plaza Real in front of the great Manila Cathedral that Bailey had not had the privilege of seeing before. The skies were now bright and clear so that the fussy Spanish ladies with bonneted skirts could go out and attend the affair at the behest of the colonial government. The ceremony was supposed to be a dignified affair, not a funereal occasion for mourning Spanish pride, wherein the Iberian conquistador could show the nobility of his race by proving that he could hold his head up high even in the worst of defeats. Presiding over the affair on the Spanish side was the new governor-general Fermin Jaudenes, whose native Latin belligerence had to be reined in by Montojo in order to guarantee the solemnity of the proceeding. Toward this end he had to enlist the support of the Archbishop, who gave blessings to his threat to pack Jaudenes in the cargo hold of a ship bound for the Canary Islands if he did not observe proper decorum during the occasion. Heading the American camp was Maj. Gen. Wesley Merritt who could hardly suppress the raw pleasure of bringing an imperial power to heel, just as his illustrious predecessors had done to Great Britain during the War of 1812.

Alighting from a carriage, he made a grand entrance to the middle of the square striding shoulder-to-shoulder with Admiral Dewey who had arrived separately. They were followed only by an aide who acted as the interpreter. Mounted officers kept to the sidelines so as not to distract the crowd's attention from the top brass making a triumphal crossing of the colony's main square.

The Spanish high command was waiting at one end of the square, arranged in a row against a backdrop of assembled colonials: Jaudenes and Montojo in the middle, flanked by lesser officers and local bureaucrats. As soon as the American top brass stopped in the middle of the square, Jaudenes and Montojo strode to meet them in their role as the surrendering officers.

In the shadow of the Manila Cathedral, the two Spanish commanders saluted their conquerors with their swords, which made an audible whoosh and glinted in the air as they were unsheathed in unison. Dewey nodded impassively while Merritt stared at them imperiously down his nose.

"Upon the authority of His Majesty, the King, I offer the surrender of my troops and my government," Governor-General Jaudenes said.

"And the city," added Merritt.

"The city," affirmed Jaudenes, if a bit uncomfortably.

It was supposed to be a confrontation between Merritt and Jaudenes, each heading his respective delegation. But the eyes of the crowd, Spanish and American, gravitated towards the supporting characters, Dewey and Montojo, the two protagonists in the Pacific theater of the war. It was the first time they had met each other after trading hundreds of tons of shells, and the confrontation proved anti-climactic. Dewey looked decidedly unprepossessing, almost grandfatherly, far from the sly, audacious commander who could calmly sail deep into the enemy's lair and send a whole fleet to the bottom of the sea, with breakfast being served in between. His silver hair and silver moustache gave him the look of a retired warrior. He had none of the trimmings of his command, coming in plain white dress coat, an admiral forced to attend a grand ceremony against his wishes.

"We likewise tender the surrender of the navy under my command," Montojo said to his counterpart.

"I see that it has surrendered," Dewey said laconically, knowing that the Spanish navy was, for all intents and purposes, nonexistent. His reticence might have been due to his being hard of hearing.

Montojo flushed at the remark. "Being in charge of the defenses of Intramuros, I have ordered that all guns be silenced and our gates be thrown open."

"It is thus that we have entered."

"Señor General Merritt, may we wish to be clarified on the terms of our surrender," General Jaudenes asked. "We have been granted safe passage for all Spanish nationals and dependents outside the colony. All properties of the Church and those of private citizens will be respected. And there will be mutual exchange of prisoners."

"The conditions contained in our letters remain unchanged," Merritt answered firmly. He proceeded to review the terms of settlement arrived at during the secret negotiations. The officers would be allowed to retain their sidearms and private horses; the churches and schools would be left inviolate; the *indios* would be kept out of the ceremony for Spanish honor's sake; and that the evacuation of Spanish soldiers and officials to other Spanish possessions around the world would await word from Washington. Matters of politics were left for higher authorities of both countries to decide. "The U.S. Army will take control of all public offices and respect private property. The rights of Spanish citizens and subjects alike will be respected," Merritt summed up the agreement.

"Aside from the officers' sidearms, may we be allowed to take down some of the guns in Fort Santiago."

Merritt was stunned. "No, the city must retain all its fortifications. General, I cannot see how you could have misunderstood the conditions."

"Pardon me for being unfamiliar with the terms," said Jaudenes humbly. "It was the previous governor-general, Señor Basilio Agustin, who participated in the negotiations. And I handled only the last stages."

"That is understood," gently interposed Dewey.

Montojo glanced at the governor-general, his nominal superior, and seized command of the ceremony. "The terms will remain as they are. They are very much understood," he said in a voice heavy with reproach.

As far as the Yankees were concerned, the terms were similar to those given by Union General Grant to Confederate General Lee at Appomatox; and while congratulating themselves for being generous, they were offended that the Spaniards would haggle for better terms.

"We yield with dignity to a better army to prevent further harm and suffering to our citizens and our subjects," said Jaudenes, meekly.

Dewey nodded. He was eyeing Montojo solemnly, trying to get his measure of the man. What he saw confirmed his previous assumption that his Spanish counterpart was better dressed than armed.

More fussy than an ilustrado, Montojo was decked with all the raiment of his office. Aside from the epaulettes with dangling locks and coils of aiguillette cord that festooned his chest, he sported a gilded sword with a handle intertwined with gold cords. He donned a plumed hat that was worn during formal occasions, an elongated affair shaped like a sail ship, with fore, aft and bridge, the feathers providing the sail. He wore a sash running diagonally from shoulder to waist, pinned with medals of every shape known to geometry: star-shaped, cross-shaped, gear-shaped, round, square and one odd configuration that recalled an oyster. Admiral Patricio Montojo, in his hour of defeat, was more ornate than a bagpipe.

Only Merritt's attire came close to matching the panoply of the Spanish outfit. He wore an officer's cap with the eagle insignia pinned on the forehead part, dented on both sides like a buckled pot. Over his plain khaki, he sported shoulder plates with two stars, crossed swords on the collars, a belt with gilt-edged buckle, a curved saber with an arched handle, and boots equipped with spurs of "gun" metal. Until the last minute, he had planned to enter the Plaza Real astride a stallion furnished with the so-called McClellan saddle, a thin bag of leader with buckled straps and conical footrests. He agreed, however, to ride a plain carriage out of consideration for Admiral Dewey who had no fondness for ceremonies.

Bailey observed the proceedings from the sidelines, positioned near the entrance to the Manila Cathedral where the Navy contingent was assembled in parade rest. His attention was focused on Admiral Dewey whose gentle manners impressed him as noble, far more than the pomposity of the other officers, including Merritt. "The old man's mild as goose milk, he's not at all cross at Montojo."

"That's because they're surrendering, you can't be hard on a surrendering army," explained Wolf, the scholar of the group. "They're doing it by the book, giving an honorable surrender."

"Poor ol' Admiral Montojo. He looks so dignified in defeat."

With mixed reactions from the crowd, the ceremony reached its climax. The governor-general handed over the Spanish Army's standards to General Merritt as head of the conquering legion, and the latter had his hands full propping up the ornate banners embroidered with the images of a lion and a seahorse in gold thread. Once again, Jaudenes saluted with a flourish; whereupon Merritt, sweeping the folds of the banners aside, responded in kind. Montojo did the same with his naval ensign, frayed, singed at the edges, which Dewey received reluctantly, knowing how much it meant to the proud Spaniard. He planted the standard firmly at his side, let out a fleeting smile and saluted – the smile being his way of conveying his respect and appreciation.

Away from the scene, at the edge of the plaza, the Spanish flag was hauled down a towering pole, a sail of symbolism on a mast of defiance, emblazoned with the yellow and red colors of the kingdom and inset with the royal coat-of-arms, the emblem of Spanish sovereignty over a colony that had borne its rule and vanity for 300 years. The Americans cheered spontaneously, except Bailey. The Spaniards grieved. The monks doffed their hoods to reveal their bald pates. The soldiers clenched their faces in bitter anguish. The fashionable ladies – panniered by whale bones, stuffed and sheltered by parasols – dabbed their eyes with silken handkerchiefs. The kingdom on which the sun never set was about to lose its Oriental frontier and retreat into the horizon across two oceans. Mexico was gone. South America had splintered into independent states. Cuba was good as lost. Spain might as well be a banana kingdom.

"Well," Wolf concluded, "that is as it should be."

It was a great moment in the history of the United States. The ceremony took place only within hours after the Spanish surrender in Cuba at 4:30 p.m. on August 12, 1898, giving allowance for the 12-hour difference in the two countries' time zones.

The occasion put an end to the careers of several historical figures. Admiral Montojo sailed away to Spain where he was to face further ignominy in the hands of a court martial tribunal which sent him to prison for losing a naval battle in so disastrous a fashion.

He was followed by the short-lived governor-general Jaudenes who evacuated the Fort Santiago barracks, leaving the fortifications of the city intact. Merritt gathered his standards to return to the United States, leaving the Eighth Corps in the hands of General Elwell Otis. The Archbishop of Manila and his court packed up and headed for the Vatican. After the evacuation of the high-ranking colonial officials aboard private commercial vessels, the ordinary Spanish bureaucrats and civilians were left to their own devices, facing the risk of retribution from the restive natives eager to take over.

Dewey stayed. He continued faithfully to discharge his subordinate duty of providing back-up and logistics to the Eighth Corps. Among his men, Bailey and his *Olympia* crewmen would remain longer than the four months it took to beat Spain. Rather than diminishing in number, the troops stationed in the islands increased over the years to more than six times its original strength, 65,000 men or two-thirds of the American standing army.

What was the reason for the escalation? Why ship in more troops when the Spaniards were leaving in droves? The reason had something to do with the *indio*s who were kept out of the gates of Intramuros.

The lowering of the Spanish flag from the skies over Intramuros was the only sight the Filipinos ever saw. It was not because they were not eager to witness the end of a 300-year rule. Nor was it because they were uninformed. The bombardment, the opening of the gates, the entry of American troops into the Walled City – all alerted them to the momentous occasion. When the Spanish flag came down its towering mast, they surged towards the gates cheering and shouting but they were pushed back by the cordon of American guards toting Springfield rifles. No seat was reserved for them in the proceedings: that was the reason.

Aguinaldo's revolutionary army made an attempt to attend the surrender ceremony. The departure of the Dewey's squadron from Sangley Point and the build-up of troops outside the Walled City on the eve of August 13 likewise alerted him that something was up. But when the bombardment of

Manila began, he knew better than to throw his ragtag army into the midst of the conflict. Rather than risk being caught in the crossfire, he sent a patrol under General Antonio Luna to reconnoiter the battlefront. They were accompanied by Dr. Joaquin Calderon who knew how to deal with the Americans and together, the two ilustrado officials observed with growing alarm the swiftness of the Spanish army's collapse. In a matter of hours, the bombardment ceased and the American had the city surrounded. Then, the gates of the city were flung open and, lo and behold, the Americans were presiding over the surrender of the Spanish government – something the insurgents had shed thousands of lives for. The keen-eyed Calderon noted something suspicious about the summary battle. Although not a military man, he noted that the half-hearted resistance of the Spanish troops, who had dealt brutally with the local insurgency, was so out of character that it betrayed an arranged match with a predetermined outcome. It was nothing short of a charade.

He kept passing on his observations to insurgent commander Luna who led the 12-man patrol. Huffing and aching, he tried to keep up with the group as it hiked the beaten fields towards Manila fast on the heels of the Eighth Corps. He trudged down the rough road that had been churned to muck by the passage of an army. Half a mile outside Intramuros, he urged Luna to wait until the American sentries started admitting the throng of civilians before pressing on, anxious to avoid a confrontation between the Yankees and the insurgents.

He had trouble restraining the fiery ilustrado. Inflamed by the sight of the gates slamming shut on the Filipino colonials, Luna plowed through the crowd, his upturned moustache sodden by the rain. He ran onto a Springfield rifle brandished by an American sentry swaddled in a raincoat.

To Calderon's relief, Luna's ignorance of the English language dampened his aggressiveness. "Ah, señor ... will you allow us to get inside," he said in vulgar Spanish.

"Back off, buster."

"We are from the revolu-"

"One more step..."

"Aguinaldo' s headquarters."

"I don't give a damn where you are from, just get out-ta..."

Luna lunged to hit the Yankee sentry but was promptly seized by Calderon and two other aides. "Let them be. They're armed." Then, in his own diplomatic way, Calderon interceded with the sentries. "Sir, we're officials of the revolutionary party of General Aguinaldo, we have been recognized by Señor Admiral Dewey as combatants, and we would like to attend the ceremony inside or whatever there is of it remaining."

The Yankee sentry softened. "I'm sorry, sir, but I'm under orders not to admit locals, especially you people." He scanned the distinctive features of the insurgents, their bandoliers, boots, Luna's scrambled-egg cap, and the straw hats of the other insurgents. "I don't want any trouble with you people, but I hope you understand. I'm just following orders."

"How about just the two of us, me and General Luna, we're unarmed. They won't even notice us."

"I have my orders," the sentry said firmly. "The answer is no."

In contrast to Calderon's supplicatory manner, Luna stiffened and clenched his teeth. *"Que demonio,"* he grumbled. *"Hijo de puta."*

The sentry stood his ground, his rifle at the ready.

To Dr. Calderon, who narrated this scene to Philippine historians for posterity, this episode was symbolic of Yankee intention in a way more vivid than Dewey's ambiguous hospitality on board the *Olympia*: there was another man of the house now and the Filipino was being shut out.

192

11

TEARS OF A FRIAR

Families were broken up during the evacuation of the Spanish nationals. Most chose to depart for Spain and the Latin American states to rebuild their fortunes. A few opted to remain.

At the height of the exodus in the last week of August 1898, Joaquin Calderon went in search of his father. He was looking for his only remaining connection to the past. A widower at the age of forty, his wife having died after giving birth to Estrella, he still had a surviving parent, and he was Spanish. Considered a mestizo, he had half the blood of a Spaniard running in his veins, a fourth Chinese and the remainder *indio*, but such lineage didn't suffice to win him the citizenship of his pure-blooded father. Nonetheless, he was able to parlay his Spanish parentage to gain a first-class education which considerably advanced his status in society. Next to pedigree, education was the straightest route to privilege. After becoming a doctor, he lived in the periphery of a society at whose center stood the Spaniards, with the brown-skinned illiterate *indio*s far removed to the margins. It was not the policy of the Spaniards to divide the colonial society into castes, but the habits of three centuries had turned prejudices into custom. Now, the old order had been shattered. Joaquin Calderon looked for his Spanish father to bid a fateful farewell which was far more conclusive, more yielding to estrangement, than any ordinary separation among family members.

He found the Manila harbor in a different kind of mess. The first batch of departing Spaniards was gathered at the pier, heavy with baggage. They had brought with them personal belongings plus souvenirs of their ties to the islands, which piled up at the pier waiting to be loaded aboard departing ships. They lay in bundles everywhere – chests, furniture, icons, paintings, statues and other bric-a-brac – some already stacked on pallets or wrapped in hemp nettings, ready to be hoisted or manhandled to the cargo holds of the outbound ships. A statue of the Virgin Mary wearing a crown studded with jewels, an icon that commonly graced the living rooms of devout Spanish families, was caged in a crate to keep it from breaking during its transoceanic journey to a new home. Everywhere bustled Spaniards of all ages, many of whom had never ridden a ship, much less been to the mother country, they having been born and raised in the colony. A gaggle of children tugged at the skirts of their mothers who were carefully packing Chinese porcelain in straw-filled crates. Never before had Joaquin witnessed so many pure-blooded Spaniards gathered in one place, nor could he imagine a more inauspicious occasion to deliver his greetings. How could one measure the sadness of an entire ruling class being booted out of a country which it had occupied for hundreds of years? How could one plumb the feelings of a native-born Spaniard, raised in the luxury of a vast hacienda, who was suddenly informed that the land which his forefathers had passed down generations was not their own? It was a mind-boggling realization. It was a cruel destiny.

He found a Dominican friar with a shaven pate bending over a wooden chest. It was under his tutelage that he earned a degree in biology, preparatory to a course in medicine.

"Ah, padre, padre Sebastian," Calderon greeted him in a reverential tone. *"Tengo mucho gusto encontrarte a usted.* I'm glad I've found you."

The old man turned around and acknowledged the chubby figure: "Ah, Joaquin, my son."

"I have been trying to locate you in the crowd, father."

"Oh-ho, but I had to make the rounds of the convents to pick up some precious belongings."

"You are really leaving?"

"Yes, my son. *Yo dejo para* Argentina."

The two men looked at each other, across a gulf of unspoken emotions. From the terms of endearment they used to address each other, it was obvious that the terms "Father" and "Son" carried a far more intimate meaning than they would openly admit. Calderon was sad to see the father leave his mission, where he had reaped worldly and spiritual rewards and pains, and the father was equally sad to see the son stay behind, cut loose from the care and patronage of a superior race.

"Can you stand the long journey? Why not wait till the rainy season is over?"

"Joaquin, I'm too old to stand in wait. Time is not patient with men like us."

"I just want to make sure you're safe."

"Ah, I put my fate in the hands of God. Be good, my son. And don't join the rebels."

Calderon didn't openly admit to his membership in the underground. "I do my duties as a doctor without choosing sides."

"Como esta Estrella?"

"She's a teenage girl now. You should have seen her lately, big and lovely, just like the mother she had never seen."

"I am glad that you were able to make it on your own, after all the problems that I brought your mother, God bless her soul. If only it were possible, that I could have taken you under my care... it just wasn't possible."

Calderon bowed his head in a gesture of respect. He could not find the right words to say in response.

"I left my collection of books with the rector, too heavy to justify the cost. You may be able to get them from him." The friar changed the subject.

"Do they include the works of Louis Pasteur?" asked the doctor.

"The medical textbooks are intact. That's my gift to the University."

The chests which contained the friar's worldly belongings were being carried aboard a three-masted ship by a pair of laborers who continued doing a yeoman's job for the departing master. Before boarding the ship, the father turned to bless his son: "God bless you, son..."

"My prayers for a safe voyage, father."

The sail ship then weighed anchor and sailed into the sunset of Manila Bay, carrying the colony's high officials across the ocean whence their ancestors came. Its silhouette crossed the face of the sun to eclipse it on the horizon. Calderon sensed something significant in the tableau: the sun setting on Spain's Empire.

———————————

12

FIVE HUNDRED BOLOS

At his Escolta shop, Carlos "Caloy" Calderon busily hammered a piece of red-hot iron into a blade on top of a galleon-era cannon that he used as an anvil all the while impatiently waiting for a visitor from the Katipunan. He marked the hours by the peal of the San Agustin church's bells which rang at 10:00 a.m., and by the hoot of an outbound launch at a nearby Pasig River wharf which departed regularly at 1:00 o'clock p.m., but still no Katipunan messenger showed up. Had he been waylaid by robbers or vengeful Spanish stragglers? Carlos wondered.

"Estrella, please take down the cloth you hung out to dry," he called his niece, Joaquin's daughter. "They'll be blackened by smoke."

"I'm dyeing them, *tio*. They need to dry out."

"Would burnt fabric look good? Take them down, I'm expecting a visitor."

Estrella did not answer as she went about her business making quilt in the adjacent clinic of his father Dr. Calderon, Caloy's half-brother.

The man Carlos was waiting for finally showed up around 4:00 o'clock that same afternoon. He looked like an ordinary working man, barefoot, with the pant legs of his trousers rolled up. All Katipunan rebels looked ordinary, for that matter. Carlos was at the door before his visitor could stop knocking.

"Seguismundo," he recognized the man.

"El Jefe asked me to give you this," said the visitor in a conspiratorial tone, pulling out a folded piece of paper out of a bag made of woven straw.

"Read it to me, dammit," Carlos barked, shutting the door behind them. "You knew very well it's not intended for Joaquin."

"I – I can't read either," Seguismundo said.

"I don't know how you ever became a messenger," grumbled Carlos. His comrades seemed to think that having an illiterate messenger enhanced the secrecy of rebel communications. "Sometimes, I wonder if those ilustrados in the movement have brains either."

"Maybe, the doctor..."

"Too bad, my brother is not around. Let's see." Carlos turned the document around. "Let's decipher this ourselves, Segui."

They could not make heads or tails of the handwritten letter that was in Spanish. But they could make out the map sketched on the back, which was a diagram of an area inside of Intramuros. "This looks like a wall ... that's Intramuros, here is the Pasig. And that's San Agustin church in the middle. He's there!" Carlos stubbed his finger on a spot highlighted by a cross. "He's *here?*"

The Katipunan messenger nodded. "But I don't know how he looks like ... big ... about thirty-five."

"I've seen him. Are you sure he's the man we're after?"

"Esteban Zaragoza. He's the leader of the firing squad who shot Rizal."

"What does El Jefe want?" asked Carlos.

"An eye for an eye. Blood debt," Seguismundo muttered.

"That's what I feel all along, Segui. Zaragoza is dead meat."

Despite having got rid of their colonial masters, the revolutionary movement Katipunan had not settled all scores with the Spaniards. Their most visceral grudge remained an open wound: the murder of Jose Rizal. Carlos himself continued to see a recurrent image of Captain Zaragoza signaling the firing squad to shoot with a downward flourish of his sword. He also realized that he once literally had the man in his grasp, by one leg in fact, but the rest of him got away by the grace of a surgical saw. Now, his quest for vengeance just got the imprimatur of the revolutionary council itself, as reduced to a cryptic order sent to him by a messenger which in their mutual illiteracy they had trouble decoding but for the illustration therein that indirectly conveyed the message. Except for the Church, there was no longer any surviving Spanish institution that could answer for Rizal's death. Esteban Zaragoza was a tangible, living symbol of the hated regime whose blood must be shed to give the natives a measure of justice.

He needed no encouragement. The execution was seared in his mind, and he could never forget how the man looked like. "Big, tall, dark. He will stand out in a crowd, minus one leg."

Katipunan spies reported that Esteban Zaragoza was staying with the friars of the San Agustin monastery where he was trying to auction off his sword collection and other belongings while waiting to be repatriated to his native Spain. The same informants often saw him on horseback ambling around the church after the bells tolled the angelus, as if he were still a Guardia Civil on patrol, and they timed their ambush at the moment he rode into the square outside. In jumping the notorious killer, Carlos was to have help from four rebel bolo men who would join him at a designated rendezvous just outside the Walled City. The courier Seguismundo himself would wait with the men until Carlos showed up at the appointed time later that evening.

Having drawn up a plan that included an escape route out of American-held Intramuros, Carlos killed time by resuming work on the piece he was forging. He needed to expend excess energy and to steady his nerves as he felt a surge of adrenalin in anticipation of the night's mission. He was a prolific blacksmith crafting implements out of scrap metal. He proceeded to heat a piece of iron in a glowing bed of coals, feeding the fire by pedaling a foot-operated leather stoker, till the piece of work glowed into a fiery red color, which he then picked with a pair of tongs to lay on top his improvised anvil, to be beaten and molded into the desired shape: e.g., a chain link, a window grill, a horseshoe, carriage wheel parts or, most commonly, a bolo blade. He was content with this humble means of livelihood, the only kind he could ever aspire for in this highly segregated society. Unlike his elder half-brother Joaquin who had had the fortune of having a Dominican friar for a patron, he never enjoyed formal education of any sort. To begin with, the Spaniards never established a system of public education in the islands during their centuries of rule. Building schools took a backseat to building churches, of which there was one or two in every town, and learning the alphabet was neglected in favor of rote memorization of Spanish and Latin prayers. The nearest thing he had to schooling was the two years he spent washing the floors of a Dominican university.

He worked with his hands to supplement the income of his family whose farm in Bulacan province never produced enough to support a clan encompassing three generations housed under one roof. He never enjoyed the love or company of his father, a small-time *hacendero* or landlord who disappeared during a typhoon in the 1870's. In contrast, his light-skinned half-brother Joaquin flourished from the love and largesse of the Dominican friar, who was also close to his mother. While Joaquin enjoyed the privilege of a foreign education in a university in Barcelona, Carlos refined his craft by the sweat of his brow until he was able to open a shop in Escolta, catering to rich Chinese traders.

Carlos was selflessly supportive of Joaquin's decision to

become a doctor. When the stipend being sent by the Dominican friar ran short, Carlos made up for the shortfall by the toil of proletarian work. The ultimate guarantee of security for a Filipino family then was producing at least one ilustrado or, better still, a priest from the brood. The family succeeded in bringing up Joaquin to be a shining example of a Filipino aristocrat, but at the cost of keeping his younger brother toiling among the ranks of the Filipino underclass.

Carlos stopped working at 6:00 o'clock as the church bells tolled the angelus. It was time to go. He lamented that the iron he had chosen was hopelessly bad, filled with impurities that rendered it brittle. For the night's mission, he decided to arm himself with a treasured fighting weapon that he had never used except as wall decoration – a glinting scimitar with a curved blade, made by a Moro craftsman in the south, known locally as a kris. Said to date back to the 16th century, it was given to him by a Chinese trader who in turn had bought it from a Spanish soldier in Mindanao.

He took the weapon from the wall, wiped its razor-sharp blade with a piece of cloth, and smelled its sinuous length adoringly, wishing that he could discover the magic of its creation. The purity of its steel gave it a crystalline hardness, a quality he could never match in his forge. He slid it carefully into its wooden sheath and tied it around his waist.

"Where are you going, Uncle Caloy?" Estrella asked.

"I'll just go buy some feeds for my fighting cocks, hija," answered Carlos.

"With *that* sword?" she inquired, gesturing at the blank space on the wall.

"Estrella, you can't travel safe nowadays, with all sorts of armed men around. So, make sure to lock all doors and windows and check also your father's clinic."

"Are you going to see papa tonight?"

"I don't know. But I'll ask him to buy more fabric for you if I see him."

The narrow cobblestone alleys were deserted by seven

o'clock at night, the only signs of life coming from the flickering light of oil lamps leaking through the windows of surrounding houses. With a torch to illuminate the way, Carlos followed the abrupt twists and turns of the street. An occasional lamp post burning coconut oil dimly lit part of the way.

At the designated spot between gates of the Walled City, he was joined by four other rebels in the company of the Katipunan courier Seguismundo. They were all dressed in the drab clothing of working class civilians, the better to melt into the church-going congregation attending novenas at San Agustin church. They made it past the American sentries at the gate without incident.

The bolo men tarried awhile in the shadows of a nearby building while Carlos scouted the vicinity of San Agustin church and the grounds of the nearby monastery, peering through its wrought-iron gates. The church was abuzz with the drone of prayers, illuminated by numerous flickering candles that made its stained-glass windows glow like Chinese lanterns in a dragon festival. The belfry was eerily silent, towering like a ghost over the humped roof. So far no sign of their quarry, nor was anybody else loitering about who could interfere with their plan.

Cocking his ears, Carlos heard the clatter of hoofs that came from a heavy carriage which presently emerged from behind a street corner. It was much bigger than the ubiquitous one-horse calesa ferrying ordinary folks, being driven by a pair of horses that could pull a lot of weight. It had been a while since he had seen such a carriage, which was the preferred mode of transport of Spanish bigwigs and high-ranking clergymen. As it sped past him, he saw that its passengers were not clerics but intoxicated soldiers whose loud voices rose above the din of hoof beats. Yanquis.

He looked in vain for his target in the dimly lit church plaza and monastery grounds. He expected to see a lone figure on horseback, draped in the cloak of a Cavalry officer. When nobody matching the description showed up, Carlos was assailed by doubts about the accuracy of the Katipunan intelligence, given that the people who supplied the information were mostly illiterates. They could not easily presume to find a one-legged horseman because the captain might be wearing an artificial leg. For all he knew, the supposed sightings of Zaragoza might have just been figments of the imagination of the rebels, who had never witnessed the execution of Jose Rizal nor ever tasted the rap of the captain's swagger stick. They could not be expected to retain as clear an image of the man that had been imprinted in Caloy's mind by virtue of his having personally witnessed the traumatic event. Presently, the hoof beats of a lone horse echoed from the dark reaches of the church compound, resonating against the walls and columns of nearby edifices, perking up the ears of Carlos.

He crept along the wall of the monastery towards a corner, his comrades following him in a single file. They hoped to surprise the horseback rider as soon as he turned the corner. Suddenly, he saw the man. It took only a split second for him to recognize the silhouette of Esteban Zaragoza astride a horse, looking none the worse for his amputation. In fact, he looked whole again for he had boots on the stirrups at either side of the horse. He must have fitted himself with a false limb made of wood or bamboo.

Astride the horse, he looked unreachably tall and imposing. It was then that Carlos realized his disadvantage, having to joust with a man on horseback, something only a military officer could have known. The battle was joined earlier than expected. No sooner had Carlos drawn his scimitar than the man unsheathed his saber to meet the threat – and then charged. This was no ambush! The man's well-honed instincts for danger sharpened further by paranoia must have been aroused by the bustle around him as the assassins prepared to close in on their target, clumsy amateurs that they were. Neither amputation nor retirement had dulled the Guardia Civil captain's reflexes. With one smite of his saber, he cut down one rebel bolo man who crept up to him from the side, sending him reeling mortally wounded into the path of another, even as he pivoted his horse with a tug at its reins in time to parry another attacker whom he dispatched with a thrust to the back with his blade. Now it was three against one.

Before Carlos could even deliver a blow, two of his companions were down, dead or dying and he was left with only two comrades to help him do the job. With one desperate flail of his kris, Carlos managed to snap the reins from the horseman's hand, while a comrade stabbed the rump of the horse, which bucked and neighed in panic throwing its rider to the ground.

Unhorsed, the captain totally lost all his coordination as his artificial leg broke off leaving him sprawled on the pavement. From there on, it was a mismatch, with the captain losing his grip on his saber which Carlos kicked away. At the moment when he had the man's life in his hands, he hesitated. He allowed the man to lift himself on three limbs. Then, the thought of the bound patriot dying under a hail of bullets filled him with deadly resolve. "This is for … Jose Rizal," he blurted out as he stabbed at Captain Zaragoza on the torso. The gurgle of a blade penetrating a man's body and Zaragoza's muffled cry told them they had done their mission.

They were overtaken by the sounds of hoof beats and the footfalls of shod feet running on cobblestones which grew louder toward the scene of carnage. The noise was ahead of a squad of foot soldiers followed by a carriage pulled by a team horses. The approaching figures ordered Carlos and his companions to halt and identify themselves, followed by gunshots when their commands went unheeded. The gunfire felled another comrade.

Carlos and his lone surviving companion fled the scene, leaving behind their weapons and the bodies of their fallen comrades. "Go ahead, Segui!" he shouted at the courier Seguismundo. "Tell El Jefe we did it!" However, as he picked up himself to flee in another direction, a lucky pot shot from one of the riflemen hit the retreating Carlos on the thigh. Carlos stumbled, groaning. Seeing it was only a flesh wound, he struggled to get up.

One of the soldiers shouted: "Jesus Christ, a massacre." Undoubtedly, a *yanqui.*

"More like an ambush," another soldier said in a low voice.

"You think it's an ambush, Wolf?"

"One Cavalryman... a Spaniard... three natives... all fighting with knives."

"It must have been something to watch."

"A brave man, this one-legged Spaniard. Fighting with his sword against three men," Wolf continued. "That's the kind of fighting that has been going on in this colony since before we landed. Apparently, they are still at it."

The soldiers were American sailors of the Asiatic Squadron on shore duty. They chanced upon the assassination only because they saw the riderless horse galloping away from the open monastery gate.

"Look! There's one of them gooks trying to get away!" another soldier shouted pointing towards Carlos who was limping along the monastery's perimeter wall which he was unable to scale.

Presently, the *yanquis* were upon him. The lead soldier had his rifle pointed at him but when he saw that he was unarmed and that his leg was bloody, he let his guard down. The second soldier was a big fellow who wasn't even carrying a rifle and who simply watched the wounded man writhing on the ground. They were Bailey and Wolf who had stumbled upon the scene after a night carousing with the goddams.

Carlos was brought to a small Navy outpost in San Cristobal, on the shore of Manila Bay just outside the Luneta ground where Jose Rizal was shot. The place was to be significant in the latter century as the site of the stately U.S. Embassy. There, his identity slowly emerged under the tender mercies of his captors who had to hire a nearby fisherman to interpret his Tagalog ramblings. One detail stood out to his chief interrogator Barton Bailey: this guy was the brother of Dr. Joaquin Calderon, the very same man who was pounding hard at the anvil when Bailey visited the Escolta clinic months before, the snobbish uncle of Estrella. For which reasons, Bailey made sure the man's wound was dressed and his person guarded as if he were one precious prisoner who held the secret to El Dorado.

Without letting on the wild thoughts that played in his mind, Bailey prodded his captive: "Do you recognize me?"

Carlos looked at him and nodded.

"Why did you kill that fine Spanish officer?"

Carlos did not answer. It was useless telling them that he wanted to avenge Rizal's death.

"You don't fight a Cavalry officer on horseback on your feet, with nothing but bolos. You will be cut down. You have to shoot him."

Carlos shook his head. Well, we cut him down, with our bolos, not with a rifle, he wanted to say but kept mum.

"What you did was a crime against American authority," continued Bailey. "We are now in charge. You will stand trial for murder."

Bailey, in reality, was unsure about his authority to hold the prisoner. This was the first time they had taken a Filipino captive for criminality, and he had absolutely no idea what to do with him. If not for the ulterior motives playing in his mind, he would have preferred to let go of the wounded Carlos as an unwanted burden.

In the following days, while the prisoner was in limbo, Bailey looked after him with unusual solicitude. He visited him often in the yard of the San Cristobal outpost, formerly a tool shed, bringing him food and water. There, sitting on a wooden box across from Carlos who was perched on his canvass cot, Bailey asked to be tutored on the niceties of the Tagalog language, spiced with a smattering of Spanish expressions which both of them understood. Carlos gladly obliged the *yanqui*, hoping that he could exploit the relationship later to win his freedom. The American's motives in learning Tagalog was unclear, but he was one quick study. They progressed from the usual polite greetings, to cuss words, to practical words about daily conduct and commerce, then, finally, at Bailey's instance, to utterances about love and courtship. He learned to say *"Ini-ibig kita"* (I love you), *"Ang ganda mo"* (How beautiful you are"), *Ikaw ang ligaya ng buhay ko* ("You are the joy of my life") and many other such romantic phrases welled up from the heart of the enamored. His motive was getting obvious... but not to Carlos.

———————

Bailey borrowed a horse from a mounted infantryman of the Eighth Corps at their camp near the bay shore a mile south of San Cristobal. He carefully parted his hair before donning the floppy hat of the infantry. Dressed in a khaki uniform with a fedora and knee-high boots, he paid Estrella Calderon a visit, the culmination of his week-long Tagalog lessons. Soon enough he found himself in front of Dr. Calderon's clinic, and seeing the lovely señorita seated by the window of the residence upstairs, he blushed in spite of himself. With a flourish, he alit from his horse, doffed his hat and, with a sidelong glance at the window, knocked on the door.

Estrella demurely looked out of the window. *"Que esta?"*

The Gringo visitor answered in polite Tagalog: "Si Bart Bailey po."

Estrella was stunned. She gaped at the apparition as if to ascertain whether some *indio* impostor donning a Gringo uniform was impersonating Bailey. But she could not be mistaken. It was indeed his father's Gringo friend.

"Papa no esta aqui, señor."

Bailey, who was expecting Estrella to say, *"Tuloy po kayo"* (Come in), lapsed into English: "No, it's not your father I want to see. It's you, Estrella."

Estrella was taken aback at the mention of her name, and protested in Tagalog: "No, no, Señor Bailey. You can't come in here. There's nobody here. I'm all alone. Wait till papa or Uncle Caloy is here."

With more reason he wanted to pay her visit. "Señorita, I have news for you. It's about your uncle, Carlos Calderon." He said gravely.

At the mention of her uncle who had gone missing, Estrella became alarmed, then curious. She had been without company in the house for more than a week, save for an occasional visit from her father, such that she had to spend the night in a neighbor's house. That Gringo Bailey was the bearer of news regarding her uncle's whereabouts was of such overriding concern that she rushed downstairs to open the door, momentarily shedding her maidenly reserve.

"Uncle Caloy? What about Uncle Caloy?" she asked Bailey as soon as he stepped inside the door.

"Ah, um, it's like this …

"You speak …"

"Allow me to speak, this poor American, ah, in your tongue, my sweet señorita … May I take a seat?"

Seated nervously in a rattan chair, fiddling with his hat, Bailey recounted to her the predicament that her uncle was in, with small doses of exaggeration to enhance his own importance. The graver the situation he made it out to be the more he appeared like a knight in shining armor. Her uncle was arrested for killing a Spanish officer and was himself wounded. He was being held in prison and was certain to be tried for murder, for which crime he faced a possible death sentence by musketry – a term which Bailey took care to explain in convoluted Tagalog to make sure she understood its gravity. "Like being shot by seven officers firing seven rifles all at once." But, not to worry, Bailey was trying to defend him to spare his life and possibly win his release. In truth, nothing of that kind was in the works. Carlos was found to be a rebel officer and his killing of a Spanish soldier was deemed to be in pursuit of a political grievance, hence, a pardonable offense.

Estrella was reduced to a whimpering wreck. "What would become of me now? I have to go to the province and tell papa."

"No, you can't ... I mean, you don't have to," Bailey tried to manage the situation.

"Uncle Caloy's the only reason why I'm staying in Manila. He looks after me while papa is away, which is most of the time."

"If you're going to allow me, we'll work for his release. First, we'll convince General MacArthur that he was acting in self-defense. That he was continuing his war against the Spaniards without knowing that the war is over. Something of that kind. Then, we'll ask a member of your family to guarantee that he's not going to make any more trouble. Then, he will be released. And that's it."

As Estrella daintily dabbed her eyes and nose with a handkerchief, the Gringo sailor kept staring at the comely señorita, bewitched by her coyness and innocence and her *mestiza* good looks. Having the mixed bloodline of his father she was blessed with fine facial features, a fair complexion, and a voluptuous figure, needing only the refinements of fashion to attain the perfection of a fairy tale princess. He had never been so enamored before, the first time he felt an all-consuming love for a woman, especially this exotic virgin of the Orient sea. His raw passion recalled that of Spanish friars before him who were largely responsible for the colony's mestizo population.

Guileless as she was, Estrella didn't go along with his loaded suggestion that she cooperate in freeing her uncle. She could not go out of the house with a Yankee unchaperoned lest she spark a scandal, agitating the whole neighborhood and her papa into paroxysms of outrage. No, she could not visit the Yankee camp without prior approval of her father.

Having thus outsmarted himself, Bailey didn't press too hard so as not to run afoul of local sensibilities, but instead made haste slowly. During the next few days, he practically deserted his post to return surreptitiously to the clinic, where he reported to Estrella the condition of Carlos and the efforts he was making to win his release, which in truth was almost nil for he didn't have any influence over his superiors. By and by, he brought with him not only tidings but also flowers, fruits and trinkets. His motive became all too apparent to Estrella as well as to her neighbors such that, on their own, they banded together to keep guard on her chastity, paying untimely visits during Bailey's afternoon calls apparently to check if anybody was in the clinic, or at work in the iron shop and to volunteer for domestic chores. Thus, while Bailey was spinning his self-serving tall stories, an old woman would drop by to help Estrella sweep the floor. Then, another would appear to do the cooking, ostensibly upon her father's prior request.

Bailey, however, was smarter than the neighbors.

Learning that she did the marketing for the household, he advised Estrella that she could buy the freshest apples in the market adjacent to the Luneta park, being imports from the distant port of Hong Kong brought in by American supply ships.

"Apples? I've never seen apples before!" the girl rejoiced.

"They're the sweetest thing in the world, darlin' and we have a saying that: 'An apple a day keeps the doctor away.'" Doctor Calderon, that is.

"Oh, really?"

This is it, the game's up, Bailey thought wickedly.

Beguiled by the idea of tasting the enchanted fruit, which she had heard about only in stories (particularly, in the Bible), Estrella proceeded to the bustling marketplace outside the Parian Gate, reeking with the pungent smell of vegetables, fish, slaughtered pigs and spices, a business cornered by Chinese traders sporting braided pigtails. And where were the apples? They floated right before her eyes, two ruddy orbs, dan-

210

gled by a grinning Barton Bailey, who suddenly materialized in front of her.

Instead of being put off by his trick, Estrella was amused and for the first time let on that she liked him in the anonymity of the crowd. From there on, it was smooth sailing for Bailey, who drew little resistance when he invited her for a stroll around the broad expanse of Luneta by the Bay. He was wearing mufti to escape detection by patrolling military police and she a blouse and pleated skirts without the umbrella-like underpinnings fashionable among the upper-class women of the day, which suited Bailey just fine, for it accentuated her shapely figure. They walked under the ancient banyan trees, with their expansive canopies and gnarled trunks, picked flowers near the site of Rizal's execution – marked only by a bald spot in the trampled grass – and, toward sunset, showered petals on the stream which ran through the moat bordering the stone wall of Intramuros.

At twilight, they walked hand-in-hand along the shore of Manila Bay, and espying a storm-swept coconut tree whose lower trunk was bent almost parallel to the ground, Bailey scooped up Estrella by the waist and gently sat her there. She let out a yelp but didn't protest too much, steadying herself by placing both hands on Bailey's shoulders, while the latter held himself still. It was then that they exchanged vows of mutual devotion for all times and sealed a contract of love with a kiss.

Bailey was eventually caught red-handed by Joaquin Calderon. One day, while he was boldly waiting for Estrella at the clinic to take her out on a date at the Luneta, unmindful of the hostile reaction of the neighbors, Bailey saw a calesa stop outside the door. Out stepped a rotund mestizo with a walking stick that was intended more for swagger than for walking. It was Dr. Calderon who before he could cross the street was stopped by a neighbor who whispered something in his ear. Nodding gravely, Calderon sauntered briskly to his clinic with a grim countenance. He shoved the door open and came face-to-face with his Gringo friend Barton Bailey whom he greeted with a baleful glare magnified by his monocle.

"Good evening, sir. Howdy do?" Bailey faced him, grinning sheepishly.

"Papa!" exclaimed Estrella from the top of the stairs, more in surprise than in greeting.

"Out," the doctor said curtly, thumping his cane. "Out of my house!" he barked at Bailey.

Thus ended Bailey's romantic interlude.

A confluence of events conspired to extricate Carlos Calderon from Yankee captivity. In a matter of weeks, his misfortune turned to good luck. Neglected in the ramshackle prison by the bay, he attracted the attention of a navy chaplain who took pity on him and referred his case to General Arthur MacArthur of the newly formed Eighth Corps, soon to be Provost Marshal of Manila. The general took particular interest in Carlos's skill as a metal craftsman, which he found relevant to the American objectives in the islands. If ever the Americans were to engage in a war of conquest, then they would be facing the same enemy as Carlos Calderon, who was adept at using the bolo. Carlos was more than that. He was also good at making bolos, a skill in which he had very few peers, if any. Therefore, General MacArthur resolved to "turn" Carlos, that is, co-opt his loyalty so that he could be an asset to the Americans.

"Let me see the guy," MacArthur asked to see the prisoner at the Navy outpost, which was just outside the walls of Fort Santiago where the Army Eighth Corps was quartered.

Carlos was brought before him. By this time, his leg injury had almost healed and he was able stand and walk on his own.

"Hey-you, fella," the general barked at Carlos gruffly. "What can you do?"

"I'm a blacksmith, sir," answered Carlos in broken English. "I do iron works. Horseshoes. Grills. Bolos."

"How about cannons?"

"Oh, no," Carlos laughed, shaking his head. "They're much too big for me."

"Knives?"

"Bolos."

"What?"

The word bolo required description – a thick, rugged machete forged to one's desired length – good for chopping anything such as firewood, sugar cane and coconuts or, lately, for killing Spanish soldiers.

To illustrate, Carlos drew a bolo on the sandy dirt floor of the Navy outpost with a stick. It was a faithful reproduction, albeit on a larger scale. "Bolo," repeated he.

The drawing pricked the American officer's interest. He stroked his chin with his hand, warming up to Carlos. "And that was what you used in killing the Spanish officer?"

"It was an act of justice," Carlos answered defensively. "He owed a blood debt to the Filipino people."

MacArthur didn't dwell on the cause of Carlos's arrest. A Civil War hero without formal schooling in the military academy, he was beguiled by the unorthodox tactics of the Filipino rebels. Some unfathomable stroke of prescience made him grasp the worth of this artisan. And it was this: if they were to dig in and fight a colonial war, they would have to resort to the tactics and weapons employed by conquistadors of yore. In hand-to-hand fighting, a bolo was more versatile a weapon than a bayonet. A bolo would also come in handy blazing paths through the jungle. The long supply route to the islands made it imperative for the expeditionary forces to source some of their hardware and armaments locally. In any case, swords were no longer being produced back home in sufficient quantities to equip an army, having been relegated to ceremonial use, nor were Army conscripts being trained in sword fighting anymore, apart from what remained of the Cavalry. A regression in military tactics was needed for a successful campaign in this theater of war.

Yes, Carlos Calderon, the bolo maker, suddenly became a very important person indeed. Forthwith, MacArthur ordered him to produce a dozen bolos as punishment for his crime, after which he would be freed. It was an indirect admission by the Americans of their lack of authority to continue detaining him. In the absence of a civil government to supplant the Spanish bureaucracy, it was doubtful that the Americans had anything to gain by turning him over to the local authorities for prosecution. He had not offended the Americans but committed a political crime. He could be subjected to a mock trial, such as what happened to Jose Rizal, and shot. In which case, they would lose an asset of intrinsic military value.

Carlos seized this chance to win his freedom with both hands. With whatever scrap metal he could salvage from the shore, such as pieces of Montojo's navy, he got down to work transforming his erstwhile prison into a workshop. First he made the commonplace utilitarian bolo, with a thicker, wider, but shorter blade, ideal for chopping down small trees. Next, he made the "anti-personnel" variety which had a thinner, narrower but longer blade. Finally, out of shell casings, he forged a curved bolo, similar to the *kris* he used to dispatch Esteban Zaragoza. But not quite. The shell casing was made of brass which contained more copper than steel, making the kris more suitable for ceremonial rather than functional use. MacArthur was so pleased with his prototypes that the captain ordered for more, thereby prolonging Caloy's detention. But it didn't matter. He could parlay the delay into goodwill.

General MacArthur calculated that aided by a handful of apprentices and helpers, his war-making asset could equip a brigade with jungle-fighting capability in no time at all. His unconventional thinking and serendipitous foresight would go a long way in outfitting the American expeditionary forces for a new kind of war that was dawning in the Pacific, which defied classic military tactics. Thus far, the U.S. Army had successfully fought the Spanish Army in conventional warfare in Cuba that followed the strategy of Clausewitz, reaping victory after victory in what was to become known as the "Splendid Little War." Nobody could anticipate that the mettle of the world's newest military power would be tested to the limit fighting countless "little wars" in these islands. *Guerilla* warfare literally meant just that: the diminutive of war ("guerra"), and it was here that the word would enter the American vocabulary. In a week Carlos made two dozen bolo blades for General MacArthur and was freed as promised to set up a bolo factory in Manila.

As Estrella watched with mouth agape, Carlos alit from a two-horse carriage driven by a Gringo. He walked with a limp as he turned to wave at two other American escorts inside the military carriage, one of whom resembled Barton Bailey. Her uncle did not look like a prisoner at all but a valued commuter, driven right up to his doorstep. "*Si, señores, gracias.* One hundred for the first order," he said in English. "*Hasta la vista! Mabuhay! Viva los Americanos.*"

The neighbors and passersby watching the sight were equally amazed. Wasn't he rumored to have been taken prisoner by the Americans after killing a Spaniard?

"Uncle, what happened to you – you're limping! Did the Americans hurt you? Papa has been so worried."

"Don't bother me, I'm going to be very busy!" Caloy growled irritably as he strode inside his shop. His mood abruptly changed as soon as the Americans vanished from view. "*Hija,* did anybody work in my shop while I was away? Are my tools and materials still there?"

In spite of her uncle's petulance, Estrella was happy: her dear Gringo muchacho had made good his promise to free her uncle. He had proved his love for her.

In the next few days, his outlook on life changed: he was now focused on the business side of the war rather than the politics that was its impetus. The racket that emanated from the shop stirred curiosity in the neighborhood. *One hun-*

dred for the first order. Good Lord, he was going to be rich!

The first order for fifty bolos became a hundred, then two hundred, then a thousand – enough to equip a whole brigade. Carlos Calderon became the busiest artisan in town.

In an effort to disguise his relationship with the Americans, Carlos at first made it known to everybody that the bolos he was producing were intended for Aguinaldo's army based in the neighboring province of Cavite.

Joaquin would have none of it. "I know you were taken by the Gringos and something happened along the way."

"Only Aguinaldo needs bolos, the Gringos have powerful weapons," Carlos retorted

"I now El Jefe – inside and out, literally," said the personal physician of the revolutionary general. "And he has no need for more bolos because he has more than enough! In fact, he has just made an order for 20,000 rifles in Hong Kong."

"My brother, why are you so curious about my work? Haven't I been doing this for twenty years?" Carlos protested amidst the racket of clattering hammers wielded by a dozen assistants.

"You've not worked on a single order in such quantities."

"Listen" – Carlos steered his older brother out of the workshop toward the adjacent clinic – "if indeed I'm working for the Americans, is that a problem? We are not at war with them."

"But soon will be. Their intentions are as clear as daylight. Why did they receive the Spanish surrender alone? They kicked us out, me and General Luna, as if we were the enemy."

"Ah, politics. I don't know nothing of politics."

"These bolos..." Joaquin tapped the bunch of blades arrayed on a stand without their handles. "These bolos will be our curse."

"Well, there's no getting away from them Yankees. They're even courting Ella."

216

"Who?"

"Well, I'd rather have her tell you. Hey, Ella, my dear..." Carlos called her niece who was eavesdropping on them while cleaning the house. "What's the name of that American suitor of yours? That little Gringo?"

Estrella smiled bashfully but did not say a word.

"What's going on? Tell me!" barked the father.

She merely giggled and ran upstairs, to the father's further annoyance.

The ilustrado doctor was not against his daughter's marrying a white man. In fact, he wanted her to take a Spaniard for a husband so that the mestizo bloodline of the Calderon family would be enhanced. However, as much as he would like to gain the goodwill of the Americans, he frowned upon the prospect of her daughter being wooed by a Yankee sailor. Not this kind of white man.

The sordid episode illustrated the contrast between the two brothers: while Carlos was able to inaugurate an easy friendship with the Yankees in so short a time, Joaquin found it impossible to forge anything other than a shaky alliance of mutual convenience. He had nothing in common with the low-born, vulgar, war-mongering farm boys exemplified by Bailey. They had none of the cultivation of the Spanish colonists who had the benefit of a Catholic education, if not European schooling and whom he regarded more as estranged brothers than as blood enemies. To learn that a Yankee was courting his daughter was an aggravation he could not stomach, a public scandal that would bring stigma to the family. Not so with Carlos Calderon. In stark contrast to his supercilious brother, Carlos had many things in common with the Gringo newcomers: their uncouth manners, their rural backgrounds, their pedestrian lifestyles separated only by the barrier of language. The tale of two brothers would parallel the saga of the revolution.

13

A FEAST OF ISLANDS

Washington, D.C.

On October 1, 1898, an ilustrado turned up at the White House. History records that on that day an emissary from Aguinaldo named Felipe Agoncillo (1859-1941) sought an audience with the president of the United States.

His mission was to forestall the inevitable: recolonization. This simply meant recalling home the Yankees that had dealt Spain a crushing blow, thereby catapulting the U.S. to the ranks of world powers, an historic achievement by and of itself. While the Filipinos were happy to be rid of their repressive colonial master, they were not about to fall under the sway of another power, especially one with whom they had nothing in common, with a different language, incompatible beliefs and divergent history. Allowing the Yankee culture to take root in this country was hardly a step forward in its civilization.

It didn't help the cause of the insurgents that Aguinaldo's Declaration of Independence hardly found a listener in the outside world. It was a shout in the cave: loud but muffled. Undeterred, Aguinaldo sent his best men around the world in the hope of winning recognition, specifically from France and the United States, the bastions of democracy. And what better emissaries to send than those illustrious ilustrados who copied the foppery of European gentry, if twenty years behind? Had Aguinaldo chosen to go himself, he would have been greeted more with curiosity than sympathy, something like sending Crazy Horse in full regalia to plead for independence for his people. He showed good judgment in his choice of Felipe Agoncillo, an educator and scholar.

The mission was destined to fail. For while Agoncillo was cooling his heels at the White House – shining his pince-nez, straightening his cravat, and twirling his moustache with a chopstick – Spanish and American diplomats were locked in negotiations inside a palace in France. They were haggling over the terms of a settlement that was to be known as the Treaty of Paris, which would govern the disposition of Spanish colonies around the world as a price to pay for losing the war, particularly the colonies now in American hands, e.g., Puerto Rico, Cuba, Guam and the Philippines. Being the most valuable asset for its sheer size, the Philippines occupied the attention of the negotiators.

The emissary was not discouraged. At pains to show his good breeding, he strutted into the office of McKinley, escorted by Assistant Secretary of State Alvee A. Adlee. A towering figure for a Filipino at six feet, he had to leave his top hat as well as his cane with an attendant to avoid hitting the chandelier.

In the president's office located at the main residence of the White House, Agoncillo faced the Great White Father, the man who was to dictate the fate of a different breed of Indians. He stood in awe of the man by whose command a kingdom was crushed. One couldn't look farther up the totem pole of Yankee politics, and it was to his attention that Agoncillo brought his people's long pent-up desire for independence. He opened his plea with a belabored account of centuries of Spanish misrule, citing the poverty of the peasants, the excesses of the friars, the cruelty of the Guardia Civil. The Philippines had been a colony longer than America had been a nation. For when the pioneers from England founded a settlement at Jamestown in 1607, the Philippines had already been in Spanish hands for nearly half a century.

Then, he pointed out one stark fact: "Your consul in Singapore, Spencer Pratt, expressly promised independence to our people if Aguinaldo would join forces with the Americans against the Spaniards. We kept our side of the bargain. We had the Spaniards bottled up in Intramuros."

McKinley nodded attentively. Of course, he had never heard of Spencer Pratt. Or Intramuros, for that matter. And he didn't consider the word of a consul binding on the United States government.

"Admiral Dewey, he has repeatedly told us in Manila that he had no interest in holding Philippine territory. That is what we want to see. But apparently, the occupation forces of General Merritt are there to stay, which is against the desire of our people."

The gentle McKinley made no comment. He didn't wish to offend.

At the end of the meeting, the emissary tried to wangle a small concession: "Can I at least speak to the Peace Commission in Paris? Can I get a seat at the negotiating table where the fate of my people is being discussed?"

According to McKinley's biographer Margaret Leech, the only response of the U.S. president was to ask Agoncillo to put his demands in writing so that his cabinet could study them. That was characteristic of McKinley. He preferred to sit on a problem until a crisis forced a decision, as he had done in the run-up to the declaration of war on Spain. He could afford to sit on Aguinaldo's demands forever, there being little political risk involved. As far as he was concerned, the opinion of the colonized people had no bearing on the peace talks.

After his audience with McKinley, Aguinaldo's emissary proceeded to Paris to pry on the negotiations between the

Spanish and American negotiators. The Spanish ambassador opened the door, cried out at the unexpected presence of an *indio*, then slammed the door shut with a sigh. Thus, ended Agoncillo' s mission.

The two sides haggled over the terms of settlement, without regard to the interests of the peoples affected by the treaty. It was agreed that Guam, Cuba and Puerto Rico would be ceded to the United States. But the Spaniards were not quite willing to yield their precious Oriental colony without compensation. The Americans agreed to pay for the Philippine Islands, $20 million, which they considered a little more generous than the 43 cents in trinkets that they forked over to the Indians for the island of Manhattan. Spain grabbed the money with both hands, considering its Pacific colony as damaged goods hopelessly mired in rebellion. In due time the Treaty of Paris was signed, distinguishing the United States not only as a world power but an imperial power as well, with colonies of its own.

When the signed treaty was presented to the United States Congress for ratification, an outcry erupted that set the tone of the Philippine debate for years to come. Apparently, not all congressmen shared McKinley's imperial ambitions made in pursuit of a policy grandiosely called Manifest Destiny. There was something wrong with the policy that was incompatible with the ideals of the Founding Fathers. It provoked questions about the role of America in world affairs, whether it should aspire to the role of an imperialist or as a liberator of colonized peoples. At issue was not the $20 million compensation demanded by Spain, which was by no means a pittance, but the morality of inheriting eight million rebellious Filipino subjects and keeping them under American tutelage.

No opponent of the treaty was quite so zealous as Senator George F. Hoar (1826-1904). He supported the Aguinaldo government not out of love for the Filipinos but out of love for American ideals. At the floor of the Congress, he explained that it was immoral to colonize a people who had an "organized army, a congress, courts, schools, universities, churches, statesmen who can debate questions of international law like Mabini and organize governments like Aguinaldo... aye and patriots who can die for liberty like Jose Rizal." He even went so far as to recite Rizal's poem *Mi Último Adiós* to bring home the point that the Filipinos had leaders every bit as qualified to run a country as Benjamin Franklin and Thomas Jefferson. During the deliberations on the Treaty of Paris, Hoar attempted to ram through the so-called Vest-Gorman Amendment that would "establish a form of free government... securing the rights of life, liberty and property" in the islands. This was defeated 53 to 30. Fighting harder, he proposed another amendment that would "give consent of the Filipinos as a prerequisite to establishment of a government." Again, this was rejected.

As a compromise the Congress approved the non-binding McEnery Resolution which promised vaguely to set the archipelago free "in due time" when it would "best promote the interests of the United States and the inhabitants of the islands." It passed 26-22.

With all attempts to derail it foiled, the Treaty of Paris was finally put on the block for ratification by the Senate. It passed, 57 to 27, with Hoar being only one of two dissenting Republican senators. Together with McKinley, he was a lonely voice in the Republican Party, which tended to play hardball on foreign affairs and which had stampeded Congress into declaring war against Spain.

The approval of the treaty did not end the outcry. Public opinion was divided on the issue of "imperialism," the first time the word became current. Given that the United States was born of the blood of patriots who fought against British colonialism, the question of joining the ranks of imperialists drew impassioned comments from Americans of all stripes.

There were those who supported the acquisition of the Philippines as a U.S. colony. "Common sense tells us to keep what has cost so much to wrest from an unworthy foe," so said the Baltimore *American.*

The New York *Tribune* of Whitelaw Reid agreed: "Having once freed them from the Spanish yoke," it said of the Filipinos, "we cannot honorably require them to go back under it again." Presumably, the United States would be a more benevolent master than Spain.

By far the most convincing proponent of imperialism was Chauncey Depew, a spokesman of Big Business, who advanced a sophisticated theory that hit the Americans where it mattered, right on the pocketbook. The Philippines' strategic location provided the U.S. access to the huge Asian market and furnished a strategic geographical stepping-stone for channeling America's excess produce by way of export to the burgeoning Asian market. "The American people now produce two billion dollars worth more than they could consume. We stand in the presence of eight hundred million people," he said. On the other side of the debate, the opponents of imperialism were no less vociferous than the advocates. They banded together as a group called the "Anti-Imperialist League," which counted among its members former president Grover Cleveland, John Sherman, Andrew Carnegie, and Mark Twain. The League published pamphlets, buttonholed officials and otherwise made life miserable for William McKinley. The more fervent members scuffled with the police and trooped to the harbors to taunt soldiers departing for the Far East.

A country that values freedom could not "play king over subject populations without creating habits of action most dangerous to its own vitality," argued League member Carl Schurz, editor of the *Harper's* weekly.

Andrew Carnegie took up the cudgels for the dissenters in Big Business. While he agreed that imperialism would open up the Asian markets for exports, he pointed out that it would also open up America for imports. It would be disastrous for millionaires like him to see America flooded with cheap sugar, tobacco, flax and hemp from the Philippines. Fired up by visions of cheap imports swamping domestic business, Carnegie spent his own personal wealth to fund a crusade against the imperial cause. "You have brains and I have dollars," he wrote his ally Schurz on December 27, 1898 to encourage him to run anti-imperialist editorials. "I can devote some of my dollars to spreading your brains."

The activities of the Anti-Imperialist League exasperated the McKinley administration. "Andrew Carnegie really seems to be off his head," Secretary of State John Hay complained to Whitelaw Reid of the *Tribune* on November 29, 1898. "He writes me frantic letters signing them Your Bitterest Opponent. He threatens the President not only with the vengeance of the voters, but with the practical punishment at the hands of a mob."

Vice President Theodore Roosevelt was blunter. "It is difficult from me to speak with moderation of such men as Hoar," he wrote to Senator Henry Cabot Lodge on January 26, 1899, referring to the senator who had opposed the Treaty of Paris. "They are little better than traitors."

The majority of the American people agreed with Roosevelt and the imperialists. There was a lot more to be gained than lost from maintaining colonies. After all, the Great Powers – Britain, France, Germany and Japan – found the policy essential to their prosperity and justified by necessity. A large swathe of the planet were colonies of any one of the Great Powers, e.g., India, Indochina, Indonesia, Korea, Burma, Black Africa, Egypt and Arabia. Another world power, Russia, did not merely acquire colonies but annexed adjacent territories to become an imperial behemoth straddling two continents. Surely, this business of imperialism could not be all that bad. If that was what it took to secure America's Manifest Destiny, then America had no choice but to abandon the venerable principles of its Founding Fathers and start collecting colonies, too.

President McKinley registered his support for the Treaty of Paris negotiated by his envoys but stood aloof of the raging debate in the Senate on its ratification. He had no taste for public spats with fire-eating dissenters whose rhetoric provided good copy to the Yellow Press. He let warring voices in the Senate drown each other in the mad debate preceding the vote. But when he thought that the fate of the treaty hung in the balance, he let his voice be heard over the din.

The occasion was provided during a visit by a delegation of ministers from the Methodist Episcopal church, to which denomination the president belonged. The ministers gave him their spiritual blessings, thinking that the Philippine Islands was virgin territory where missionaries could find new converts to Christianity. As the ministers walked out of the White House, McKinley called out: "Hold a moment longer! Not quite gentlemen! Before you go I would like to say just a word about the Philippine business."

As the *Christian Advocate* reported at the time, McKinley related to the Methodist ministers: "I walked the floor of the White House night after night until midnight. And I am not ashamed to tell you, gentlemen, that I went down on my knees and prayed to Almighty God for light and guidance more than one night. And one night late it came to me this way – I don't know how it was, but it came ... that there was nothing for us to do but to take them all, and to educate the Filipinos, and uplift them and civilize and Christianize them, and by God's grace do the very best we could be for them, as our fellow men for whom Christ also died."

With that decision "I went to bed and went to sleep and the next morning I sent for the chief engineer of the War Department, our mapmaker, and I told him to put the Philippines on the map of the United States and there they are, and there they will stay while I am President!"

———————

Uncle Sam got quite a handful from the King of Spain. For a bargain price of US $20 million, he acquired an archipelago the size of New England, with a population of eight million souls. Comprising the territory were 7,109 islands, counting the vast number inhabited only by birds and monkeys but excluding those that surfaced only at low tides. There was no need for Uncle Sam to consult with the inhabitants of the islands in order to acquire valid title to the territory, as the rules of the Great Game went, for the signatures of the belligerents on the treaty were all that were needed to effect the transfer. The Filipinos had no say on their own fate. Uncle Sam had a Torrens title over the archipelago sealed by a treaty and enforceable by force of arms.

Now, Uncle Sam could drop his false pretenses of being the Filipino's friend and ally: he was now free to crack the whip as the new colonial master.

For the Filipinos, the transfer of sovereignty to yet another foreign power was just another chapter in its long history of subjugation. Their first contact with foreign powers took place on March 16, 1521 when Ferdinand Magellan, sailing for the Spanish crown, sighted one island in the archipelago after drifting aimlessly across the Pacific Ocean in search of the Spice Islands, a voyage that was to end in the first circumnavigation of the globe. Magellan found clumps of villages that flourished on fishing and barter trade between islands. He exchanged gifts with the natives, Christianized a few and, filled with imperial vainglory, fatally involved himself in tribal feuds. After winning the allegiance of the chieftain of the island of Cebu, he quarreled with the warriors of the island of Mactan, led by Lapu-lapu, who had refused to send him tokens of their obeisance. Whereupon the Cebu chieftain urged him "to fight and burn the houses of Mactan to make the King of Mactan kiss the hands of the King of Cebu, and because he did not send him a bushel of rice and a goat as tribute," so related Father Pigafetta, one of the members of the expedition who chronicled the voyage.

Eager to force Lapu-lapu to bend to the Spanish crown, Magellan gathered a raiding party composed of sailors from his fleet and a group of Cebu warriors, then invaded the island of Mactan. Unfortunately Magellan, though a great navigator, proved to be an inept conquistador. He got into trouble right upon approaching the beach of Mactan in a flotilla of boats where he got bogged down in the surf. Then, as he waded through the water, Lapu-lapu's band of warriors rushed from behind a coconut grove to meet the invaders. They ganged up on Magellan whom they identified as the leader of the invading force from his fancy martial attire consisting of a finned helmet and plates of armor. He was soon struck by a poisoned arrow on his exposed right leg. Then, the blows of a scimitar from the hulking Lapu-lapu knocked off his finned helmet. The shaft of a spear smote him on the face so as to stun him out of his balance. Then, as he struggled to fend off the blows from an enraged Lapu-lapu, another warrior came from behind and slashed him on the calf which was left uncovered by his armor. He tumbled to the sand to receive the coup d' grace from the Mactan chieftain.

"They killed our mirror, our light, our comfort and our true guide," mourned Father Pigafetta who watched the battle from a ship anchored at a distance.

Thus, ended the first Western attempt to colonize the archipelago.

After the Battle of Mactan, the remnants of Magellan's fleet returned to Spain to report the discovery of an hitherto uncharted group of Pacific islands as well as the tragic fate that had befallen their leader there. Magellan was eventually credited for circumnavigating the globe and "claiming" the Philippine archipelago for the Spanish crown; if so, it was his spirit that completed the voyage around the world because his body remained in the islands. It was never in fact recovered where it fell. Lore has it that its head was preserved in a jar inside a hut in Lapu-lapu's island where it lay as a trophy for half a century – smoked, salted and pickled – and regularly displayed at pagan rites.

Spain was not discouraged but, on the contrary, challenged by the fate of Magellan. It sent a series of expeditions to the Philippines over the next forty years composed of able and well-armed warriors. But while they were good conquistadors, they were poor navigators. One after the other, the trans-Pacific expeditions floundered in storms, were aborted by mutinies or vanished into infinity to fates unknown. Finally, in 1565, King Philip II dispatched a determined force headed by Miguel Lopez de Legazpi who had the qualities of both a navigator and a conquistador. He arrived in the islands in good shape and immediately set about conquering one tribe after another. In a campaign lasting from 1565 to 1572 Legazpi subjugated the major islands of the Philippines where the population was concentrated, with a little help from Christianized natives. His biggest conquest was a flourishing port settled by the Tagalog tribe in the estuary of the Pasig River, in the western side of the main island of Luzon – the village of Manila – where Legazpi built a fort called Intramuros, the seat of government of the colony and Spain's farthest harbor. It was at this point that King Philip II boasted that he ruled an empire "where the sun never sets" – a boast later echoed by England – for while it was noontime in Madrid it was midnight in Manila, and vice versa. From the arrival of Legazpi to the appearance of Dewey, the islands never experienced a moment of freedom, a good 333 years of bondage, which explained Aguinaldo's fury at the American takeover.

The colony that McKinley bought at a bargain was not so pristine as Louisiana on the day it was purchased from Napoleon for $11 million, or Alaska, for that matter, when it was bought from Tsar Alexander II for $7 million. Most islands of the archipelago were unspoiled by the feudal rule of the Spaniards whose unenlightened parsimony left the islands undeveloped. Relatively young in geological time, the archipelago was the exposed spine of an underwater mountain range, which was constantly being remolded by earthquakes and volcanic eruptions. Its shores were continually lashed by typhoons that washed out entire villages and hampered communications among inhabited islands. Its soil was a life-giver to myriad species of plants and animals. What it lacked in arable area or mineral wealth was made up for by its rich biological diversity.

In a study published early in the American rule, naturalist Ron E. Dickerson found the Philippines a haven for tropical wildlife, many found nowhere else in the world. He counted 300 species of wild animals, 750 species of birds, 3,000 species of timber and 10,000 species of flowering plants and ferns, many unnamed and found nowhere else in the world. Among the rare plants that Americans considered a matchless treasure were 900 species of orchids that Dickerson had meticulously catalogued. He also credited to Uncle Sam's natural treasury 2,500 species of beetles, 1,825 species of butterflies and moths, and a worrisome 40 species of termites. To his disappointment, however, he found not a single species of tiger or elephant that American high officials could shoot in leisurely safaris as one of the delights of empire enjoyed elsewhere by Englishmen in the British Raj.

In the coming conflict, the wilderness proved a bane rather than a blessing to the troops of the Eighth Corps. For it was in the jungle where most of the battles in the Insurrection would be fought, a setting that would confound even veterans of the Indian Wars.

Toward the end of 1898, the Americans didn't know the nature of the country they had taken over from the Spaniards. After the Wild West was largely won, its new frontier was pushed farther to the West, right across the Pacific Ocean. And its deep interior was inhabited by wild tribes as well such as the Igorots and the Ifugaos of the Cordilleras which practiced head-hunting, the Aeta pygmies of Bataan living in Stone Age conditions and the fierce Muslim Moros of the south who over the centuries had defied the sword and the cross and never yielded themselves to Spanish rule. The relatively civilized rebels of Aguinaldo, recruited from the majority Christian communities that had submitted to direct Spanish rule, represented the tamer face of the general populace, amenable to the influence of politics. Not so the so-called non-Christian tribes who were to rear their heads later in the conflict.

Aguinaldo himself was spoiling for a fight. Snubbed by the great powers at Paris, he was equally determined to assert his freedom. He began preparing for battle early in January 1899. At the time, he had absolutely no idea about modern battlefield tactics that might prove effective against the Americans. Accordingly, he started with small, tentative steps. The previous month, Aguinaldo had relocated his government to the town of Malolos, province of Bulacan, 25 miles north of Manila, feeling the heat from the American naval base in Sangley Point, which was located right behind his old headquarters in Kawit, Cavite. There was no special military reason for his choice of Malolos except its distance from Manila. To cover his tactical retreat, he followed the advice of his able commander General Antonio Luna to dig entrenchments on the suburbs of Manila, beginning three miles from the walls of Intramuros. Trenches were simple defensive works that had proved effective against Cavalry in recent military conflicts, as Luna had learned, which the Filipinos were well-equipped to do, needing only picks and shovels. It was by the use of the Cavalry that the Americans were able to conquer the West, and they were expected to use the same tactics in the islands. In short order, the rebels were able to excavate twin lines of trenches north of Manila to cover their positions. They were to form the demarcation lines between American- and rebel-held territories.

The Americans were expected to make short work of the rebels. The victories of their Army and volunteer Rough Riders in Cuba, of their navies in Santiago Bay and Manila Bay, convinced the Americans that they could not possibly have any trouble repelling the mosquito resistance offered by the insurgents. The state of their ragtag army was laughable, armed with stolen rifles of various vintage and bolos, transported by carabao-drawn carts, or so it seemed. After years of indecisive battles, the revolutionary army was a spent force. It was never able to defeat the decadent Spanish army and surely would not last longer than Montojo's navy in a clash with the U.S. Army. When a Cavalry patrol sighted Luna's trenches, it reported the same as an annoyance to U.S. commander General Elwell Otis at the U.S. Army headquarters in Fort Santiago. General Otis promptly ordered the patrol back to the countryside to serve an eviction notice on Luna.

Unwilling to provoke a clash at that point, Luna dropped his shovel and proceeded to dig new trenches two miles farther north, in the town of Caloocan. Again, Otis protested but this time Luna, a hot-tempered ilustrado, stood his ground. By the end of the year, Luna had streaked the Caloocan hinterlands with 10 miles of trenches, manned by 2,000 troops armed with Mauser rifles, old cannons and Gatling guns. Trench warfare was then a new-fangled military concept which he had imbibed from reading German military treatises during his student days in Barcelona. Unsure of his own strength, General Otis grudgingly allowed the trenches to stay but kept them under tight watch.

For six months following the Spanish surrender, there was enough space between the two forces to go around without a clash. Soldiers of the Eighth Corps caroused in the bars of Manila that catered to sailors and European merchants, guzzling rivers of beer and a home-made brew, the *lambanog,* made of fermented sap of sugar cane or the coconut tree. Their drunken brawls spilled to the cobblestoned streets so as to drive Manila residents indoors after eight o'clock in the evening, the time when the church bells of Intramuros tolled vespers. A self-imposed curfew only marginally restored calm to the capital at night.

The new colonial overlord immediately grooved into the decadent lifestyle of the departed Spaniards. A siesta became the order of the day for the American top brass and horseback riding the recreation of choice during idle hours. Inside Intramuros, where the U.S. Army high command was billeted, Otis lounged blissfully in his palatial apartment at the San Agustin abbey, Montojo's erstwhile quarters. He managed military and civil affairs by delegation while poring over maps at his military headquarters. He made quite a record of never going to the countryside during his entire two-year tour as military governor. The task of policing his realm he left to his able deputy, General Arthur MacArthur, Provost Marshal of Manila and field commander of the Eighth Corps. With their overwhelming military superiority over the Filipino insurgents, the two generals did not anticipate any difficulty in pacifying the islands. After all, they had cut their teeth fighting the far more savage Indians in the West.

Meanwhile, Aguinaldo, determined to assert the sovereignty of his people over the land, set himself to the task of organizing a government that the outside world could respect. He instructed his ilustrado advisers to draft a Constitution that would lend his government democratic features. On January 21, 1899 he proclaimed the adoption of a new Constitution for the country, one which provided for separation of powers, an elected assembly and a cabinet of seven men. At the urging of the educated elite, he quickly appointed the members of his cabinet and caused a rump parliament to be elected among the provinces he controlled, a nationwide election covering the entire archipelago being well nigh impracticable to hold under wartime conditions. With the rudiments of government in place, he announced the formation of a new Philippine Republic and thereby staked a claim on a seat among the League of Nations. He inaugurated his republic inside the basilica of Barasoain in the province of Bulacan, where a crowd gathered to observe what was both a political and a religious experience. History records President Aguinaldo presiding over the ceremony in the third week of January 1899 inside the basilica, arrayed in the military uniform of a field marshal, with blue-striped pants, a gilded sword, and a braided cap – a faux pas that didn't quite suit the democratic image he wanted to project. For he made it appear that he preferred to rule by military force than civilian authority.

The durability of the republic depended less on the wiles of Aguinaldo than on the will of the Americans. To them it was a provocation of the highest order. They were expected to crush it to assert their authority over the entire archipelago sold to them by Spain. The days following the inauguration of a republic found the Americans in high dudgeon. The smug tolerance that they exhibited in the face of Luna's diggings turned into downright hostility. A test of strength appeared inevitable sooner rather than later. Little by little, they vacated their camps in Fort Santiago and Sangley Point to confront Luna's trench lines in Caloocan. Instead of digging trenches, which tactic they abhorred as self-defeating to their Cavalry, they built strongholds inside church compounds that dotted the countryside and seized natural positions along riverbanks. By the end of June they had run smack of the insurgent's forward defenses along the San Juan River, a tributary of the Pasig. There, they sat out the last days of the peace till one side fired the first shot.

On the south bank of the San Juan River, at least 5,000 infantrymen under Gen. Arthur MacArthur were encamped ready for combat at a moment's notice, equipped with Fletcher and Hotchkiss mounted artillery, air-cooled machineguns and Danish-made Krag-Jorgensen rifles, which were among the best weapons of any army in all the world. Their discipline was demonstrated by the ritual that they followed called the "kit inspection." The infantrymen dropped their backpacks to the ground for inspection and officers examined every component – knife, canteen, blanket roll – to see if it was in proper condition. They executed snappy maneuvers with their rifles all in perfect unison, undoubtedly to impress the observer with their discipline and training.

On the north bank of the river was the ragtag army of General Luna, composed of 10,000 men, equipped with obsolete Mauser and flint-lock rifles, galleon-era cannons and bladed bolos forged in the foundries of Bulacan. They were hunkered down inside the trenches with the added protection of breastworks made of earth and firewood. They had been whipped into an organized force by the Spartan discipline of the martinet Luna, but their discipline was of an evanescent nature, quickly evaporating as soon as Luna turned his back; whereupon, they would abandon their lines to visit their sweethearts in the barrio and return at daybreak to man the trenches.

The opposing lines watched each other across the river and waited for a casus belli to break the impasse. It didn't take long for the situation to come to a boil, sparking what became known as the Insurrection.

PART TWO

The Insurrection

Take up the White Man's burden
  Ye dare not stoop to less —
Nor call too loud on Freedom
  To cloak your weariness.

-   *Rudyard Kipling*

*"We have hoisted our Flag, and it is not fashioned
of the stuff which can be quickly hauled down."*

-   *Theodore Roosevelt*

14

FIELDS OF DOOM

Joaquin Calderon was celebrating his 41st birthday on the night of February 4, 1899 when the first shot of the "Insurrection" was fired. The celebrant didn't enjoy the feast at all. He worried about his daughter whom he had left behind in Manila, 25 miles south of his hometown of Malolos where he was hosting the party. He smarted from the snub of General Aguinaldo, now president of the newly minted Philippine Republic who had refused to drink with his guests and left early. What was there to celebrate now but the graying of his hair? Soused to the gills with tuba and stuffed to bursting with native delicacies, he tried to appear cheerful in the company of his guests, a mixed bag of ilustrados, army officers and relatives. But he was too well-bred to be a killjoy at his own birthday bash so he indulged his appetite and drank more wine than he would customarily imbibe. Whenever he heard the laughter of his women guests, he was reminded of his 17-year old daughter Estrella from whom he had been separated by the inexorable march of events. How was she doing in the occupied city, stranded alone with his not-so-dependable brother Caloy, he wondered? Did she remember to take precautions at night, locking up the clinic and snuffing out all the oil lamps?

His birthday was yet another opportunity to showcase his family's standing in Filipino high society. The Calderon ancestral home on the outskirts of Malolos had lately become the gathering place of high officials in Aguinaldo's cabinet. Many regarded Dr. Calderon as the most illustrious physician in the land, being President Aguinaldo's personal physician, his minister of health, and an intellectual in his own right. Among his peers in the cabinet, no one could recite the *Mi Último Adiós* as movingly as the widower doctor whose rendition of the poem seemed to capture the soul of its author, coming as it was from a colleague who had brought the poem literally to the light of day from the insides of a lamparilla.

Gathered around the main table were his educated friends along with a few military officials who stood out for their ill breeding. His guest list was not as exclusive as he would have preferred. As a cabinet official whose hometown was now the seat of government, he had to play politics and issue invitations to such people as the town officials and military officers. The proletarian guests who crowded the yard of his house did not even bother to wait for an invitation and had simply followed the aroma of spices wafting out to the streets of the community. Next to Aguinaldo, he sorely missed his long-time buddy, General Luna, who was then manning the trenches outside Manila. He missed Luna's sharp wit and vulgar jokes that shocked as much as they titillated him, particularly his stories about the sex lives of the friars and his misadventures in Barcelona. The conversation among his guests ranged from old wives' tales to the braggadocio of military officers that grated in his ears. What a disastrous night!

In one entertaining interlude of the evening, the band played an upbeat tune of the *curracha*, which drove a number of tipsy guests off their seats to the dance floor. It was a rhythmic folk dance somewhat like the flamenco of the Gypsies but with less hand motions on the part of the men who mostly held their hands akimbo as they strutted after their partners imitating the moves of an ardent rooster. The celebrant enjoyed watching his guests dancing, but when asked by one stately lady to dance, he politely declined, being one rare

Filipino gentleman who could not dance. Dancing was one of the social graces that neither his elders nor friends taught him as a young man, his excess of blubber making him clumsy and sluggish even then. Content to watch at the sidelines, he simply tapped his feet to the beat of the music and vicariously joined in the fun.

As he prepared to excuse himself and retire to his bedroom while his guests were thus occupied, a cabinet peer, Felipe Buencamino accosted him.

"*Compadre*, why don't you dance the *curracha*, too?"

"Me, ha, ha, I don't dance," chuckled Calderon.

"You mean you can't?"

"Had one drink too many."

"Calderon!" barked a general. "Why don't you dance, bounce up and jiggle your belly like this!"

The celebrant determined that his guests wouldn't relent unless he obliged. So he boldly sauntered to the stately lady whom he had refused earlier, bowed politely, and took her to dance. After negotiating the rudimentary steps without mishap, he steered her rather nimbly to pair with Buencamino, and made his escape.

In his bedroom, he retched into a chamber pot and flopped down to bed. An hour or so later, Calderon was awakened from his drunken slumber by the discordant noise of the band, the footfalls of hurriedly departing guests and the hoof beats of galloping horses which came blowing down the open window of his bedroom.

"*Guerra*! It's war! Pass the word. We're at war with the Americans!" shouted one messenger on horseback who had slowed down to a trot then galloped past his window.

The news was enough to rouse Calderon from what remained of his stupor. After combing his hair and straightening the evening dress which he slept in, he hurried out of his bedroom to the nearly deserted sala of his house. The members of his household and some guests, women mostly, were huddled near the windows looking out. Seeing that the men folk had gathered at the foot of the stairs, he went down to join them. His first sober thought was of his daughter, Estrella, who was stranded in his clinic outside the Walled City, then of his brother Carlos whose foundry business stood the risk of being commandeered by the Americans. Finally, he thought of his bosom friend General Luna, chief-of-staff of the revolutionary army, who stood in the way of the Americans leading his poorly armed army of peasant conscripts. They could be among the first casualties of war. He didn't worry about General Aguinaldo whose life was not in immediate danger at his headquarters in nearby Barasoain.

Calderon saw that two of the mounted soldiers, an officer and his aide, had pulled over to speak to one of his guests, a general.

"El Presidente, is he here? General Luna sent us to report to him," said the officer.

"He was here earlier, but not in this house," Calderon answered. "Tell us what's happened before you go," he urged the harried officer. "The President will have heard the news by now from your comrades."

"The Americans have broken through our lines across San Juan River. They also attacked us in Caloocan. Big battles are going on all over the front and we have suffered heavy casualties, but we're trying to hold our ground... Please, Senores, I must be on my way, El Presidente will be waiting to hear the news."

Having sent the officer on his way Calderon conferred with his remaining guests. The military and civilian officials among them were in a hurry to get back to their posts in light of the emergency at hand. It was almost daybreak and Calderon bid them Godspeed as they excused themselves.

Upstairs, the stately lady, Teodora Agoncillo, wife of a cabinet minister, was crying in her chair. "Jesus, Maria y Josef! What will happen to my husband now?" she lamented.

The band members stowed away their instruments. The departing guests said their goodbyes with a few asking their host what they should do.

"Let's pray for our soldiers, that they might survive the battle unharmed," Calderon addressed them solemnly, "and that they emerge triumphant over the enemy and bring us the freedom we have sought for so long." Then bowing his head, he led them in saying the Lord's Prayer: *"Padre nuestro, que estas en los cielos..."*

After the last of his guests had gone, he gave instructions to the housekeeper, a spinster aunt, that his horse be saddled and ready early on the morrow, determined to fetch his daughter in Manila which was now in hostile hands. In the meantime, he needed to retire to his bedroom to rest and perchance to steal a few hours' sleep. It was going to be a long day tomorrow.

Breakfast was ready when Calderon emerged dressed from his bedroom. He had quietly done his ablutions preparatory to taking his seat on the table and much earlier than he was wont. Eating sparingly over his aunt's protests, he announced that he was ready to go. He told her to stock up on root crops and bananas as there might be hard times ahead. And yes, he was going to bring Estrella to safety.

At 7:00 o'clock a.m., Calderon was under way astride his horse, a squat equine mongrel strong enough to support his weight but not much faster than a carabao. Compensating for his bulk, he traveled light, bringing only the barest necessities such as his surgical kit and a change of clothes in one bag. He had already decided on his itinerary before retiring in the wee hours of the morning. He planned to pay a courtesy call on Aguinaldo and get his marching orders before proceeding to the front where his filial as well as his official duties awaited him.

En route to Aguinaldo's headquarters, he took a short-cut through a trail which traversed part of the Calderon farm holdings. The small hacienda inherited from his maternal grandfather had more than doubled in size courtesy of Padre Sebastian who arranged for a large parcel of an adjacent friar estate to be let to his mother. Calderon surveyed with his eyes the vast farm planted to coconuts, sugarcane, and rice with proprietary interest. The revolution had evicted the Dominican friars from the estate whose ownership would now redound to the welfare of those who actually tilled the land. Calderon had looked forward to this day when he would enjoy the fruits of the land and become truly rich. But this day was bound to be fleeting. The Americans were threatening to dispossess him of his patrimony.

As he approached Aguinaldo's headquarters, he was startled by the sound of gunfire. He was relieved to discover that the shots were not fired in anger but in celebration of freedom. They came from the direction of revolutionary troops applauding El Presidente who was addressing the assembled soldiers in front of the Barasoain church where Aguinaldo had inaugurated his government two weeks before. The slight, brush-haired leader, in his field marshal uniform, was reading a proclamation from a platform in front of the church. Albeit diffident in manners and unimposing in physique, he was capable of inspiring his troops with homespun eloquence when he addressed them in his native Tagalog. The soldiers cheered him at salient points of his speech, the expression on their faces shining with admiration and loyalty to their leader. At the end of his speech, they collectively raised their arms in salute, rifle in one hand and bolo in the other, and let out a concerted cry of defiance which made Calderon's flesh creep as he watched from his horse. *"Mabuhay si Presidente Aguinaldo! Mabuhay ang Republica ng Filipinas!"*

Calderon felt a surge of sympathy for the unlettered foot soldiers who were to bear the brunt of the battle and on whose shoulders rested the hopes of an entire nation.

He stayed in Aguinaldo's headquarters long enough to attend an emergency cabinet meeting which barely made a quorum, with half of ministers failing to show to up. In the

242

privacy of his headquarters, the leader looked somber so unlike the peppery figure who had just delivered a rousing speech to the troops outside.

"All depends on Luna now," he sighed tiredly. "I hope he could hold his own against the *yanqui*."

"Antonio is a capable general," said Calderon.

"A fine soldier. But with their superiority in weapons, we don't stand a chance."

"Let's pray that our men prove equal to the challenge."

"I want him to withdraw and prepare new defense lines in the countryside closer to our supporters and jungle hideouts. If the *yanquis* chose to make pursuit, we can ambush them and interdict their supply lines," mulled the general aloud.

Calderon was scared by the note of pessimism in Aguinaldo's voice. "You want me to carry a message to him?"

"If you're up to it. I heard you got drunk last night."

The doctor laughed. "I drink usually in moderation, only last night it was my birthday ... I got drunk because my dear Jefe was not around."

Aguinaldo replied in kind, "I heard the *yanquis* timed their attack to coincide with your birthday to make sure nobody will be manning our lines."

"Oh-ho. Their gamble didn't pay off because nobody came," Calderon retorted.

"Paterno wasn't there?"

"Also Agoncillo, Pardo de Tavera, Antonio Luna," he ticked off the fellow ilustrados who snubbed his party.

"We can't expect General Luna to be around. He is manning the trenches in Caloocan, holding the line against the *yanqui*."

"That's where I'm headed, sir. To take a look at the situation, if anyone needs medical treatment."

"I hope he could hold on, but I doubt it. If I had my way, I'll be fighting a running battle across several fronts to take advantage of our numbers and familiarity with the territory. We should pick our fights, constantly harass them with hit and run tactics instead of battling them head-on. That is my strategy. Based on my humble experience fighting the Spaniards for the past two years."

"But Luna learned his military tactics from Europe – from the best Prussian strategists – he's doing it by the book."

The ilustrados had the habit of imposing their learning on the home-grown leaders of the revolution on the ground that they knew better, even on matters of military strategy. Calderon had as much faith in Luna as he had reservations in respect of Aguinaldo's unconventional methods.

"If it worked against the Spaniards, it's bound to work against the *yanqui*," hazarded Aguinaldo.

"We are up against a different kind of enemy equipped with the most modern armaments in the world. We need modern tactics," said Calderon.

Unable to fathom the military mind, Calderon had no idea that what Aguinaldo was espousing, guerilla warfare, was the future of war. Afraid that he might speak out of turn on a matter beyond his expertise, the doctor excused himself. He would be more useful at the front near Manila tending to the humanitarian needs of the casualties of battle. As he left Aguinaldo's headquarters, he worried that El Presidente's pessimistic, if not defeatist, frame of mind did not augur well for the prospects of the fledgling republic.

Calderon spurred his stolid horse to a trot along a dirt road marked with parallel ruts, the signature of carabao-drawn sleds which was a common means of conveyance used by peasants in the provinces. He dared not take the railroad that skirted the coast from Manila to Dagupan in the north. To do so was to risk capture by the Americans who had commandeered the steam-powered locomotives at the Manila end of the line. So he chose to travel the slow but dependable foot trail toward the capital.

By midmorning, he came across signs of war. First, he encountered civilian refugees evacuating on foot and onboard calesas and more carabao-drawn carts. He pumped them for

244

information of the battle they were fleeing from, but their conflicting stories served only to confuse him. Next, he met retreating troops composed of the walking wounded and the seriously injured carried aboard carts or borne by their comrades in hammocks slung across bamboo poles. The retreating soldiers knew more and their stories depressed him. Calderon dismounted to tend the wounds of the gravely wounded under a hastily built tent. The demand for his services detained the doctor in his makeshift field hospital for three days, during which he saved dozens of lives and let go of dozens more. Even for a doctor inured to suffering, it was a harrowing experience that made him doubt the adequacy of his training.

———————

    The San Juan River, a tributary of the Pasig, formed the boundary between the Filipino and American forces until February 4, 1899. It was spanned by a bridge of masonry supported by stone arches anchored on piers dug into the riverbed. For several days prior to the outbreak of the fighting, the two sides engaged in a war of words that wore down their patience in what was tantamount to a psychological war of attrition. Apart from the ritual taunting that enriched the vocabulary of the soldiers on both sides, they harassed each other's supporters passing through the bridge. Relatives of insurgents crossing the bridge on their way to Manila were forced to submit to groping body searches by Yankee sentries, including the women, a practice that outraged the straitlaced rebels watching from the opposite bank. In retaliation, the Filipino soldiers accosted the native runners of the Yankees who crossed to their territory to forage for provisions for the U.S. Army. They subjected the runners to equally humiliating searches or robbed them outright in full view of the Americans. On several occasions, both sides were at the brink of shooting each other but just managed to stand down at the last minute.

Maj. Gen. Elwell Otis could not launch an attack on his own initiative. He was under instructions to wait for the ratification of the Treaty of Paris before opening hostilities. The treaty would seal America's claim to sovereignty over the Philippines thereby bolstering its right to stamp out all attempts to undermine it, from within or without. Come January 1899, with the treaty in hand the way was clear for the military. General Otis was given full authority as theater commander to start hostilities whenever the situation demanded.

Tempers were running high at both banks of the San Juan River on the night of February 4, 1899. The troops on the southern bank, consisting of the First Nebraska Regiment under the command Lt. Col. John M. Stotsenberg, had been sufficiently provoked that their sentries were raring to shoot the first target to present itself. At that time, the field commander of the Filipino army, General Antonio Luna, was absent from the frontline having gone to Dagupan in Pangasinan province to visit his relatives (of which fact neither Aguinaldo nor Calderon was aware). Thus, discipline among the Filipino troops was expectedly lax. Earlier in the day, a native runner in the American's employ was robbed of a cartload of supplies at the Filipino side of the bridge and forced to swim back to the American lines across the river. Worse, the rebels laughed and yelled insults at the hapless swimmer who struggled to keep himself afloat in midstream where the current was strongest so that he had to be rescued by an American soldier. Most aggravating of all, they hurled invectives and pebbles at the rescuer for spoiling their fun.

The following night, a Saturday, a Filipino rebel impulsively ran across the San Juan Bridge in hot pursuit of a stray dog he was trying to skin for supper. An alert sentry saw the approaching intruder and followed his progress with the bead of his gun sight. Before the Filipino soldier could realize his mistake, Private Robert W. Grayson of the First Nebraska Regiment opened fire with his Krag rifle as duty required him. The dog survived but the rebel lay crumpled on the bridge, dead or dying.

Commanded by lesser officers, the Filipino troops manning their end of the bridge and the adjacent riverbanks returned fire with Mauser rifles and a Gatling gun. Across a broad front ten miles long running along the banks of the San Juan and Pasig Rivers, the Americans responded in kind and then some. Volunteer regiments of the Eighth Corps named after the States of the Union – e.g., Tenth Pennsylvania, First California, First Idaho, 20th Kansas – unleashed their Fletcher 3-inch artillery, Hotchkiss rapid-fire cannons, and an assortment of small-arms fire upon the Filipino troops positioned along the opposite bank of the river. Flames spurted from the bores of cannons, illuminating the river. At the receiving end, shells plowed through the breastworks of the trenches and exploded, sending boulders, timber, and dirt flying including the body parts of soldiers who hunkered in them. The Filipino troops who did not flee their posts cowered at the barrage relentlessly pounding on them.

In the northern town of Caloocan, the Tenth Pennsylvania joined the battle from an impregnable position inside a church compound surrounded by a six-foot tall stone wall. The holy edifice was a natural fort with its walls of sun-baked bricks made to last a hundred years. Its builders never in their wildest imagination intended it to double up as a fort but the Americans quickly recognized its military uses. From behind its stone walls, a dozen pieces of wheeled artillery blasted rebel positions with a steady rain of shellfire. Colonel Howard B. Douglas directed his gunners from atop the bell-tower which offered an unobstructed view of rebel positions.

Logistics forced the Yankees to abandon conventional tactics that had proved effective in their recent wars: they deployed no Cavalry for the simple reason that they could not ship sufficient number of horses across the ocean, as they would most likely die in transit; nor could they rely on the local breed used for pulling calesas which were squat and sluggish. Instead, they depended on their artillery to soften rebel positions before sending masses of soldiers on foot.

In the wee hours of February 5, 1899, the fighting abated to sporadic exchanges of small-arms fire as the opposing camps re-assessed their positions. But at daybreak the battle gathered in intensity as more American units swung into the offensive. The U.S. Army led by General Arthur MacArthur, provost marshal of Manila, advanced towards the concentration of Filipino forces in Caloocan where it relieved Colonel Stotsenberg's embattled Nebraskan volunteers from further pressure. From their camp in the vicinity of the Walled City, General MacArthur's 5,000 regular army troops had to cross the Pasig River and its tributaries on foot to reach the battlefront. The natural barrier offered by the river which the Filipino forces had exploited to their advantage hardly slowed the American advance. Where no bridges spanned the Pasig River or its tributaries, the Yankees simply fashioned pontoons made of bancas strung together to enable them to cross with their heavy equipment. MacArthur split his forces in a classic pincer movement with one smaller arm proceeding to seize the waterworks in Navotas a mile north of Manila, while the bulk of his forces deployed further to the northeast then wheeled around to outflank the entrenched Filipino defenders.

At the San Juan Bridge, the close combat between the protagonists lasted only as long as the darkness. Through the night, the Filipinos kept the Americans at bay firing their odd assortment of weapons with wild abandon, feeling secure in the dark and the protection afforded by their trenches. As soon as the sun shone on their dugouts and bare heads, the firefight became a one-sided affair as the Yankee artillery spotters zeroed in on the Filipino entrenchments wreaking havoc on the latter's defenses. The demoralized Filipinos fled their trenches which were a magnet for American artillery. After the artillery barrage had softened up the Filipino positions, Colonel Stotsenberg stormed across the bridge with his 2,000 Nebraskan volunteer foot soldiers, their State colors flying. With the well-armed Yankee horde hot on their heels, the Filipino troops ran for their lives to the safety of the nearby hills and in such disorder that they had to leave their dead and wounded at their wake.

General Luna arrived at the front to find the situation at the San Juan battlefield beyond redemption. He managed to rally the remnants of his forces withdrawing them farther north where he hoped to check the advance of General MacArthur's regulars. He did so by dint of his indomitable willpower. Hurrying back to the front from an ill-timed visit north, he encountered Filipino troops fleeing the battlefield and lost his temper. He ordered them to return to their positions beating a few with his riding crop and threatening to shoot the others. He marched back to the battlefield, leading platoon after platoon of re-animated troops. He himself seized a rifle and took a pot shot at the advancing Yankees, inviting everyone to find their own targets.

The sight of the mustachioed commander leading the countermarch inspired the shell-shocked troops to fight in spite of the odds as they had done against the hated Spaniards. Rather than be killed by their own leader, they fought back against the Americans who had by this time overrun the trenches. The counterattack, however, proved more costly than the retreat, handing the Filipino forces a fleeting but Pyrrhic advantage. Soon thereafter, the Filipino forces were driven back to where they came from. This time not even Luna could turn back the tide of the American advance, and he was finally constrained by sheer military necessity to direct an orderly retreat into the woods.

In the middle of the day, another catastrophe was visited upon the overwhelmed Filipinos who had fallen back to lick their wounds in the hinterlands. This time, their tormentors were the cruisers of the Asiatic Squadron whose main guns had the battlefront within range from their anchorage in Manila Bay. The huge shells from the eight-inch cannons wrought as much havoc as boulders thrown from a volcano. When the 500-pound missiles landed, the Filipinos gaped in awe to see them gouge craters deep enough to be their graves. They uprooted trees and massacred men and animals within a 30-foot radius. No wonder, Montojo's fleet went down so quickly!

Luna set up camp in the shelter of the woods 12 miles north of Manila, off the coastal barrio of Navotas. From scattered reports of officers and runners, who were able to monitor the movement of American troops, General Luna learned that another U.S. Army formation had taken the Navotas waterworks but remained dug-in there. Meanwhile, the U.S. Army forces they had been fighting the whole morning had checked their advance but did not pursue them into the jungle. This was just as well. Stunned by the ferocity and firepower of the U.S. Army, the Filipino soldiers realized that they had a formidable enemy at hand, far more powerful than the Spanish army against which they had skirmished indecisively for years.

The fighting ceased by noontime and silence descended over the ten-mile front. The terrain had changed in a few hours' of fighting: craters gaped where grass grew thick before; the breastworks were leveled and the trenches collapsed in several places; the jungle canopy showed gaps where the shelling had felled trees. The dead, mostly Filipinos, lay where they fell: in the trenches, across the fields, by the riverbanks, and in the water itself.

During the lull in the fighting, Luna ordered his men to scour the battlefields for weapons and equipment that could be salvaged for his arms-strapped army. It was then that his hold over his army began to slip. The Caviteños under his command – natives of Aguinaldo's home town of Kawit – balked at leaving the safety of the woods to return to the battlefield to scavenge for stray firearms and junk where they would be exposed to enemy fire. They dug in their heels even as Luna let go of his notorious temper and threatened to shoot them for cowardice.

"I don't give a damn if you come from the hometown of El Presidente. You are all under my command, and for as long as I am in command of this army, you will obey my orders!" he railed.

The Caviteños stood pat, huddled together in the woods.

"Attention! All officers, step forward. I'm giving you one minute to assemble your men in formation in front of my tent – one minute! Or else, all of you will be disarmed and, by God, under my authority as theater commander, shot."

The Aguinaldo boys started to waver, some preparing to cut and run into the surrounding jungle.

"There will be hell to pay."

Luna stepped into his tent and huddled with his Tagalog generals to assess the crisis. "A machinegun will do the job," he muttered at one point.

One Caviteño officer, himself unable to assert his authority over his men, followed Luna into the tent to explain that his men had been badly mauled across the Pasig River, that their morale was at its nadir, that they were emotional wrecks after coming under the kind of bombardment they had never experienced before, and that, for the sake of preserving Luna's authority and prestige as field commander of the republican army, he should not humiliate himself by breaking his pick on the back of the recalcitrant troops.

"Leave the matter to El Presidente, please, let's not risk a breakdown of authority here," said the Caviteño officer, Major Diego Dimayuga. "It will be the end of everything. Let us just say that the Caviteños are ... sick and exhausted ... in order to save face."

"As much as I disapprove of the men's behavior," General Artemio Ricarte seconded, "I agree with Major Dimayuga. Let us not risk a shootout here among brothers in arms. We will deal with them later when the situation calms down. If we force them now and they resist, it will be the end of our struggle."

Luna listened to his officers' entreaties with barely suppressed rage, his jaw muscles tightening as he audibly gritted his teeth. But in the end, swayed by his officers, some of them town mates of the insubordinate troops, he swallowed his pride. He was not prepared to split the republican cause in its first test against the Americans.

"This is not the end of it, there will be settling of accounts later in Malolos. All those who disobeyed will be punished," Luna vowed. Leaving his tent, he cracked his horse whip and addressed the mutinous Caviteño soldiers assembled outside his tent: "Since you are all exhausted and weak, I order you to retire to Malolos immediately and there report to General Aguinaldo, all of you! None of you will remain here! You will all stay in Malolos until further orders. Get moving!"

The Caviteño troops led by Major Dimayuga filed out into the woods in disorder, watched by Luna in utter contempt. Their wretched condition became obvious when some of them had to pick up their wounded and drag themselves along the road in a slow hike towards Aguinaldo's headquarters in Malolos, more than ten miles away. They were obviously shell-shocked, a phenomenon that not even Calderon could recognize. They were not so much rebelling against Luna as shrinking away from the bombardment. They were not fleeing the front as much as they were returning to their mothers and fathers, wives and children.

The toll in human lives and limbs sustained by both sides during the opening battle of the Philippine Insurrection was heavy, compared to the casualty rate of the Spanish-American War. According to contemporary American historian James Le Roy, writing in 1914, the U.S. Army suffered an estimated 50 dead and 185 wounded, while the Filipinos suffered over 1,000 dead and 3,000 wounded. Despite the lopsided outcome, the fighting was the heaviest that the Americans had encountered in the Philippines or in the Caribbean, for that matter. During the Battle of Manila Bay, not one American was killed and only a handful was injured, mostly from heat exhaustion. In the mock battle for Intramuros, the Americans sustained about five dead due to the vainglorious folly of General Merritt who, in an effort to upstage Dewey, let an ersatz battle turn into a shooting spree. Against an ill-equipped and poorly-trained rebel army, the Americans suffered 50 killed and scores wounded, despite being better led and enjoying overwhelming superiority in firepower, including heavy artillery and naval guns that rained shells upon the hapless Filipino defenders.

More was to come.

———————

It took Joaquin Calderon three full days to reach the outskirts of Manila because he kept meeting wounded soldiers and deserters along the way. From each he wrung out tidbits of information about the ongoing battle, invariably bad news. Meeting a straggler who looked as if he had just emerged from a tiger's cage, he brought him under a tree to dress his wounds and apply splint to his broken arm, and thus incurred more delay. More such survivors of war stumbled into view. In their stricken voices, he heard the plaintive cry of Estrella. In the look of death that hooded their faces, he saw the mortal peril facing his family and his country. The bells tolled tragically for the Filipino cause, the echoes of which rode the winds of war to visit the poignant news upon many a household of the death of sons and brothers who had volunteered to fight for the revolution.

Calderon waited until the bombardment subsided before daring to go any farther. Walking out of the woods, he beheld a countryside strewn with the wreckage of war: mangled corpses, burning huts, a disemboweled horse, broken gun carriages, detached wheels, abandoned weapons... Then, from the screen of black smoke that shrouded the battlefield, emerged a parade of ghosts, the wraith-like figures of Filipino troops staggering out of the scene of battle, shaken and witless. A few simply dropped to the side of the road to faint or expire, completely sapped of spirit, if not life. He arrived too late to observe the actual fighting, but he felt the heavy air of defeat weighing down the spirits of every surviving compatriot he encountered. He could not make out the enemy in the distance clouded by smoke that crept close to the ground. But he knew they were still there from the gunfire and occasional shell exploding on the nearby fields kicking up grass and dirt. He gave up all thoughts of proceeding to Manila that day. Instead he re-entered the nearby woods where the survivors and the walking wounded had sought refuge with the hope of finding some semblance of organization among the remnants of the defeated Filipino army.

Spotting a cluster of tents in a clearing deep in the jungle, he dismounted, tied his horse to a tree, and went in search of an officer. He found his way obstructed by a trench that he mistook for a canal of Manila's shattered waterworks. The sight of bodies sprawled inside the canal made him realize that it was some form of military defense work dug into the ground that the Americans had turned into their grave.

Now, he had a problem. Being heavy and sluggish, he couldn't cross the trench unaided.

"Hey, excuse me, I'm Dr. Calderon," he said in Tagalog to the men shoveling earth to the trench from the opposite side. "Will you put a plank across this pit please?"

"Jump, mister," the men said in blunt Tagalog.

"It's simply too wide for me, you see. That piece of wood will do."

The men continued shoveling.

"Listen, my services are needed here. I'm the minister of health and I've been sent by El Jefe to attend to the soldiers here."

Grumbling, a peasant soldier laid a piece of timber across the trench. "There."

"That wouldn't do," said the doctor.

254

"What exactly do you want? A bridge?"

"Something that won't slip or break."

The soldiers spanned the trench with planks of wood salvaged from a broken carriage which they then leveled and firmed up by stamping on them. "Thank you very much," said Calderon, showing good breeding. "I will be back later to set up my field hospital."

When he reached the clump of tents, he asked a group of troopers to take him to the most senior officer in the camp. He didn't want to have to take a look into each and every tent in the sprawling bivouac. Again he found everyone too busy to entertain him in the manner befitting his high station as a cabinet minister. Then, he espied a familiar figure emerging from a tent flying the republic's tricolor. The doctor's face broke into a wide grin for the first time in three days that his mouth hurt. It was his bosom friend General Antonio Luna, all right, who looked none the worse for his recent drubbing. Calderon was proud of the only ilustrado general in the insurgent army who was sure of his place in Aguinaldo's government and equally fearless of the Americans.

"Ah, Joaquin, it's you!" Luna greeted him first because the doctor didn't know how to address him in his new position as chief-of-staff of the republican army.

"General, why do you camp out in the mud?"

"Oh, I'm so glad to see you, compadre. How are you? Aren't you afraid to come?" Luna was effusive as ever.

"I came here to help out."

"To dirty your hands. I'm sorry, things are not so tidy in our camp."

"Not that I mind the dirt, general. Things are dirtier in the hospital where I work."

"Come on, Joaquin, call me Antonio."

Calderon promptly checked the general's health but found him robust and rock solid. He then ventured into matters extraneous. "Tell me, Antonio, is it dangerous to go Manila? How do I get there?"

"What?" Luna feigned shock. "You want to attack Manila? Compadre, you're braver than I am!"

"My daughter is there."

"My godchild, Estrella?"

"Yes, Antonio, and I'm terribly worried. She's alone, she's got no money and I don't know what will happen to her in the hands of the Americans."

Luna turned serious. He scratched his moustache pensively. "Let me see ... no, no. It's dangerous, my friend. You'll be arrested, if not shot."

"They won't harm me. I've been helpful to them."

"Joaquin, you're a minister now. All officials of the republic are wanted men. To the *yanquis*, we're no better than bandits."

"How about Estrella?"

"Let me worry about her, I'm her godfather and I'll ask some people over there to look her up. Don't make things worse by going there alone and getting captured. Stay with me and we'll solve your problem together."

Reassured, Calderon turned his mind to the immediate consequences of defeat. "What's going to happen now, Antonio? Is there hope for a settlement?"

Luna turned gloomy. "The *yanquis* are far more formidable than the Spaniards. They're good soldiers, well-armed, and well-led. They mauled us pretty bad. But we have no choice but to fight. What's there to settle if what they want is to colonize us again under the Treaty of Paris?"

"How many men have we lost?"

"I don't know. I can't keep count, many were killed in the trenches, some deserted, others – Aguinaldo's boys – they won't follow my orders. I should line them up against the wall for treason."

"The Kawit soldiers recognize only Aguinaldo as their leader," affirmed Calderon.

"It was the most humiliating thing, I tell you, not being obeyed by your soldiers in the middle of a battle. Under ordi-

256

nary rules, they should have been shot. Only I didn't want a mutiny to add to our troubles."

"Maybe you should take that up with El Jefe. Let him deal with those Kawit boys."

"With better discipline, we could have inflicted more casualties and minimized our own."

"The best way to avoid casualties, I believe, is to reach a settlement with the Americans, negotiate a truce," repeated the doctor.

"That I don't know, Joaquin!" Luna threw up his hands in exasperation, pacing around his tent restlessly. "I'm not a diplomat as you very well know. Fighting is the only thing I'm good at."

"Okay, going back to my daughter..." Calderon changed the subject. "Help me get her out. We have to get her out of there, whatever it takes."

"Stick around for a while, I need your help. Your daughter may be safer in Manila for now. Take care of my wounded men and I'll find a way to get you to Manila at a time of our choosing. Excuse me, compadre. I'm in the middle of a meeting..."

Luna went back inside his tent to resume a strategy session with two of his more tractable generals, namely, General Pio del Pilar and General Artemio Ricarte. The two outstanding officers had bravely fought the Americans, extricating their troops in an orderly withdrawal to the hinterlands of Navotas. They discussed and argued animatedly into the night.

Calderon silently rooted for them. He had a lot more at stake in this war than ordinary Filipinos. Having put himself through school at a great sacrifice for himself and his family, he had nothing to gain from a prolonged war. His clientele in Manila consisting of rich businessmen and mestizo heirs had all but disappeared. The lost income could not be recovered by placing himself in the service in Aguinaldo's army, which was more of a patriotic duty than a lucrative pursuit. He earned nothing therefrom except an increased share of the friar farm that his family had taken over in Malolos, with the help of the insurgents who were now applying most of its produce to the revolutionary cause. One side had to win somehow, and soon. From the lopsided result of the initial hostilities, it looked like the Americans would make short work of the republicans, unworthy the thought might be. That got him thinking: Would the Americans allow him the same privileges that ilustrados had enjoyed under Spanish rule – such as land ownership and freedom to travel abroad? Would they let him practice medicine freely? Or would they instead drive him into exile as the Spaniards had done with some rebels whom they banished to its remotest territories to die of homesickness? Such questions constantly preyed on his thoughts even as he worried over the fate of his daughter.

For all his faith in the martial ability of General Luna and the righteousness of the Filipino cause, he was convinced that they were fighting windmills. Given the halo of invincibility that even General Luna ascribed to the U.S. Army, pushing on with their insurrection would only subject his people to unremitting misery. The ragtag Filipino army was hopelessly overmatched by the American military machine just like the Indian tribes that Uncle Sam had massacred to the brink of extinction, with intermarriage completing the process. For a mestizo such as Calderon, it was preferable to submit to American domination rather than risk the prospect of being decimated as a race.

Calderon stayed two weeks in Luna's jungle bivouac to tend to the sick, the wounded, and the shell-shocked. He did this in discharge of his duties as minister of health of the embattled republic, in fealty to his oath as a doctor at a time when so many of his countrymen were in dire need of medical attention, and out of friendship for General Luna. He set up a field hospital inside two tents given to him by General Luna who could afford him nothing else by way of amenities. For all his fussiness and cranky nature, he never uttered a word of complaint.

He scoured the battle zone for supplies and materials and conscripted tractable soldiers to serve as his assistants. As the first order of business, he inventoried and sanitized his surgical kit. The tools of his trade – knives, scissors, scalpels, forceps and the dreaded saw – were his most prized possessions, which made the whole of his person as a professional. Next he and his assistants jerry-built a surgical room in one of the tents with an operating table fashioned out of the flatbed of a broken carriage. Last but not least, he sent his assistants to forage for herbs and other medicinal plants in the surrounding jungle, supplemented later with Chinese pharmacopoeia smuggled in from the Parian district outside Intramuros. Forthwith, he then proceeded to inflict his expertise on the casualties of war.

His tent saw carnage almost as gory as that seen in the battlefield. Many a patient emerged from his field hospital with missing or attenuated organs. Gangrenous limbs he simply amputated with his redoubtable saw for want of antibiotics. Gaping wounds he promptly sewed up using *lambanog* (a native whiskey favored by the troops) both as disinfectant when applied locally to the wound and as anesthetic when taken orally. Festering sores were wrapped with the pulp of leaves known to have disinfectant properties. He made splints of bamboo for the more fortunate ones who suffered simple fractures. For those suffering from malaria, dysentery and other unsightly maladies, he let them drink a potion made from a mixed brew of ginseng root and other spices boiled in a clay pot. And to those suffering from mortal injuries and had to be triaged, he prescribed prayers. The inevitable ululation that emanated from his tent rode the wind far afield demoralizing the able-bodied troops within hearing distance.

There was one interruption in his duties that broke his stoic reserve. Somebody stole his saw.

When he reconnoitered the field for the trusty instrument, he found it in the hand of a soldier cutting firewood.

"Hey, what are you doing with my saw?" he shouted.

The soldier cast him an impatient look that said: Why, of course, cutting wood, what else can a saw do?

Reading the look that conveyed the abysmal ignorance of the foot soldier, Calderon huffed: "That's my surgical saw! That's for cutting flesh and bone, human legs, amputation. Do you understand?"

Calderon reported such aggravations to General Luna to impel him to punish the soldier severely. Instead, the martinet Luna laughed uproariously. "Ah, that's the kind of soldiers I have, so ignorant but very, very resourceful!"

Luna then sought to mollify the doctor by informing him that they would be leaving for Manila on the morrow to fetch his daughter. Calderon balked. Such was his preoccupation with his duties that he was unprepared to leave dozens of patients in his tents needing critical medical attention – even if that meant prolonging the threat to his stranded daughter.

"We can't, we must leave tonight," said Luna. "You have a couple of hours to dispense with your urgent cases. Let your assistants attend to the others. You don't have to pack anything."

"What about my instruments?"

"Leave them behind. You can retrieve them later."

"What!? Do you realize what I will be missing? Don't you know I started collecting some of them while we were in Barcelona? I had to scrimp on meals just so I could afford to buy them – *you* know that very well."

"Don't worry, compadre," Luna said soothingly to his agitated friend. "If necessary, we'll raid an American hospital just so we can replace your instruments with more modern ones," added the general only half in jest to stop his friend protesting.

Calderon excused himself to return to his work. Having attended to the last of his serious cases, he admonished his assistant not to lose sight of his instruments, especially the bladed ones that could double up as tools in carpentry.

As soon as darkness fell, Luna, Calderon and their party of one hundred made their way toward Manila. It was a military operation intended to impress upon the Americans that the insurgents were far from defeated. The plan was to sneak into the occupied capital under the noses of the Americans and set fire to establishments right in their backyard. In the tactical opinion of General Luna, the Americans were now stretched so thin and were bound to be complacent after their initial victories that they would leave their rear unguarded. The conflagration was their way to show the people of Manila that "we are still in business." Calderon marveled at the boldness and simplicity of Luna's plan. Whether Calderon realized that the conventional Luna was beginning to hew towards Aguinaldo's hit and run tactics, he didn't say.

15

FIRE IN THE NIGHT

Two weeks on after their occupation forces trounced the Filipino insurgents, the Americans rested on their laurels believing that they had dealt the insurgent army a decisive blow, one telling enough to make them knuckle under and cozy up to their new masters. After all, it was the way the Spaniards colonized the islands, by making an example of a few tribes and overawing the rest. Without enough troops to carry out a full-scale offensive, the Americans desisted from hot pursuit choosing to fall back to the near bank of the Pasig River which was easier to secure. Meanwhile political commissars scouted around Manila for native collaborators or turncoats willing to occupy symbolic positions in a new colonial government. To impress the Filipinos that they were magnanimous in victory, the Americans made no arrest of suspected insurgents or their supporters and instead looked after the nitty-gritty of running the business of government: getting the railways, post office, telegraph lines up and running again, and preparing the ground for institutions that had to be built up from scratch such as, for example, a public education system. The best way to conquer the people, argued Provost Marshal MacArthur, was to show them they could run the place much better than the Spaniards. Or so it was thought.

Also in February 1899, McKinley dispatched to the Philippines the Schurman Commission headed by Jacob G. Schurman, president of Cornell University, to study the peculiar conditions of the former Spanish colony and recommend a form of civil government best suited to the needs of the Filipinos. Being a latecomer to great game of imperialism, Uncle Sam had several working models of colonialism to emulate, notably the British Raj in India. But being famously of a nation that was a former British colony, the political leaders of the United States wanted to inaugurate in the islands a type of nation-building that was more in accord with the ideals of its Founding Fathers. McKinley therefore issued instructions to the Schurman Commission to "ascertain without interfering with the military authorities what amelioration of the condition of the inhabitants could be accomplished and what improvement in public order was practicable" in order to win the allegiance of the populace. Almost everybody at the time missed the qualification "without interference with the military authorities." It was a conciliatory plan that on its face ought to sell well to the natives.

The Americans did not reckon with Luna. Adamantly against surrender, he wanted to settle the issue in mortal combat. He was one ilustrado who was utterly devoid of colonial mentality, who did not believe that the intentions of colonial powers were inherently good, and who was fired with the nationalism that was then sweeping South America. He wanted outright independence and to achieve this, he vowed to shatter the Yankee's mantle of invincibility with one blow.

His torches, thrown in the right places, would do the job.

General Luna's raiding party of a hundred men infiltrated Manila under cover of darkness on the night of February 22, 1899. He had divided his raiders into four groups consisting of 25 men each and sent them on separate roundabout routes into the city to mask their total strength as well as their ultimate objective. Luna's aim was to strike a blow at the Americans' rear, right in the tranquility of their camps. It took Luna and his men three hours to reach the occupied city from their jungle hideout, just in time to catch the Yankees sleeping.

Dr. Calderon tagged along with the raiding party as Luna had promised, on a personal mission to extricate his daughter from the occupied city. He was unaware that Luna's raiding party had ample support from within Manila itself: insurgent troops caught behind enemy lines by the outbreak of hostilities, as well as resident Katipunan veterans who were spying on the Americans while performing their normal routines.

Joaquin was not surprised by Luna's boldness. It was entirely in character, given his friend's combative temper which Joaquin had observed first-hand during their student days in Spain where Luna gained notoriety for his propensity for getting into trouble with friends and foes alike. In Barcelona in the 1880's, for instance, he was provoked into anger by a Spanish editor who had written satirical comments about his country being a land of savages. Taking up the cudgels for his countrymen, Luna stormed the editor's office and challenged him to a duel, which was fortunately turned down by the latter. In Paris, a watering hole for Filipino exiles, he was arrested for mauling a Frenchman in an altercation over Spanish politics and was jailed accordingly. His French attorney, who had a natural empathy for revolutionaries, appealed to the judge for clemency on the ground that Luna was a "barbarian who didn't know how to win an argument with witticisms." The unusual plea won Luna his freedom. Now, as field commander of the insurgent army, he put his pugnacity to good use against the Americans.

Calderon joined the group of raiders led by General Luna himself upon the latter's invitation. The general was grateful for the example set by Calderon to all ilustrados, going out of his way to visit the ordinary troops in the battlefront at great danger to himself, something their colleagues in the cabinet never did, preferring to fight their battles on the political front where they vied for the ear of Aguinaldo who seldom, if ever listened. Wanting to return the favor, Luna decided that he himself would accompany his noncombatant friend to rescue daughter Estrella while directing his band of one hundred in their surprise attack their behind enemy lines. He got more than he bargained for.

General Luna's group took a roundabout route to Manila involving prolonged hikes, river crossings, boat rides, and detours along difficult terrain. Their sortie was made more difficult by Calderon's constant whining and kibitzing. If he were not complaining, he was slowing them down as he had difficulty keeping up with the group.

The first leg of the journey involved hiking over hilly terrain from their encampment to the Marikina River, a tributary of the Pasig where five dugout canoes awaited them at the far bank. Luna wished they, or at least Calderon, had made the trip on horseback for it took them longer than usual with the portly doctor bouncing along. They paddled downstream towards the Pasig helped along by the current, thereby making good time. Their passage through the upper reaches of the Pasig was similarly smooth and without incident. It got increasingly trickier the closer downstream they got to Manila as the raiding party had to pass through several bridges. They had to stagger their passage under the bridges, one boat at a time, so as not to attract the attention of the American sentries. Keeping close to the far bank, they passed by Malacañang, formerly the Spanish governor-general's summer residence, which was brightly lit and crawling with Yankees, being now the luxurious nest of General Arthur MacArthur. They were now only several hundred yards away from their destination, Escolta near the Parian district in Binondo, where the doctor's clinic was located.

The doctor parted the wall of grass and faced the breadth of the Pasig River at 7:30 o'clock in the night. It was a major artery for steamboats and trawlers that carried goods from Manila inland. With all bridges in the hands of the Americans, they were warned by Luna to be prepared to cross the river by boat or to wade across in complete dark. The glow of a crescent moon and the shower of starlight flickered against the surface of the river to bare the silhouettes of passing boats ruffling the face of the waters. The current carried away mats of water lily, ripped out from either side of the river where they grew in abundance. Their faces screened by blades of grass, they raised their torches so that their waiting comrades might be able to detect their arrival.

The rendezvous was the stump of a broken pillar where a bridge once stood sticking out to the sky straight as an obelisk. They waited for an outrigger boat to come paddling along the bank in keeping with a pre-arranged plan; but as the hours passed nothing came out of the dark.

Calderon scanned the bank with his monocle. "What are we going to do now? What if they don't come?" he asked, pessimistic as usual.

"Damn," muttered Luna.

"And if they don't come we can just proceed to the bridge over there and cross one by one like ordinary travelers."

"They will come."

Exhausted by the ten-mile trek over winding trail, Calderon started complaining about the mosquitoes. He slapped and scratched himself repeatedly. "Pretty soon, I'll have allergy."

"It should not be a problem for you finding a cure for it," said Luna bitingly, equally impatient.

"Maria y *Josef,* I thought everything has been arranged. What's taking them so long?"

Calderon expressed his impatience by fussing while Luna steamed in silence.

"I hear something..." said the doctor.

The water splashed and rustled by the river bank. The snout of a boat slid over the grass, followed by a figure holding a lantern.

"Okay, let's go," Luna sprang into action and rattled off directions. "As soon as we cross the river, I'll drop you by your daughter's house since you can't be with us. Just make arrangements to meet with us here at 7:00 o'clock tomorrow morning. The rest will follow me. Everybody aboard."

Calderon wended his way down the bank of the river grabbing at the roots of bushes to steady himself, then tugging at the coat of Luna who trudged down the slope with sure steps, nimble as a mountain goat. The finicky doctor kept complaining about everything along the way, most especially the dirt. In this clandestine mission, he gave Luna as much problem as a battalion of sneezing spies, and Luna was only too eager to drop him off at the opposite bank of the river where the need for silence and secrecy was most acute.

The portly doctor was relieved to find four outrigger boats lining the bank of the river, afloat over a bed of ripped water lilies. He heaved himself upon the outrigger of one boat then plopped inside, throwing the pilot into the water with a splash and almost capsizing the vessel. "Whew," he sighed triumphantly as the vessel righted itself.

Luna fished the pilot from the muddy water, draped with strands of water lilies. "Have patience with the man...*esta cacique.*"

During the boat ride Calderon pumped General Luna for more information regarding the raid to no avail. Luna told him bluntly it was none of his business and that he had no need to know the details.

"Compadre," General Luna had admonished his friend, "the less you know the better for you and for *us*, in case you're captured by the Gringos. Just be there tomorrow morning at six o'clock"– referring to the estero where they had docked – "if you and Estrella want to join us in our getaway. That's all you need to know." Then he added: "Bring a basket and do your marketing for cover. God knows we can use some supplies where we're going." For the morrow was a Sunday, market day; the esteros will be crowded, the perfect place for a getaway. Even the noncombatant Dr. Calderon could appreciate Luna's tactical sense.

The party paddled ominously across the river in four boats. The distance was about 200 yards in a diagonal line toward the opposite bank which they could reach only by riding the strong tidal currents. The oarsmen plowed the water furiously with their paddles to take advantage of a shroud of clouds wafting across the face of the crescent moon and the stars. With the water swishing under the rhythmic chopping of the paddles, the doctor refrained from touching the water because he knew very well its unsanitary condition – murky, foul – defiled by a combination of mud, sewage, garbage and decayed plants. He noticed other perils more serious than disease. As they rode down the current they drifted closer to the heavily guarded wall of Fort Santiago looming at the mouth of Manila Bay, and they inexorably gravitated toward the stately bridge leading to the Parian Gate, a skeletal structure of wood and iron aglow in the illumination of torches.

Calderon saw the lead boat veering towards the near bank, traversing the expanse of the Pasig River diagonally. Downstream near the mouth of the river, he could just make out the silhouette of the walls of Intramuros against the moonlit sky. They had to paddle furiously to stay on course and avoid collision with other river traffic as the tide was changing, creating cross-currents and eddies in the middle of the river. They reached the riverbank without mishap and docked at an estero, a drainage canal where small boats moored to offload passengers and cargo. The church bells tolled the vespers as they were about to disembark, 8:00 o'clock.

Before they could enter the field of light under the bridge and thus be seen by the guards, the lead boat came within reach of the opposite bank, only to get entangled in a thick carpet of water lily. The oarsmen's paddles simply got entwined with the tenacious creepers which obstructed river traffic as surely as a coral reef, and they had to grab at lengths of vine to enable the boat to worm through the thicket of floating reeds. It was muddy out there, with nary a firm foothold on the bank, Calderon observed the distance. His boat came to a stop three yards from the bank. "And so?" he said, suspended in anticipation.

"Okay, everybody jump," Luna answered.

"Are you crazy?"

"It couldn't be more than waist-deep, come on, follow me."

Luna led the way. He jumped into the waist-deep water and waded toward the bank, ripping off strands of reeds.

Calderon had an unexpectedly easier time because he floated. In his hurry, driven by his distaste of the water, he dropped something. "Oh, my monocle!"

"Move your ass, buddy."

"Wait, help me find my monocle." The doctor sank down to probe the depth with his hands, groping through the filthy water. *"Por dios, por santo!* Somebody find my monocle!"

For all his distaste of the foul water, he scoured the depth with both hands, feeling the roots of the plants for anything glassy.

"Come on, Joaquin, we'll find some replacement for it."

"It's gone, I won't be able to perform surgery anymore. And I paid a hundred pesetas for it in Spain!"

"No use crying over it."

"Just a little more time..." Joaquin continued probing.

"Goddamit, Joaquin! We're in the middle of an operation, we can't be bothered by the loss of such useless instrument. If you insist in looking for that goddamned glass of yours, we'll leave you behind."

The doctor stamped on the bank, overwhelmed by the loss of so precious an instrument, even more valuable than his stainless scalpel. It was almost like losing his winged moustache.

It took more effort for him to keep up with his comrades as they crept under houses on stilts and climbed over fences – these people seemed to enjoy picking the worst possible route to the city – until finally they found themselves in the clean pavements of Paco. Here, they decided to break into groups to avoid catching attention, with Calderon hiking off on his own. He was the odd man out, the one whose size and constant whining were bound to expose them to danger, nevermind his usefulness as a doctor. And besides he had his own personal mission of finding his daughter and bringing her to the safety of the countryside.

"Take care, 'padre, and see you at the river," said Luna.

Calderon could hardly say a word in his exhaustion.

"I'll find a new eyepiece for you. The first American I'll shoot is one with a poor eyesight."

Calderon walked away. He loved being humored by Luna especially in times of trouble. They parted ways in the street of Escolta.

"*Vaya con dios,* Antonio."

"You be careful and take good care of my goddaughter," replied Luna as he and his men slipped into the night.

Calderon's clinic was only a few blocks away from the estero. But with an abundance of caution he avoided the main street by making a detour through the district's narrow side streets and alleys, which roundabout route took him much longer to reach home. As he turned a corner to the street where his clinic was, he was surprised to hear church bells ringing in the distance. It can't be vespers for it was almost nine o'clock already. Then he realized that the insurgents were using the church bells to signal the launch of an attack, just as they used to do during past rebellions. Calderon made a sign of the cross and said a silent prayer for General Luna and his men, quickening his pace as he neared the safety of his home.

Soon, more bells from near and far joined in, this time to raise a fire alarm which brought the curious and the alarmed out of their houses and into the streets. This was no

270

ordinary fire as it seemed to be occurring simultaneously all over Manila and the clamor of the bells was now punctuated by sporadic gunfire. Later, Calderon heard hoof beats and the clatter of carriage wheels before sighting a fire wagon from the local fire station speeding in the direction of the nearby port area. He craned his neck and saw a faint glow lightening the night sky above the vicinity of the port of Manila where the warehouses were stocked with supplies for the U.S. Army. That must have been the target of General Luna and his group who had been his companions until barely an hour ago.

The raid caught the Americans totally by surprise. Apart from the port area warehouses that were vulnerable for their lack of security, the raiders set fire to the barracks housing the volunteer regiments of the U.S. expeditionary forces in Santa Ana and Santa Mesa, both located some distance from Intramuros. In addition, the insurgents burned down some commercial establishments patronized by the Yankees together with a few colonial government buildings outside Malacañang. The destruction was far more extensive than planned because the conflagration took on a life of its own as it spread to nearby buildings and houses. Except for a few raiders who went missing, the insurgents suffered no other casualties. The Americans reported several dead and many injured among their ranks, the former mainly sentries hacked to death by the raiders and a few sleeping soldiers caught inside the burning barracks.

The success of the deadly raid stunned Dr. Calderon as it exceeded his worst expectations. Privately, he would rather have nothing to do with such violence that compromised his principles as a doctor. He even worried that the Yankee Barton Bailey might be among the victims, the likeable fellow that he was. But the patriot in him silently rooted for Luna and his men who just two weeks ago had suffered grievously at the hands of the rampaging Yankee.

16

ESCAPE TO MALOLOS

Carlos Calderon had scheduled delivery of the first installment of General MacArthur's order for 1,000 bolos on the evening of February 22nd, which unfortunately for him was the same night General Luna's raiders attacked Manila. He was instructed to deliver the bolos to the logistics command of the Eighth Army Corps located inside Fort Santiago where he would be paid in cash. As pre-arranged Carlos was to enter the Walled City at the Postigo and was therefore surprised to see the drawbridge raised and the doors barred. While en route to Intramuros on a bullock-drawn cart laden with his precious cargo, Anselmo, his assistant wondered aloud why the church bells tolled the angelus twice that night at widely different intervals. Carlos heedlessly dismissed the oddity as a sign of the unsettled times but began to worry when they heard gunfire and the pealing of more church bells in the distance. Was Manila under attack? Now, seeing the drawn bridge and barred gates of the Postigo, he cursed his compatriots for their poor timing which threatened to jeopardize his lucrative business deal with the *yanqui*.

Carlos jumped from the cart before it came to a full stop at the edge of the moat, hollering at the American sentries on the ramparts above the gate who had their rifles trained at him.

"Don't shoot! My name is Calderon. I am expected by General MacArthur. I'm delivering supplies to the U.S. Army!" he shouted in broken English mixed with Tagalog, waving his gate pass at the Yankees.

After a few interminable moments, the gate opened and the drawbridge was lowered to the rattling of chains and creaks of rusty hinges. Before Carlos could board his cart thinking they were being allowed through, a Yankee officer accompanied by four riflemen marched across the span toward them, signaling them to stay put with his open palm.

"Are you Carlos Calderon?" The American officer tried to ascertain.

"I am, indeed," Carlos replied handing his gate pass to the officer who scrutinized it.

"Intramuros is now off limits. You cannot enter. You have to unload your cargo here," was the peremptory reply.

"What! What about my money?" Carlos asked, close to panic. "I was promised payment upon delivery."

"Come back for it tomorrow. Those are my orders," the officer curtly answered in a tone that brooked no argument.

Carlos looked at the officer, at the soldiers who had their rifles at ready, then at his cart with its cargo of 250 bolos. He looked back across the Pasig towards Manila which was calm and peaceful when they left barely an hour ago; now it was agog with the pealing of church bells and gunfire, ablaze in several places. Reluctantly, he asked his assistant to help him unload the bolos which were bundled inside four burlap sacks secured with rope.

To cover the people on the bridge, the sentries sandbagged atop the gate raked the distant figures with gunfire, aiming at the shadows scurrying between the buildings which they presumed to be those of rebels. Carlos was both scared and relieved by the bullets flying over his head. With his assistant, he hauled off one heavy crate from the wagon, struggling under its weight and cowering under the steady fire of Krag rifles. He handed one of two crates containing sheaves of bolos to the impatient Yankee officer. But as he attempted to follow the soldiers to the gate, in order to take payment from a quartermaster behind the walls as was the longstanding practice, the two infantrymen with drawn guns stopped him on his track. "You can't come with us. Get back..." the officer drove him away as the drawbridge began to rise to the sound of jangling chains.

"But you haven't –"

"Begone, sir!"

"–paid me yet..." Carlos protested.

The staccato burst of the Gatling machinegun rattled Carlos out of his wits and he scampered back to his wagon cursing. He gritted his teeth under his breath as he and Anselmo saw the product of their labors vanish behind the gate.

"Damned Gringos! Damned *insurrectos!*"

Unbeknownst to Carlos his transaction with the Americans was being observed by the very insurgents whom he was cursing. Some of General Luna's raiders reinforced by Manila-based insurgents were lying in wait in the shadows outside the walls of Intramuros. They were part of a blocking force deployed around the perimeter to ambush any reinforcements that the Americans might send out during the attack. When the Americans hesitated to join the battle, being yet untrained in house-to-house combat, much less guerrilla tactics that were slowly entering the consciousness of military strategists, the raiders set fire to more houses to provoke them into coming out of their impregnable position. Noticing that the Yankees were staying put behind the barred doors and drawn bridge, the insurgents prepared to withdraw from their sector only to espy the curious incident of a bullock cart making a delivery to the Americans.

Dispossessed, a despondent Carlos wheeled his cart around. He cursed the rebels again for attacking the Americans before they could pay him. He condemned his poor timing and ignorance of the rebels' plans. What rotten luck. Next time the Americans placed new orders, as accumulate the bolos they must, he was going to double his price. His spirits lifted momentarily at this thought, but sank again when it occurred to him that the fighting might not be over yet by tomorrow. It was then that he saw their way blocked by insurgents brandishing rifles and bolos.

"Halt! What did you deliver to the Americans?" asked an insurgent officer who was wielding a pistol.

"Nothing, comrade!" blurted out Carlos, flabbergasted.

"Don't lie, running dog!" was the officer's biting reply in Tagalog. "They lowered the drawbridge just for you."

"Well... nothing harmful, amigo," Carlos groped for words as his brains raced for a plausible explanation while his assistant cowered beside him. "Just *zacate*, sir. They were forcibly taking my grass fodder for their horses..."

"I'm not buying that. The Gringos wouldn't open their gates in the middle of an attack just for a cartload of *zacate*. We are taking your cart and you're coming with us."

"But I'm telling the truth," Carlos protested. "I'm a Katipunero myself. Do you know who I am?"

"In that case we'll shoot you for treason," the officer retorted.

"My name is Carlos Calderon, brother to Dr. Joaquin Calderon who is El Presidente's personal physician and a cabinet member in the revolutionary government. El Jefe himself knows me personally. You must have heard of our family name, amigo," Carlos rattled off his connections, gaining in confidence by the second.

"That's him, the blacksmith Caloy," one knowing insurgent whispered to his lieutenant.

"Aha, a blacksmith," the insurgent officer seized on the tip, then turning to Carlos, added: "Those bundles you unloaded, weren't they weapons, like bolos perhaps, hah, señor?"

"I told you it was fodder. Why don't you believe me! I was only trying to make a living, doing something harmless. Didn't you see?" Carlos expostulated.

"Don't play around with us, señor. Whatever you say it was, we caught you giving aid and comfort to the enemy. For now, I'm placing you under my custody. Save your explanations for our superiors at the headquarters."

The lieutenant ordered one of his men to take the reins from Calderon who was told to sit at the back. The officer and the rest of his men piled aboard the cart which trundled toward the Parian Bridge, later joined on foot by other fleeing comrades. Carlos was going to face an investigation and trial in the hands of his peers.

———————

When Joaquin Calderon arrived at his clinic, it seemed deserted. The gate to his brother's foundry next door was also locked, with no sign of activity within. Beginning to get worried he banged at the clinic's door calling out his daughter's name. Finally, Calderon heard the bolt being unlocked from the inside and the door swung open.

"Papa, papa!" Estrella burst out of the door.

By this time Calderon's impatience had considerably dampened his delight. "Ella, what have you been doing? Why won't you open the door?"

"I was hiding upstairs because our neighbors told me not to open our doors, and not to admit any yanqui because we are at war with the Americans."

Calderon gently led her back to the house. "They're right. That was the right thing to do. I'm sorry I was impatient."

"Pa, is it true we're at war with the Americans?"

"Yes, *hija*. There's a war going on. That's why I have been detained in the province for so long. I left Malolos two weeks ago, but fighting broke out and I had to attend to our wounded, dozens, hundreds. And now Manila is burning, torched by our own soldiers."

"All these fires? Set by our own soldiers?"

"War is terrible. War makes people do crazy things."

Calderon made a cursory inspection of the house, first his clinic, then the foundry. He noticed something amiss. "Where's your Uncle Caloy, by the way? Has he been taking care of you?"

"Yes, papa. He never left the past few days busy making bolos for the army. Tonight was the delivery date, that's why he isn't here."

Which army? Calderon wondered. He remembered the day his younger brother returned from detention in the American camp and how he immediately got down to work making great quantities of bolos. Though he wouldn't admit it, the big order came from the Americans and tonight the deal must have been consummated with the delivery of the goods.

"If we are at war with the Americans, why does Uncle Caloy look up to them as if they are his friends?"

Calderon was stumped. "That is the question."

"He was escorted here by the Americans, and he keeps mentioning American names."

"Barton Bailey?"

"No, he's mad at Bart Bailey."

Calderon glared at her.

Estrella bit her tongue, having let the cat out of the bag.

"Bart? You call him Bart?"

She simpered.

A swirl of imagined scenes crossed the doctor's mind. "What have you been doing while I was away? Flirting with a *yanqui* soldier?"

"No. Uncle Caloy hates Bart even if he's friendly with the Americans. He can't come near me. There's nothing between us."

"I've talked with some of our neighbors. They say he's already taken to calling you pet names... Estrelle... sweet señorita," he mimicked. "How am I supposed to interpret that?"

In spite of herself, Estrella giggled upon hearing Calderon's impersonation of Bailey.

"Don't play games with me, *hija,* I'm your father. There is something going on here. Tell me, he's been courting you, is he not?"

"I don't know, I don't know! I don't want to talk about it." Estrella exclaimed, stamping her feet.

Calderon's inability to penetrate his daughter's maidenly reticence drummed into him the inadequacy of his role as a parent, underscoring the loss of her mother 17 years before. He looked for other evidence of Bailey's knavery that would pin her down and soon found something incontrovertible that sent him trembling with rage. From the most private corner of the house, i.e., the living quarters at the second floor, he found a hat of a Yankee soldier, with a dimpled crown and crossed rifles insignia on the front. He went down to confront Estrella with the damning evidence, only to be interrupted by the sound of hoofbeats and banging outside the door.

That same night, a Cavalry company sallied out of the Santa Lucia Gate of Intramuros to scour the city for insurgents. Initially rattled by the insurgent's unorthodox war tactics, General Otis hurled down the gauntlet at the audacious raiders and sent mounted troops to engage and kill the attackers. They could not, however, find the rebels who just melted into the dark, as ephemeral as the mist over a camp fire. The Cavalry soldiers instead took to escorting, then assisting, the fire wagons that spread around to squirt their limited water supply into the conflagration. Four of the horsemen broke

278

away to infiltrate a neighborhood in Escolta where there was no disturbance of any kind but where the flames of passion burning in the heart of one of them irresistibly led them. Wearing the uniform of the 20th Kansas Regiment, Barton Bailey came upon a small clinic at the end of a row of buildings with canvas awnings. Its door was heavily protected by planks of wood that covered its entrance as protection from burglars who prowled the streets at night in these lawless times. He was intent in saving one trophy of the war that he feared might fall into the hands of the wrong persons. He found a familiar side entrance that was barred by an iron door secured by several padlocks and, with the urgency of a fireman trying to save somebody from a conflagration, hammered the door with his rifle butt, taking down one rusty padlock at a time, entertaining neither fear nor doubt in the company of other combat-ready Americans.

As he entered the darkened premises, bareheaded, without his dimpled cap, he became almost reverential, scenting the presence of the sweet señorita who had graced his recent dreams. He felt the warmth of her presence in the abandoned kitchen, with pots still sitting on earthen hearths, in the deserted bedroom upstairs with empty closets, behind the stained draperies hanging out to dry in the backroom. His Army-issue boots, heavily wrapped with leggings, squeaked on their creases as he tiptoed in the still surroundings, hoping to see his gal. He found a comb made out of an oyster shell on a table. He picked it up wistfully. "Estrelle," he murmured. "My darlin' Estrelle."

"Nothing but pots and pans around here," growled Wolfgang Messner, his left sleeve torn and soaked in blood. He used his Krag rifle as a cane and kicked things around in search of something precious. Two other soldiers stayed outside to stand guard.

"Don't touch anything, Wolf. This is my darlin's home. My sweet señorita..."

The giant German, wearing ill-fitting Army uniform, stared at him transfixed.

A stir behind a curtain jolted the German into swinging his rifle in its direction. "Halt! Who goes there?"

The portly figure of Joaquin Calderon emerged from the shadows holding a bundle of clothes.

"Hold it right there, mister, or I'll blow your brains off!" exploded Wolf.

"Whacky!" exclaimed Bailey. "Good to see you, sir. Are you alone?"

"Barton ..." Joaquin Calderon greeted coldly. "I heard you calling my daughter." All this time, Estrella was locked up inside Caloy's tool shed to guard her chastity from what the father thought were ravenous Americans.

"Ah, yeah, Estrelle ... how are you doc?"

"Why are you calling my daughter?"

"It's this, doc," Bailey groped. "We came here to rescue your daughter, as a matter of fact."

"So, this is...," butted in Wolf.

"Estrelle's father."

"I see, what do you want me to do with him?"

"Don't touch him, Wolf, he's a friend. He has a very nice daughter."

Calderon was absolutely fearless, first, having taken his measure of Bailey in their first meeting and, secondly, being in the premises of his own house. "You seem very familiar with my house. Have you been here before in my absence?"

"Here? No, of course not. This is my first time here."

"How did you get to know my daughter then?"

"Oh, she visits me in the camp."

"My daughter will not do that!" Calderon indignantly defended the honor of his daughter. "No virtuous Filipina will ever do that!" Then, he produced the cap that he had found in his daughter's boudoir and tossed it toward the bareheaded Bailey. Tell that to the Marines, he seemed to say.

They rode a cart at the tail end of a procession of refugees headed toward the town of Malolos, where Aguinaldo maintained his headquarters. As they approached a small wooden bridge spanning a stream, the doctor spotted Luna at the opposite bank scanning the column of refugees with a pair of binoculars.

The general, astride a horse, beamed as he watched the carabao-drawn cart bearing Calderon and his daughter cross the bridge, laden with belongings such as a grandfather clock and chests of clothing. His display of amusement only irritated the doctor who did not find the behavior apropos to the circumstances of their escape where they risked life and limb to find safety. He was mad that the general had failed to meet him earlier in the morning at their agreed place of rendezvous by the Pasig River. More seriously, Luna seemed to have treated rather cavalierly his promise to replace the doctor's lost monocle.

"Hurry! Hurry!" Luna shouted jokingly from a distance. "We're going to blow up the bridge."

"Papa, look, it's my godfather, Uncle Tonio!" Estrella screamed with delight.

"Hello, compadre Joaquin, and Estrella, my *niña bonita,* I'm glad you all made it."

Calderon pointedly refused to answer his greeting. "Hold on to that clock, *hija,* or it would fall," he said in a loud voice, calculated to get past the ears of Luna.

"I never had any doubt you'll make it, Joaquin."

Calderon looked distantly ahead.

"What's the matter? Are you not glad you made it?"

"You left me behind," the doctor grumbled.

"Oh, you see, Joaquin, the *yanquis* reacted quite quickly to our attack so we had to make an early exit in the morning. Everything did not go down as planned," Luna explained in a low, grave voice.

Calderon was not mollified. "How about my monocle?"

"What?"

"My monocle! You promised to replace it."

Luna fumbled the leather bag hanging from his saddle. "Oh, but the *yanquis* don't wear monocles, I could not find any. But I did find a telescope."

"Ha-ha-ha," laughed the soldiers all around, followed by their commander.

"This may be a poor substitute for your glass but you can look farther ahead with it." Luna extended a small telescope, the kind used by pirates, but Calderon tapped it away without a word.

Luna's ribbing provided gaiety to the troops who were otherwise exhausted by the night's fighting, all at the expense of Calderon. These were all vulgar, ill-bred people, the polished mestizo steamed. He could not understand how an ilustrado like Luna could thrive in their company and still remain respectable. He forgave them all in his heart and turned his back on their boorish behavior.

Once back in his villa in Malolos, he questioned his daughter closely about her relationship with Barton Bailey. "He broke into our house without any regard for its owners, didn't you see? And he was familiar with the interior of the house as if he had been there several times."

"Perhaps Uncle Caloy, he must have been looking for him."

"He was calling out your name, señorita. And there was something more to it than meets the eye..."

Estrella grinned, then covered her mouth coyly.

"What have you been doing while I was away? Making a scandal in the eyes of our neighbors? Were you not taught by your aunts how to behave like a lady?"

"He is just a friend."

"How did he ever become your friend? Last time I saw him, he hardly set eyes on you. What – *Dios mio,* forgive my thoughts – what happened since then?" Calderon nagged, disturbed by the visions that eddied in his mind. "I should take this up with your Uncle Caloy."

Every mention of Bailey drew from her a shy, evasive response such that it set his father's imagination flying. As her denials wore thin, Estrella finally owned up to something. "He did visit me a few times when Uncle Caloy went missing, and he appeared in the house to offer help, and he used his connections to lead us to where he was being held, and so he helped set him free. It was all with the knowledge of our neighbors and they gave me advice. And we never talked very much because all he could say was 'Howdy? *Como estas? Donde? Gracias.'* All our neighbors will tell you that he behaved properly and nothing happened between us. Ask them. We never did anything."

Calderon was not satisfied by the explanation. He could read between the lines. Bailey was courting his daughter, that was the meaning of it all. It was natural for a demure young woman to be secretive about affairs of the heart, and he did not press for details. From hereon, he would just make sure that someone would be overseeing the affair at close quarters, and no contact was going to be tolerated while a war was going on.

The doctor was glad that he was able to get a handle on the affair at an early stage. Or so he thought. The following days, he observed some queer behavior in his daughter. Estrella would spend hours looking distantly out of the window as if waiting for someone to appear. At one time, he caught her vomiting into the sink and seizing her tummy in pain. At another time, he found her munching avidly at a green mango after skipping lunch, a diet that progressed into an addiction. To a doctor steeped in native culture, these were telling signs.

The widower father was struck down by the thunderbolt of realization: the girl was pregnant!

Grabbing a machete with one hand and a gun with the other, he stormed out of the house. "I'll look for that bastard,

Bailey, that slimy little serpent, that no-good son-of-bitch," he said with all the venom of his native language.

Impulsively, he mounted his stolid horse and trotted down the road in the direction of Manila. Five miles into his lonely trek, he was overtaken by the thought that it would take an army to get the head of Barton Bailey, one assuredly more powerful than Luna's. He was forced to stop before the wooden bridge spanning a stream near the municipal boundary of Malolos. It was being wired for demolition by a group of rebels who tied bundles of dynamites around the concrete posts and under the wooden planks. Prevented from going farther by an officer who warned him that the Americans were preparing for an offensive just a short ride away yonder, behind the screen of woods, Calderon turned back sadly, overawed by the power of the U.S. Army. He would redeem the family honor some other time when he had the means and the courage to do it.

In any event, he consoled himself with the thought that something good might come out of the affair: he could parlay Estrella's relationship with an American soldier into influence with the colonial government.

Their stay in Malolos was not free from intrigue. At the outset, Caloy's "escape" from the Yankee-occupied Manila became the subject of suspicious talk. He was subjected to an informal inquiry headed by Emilio Aguinaldo himself. Caloy's father-in-law, a village head or barrio captain, subscribed to the insurgents' tales that Carlos was caught selling weapons to the Americans, a serious accusation that threatened to stigmatize the Calderon family in the eyes of their neighbors, one of their members being a prominent official in the Aguinaldo government. According to the story making the rounds of the barrio, Caloy's guilt was sealed by the unchallenged fact that he was seen unloading the box of weapons at the Postigo even before the Gringo troops started firing. It meant that he had hauled off the cargo with evident premeditation, not under duress as he had protested all along but pursuant to some treasonable plan.

For their part, Caloy's wife and children steadfastly defended him and purveyed his version of his story to all and sundry, to wit: that he was merely delivering fodder for the horses of the Yankees' Cavalry, that the fodder contained poison to weaken and slowly kill their horses and thereby limit their ability to fight a running battle with the insurgents, all strictly in keeping with Aguinaldo's guerilla tactics. Carlos was not a traitor but one of the many passive patriots who quietly supported the revolutionary cause from behind the enemy lines while performing their daily jobs.

Challenged to prove his version of the events in front of General Aguinaldo himself, Carlos Calderon acquitted himself very well. He recounted his heroism during a breakfast hosted by Aguinaldo in the lawn of his temporary headquarters in the local mayor's residence. Behind a bamboo fence draped with crawling vine, Carlos worked the unsophisticated chief to a lather, regaling his generals about how he fooled the Americans into seizing the bundles of *zacate* grass as food for their horses, not knowing that he had dipped them in a vat spiked with sap from the cashew tree which was deemed poisonous to the animals.

"But how come you were seen unloading the box before the Gringo even started firing?" the persistent question came up, this time from the mouth of the revered General.

"If you could have seen how many guns were trained at me, including even two cannons, you would have handed over your pants as well," Carlos was quick with his repartee.

The ranking generals in Aguinaldo's staff listened to his tale with contemptuous silence, staring at him from under their capacious sombreros, and nodding penetratingly at the falsehoods being served up to them. After dismissing him, they held a private meeting where they ruminated over and regurgitated all his lies, and they marked him out for future punishment but they decided to take no action, for now at least, in deference to his elder brother Joaquin.

Having beaten the rap, Carlos sought out Joaquin and talked to him in private.

"I know where your sympathies lie. The Americans will listen to you. Please help me collect from General MacArthur the money they owe me," Carlos said to his brother in the privacy of their ancestral house.

"How dare you ask me to do such a thing! After all that I have done for you," Joaquin replied, recoiling with revulsion.

"But this is all in the family. We can use the money, you know..."

"No way, Caloy. No way am I going to risk my neck after having just saved yours. Don't you realize what you're asking me to do? It's treason!"

"But nobody will ever know," Carlos persisted. "You have connections with the Americans."

"Caloy, perish the thought. *Nunca*! Never!" Joaquin cut him off.

Although it was not beneath Joaquin to seek accommodation with the Americans, he was never going to do it for money. Never was he going to sell his loyalties for thirty pieces of silver that the Americans owed his younger brother.

The Calderon family's Malolos interlude was short lived. The Americans soon swung into the offensive, stung by Luna's audacious raid on their backyard and emboldened by the arrival of fresh reinforcements. The rearguard action fought bravely by Luna's troops served only to delay the inevitable. Soon, the Americans were knocking on the doors of Malolos, and General Aguinaldo prepared to move the embattled republic's seat of government yet again to a safer place ahead of the rampaging Yankees. Thus began the long march of Aguinaldo north of Luzon that would see him disappear deep into the jungles of Isabela where he would inaugurate a new kind of war.

Early in the fighting, Aguinaldo's cabinet splintered under the weight of the American onslaught. One faction, which counted Joaquin Calderon among its ranks, implored Aguinaldo to sue for peace or at the very least, a conditional truce. This was adamantly opposed by other cabinet members and the generals, in particular, the fiery Antonio Luna. Malolos swirled with rumors of the impending flight and in-fighting among high officials of the republic. Given the unremitting military reversals suffered by the insurgent army, rumor had it that the faction favoring accommodation with the Americans was gaining the upper hand.

History begrudges Luna credit for the nighttime raid on February 22. Historian Le Roy extolled Luna as "the most warlike of the Filipinos" and "a man with the greatest capacity for war," but disparaged the attack as a simple case of "incendiarism." It did more to damage Filipino property than American military might. Unable to hit any of the American barracks in Santa Mesa and Santa Ana, Luna succeeded in burning mostly Filipino homes and commercial centers. He did manage to inflict 50 casualties on the American side, consisting of 9 dead and 41 wounded, mostly belonging to volunteer regiments housed in barracks outside the walls, but the same only stoked American enthusiasm for war instead of sending them scrambling to board their fleet. The week following the raid, in fact, reinforcements poured into the Manila harbor from the Pacific port of San Francisco, consisting of men and matériel needed to sustain the campaign to secure the colony. This emboldened General Arthur MacArthur to plan an open-ended campaign to the farthest reaches of the colony, with the ultimate aim of destroying the spurious republic of Emilio Aguinaldo.

Fortunately for the Filipinos, when General MacArthur felt that he was ready to launch an all-out war, Governor-General Otis reined him in. Otis almost never left the comforts of his palace inside Intramuros where he conducted the war by reading dispatches from the fronts and sending messengers on horseback. It was characteristic of Otis to procrastinate on his next step, building up an excess of supplies and men to ensure overwhelming superiority while his workhorse MacArthur itched for action to press home the hard-fought gains that he had won at the outskirts of Manila. Otis's style smacked of the dilatory tactics of Union General McClellan who refused to budge from his camp on the Potomac until he had amassed a surfeit of supplies. To Otis, the Potomac was the Pasig. His differences with MacArthur would soon reach the ears of the top brass in Washington. The conflict recalled Admiral Montojo's clash with the Spanish governor-general Basilio Agustin and was resolved in much the same manner, that is, with the inutile governor-general being unceremoniously shipped back across the sea and his energetic junior commander installed in his place. As the new overlord of the colony, MacArthur did not command by proxy but instead personally oversaw the conduct of the war. His aggressive pursuit of Emilio Aguinaldo and his rebel army would set the tone of the war in the coming days.

17

PEACE ON A SILVER PLATTER

In March 1899, one month after landing in Manila, the Schurman Commission got down to serious business even as the Insurrection that broke out to greet their arrival was gathering force. They began discharging McKinley's instructions in earnest, that is: to establish a colonial government in a form that was acceptable to the locals. Apart from Professor Jacob Schurman, it counted among its members academics like Dean C. Worcester, a zoologist who had earlier spent three years in the Philippines gathering specimens and who would later stay on to play a prominent role in the colonial administration. The other members of the commission possessed equally impressive credentials: they were the ilustrado of American society, equally distinguished as the local breed.

The Commission was welcome neither to the military brass nor to the Filipinos. To Otis, it was a worthless mission, a quixotic junket that interfered with military operations even as it aggravated the shortage of fighting men. His commanders became babysitters of the peripatetic mission, dispatching soldiers to its security detail as they made high-profile visits to Filipino communities in Manila and its environs. They visited the Universidad de Santo Tomas, the upscale districts of Santa Ana and Santa Mesa which the insurgents had torched, the occupied towns surrounding Sangley Point, including Cavite Viejo a.k.a. Kawit, the hometown of Aguinaldo.

The Schurman Commission made the following offer to their rebellious wards: a legislature composed exclusively of Filipino delegates; a judiciary manned by both American and Filipino jurists; and eventually, but not for now, a Filipino chief executive. In exchange, the insurgents must lay down their arms and pledge allegiance to the American flag. They also promised that the colonial rule under an American governor-general would be a short transition period towards complete independence, much shorter than Spain's three-century imperial tyranny. Then, just in case the American magnanimity was misunderstood as a sign of weakness by the insurgents, the Commission it made clear that the United States would brook no resistance to its enlightened rule during the transition period, declaring its readiness to enforce American suzerainty over the entire archipelago such that "those who resist it can accomplish no end other than their own ruin."

The text of the ringing proclamation was published in English, Spanish and Tagalog and posted on walls throughout Manila and nearby towns beginning April 15. The following day, the posters were in tatters.

The statement was only the first shot in the so-called Battle of Proclamations, an exchange of propaganda between the pamphleteers of the warring sides that for a time generated more heat than the shooting war itself.

Aguinaldo scoffed at the motives of the Commission. "They are offering worthless trinkets in exchange for our priceless sovereignty. The *yanqui* wants to become man of the house while we are relegated as mere servants to the *entresuelo*," he said in bitter analogy. He then instructed his ilustrado prime minister, Apolinario Mabini, to compose the official text of his government's response.

"We reject the notion that the United States is the source of our rights and that we ought to be satisfied with a token offer of 'self-rule,'" Mabini began his letter addressed to

Jacob Schurman. "As far as the Filipino nation is concerned, it has declared itself free and independent, and to offer it the lesser status of a dominion is to diminish its sovereignty and take away its freedom in its entirety." As a parting shot, Mabini resorted to high rhetoric: "What a spectacle it is to see the American nation wrest away from another people, weak and worthy of better fate, the very rights which in its own case it believes to be inherent by Law, natural and divine!"

In response, the Commission promised to bring democracy into the islands and published excerpts of the U.S. Constitution, which would be the model of the islands' basic laws. Once again, Aguinaldo supporters tore off posters of the American proclamation from the city's walls and distributed leaflets saying bluntly: "Whoever believes the American propaganda allows himself to become a traitor, and traitors shall be condemned to 300 years of slavery. Don't believe the promises of a slave master."

On May 5, Secretary of State John Hay authorized the Commission to reveal the tantalizing details of the colonial administration they had in mind. The government would consist of "a governor-general appointed by the United States President, a cabinet chosen by the governor-general to include Filipino members, a general advisory council elected by a carefully chosen group of voters ... and a strong independent judiciary with the [U.S.] President appointing the principal judges among either the natives or Americans." It was an extraordinary proclamation with supreme propaganda value to the Americans. If implemented, the Schurman Plan, as it became known, would transform the Philippines into a self-governing colony unlike any other in the world.

The well-calibrated American offer had its intended effect: it divided and sowed discord among the leadership of the insurgent republic. It was an offer that was too good to reject outright and was backed-up by a credible threat. Aguinaldo's cabinet split into two factions with opposing views on the Schurman Plan: one wanted to negotiate with the Americans to test the latter's sincerity; the other preferred to settle the issue on the battlefield. Both sides counted ilustrados amongst their supporters. The hawks were led by an unusual duo: Apolinario Mabini, a paraplegic man of letters who was the insurgent republic's prime minister and Antonio Luna, the tempestuous warrior who shot down the peace plan with his pistol. The doves were dominated by European-educated ministers who had a grasp of American democracy, among them Felipe Buencamino, Pedro A. Paterno and Joaquin Calderon. Caught between the two sides was Aguinaldo who initially deferred to the enlightened opinions of the ilustrados but soon began taking his own counsel.

The doves prevailed during the initial clash. They ousted Mabini from his prime minister's seat and formed a so-called Peace Cabinet on May 15, 1899, headed by the suave scholar Pedro A. Paterno. Unable to stand the sight of Filipinos dying in the countryside by the increasing numbers, they sought to start negotiations with the Americans.

Following the reverses in the battlefront suffered by General Luna, Paterno dispatched a peace delegation to Manila to negotiate the terms of settlement within the parameters set by Secretary of State Hay. It was their misfortune to meet with representatives of the military command instead of the Schurman Commission. In an informal meeting with MacArthur at a Dominican monastery, the U.S. side made it clear to the Filipinos that no settlement was possible unless the latter first laid down their arms. "Put away your guns," MacArthur said laconically. "And we talk." The condition was unacceptable to the Filipinos as it made a settlement contingent on their surrender. The Paterno delegation went home with a heavy heart, having run into a brick wall.

General Luna used Paterno's failure to heap scorn on the doves. "Look at what they did," he blustered during a cabinet meeting attended by Aguinaldo. "They made fools of themselves. They go to Manila to bargain for our people's freedom and all the Americans say is we must surrender first.

Must we go down on our knees to ask for our birthright?"

"You should not have spoken to General MacArthur, he has a conquistador mindset. You should have spoken directly to Mr. Schurman," Aguinaldo reproached Paterno.

"It was the military officers who faced us. They themselves are not united. They must have taken the commissioners prisoners," speculated Paterno darkly, citing similar Byzantine conflicts during the Spanish times.

On May 21, a showdown occurred between the doves and the hawks that presaged the downfall of the ablest general in Aguinaldo's army. On that day, the Paterno cabinet again met to give the peace overture another try, this time with a specific request to meet with the Schurman commissioners. Aguinaldo gave a perfunctory nod to the plan, then left Malolos for the countryside to mediate in a land dispute. When Luna got wind of the meeting at the front, he rushed back to Aguinaldo's headquarters to register his opposition to the plan. He arrived in Malolos in time to see the members of the cabinet smoking their pipes to mark the end of a long meeting. His arrival ahead of a squad of bodyguards broke the sedate atmosphere that marked the deliberations in the cabinet room. He broke up the meeting hopping mad. Without bothering to ask about the outcome of the meeting, he yanked Paterno out of his chair. "What's this I hear about you talking surrender again? Have you lost your mind? Have you forgotten the sacrifices we have made in the field?"

The resulting bedlam sent the other ministers jumping out of their chairs to save the prime minister from being strangled by Luna's callused hands. In Aguinaldo's absence, they pacified the general by explaining that the cabinet had not agreed to lay down the insurgents' arms as a precondition to talks but intended to propose a ceasefire. Still, Luna was not mollified. According to contemporary accounts, Luna shoved Paterno around the room and slapped Felipe Buencamino, the foreign minister, when the latter tried to stop him.

"I won't allow talks to be held with the Americans behind my back," Luna raged at his colleagues. "I command the army and I deserve to be heard. The Filipino people want independence and I will fight to the death to fulfill their wishes, thus complying with my oath to the flag."

Luna's behavior at the cabinet meeting marked him as a dangerous man. Hawks and doves alike closed ranks to protest Luna's treatment of his fellow ilustrados. Thereafter, Luna lost the support of the cabinet which was the source of his authority. When the story reached Aguinaldo in all its gory details, he instructed his Kawit troops to keep an eye on General Luna. Calderon himself was saddened by Luna's behavior; but he did not want to risk breaking their friendship by criticizing the man's behavior.

Meanwhile, peace talks were furthest from the mind of the American top commander in the islands. Major General Elwell Otis, commander of the Eighth Corps and military governor for the islands, cabled Washington for more troops. His demands further heated the debate on the scope and purpose of the American military adventure in the Philippine Islands. Otis's demand for 30,000 more troops, on top of the 11,000 already in the islands, pushed the Philippine question to the top of McKinley's political agenda. Before the outbreak of the insurrection in February 1899, it widely was assumed that pacifying the islands would take no more than the time it took to defeat the Spaniards, 3 months and 22 days. The ferocity of Aguinaldo's resistance drastically changed the estimate. Now, it was an open-ended military operation.

The question of numbers posed political problems in Washington. In 1899, the authorized standing army of the United States was pegged by Congress at 28,000 men. McKinley's call for 125,000 volunteers on the eve of the Spanish-American War was never completely filled, and Congress saw little reason to increase the size of the Army following victory over the Spanish empire. Hence, when Otis badgered his superiors for a staggering 30,000 additional troops to put down an insurrection by natives in a far-flung Pacific territory, he was in effect talking of committing the whole of the United States standing army to his patch of jungle.

In July and August of 1899, at the height of the insurrection, there occurred an exchange of telegrams between Elihu Root, the Secretary of War and Otis, the military governor. Root tried to pin down an evasive Otis on the exact size of the military contingent that was needed to ensure victory. "Washington has to justify the numbers to Congress. We need your report on the scope and size of the native resistance to enlighten Congress of the seriousness of the problem." Otis replied that, at the rate he was killing Aguinaldo's cannon fodder, he would need between 30,000 to 35,000 additional troops. "Impossible," Root cabled, "half the size would be undoubtedly adequate force to ensure prompt victory." Otis retorted that his original estimate in fact called for an "adequate force" of "between 50,000 and 60,000 men," but for political considerations, he drove down the figure.

In 1899, Secretary Root indefinitely delayed the demobilization of the reserves who had been called to action in the Caribbean war and "prepared a measure providing for a standing army of 60,000 so elastically organized as to permit its expansion to 100,000," according to records of the time. Pressed to fix a timetable for ending the insurrection, Otis hedged. Already, the conflict was dragging on longer than the "Splendid Little War" with no end in sight.

As the military brass band was kept busy welcoming troops at the Manila harbor, Otis reorganized the Eighth Corps, which was growing fatter by the day. He divided the corps into two divisions. The First Division was commanded by Brig. Gen. Henry W. Lawton, a veteran of the Cuban campaign. His task was to exterminate the rampaging bands of guerrillas south of Manila – loose companies of brigands and patriots who had risen to the call of Aguinaldo without submitting to his leadership. The Second Division was headed by the seasoned MacArthur who did not really suffer a diminution of command because the revamp simply split up an enlarged army. His job was to press on with the hot pursuit of the organized army of Aguinaldo, which held sway in the northern provinces of Luzon.

As for the Navy, nothing could save it from its perennial role as second fiddle to the Army. In the absence of an insurgent navy, the Asiatic Squadron had no belligerent role except showing the flag and ferrying troops and supplies to the major islands of the archipelago. Not that Dewey complained. He dutifully carried troops aboard his gunboats and cruisers to the Visayas and Mindanao, the two major island groups south of Luzon. The Navy's trickiest assignment was ferrying men to Moro territories in the islands south, where fierce Moro tribes brandishing curved blades engaged American troops in hand-to-hand combat wherever they pitched camp. The Moro's resistance to pistol shots at close quarters was said to have led the U.S. Army to commission a more powerful handgun which was strong enough to repel a Moro warrior on a headlong charge – the Colt .45-caliber pistol.

In private, Dewey gained a favorable impression of the Filipinos in his year-long stay in the islands which was in character given his professional detachment to the war. In his private correspondence, he commented that the Filipinos "were more capable of running a government than the Cubans" whom McKinley had allowed to proclaim their independence. Of course, he never expressed his views in public even as the Philippine debate grew increasingly acrimonious back home. He was a good captain whose hands were steady on the rudder of political neutrality.

Finally, in May 1899, on the first anniversary of the Battle of Manila Bay, the old admiral of the Orient Seas decided that it was time to go home. So he weighed anchor off Sangley Point and sailed into the sunset. If there was any doubt as to who was the star of the Philippine campaign – or the whole of the Spanish-American War, for that matter – it was dispelled by the tumultuous welcome he received at home. As he entered the New York Harbor aboard his flagship on a clear moonless night, tugboats flying the Stars and Stripes came out to escort him, firing rockets into the sky. The Brooklyn Bridge displayed a huge streamer saying "Welcome Dewey" in luminous letters. From atop the bridge, searchlights scanned the length of the East River to illuminate his way. As soon as he disembarked, fireworks accompanied the brass band that came out to greet him along with high city and federal officials. He passed through the high rises of New York in a motorcade amidst cheering crowds. Enough gunpowder fizzled that night to sink another fleet. In Washington, congressmen fell over one another in an effort to shake the hand of the man on whom they had bestowed the rank of Admiral of the Navy, with a golden sword to match. In one of the many adulatory gatherings he attended in the U.S. capital, he spoke on the bow of a scaled-down *Olympia* jutting out of the wall of the hall. Dewey was the American hero of his time.

That was not the end of his involvement in the conflicts that his sojourn to Manila unleashed. Informed that Admiral Montojo was sent to prison for losing the Battle of Manila Bay, he wrote the downtrodden admiral a letter extolling his gallantry in battle. "I have no hesitation in saying to you what I have already had the honor to report to my government, that your defense at Cavite was gallant in the extreme. The fighting of your flagship, which was singled out for attack, was especially worthy of a place in the traditions of valor of your nation," he said. Perhaps because of his letter, Montojo was later acquitted and spent his last years in Madrid in quiet obscurity, which was the same fate that was eventually to befall George Dewey. Yet, he would not have complained. Dewey was an odd character of the turn of the century when flamboyance was a virtue, when lesser officers fell over each other to seek fleeting glory, when journalists embellished facts and more often than not invented heroes.

———————

18

ON THE ROAD WITH THE 20ᵗʰ KANSAS

At the outbreak of hostilities between American and Filipino troops, Bailey was patrolling the Pasig River aboard a small gunboat, a relic of the Spanish Navy that the Americans had salvaged and impressed into service. The gunboat's routine consisted mainly of mapping the river for navigation hazards such as uncharted wrecks and dangerous flotsam as well as monitoring river traffic. Occasionally, they would stop and board boats suspected of gun-running or smuggling other contraband. Such encounters were the only relief from the drudgery of routine river patrol and Bailey usually led the boarding party. Invariably, the boat's crew would protest that the dynamites stashed in their vessel were intended only for blast fishing or that the guns lying among the cargo were for self-defense against pirates. Bailey let go as many of the contraband as he had confiscated.

Now that war had broken out with the insurgents, it seemed to Bailey that his river patrol duties contributed nothing worthwhile to the war effort. He envied the Army grunts who were reaping the glory of combat in the countryside. He wanted a piece of the action, too.

The call to arms came none too soon. His skipper told him to report to his superiors at the San Cristobal naval station. There, Bailey found Lt. Cocker who was his commander at *Olympia's* forward main gun turret and Captain McDyer, Gridley's successor as *Olympia's* skipper, waiting for him.

"The Army needs gunners," Lt. Cocker told Bailey.

"Beg your pardon, sir?" Bailey replied wondering what it had to do with him.

"The 20th Kansas lost four gunners in Caloocan and they can't find any replacements from among their ranks. It would take too long to train new ones and reinforcements from home are still weeks away. On the other hand, the Navy has lots of gunners," Lt. Cocker explained. "I am recommending you and another gunner as replacements. I urge you to enlist at once since I've heard you've been complaining about being bored in the Navy anyway. You can name a buddy of your choice as your partner," Cocker added.

"But I ain't Kansan. I'm Virginian."

"Don't bother with State banners, this is an emergency. Tell us if you're willing to volunteer for duty in the Army, and we'll make arrangements for your transfer. And also find a partner who's willing to enlist with you."

"I haven't fired any of the Army's guns."

"It's the same kind of guns, only on wheels," said Cocker. "The Fletcher three-inch gun and the Hotchkiss two-pounder, surely you won't have any problem with them."

"Yes, I have seen them, sir, but..."

"Then, you have seen enough. Just tell us if you're interested in serving in the Army."

The Navy brass seemed genuinely concerned about helping their rival branch.

Bailey paused to think while his superiors waited, studying a map of the front where the Army were battling it out with the insurgents.

"Well, if I have to go into action, I might as well fight alongside them Sunflowers," Bailey finally said, referring to the Kansans whose State symbol was the sunflower.

"Good. Can you think of someone who's willing to volunteer with you?"

"There's Wolf Messner who's been griping about having to wash the decks while there's war going on."

"Ah, Messner, my big gun," said Cocker. "He's a good man. I must say we aren't exactly happy to part with our men this way, our best men I dare say. But Washington is slow to send additional troops, so we have to pitch in."

Captain McDyer nodded in agreement, laconic as was his predecessor Gridley.

"I'd fight with the Sunflowers as if I'm fighting with the Navy. We started this war and we might as well help the Army finish it."

Captain McDyer smiled.

With the blessings of his superiors, Bailey looked for his partner at Sangley Point, an hour ride away from Manila. He was sure the German scholar would be elated by the recommendation.

"Don't give me no sass about enlisting with the goddams. I'd soon swim across Manila Bay than join 'em chasing gooks in the jungles and boondocks," Wolfgang Messner reacted.

"You afeard of them gooks."

"Nah, got nothin' to do with that. The goddamns treat us like poor cousins and we'll gonna be left in the sidelines to shine their shoes. Besides, in the jungle you'll get loads of leeches sucking your blood dry, slimy li'l creatures."

"Oh, come on. Don't give me that nonsense. Just say you don't wanna go because you're fed up with me."

"Nobody likes you more, Gatling, especially among the people here in Sangley, though you've been living it up in Manila. But I just can't leave my buddies here and be killed in the boondocks among goddams who don't know me from Adam.

I don't want my body buried in the jungle without anyone remembering."

"You ain't coming even if it's an order?"

"What order?"

"Captain McDyer's"

"I love it here in the Navy..."

"So do I."

"So why go over to the other side?"

"Because that's an order, by Juniper. Captain McDyer asked for volunteers but the way he said it, it sounded like the whole war depended on it."

"Let me think about it. We've got enough trouble keeping the seas safe for the Army."

"That's nothin' compared to what they're up against in the boondocks. That's where the action is."

"You think we're just swatting flies here? Jeez, ferrying those people to the islands, braving typhoons, chasing Moro pirates in the South Seas. My God, just the thought of fighting them Moors hand to hand gives me nightmares. They're worse than the Injuns."

"Wolf, buddy, please think serious about it."

"I'm thinkin' and I ain't going."

The two buddies reported together to the camp of the 20th Kansas Regiment in the district of Santa Mesa, Manila. The bugle call from the stricken Army was too compelling to resist, stirring fears of a repeat of Custer's Last Stand at Little Bighorn or of the disaster at Fort Belknap involving Bailey's Dad, for that matter. Even Wolfgang heeded the call of duty, being one part a red-blooded Yankee patriot and one part a Teuton warrior.

Accordingly, the Sunflowers of the 20th Kansas Regiment became the beneficiaries of the services of two of Dewey's prized gunners and together they would do honors for their country.

The pair appeared at the gate of the Santa Mesa barracks wearing their flannel summer dress with knotted scarves. They cooled their worn-out heels as they waited anxiously for the camp gate master to meet them. By and by, they were admitted into the camp without ceremony and led into the playing field to mix with the troops doing their morning exercises. Standing out like sore thumbs in their sailor's outfit by the sidelines, they soon found themselves the objects of derision by the Kansans playing all kinds of Yankee ball games – baseball, football and a newfangled sport of unruly character called "basketball."

Some grunts interrupted their ball games to heckle at the newcomers. "Hey, ducks, what brought you here? How's fishing lately?" went one. "They've finally sent some folks to scrub the barracks floor," said another.

Bailey, being naturally friendly, took it all in stride, grinning at the ribbing they were getting from the goddams. The giant German, however, took it as a provocation and he fidgeted uncomfortably, his face flushed red.

Later, at the quartermaster's building where they were sent by a sergeant, the pair shed their Navy uniforms to put on Army suntans. They were decidedly more complicated than their plain sailor's flannels, with countless pendants and attachments to boot. Bailey put on a pair of trousers with a buttoned-up fly, a high-collared tunic, a webbing cartridge belt lined with bullets, low-heeled shoes with leggings and a creased fedora. Strapped to his belt was a jungle knife that proved more serviceable in the field than a bayonet. Hanging on a sling from his left shoulder was a wineskin-like canteen filled with potable water or, if one can get away with it, whiskey. For insignia, he wore the chevron of an artillery sergeant on his left sleeve, the trinkets of crossed rifles on his collars and a sunflower patch symbolizing the State of Kansas on his breast. Finally, he was given a Krag-Jorgensen rifle made in Denmark that was the choice weapon for the infantry at the time, one preferred to the Springfield. To an artilleryman the rifle was superfluous and Bailey kept his most of the time in the limber of his mounted cannon. Standing before a postage-stamp size mirror on the wall, he examined patches of himself and immediately fell in love with his uniform. Estrella would surely be pleased to see him in this get-up.

"Attaboy, it ain't me! Don't I look smart in this, Wolf?" Turning to his friend who was similarly dressed, he remarked: "Oh, Wolf, you're a beaut. You'd sure beat Montojo in those suntans. Come up to the mirror here, take a look at yourself. No more ducky get-up like they say. What would the old gang say if they see us now?"

The blond German felt uncomfortable, preferring the loose, light Navy uniform without the frills. He groused.

Dressed to the nines, they left the quartermaster's building to join the Sunflowers in the parade grounds from whom they got a different reception. They ceased to be the object of ridicule by the Kansans who could hardly distinguish the erstwhile sailors from their fellows. The same men who had taunted them at the playing field now did a double take and complimented them. "Nice-looking chaps there," said one. "So, you're leaving the Navy to join us, huh?" remarked another. "How about joining us for some basketball?" This last one addressed to Wolf.

The pair were encouraged by the change of attitude among the Kansans. Wolf was especially heartened by their display of warmth noticing that the grunts shared a lot in common with his Navy mates, many of whom were farm boys. He also wanted to play their ball games, particularly the unruly new sport called basketball in which he had a height advantage.

At ten o'clock in the morning, the whole regiment was called to formation to undergo a kit inspection, preparatory to its deployment to the battle front. The two new recruits wad-dled uncomfortably in their unwieldy uniforms strapped with

all sorts of appendages, which seemed to tinkle and clash together. They felt like peddlers in the marketplace laden with all
kinds of trinkets. Assigned to the artillery unit, they stood behind their Fletcher cannons as the regimental colors were paraded around. Soon the officers broke ranks and approached
to inspect their men.

Chief of the whole shebang was Colonel Frederick
Funston (1865-1917), a man out to win honors for his backwater State, imposing in his erect stance, tanned face and grizzled
features. He scrutinized every man in every squad of every platoon in every company with eagle eyes, taking note of imper-
fections in his men's uniforms and bearing, however slight,
which caused him repeatedly to break his stride and snap his
swagger stick in order to call a man's attention to a rule infrac-
tion. His absolute command over his troops was reflected in
the silence that gripped the assembly, motionless as a patch of
sunflowers on a windless day.

At the back of the assembly, Funston gave the artillery
unit a similar treatment. He took particular notice of the two
Navy hands who stood out despite their suntan uniforms. He
found several accessories misplaced: such as the crossed rifles
being on the collars instead of on the cap, the jungle knife
latched to the right hip instead of the left, and the canteen
slung from left shoulder to right hip instead of the other way
around.

"You're the ones from Sangley?" asked the 34-year old
colonel, his prematurely gray beard accentuating his frown.

"Yes, cap'n, sir" answered Bailey, stiffly erect.

"Don't you see anything wrong with your uniform?"

"It's splendid, cap'n."

Funston turned his attention to the slouching Wolf.
"How about you, sergeant?"

"Sir, no, sir," the German answered his gaze, "but it's
kinda heavy on the sides."

"Go back to the barracks and ask the quartermaster
what's wrong with the uniforms they gave you."

From their first day with the Army, Bailey noted that Funston was no different from Gridley in the way he ran a tight ship in his Santa Mesa camp. He made sure his men were fit for the hard grind ahead by requiring them to undergo taxing drills every other day, all in the manner of Roman legions being trained to fight the barbarians. They had to run over obstacles, crawl over mud, dig trenches, scrabble with one another, swing from ropes and, of course, practice shooting at targets. This they did on rations consisting of rice and carabao meat, supplemented occasionally by imported treats. Their recreation consisted of ball games which tested their coordination and endurance while instilling in them the spirit of teamwork. Breaking in the newcomers from the Navy took all of three days, at the end of which Bailey felt sufficiently fit to meet the enemy in battle. Only there was not going to be any fighting soon.

He constantly pined for his weekend furloughs which enabled him to steal a visit to Estrella. This he soon supplemented by clandestine late night breakouts which he accomplished by climbing the roof of his barracks and swinging over the top of the fence while grasping a limb of a tree, an undeniable demonstration of the wondrous effects of his training. In his nighttime sallies, he deliberately left behind Wolf Messner, not only because it would increase the chances of detection by the no-nonsense Kansan sentries but also because he was jealous of his Aryan looks and gift of gab. If Estrella came to see Wolfgang's blond hair and his blue eyes – or worse, hear his yarns – she might switch her affections to him, and Bailey had absolutely no intention of letting that happen. This was a lone-wolf operation on an unguarded home, and he wanted to savor the taste of his romantic escapades alone.

Bailey began his conquest of Estrella in earnest during the dog days preceding the outbreak of the insurrection, sometime in January 1899. He was then on patrol along the Pasig River, an assignment that gave him time to kill and opportunities to go off the reservation. He would steal away on foot to the home of his sweet señorita, following the twists and turns of Manila's *esteros* until he arrived at the cobblestone streets of Escolta, excited and out of breath. At times, he found the girl frosty and petulant; at other times, lively and talkative; but at all times, he was filled with bliss at the mere sight of the virginal mestiza.

His transfer to the Army unexpectedly worked wonders on his appeal. For reasons only a girl's mind could fathom, she found his khaki uniform far more attractive than his Navy garb. Whenever he appeared in his crisp Army suntans, she would giggle and shed her reserve and engage him in animated talk well into the wee hours of twilight. In his get-up, the shy Gringo muchacho looked oh-so-handsome, she seemed to notice.

For conducting his courtship in the absence of the girl's father, Bailey did not endear himself to Estrella's neighbors. They kept a close watch on the goings-on in their unchaperoned neighbor's domicile, knocking on the door at odd times on some pretended errand or loitering under the clinic front awning in an effort to prolong her chastity. To Bailey it was none of their darned business.

One night in mid-January, he pursued his courtship to its culmination. He had slipped out of his Santa Mesa barracks and soon found himself outside the clinic's door burning with carnal desires. The door was opened by Estrella who was groggy with sleep as it was past her bedtime. As soon as he shut the door, he grabbed Estrella who let out a yelp which he soon smothered with a kiss to her mouth. To Bailey's pleasant surprise, she didn't resist wilting instead in his arms and kissing him back although she didn't quite know how. Bailey groped and fondled her and was about to undress her right then and there, lifting the hem of her night dress, when Estrella finally protested.

"No, no. Not here, Bart. Please, not here," she told her eager lover breathlessly. Then she took his hand and led him up the stairs to her bedroom.

All that Bailey noticed of her room was the mosquito net draped over a four-poster brass bed into which Estrella nimbly disappeared even as Bailey fumbled with the buttons of his uniform fairly ripping them away. When Bailey entered the diaphanous confines of the bed net, he felt Estrella nestled underneath a sheet and was again pleasantly surprised to see her naked and ready for him when he drew the sheet aside. Soon the room was filled with Estrella's moans, Bailey's grunts, and the bedsprings creaking merrily away as the two lovers consummated their longing for each other.

By local standards, Bailey's conquest was a feat worthy of a Dominican friar.

Then, the war intervened. On the night of February 22, 1899, insurgents set fire to the vulnerable quarters of Manila outside the walls, throwing the city into panic. Bailey was then drinking beer with Wolf and a couple of Kansans in one of Manila's lamp-lit bars whose operating hours American soldiers on their weekend passes pushed beyond their normal closing. Bailey was trying to fortify himself without getting soused for another foray into Estrella's bedroom. He was about to excuse himself when the bells of a nearby church rang raising the fire alarm. When they went out of the bar to investigate, they saw the skies above sections of Manila ruddy with the glow of scattered conflagrations. All hell had broken loose. Manila was on fire.

Soon the streets of Manila's red-light district clattered with the hoof beats of mounted military policemen rounding up the Yankees on furlough, ordering them to return to quarters. Bailey hardly paid attention to the MP's commands, pulling Wolf aside to tell him he must accompany him to check if his beloved Estrella was safe, for friendship's sakes. The two Kansans went along out of fear of ambush in the uncertain situation. Accordingly, Bailey and his three companions slipped by the MP's who were distinguished by their green and yellow patches and insignia of crossed pistols. They mounted their horses and ran into horse-drawn fire wagons with bells tinkling and soldiers running out of their barracks in panic. Bailey took his companions where his heart led him, convinced that there was one inhabitant in the city worth saving above all others.

They came upon a small clinic at the end of a rambling alley with a door heavily protected by planks of wood. He pounded open the locks and latches with his rifle butt until he was able to force his way inside but instead of finding Estrella, he ran into Joaquin Calderon. The man was holding his dented cap which he had left in Estrella's bedroom – the significance of which sent his romantic hopes crashing down: their forbidden love had been discovered and the father was there to demand an explanation. It would take a war to get back his sweet señorita.

While the Schurman Commission talked of peace, the Eighth Corps tried its best to sabotage its mission by prosecuting the war. General Otis had no intention of sharing the business of running the colony with the Filipinos, nor even of handing his position of governor-general to an American civilian, as the peace plan envisioned. It was a sentiment shared by his rival MacArthur. To them, the rebellious islands were better governed with an iron hand by military minds, just like other stable colonies in the world. They had seen in Latin America and elsewhere that when the colonizer relaxed its grip by giving the natives a modicum of freedom, the natives were quick to bite the hand that fed and compound their ingratitude by seeking independence.

Accordingly, Otis put his Army back on the warpath after licking the wounds to its self-confidence inflicted by Luna. Having amassed sufficient men and supplies at the Manila harbor, he launched the long-awaited offensive. He ordered an attack on Aguinaldo's seat of government itself, located in the town of Malolos 25 miles north of Manila, where he was inaugurated as president with much pageantry on January 21, 1899.

Otis had reorganized the Eighth Corps into two divisions commanded by his fighting generals Henry Lawton and Arthur MacArthur. Lawton was the more accomplished if not better known general, having figured in several battles in the Indian Wars and the Caribbean conflict, foremost among them the capture of Geronimo and his band of marauding Apaches in 1886. His First Division was assigned the task of pacifying the towns south of Manila, including Aguinaldo's home province of Cavite but after initial successes, Lawton was killed by a Filipino sniper in battle at San Mateo, Rizal on December 19, 1899, the highest-ranking American casualty of the war. The return of his body to the United States along with his burial at the Arlington Cemetery was an occasion for great mourning. A campaign for donation to support his widow financially collected some $100,000 throughout the country, mostly in dimes and nickels, then an enormous sum. After his burial, his widow retrieved a letter from among his belongings saying: *"If I am shot by a Filipino bullet, it might as well be from one of my own men."* The mysterious meaning of the general's letter was related to the flipside of the war, the disruptions of the Anti-Imperialist League which struck a discordant note opposed to the jingoistic tone of the Yellow Press. The league mobilized anti-war supporters in the streets and at the ports to vilify the uniformed men fighting a colonial war as if they bore personal responsibility for their actions. Their activities had a wounding effect on the morale of the soldiers prosecuting the cause of Manifest Destiny.

Lawton's tragic fate was to hang over Arthur MacArthur. He was determined to get his prey and go home alive – so that he could groom his youngest son, Douglas, to follow in his footsteps to the Army. The latter was then poised to enter West Point with only his wife Pinky to pull strings for the son. Detained by the duties in the islands, he was tasked with pursuing Aguinaldo's main force north of Manila, which was far better organized than the loose bands of rebels that Lawton faced. A veteran of the Civil War who gained the rank of colonel at the tender age 19 and who distinguished himself early in battle at Missionary Ridge, he took no chances in his pursuit of Aguinaldo unlike the swashbuckling Lawton. MacArthur's Second Division consisted of a motley collection of volunteer State regiments such as the 1st California, 13th Minnesota, 1st Iowa, 1st Nebraska and 20th Kansas – reinforced by regular army troops of the First Infantry Brigade. As they marched towards Malolos, the invading army of 10,000 men presented an awesome sight to the locals as they advanced under their State banners, backed up by machines in the form of wheeled artillery pulled by teams of horses. Never before had the Philippine countryside witnessed such a fearsome spectacle that recalled the forces of the Apocalypse.

Neither man nor nature seemed capable of stopping their advance. Along dry stretches of dirt road where the column marched at a brisk pace, the passage raised a dust storm in its wake. A blown-up bridge only delayed the column momentarily as men and their wagons managed a wet crossing. Along foot trails and off road, the going was slower and more tedious especially for the artillerymen as the wheels of their heavy guns sank into deep ruts of their own making. Up to this point in the campaign, MacArthur's army met no resistance and they passed through villages and towns without a shot being fired in anger. No welcoming party greeted their arrival except for kids and a few curiosity seekers. Most of the town folks had retreated to the woods or inside their homes where they could feign innocence while the cavalcade and its retinue passed by inexorably.

They looked unstoppable only when seen en masse. Up close, however, the rigors of the forced march through unfamiliar terrain in an unforgiving climate grated into the morale of the individual foot soldiers and wore down their beasts of burden.

At the head of the 20th Kansas, Colonel Funston bore down hard on the volunteers from the Sunflower State. He rode up and down the trail astride a gray horse driving his troops relentlessly, urging them to maintain a steady pace in order to keep up with the rest of the column.

"Get on! Push that cart over the top and get on with it. Come on now, move your arses! Faster now, try to keep up with your unit."

The tractable Kansas infantrymen found the march easy-going, being lightly equipped. But the artillery company lagged behind, burdened by their heavy equipment.

"Get movin', Wolf, didn't you hear?" Bailey prodded his partner who held the reins as their mounted field gun negotiated a steep incline. "Whip them horses some more or the Colonel will be on our backs."

"If I whip them any harder they'll die on us. Can't you see what a sorry bunch of donkeys they gave us?" Wolf retorted.

"Lemme get down and push this damn cart myself."

The two Navy conscripts were trying to propel a heavy Fletcher three-inch field gun up a sloping trail. It was heavy stuff that required the pulling power of a team of four horses, never mind that the U.S. Army classified the weapon as "light artillery." The gun, mounted on a caisson, was dragged backward by its stem, a piece of timber extending from its underside which anchored it to the ground when fired. The stem in turn was connected to a limber, a two-wheeled baggage cart carrying spare parts and charges for the cannon which were stowed in a box on top of which Bailey and Wolf sat. Roofless, austerely functional, and heavy, the tandem of wagons was pulled by a team of horses which strained against their harness while being repeatedly lashed by Wolf. The effort, however, was proving too much for the animals which had barely recovered from their ocean crossing. Time and again, Bailey had to alight from his seat to pry loose a rock from underneath the wheels or to restrain the wagon when it threatened to drag the horses back downhill of its own weight. Bailey was tempted to tell his giant partner to get off the wagon if not to assist him then to lighten the burden on the horses by walking on his two sturdy feet. But he dared not to provoke his friend who was still sore at him for getting him into this mess in the first place.

The two Navy hands had never marched in battle gear before, much less fought a land war with the Army. The hardships of a sailor's life at sea paled in comparison with the adversity that was the foot soldier's daily fare in a land campaign, or so it seemed. And they hadn't even engaged the enemy yet! There were no forced marches for sailors, no heavy lifting, no slogging through mud and rivers, no digging, no equipment getting stuck and, most scary of all, no leeches sucking you dry. The tribulations Bailey and Wolf were experiencing in all of one day began to strain their friendship to the breaking point.

"You got me into this, Bart, you sonofabitch. It's all your fault. What made you think life would be better among the goddams?" Wolf nagged at his friend.

Bailey suffered his friend's tirades in silence as the going got tougher. He couldn't help feeling guilty for volunteering Wolf into the Army with blinkered eyes. To assuage his conscience, Bailey volunteered to do the heavy lifting, such as manhandling the wagons when the strain became too much for the horses. By and by, Wolf began helping out without being told. He took his turn getting off and pushing the wagon when Bailey started to falter with his failing strength. Perhaps Bailey's uncomplaining attitude moved him to sympathy. More likely, Wolf was getting impatient at the seemingly endless journey and wanted to hurry things up a bit. For every hundred yards they covered, a hundred miles of the same godforsaken terrain stretched before them. It was as if they were chasing the horizon onboard a ship. The dirt track went on and on and on, losing itself in the woods, behind a bend, down or up a slope, but never coming to an end. Amidst it all, they kept hearing Funston barking orders.

"Move on, we have no time to waste, press on."

"He keeps hollering: 'Get on!' as if we never tire out," Wolf complained. "Doesn't the man realize we've been marching all day?"

Funston hovered as an abiding plague on everybody in the regiment.

Bailey tolerated Funston's relentless prodding as well as Wolf's constant griping. Being a veteran of the infernal Black Room of several U.S. Navy warships, Bailey was inure to hardships, even moreso than Wolf who spent his entire naval career above deck. Bailey never so much as uttered a word of complaint, although he was suffering like the Dickens, too. This was because he had one advantage over the others. The source of his inexhaustible stamina was the thought that at the end of the rainbow stood his lovely Estrella with a pot of hot kisses. The farther the Army advanced into the countryside, the closer he thought he got to his sweet señorita who could only be somewhere in her hometown of Malolos which happened to be their objective. Wolf had no such inspiration to keep him going.

"Jest think you're doing this for our country. We're conquering more Indian territory in the Far East for the glory of our country and for our sons and daughters to settle and farm." Bailey was now speaking Wolf's language, driven by the desire to shore up the latter's morale.

Wolf would have nothing of it. "I don't intend to die this way for no reason. And I don't want to die on account of your squaw neither."

Bailey was stunned by Wolf's snide remark about Estrella. Never once did he talk of his beloved girl.

"Wolfgang, leave her out of this. She's got nothing to do with this," he rebuked his friend mildly.

By mid-afternoon, the advancing column was within a day's march of their objective. They were expected to reach

Malolos just before sundown. Thus far, the Americans suffered no casualties save for some cases of sunstroke. The only American blood drawn by the locals were those inflicted by mosquitoes, gnats, mites and other blood-sucking pests – which the two transplanted sailors never had to contend with in the high seas. Breeding in the humid woods where stagnant water pooled in perpetual puddles on the ground and above in the cisterns formed by the foliage of ubiquitous bromeliads and other flora, the mosquitoes took to the air in the late afternoon swarming over the Yankee hordes. Bailey and Wolf were likewise unaccustomed to other terrestrial hazards that plagued landlubbers: the itchy nettles and spores of grass, the miasma of wet lands and decaying plants, the dust that congested their throats and nostrils, and the scorching sun out in the open. Luckily, the duo didn't encounter the one abomination Wolf had repeatedly warned Bailey about, leeches. To Wolf, they were "slimy li'l creatures that lurk about in the swamps and stick to your skin and suck your blood till you're dry." Well, the entire marching army gave the swamps a wide berth. The artillery unit avoided soggy ground lest their heavy guns get bogged down. The infantry also wore leggings wrapped around their ankles and shins. The Yankees would encounter their fair share of leeches a little later, when the fighting took them to the boondocks. There, plenty other pests besides leeches thrived in the brush, such as the tiny worm-like specimen which tip-toed head-to-tail like thumb and forefinger through the branches and leaves of shrubs and the lower canopy of the jungle, lying in wait for the unsuspecting passersby to brush past their perches, sometimes latching underneath the eyelid of their human prey. For now, in the early stages of their campaign, the route they followed to Malolos took them mostly through farm land and open country.

It was late in the afternoon of March 30th when MacArthur's column reached the outskirts of Malolos. Lacking the appetite to fight the insurgents in house-to-house combat in the dark and at the tail end of a long march, MacArthur decided to defer the infantry assault until the morning after, ordering instead an artillery barrage to soften up enemy positions. Unbeknownst to the Americans, Malolos was ripe for the taking for it was virtually undefended. Aguinaldo had decided to evacuate the town which he deemed indefensible against attack by a determined enemy whose counteroffensive came sooner than he had expected. Apart from its symbolic value as the capital of his moveable republic, Malolos had no intrinsic military significance. Only a token force of brave volunteers was left behind to fight a rearguard action that would buy Aguinaldo and his cabinet more time to get out of harm's way.

It was too tempting a target, however, for the artillery to ignore. Given his orders, Bailey positioned his artillery team in a clearing in the woods far enough from the intended target to give his shells an ideal trajectory. His Fletcher 3-mm. gun could have been taken straight off the turret of the *Olympia*. It had a grooved bore that sent projectiles spinning in the air and a so-called sliding-wedge breechblock, a loading mechanism that allowed for rapid-firing. The bombardment had no other purpose than to overawe the defenders, or the few that remained, for their effect on their light defenses was like that of a shotgun hitting a leaf. The breastworks of branches and soil were reduced to smithereens. Stray rounds fell on the grounds of the Barasoain church where Aguinaldo last had his headquarters, shearing off its steeple and burning parts of the timber on its roof.

About 500 yards in advance, the foot soldiers took potshots at anything that moved. They were arrayed in a set-piece formation of two parallel lines, the front line consisting of a row of soldiers leaning down on one knee to shoot with their Krag rifles, and the rear line composed of soldiers standing up to take a similar aim. They unleashed concerted blasts of fire in staccato intervals at the woods 100 yards away, picking off straw hats and moving figures shielded by branches and stones. Their indiscriminate firing sent civilians fleeing with their animals. By sundown, Malolos had become a ghost town, visited only by creeping smoke and the smell of burning flesh.

The Army waited until the following day to enter the town. Early at sunrise, the 20th Kansas was roused by a bugle sounding the reveille. They immediately broke camp and assembled in formation to receive their marching orders from Colonel Funston. Bailey's company entered the deserted town near the tail end of what was more or less a triumphal parade. He saw where their rounds had found their mark. Bomb craters pock-marked the main road which led into town clustering closely around the flattened breastworks that the defenders had built at the entrance of the town. Clumps of dirt strewn with sharpened bamboo stakes were all that remained of the rebel's defense line, some of which were used to patch up the craters on the road by the Army engineers who had preceded them. Bailey also saw that their shells didn't discriminate between rebel and civilian targets. Inside the town proper, they passed several bombed-out houses as well as the dead bodies of civilians lying in various Pompeiian poses where they fell. At one point, he asked Wolf to slow down when he espied a well-dressed lady sprawled dead in front of a burned out building that was still smoldering. It wasn't Estrella, thank God, but the thought haunted him. Could any of his stray shells hit his beloved gal?

Pretty soon, he couldn't help calling out to the empty houses lining the road. "Estrella? Estrella? Are you there?"

"There's not a soul around. They all lit out," observed Wolf, picking through the debris.

"Get on! Straight to the town square!" a familiar voice echoed over the sound of wheels and hooves.

"Estrella? Yahoo! Anybody knows Estrella?"

The grim procession trickled into the town plaza where they made their bivouac. Following Spanish colonial tradition, it was a square flanked by church buildings, the *municipio* or town hall and the grand houses of the town's notables. Many of the acacia trees that lined the plaza had their limbs torn asunder by the bombardment. The Barasoain church where the congress of the embattled Philippine Republic had once held its sessions was still smoldering. Swathes of the church's timber structure caught fire blackening its ribbed dome. The bell tower which stood apart from the church building like a light house was also damaged. Only the parish priest's convent escaped unscathed, which MacArthur promptly appropriated for his headquarters.

"So, this is Malolos," Bailey sighed to his partner as they surveyed the random destruction. "Estrelle's hometown."

"How did you know?" Wolf asked.

"Little da'ling used to tell me. She says when she was little, she used to run around this park with her friends. Hmmm, I could almost smell her around."

"Well, she didn't come running to welcome you with open arms," Wolf said with sarcasm.

The occupied town slowly stirred back to life later in the day as the few remaining residents stuck out their heads to test the atmosphere in town. Windows were opened and doors unlocked. They were encouraged by the fact that they had not been rounded up and no looting was committed by the invading army although many houses stood abandoned. A few curious souls ventured outdoors to take a closer look at the Yankees. Those of them who strayed farther to the town plaza witnessed the Philippine tricolor being hauled down the flag pole to give way to the Stars and Stripes. None of them was Bailey's missing princess.

————————

General Arthur MacArthur set up command in Aguinaldo's former headquarters where he found time to relax from his grueling campaign. He allowed his commanders to furlough their men within the confines of the town. With few civilians in town to fraternize with, the troops whiled away their free time playing ball games among themselves in the town plaza. MacArthur spent idle hours in the balcony of the convent watching the ball games or talking politics with his colonels. In his private moments, he wrote letters to his 19-year old son, Douglas, whose picture was prominently displayed on his writing table.

"Douglas was accepted into West Point," he told Colonel Funston proudly during an evening spent over drinks at the balcony of the convent. "His mother is so determined to see her son become an Army officer that she's moved into town to stay close to him... And with Pinky around, it's guaranteed he'll make it."

"Well, one thing running against him is his name."

"Oh, ho-ho. Douglas is equally determined to make it on his own. I know he will make us proud. He is close to his mom, but he is driven and he is ambitious, and he will one day become an Army officer."

"That guy Aguinaldo slipped away again. I wonder how we can nail him," Colonel Funston changed the subject matter.

"He can run away only so far. We'll keep on giving chase until he has his back to the sea. It's only a matter of time before we catch up with him."

"Once he's in the bag, what are you gonna do with him?"

"Following the Spaniards' example, he deserves the firing squad. But I personally want him taken alive and exiled, maybe to some island in the Marianas. I don't particularly care one way or the other. It's up to the politicians to decide."

"They're a determined lot. We can probably weaken their resistance if we promise them some kind of autonomy," said Funston.

"Only after we have instilled fear in their hearts. That's the way the British do it," insisted the general who was not versed in the subtleties of politics.

The two top officers of the corps looked out of the balcony to see campfires burning among the tents, soldiers huddling under the stars, and the horses neighing in the woods bothered by bats and swarms of harmless fireflies. "It's a long and hard campaign half a world away from home. And here we are pushing the American frontier into the Far East. I couldn't help comparing ourselves to the Roman legions carving an empire out of the most hostile parts of the world. It is our Manifest Destiny to rule the Pacific," MacArthur grandiosely mused.

"Still, it's a long way from home." Funston shared the man's melancholy.

"I miss my wife and especially Douglas, but this is the life I asked for. This is *my* destiny."

"How old is he, your son?"

"Nineteen and a handsome lad he."

Funston wondered whether the general's son, being the Mama's boy that he was, would ever amount to anything.

————————

19

CALOY'S SWEET REVENGE

The following day again started with an artillery barrage. The Eighth Corps seemed again stuck in the miasma of inactivity. Scouts from the 1st Nebraska Regiment spotted concentrations of rebels gathering two miles away, apparently trying to draw the Yankees out of the town so that civilians could reclaim their homes. Instead of going on hot pursuit, MacArthur ordered a barrage that lasted almost an hour – which Dewey's veteran gunners, Bailey and Wolf, carried out with glee to break the ennui that was gnawing at them in the camp. The rest of the troops sat around their tents to watch smoke rising over the verdant skyline, interrupted in the middle of their morning exercises. The barrage had the effect the Americans desired: civilians trickled out of the woods like termites, stunned into thinking that they were safer in their homes than out in the field. They retook their homes without further hesitation and soon learned to tolerate the presence of the conquistador.

Bailey recognized someone staggering out of the woods, a muscular man shaken out of his hiding place by the bombing, looking a bit woozy and sick: Carlos Calderon. He was struggling to stay on his feet by seizing one post of a fence after another, his eyes glazed over by the look of pure terror, his pants caked with mud. Bailey rushed down the road to meet the guy. It was the next best thing to finding Estrella, coming across the man who might know her whereabouts. He supported Carlos by slinging one arm around his shoulder and guided him toward the soldiers' lodgings among a clump of huts in a coconut grove that served as makeshift barracks.

"Carlos, do you recognize me?" Bailey shook the man. "It's me Bart, Bart Bailey."

Carlos collapsed on the floor of the hut, apparently stricken with a new kind of sickness called shell-shock, a condition that was akin to nervous breakdown suffered under intense shelling and gunfire. A lot of other inhabitants, mostly women and the aged, were also afflicted by the same malady, aggravated by the fear of the power of the apocalyptic weapons in the American arsenal.

Doused by a pail of water, Carlos woke up but he was still incoherent. He looked up at the face of Bailey, shaded by his floppy cap. "Maria, Maria," he called his wife.

"It's me, Bart. Estrelle, where's she?"

Even after he regained full consciousness Carlos became sulky, as if he were nursing an old grudge against Bailey. He refused to talk. He did not want to have anything to do with the Yankees. As soon as he regained his bearings, he left the hut without asking permission and returned to his house, a middle-class cottage of lumber and thatch, located at the periphery of the town.

For two days, he confined himself to his nearby farm, seeing to it that his wife and four children were fed. Filipino messengers of the new town council repeatedly asked him to report to the American commander at the Barasoain camp, but he curtly told them to mind their own affairs.

Finally, Bailey himself came to see him. The U.S. Army needed information from its former bolo-maker who everybody knew had close connections with the Aguinaldo government. Carlos played hard to get. Having done service to the U.S. Army, he exhibited an air of familiarity with its soldiers which would have been regarded as impudence had it come from someone else. He had debts to collect. He dunned the Yankees for the $500 they owed him.

Invited to a meeting with General MacArthur, Carlos answered brusquely: "Ask him to pay me first."

"Carlos, it's Gadawful MacArthur hisself," Bailey snapped. "You can't say no to him. That's an order."

"I'm no Gringo soldier."

"Bring it up with him at your meeting. Carlos, don't give me a hard time," Bailey pleaded.

"I will finish my harvest. When I'm done I'll come over to see him."

"You could get arrested for that kind of attitude."

"You want to arrest me? Go ahead. For the crime of refusing to see your commander? All the people here will think you're no different from the Spaniards."

"We're inviting you because we consider you a friend of the Americans. That is an honor. It is an honor to be asked to see General MacArthur."

"Señor Barton, I am a friend of the *yanqui*, no question about it, but you people don't know how to honor an obligation. Friendship is not a one-way street. You still have to pay me 500 pesetas for the bolos I delivered to you at Intramuros."

"Well, I don't know anything about that."

"Now, you know."

Bailey changed the subject and asked about something closer to his heart. "Estrelle?"

The question again sent Carlos's dander up. "Don't ask me about her."

"I have to know, I have been looking for her."

"It might be good for your health if you never saw her again."

"I-I don't understand!"

"You, *yanqui*" – Carlos pointed a hostile finger at him – "you owe my family a blood debt."

"What the hell are you talking ab-"

322

"You took liberties with my niece. You defiled the girl's honor..."

Bailey was stunned.

"... She's pregnant. And my brother will kill you with his bare hands."

Bailey was speechless. From the pit of his stomach surged a rush of emotion that he struggled to suppress for decency's sake. So, this was the reason why the man was angry with him. He hurriedly left the man's house as if to retch, bursting with pent-up emotion; then, when he was safely out of earshot in the confines of his barracks, he let go a bellyful of laughter.

Wolf heard his laughter from the open field where he was playing basketball with the Kansans. "Gatling's gone over the deep end," he observed from a distance. "Lord have mercy on him."

Bailey rushed out of his barracks to the field, jumping every few yards. "I'm a father, I'm *a* father now," he yodeled aloud.

———————

Carlos got his revenge against the Americans. Asked for information about the deployment of the insurgent forces, he pretended to cooperate. He reported that Aguinaldo's troops had scattered into the surrounding jungle in small groups, and their new orders were to engage the Americans in sporadic, pitched battles, then melt away into the woods. The tactic was called guerrilla warfare.

Carlos stood to earn a fortune from this change of tactics because the only way the Americans could penetrate the jungle was to hack their way through it using bolos. And bolos, he had hundreds to sell.

Bailey was tasked by the Army brass to take delivery of 1,000 bolos from the Filipino artisan and in turn hand over the payment – $ 200 greenbacks which a paymaster had to deliver all the way from Manila.

From the very start, Bailey had serious misgivings about his mission because he didn't really trust Carlos. "I have the uneasy feeling the guy is out to con us. He rubs me the wrong way. He just can't be trusted," he said as he rode toward the rendezvous with the artisan, accompanied by Wolf and two Kansans.

"I thought you were friends with him."

"It's Whacky Doc I'm friends with. He couldn't be more different."

By prior arrangement, they met at Caloy's farm house outside Malolos located in the middle of a coconut plantation. The craftsman greeted them with a broad smile, half-naked, oozing with hospitality, as if by some miraculous technique he had mass-produced 1,000 bolos on short notice and under the noses of his wary neighbors. He led the party into a barn behind his house where he showed them five boxes stacked on a bed of rice hay. With a crowbar, he pried open one wooden box, dug into the layer of hay and uncovered a bundle of glinting bolos – all finely crafted, complete with carabao-horn handles. With a dramatic sweep – "Tararang!" – he showed the contents to the Americans who were blown away by the quality of the blades. Then, he opened the second box and revealed an even finer collection, kris and sabers, which appeared to have been made by the best craftsmen of the south. "Here's some more, Moro style, for the Army officers."

Bailey was beside himself. "This is what the general wants! Oh, Carlos, you're a beaut." With absentminded alacrity, he handed Carlos an envelope full of money so that he could dig his hands into the cache of blades.

"I'll show you some more." Carlos disappeared into the main house.

Given two sabers, Bailey and Wolf playfully fenced with each other inside the house where they created a racket of clashing blades that ended only when they noticed Carlos's prolonged absence. They and their Kansan companions scoured the house and its surroundings but found not a shadow of the Filipino artisan. Overtaken by suspicion, the two old buddies retraced their steps to the barn and opened the other boxes and found nothing but hay, almost prompting the two men to turn their swords on each other.

"Dammit, Wolf, we've been taken in! The sonofabitch."

"That's what you get from being too friendly with them Injuns," shouted the German.

"He's gone! He galloped away on his horse," yelled a Kansan companion outside.

"What will come of us?"

"It's either the firing squad or life in the slammer. Take your pick," Wolf groused.

Bailey was court-martialed for mishandling the bolo affair, a story which went the rounds of the Malolos community and gave the people reason for merriment. Instead of being sent to the slammer, however, Bailey was sentenced to reimburse the Army the $200 that had been swindled by Carlos out of his own humble soldier's salary. He was far too valuable an artilleryman to lose. Bailey took the punishment like a man: he was not fighting this war for money alone, but in pursuit of far more sublime ideals: love and glory.

The capture of Malolos capital afforded the Americans a week-long respite from the war, during which they built up their logistics in a remote base 25 miles north of Manila. They hoarded supplies of food and ammunition while the troops cooled their heels, as it were. During this period of rest and recreation, Wolf Messner bonded closer to the Kansans at the expense of his ties with Bailey. Strains had already begun to develop between them as a result of the latter's friendship with the Calderons and mad pursuit of Estrella. Their ties of comradeship dating back to the Navy days slowly frayed as they adapted in contrasting ways to conditions inland.

One activity which drew Wolf closer to the Kansans – and away from Bailey – was a rough-and-tumble game variously called "Naismith's game" or "wrastling" or "basketball." Just to annoy Bailey who didn't like the boisterous sport, Wolf would egg him and challenge him into catching a leather ball. "Let's go play Naismith's game, Gatling. Let's wrastle."

Invented in 1891 by someone named James Naismith, the game was introduced to the American troops in the Philippines as a way of conquering their loneliness away from home. It was much easier to propagate than democracy and it instantly became a hit among the natives. The game was played on the grounds of the burnt-out Barasoain church, where two goals consisting of rattan baskets were set up – one hung on the trunk of an acacia tree, and another on the wall of a bell tower twenty feet away. Both goals were ten feet high. Constant shooting with coconuts had already burst the bottom of both baskets, which suited the game just fine.

"Come on, kid, stop brooding and play basketball," Wolf pestered Bailey. "That will turn your thoughts around."

It was the Kansans who took up the challenge. "Come out to the open field, Wolf! Let's go!"

"All right, come on, Gatling, join us."

"He's heartsick, let him be," said the Kansans who had been observing the morose Bailey.

A Kansan sergeant caught the leather ball and passed it around six other soldiers eager to join the fun. "We'll have six in our team and you'll have five since you're tall," said the sergeant.

"You can have as many as you want," shouted back Wolf. "Just pass that ball around."

With an audience of natives looking over the fence, the two teams, six against five members, played in the open field. An idle cook tossed the ball over the heads of the contending groups at the opening jump without knowing the nature of the sport. Both teams promptly scrambled for the ball, shoving and wrestling. When the dust settled, the cook found himself being shoved to the edge of the field to give way to a knot of Kansans scuffling for possession of the ball. One man managed to run away with the ball, with five others fast on his heels and tugging at his shirt. He tossed it into the basket secured to the side of the bell tower – one point scored – and the natives cheered wildly from the fence. A second "jump-ball" ensued, with Wolf gaining possession. He scored repeatedly by dumping the ball, catching it as it fell and jamming it again into the basket. The sergeant questioned the validity of the shots that followed the first one; whereupon it was agreed that Wolf's basket would be raised one foot higher on the acacia tree to keep him from reaching it on his toes. Wolf circumvented this measure by carrying a teammate on his shoulders and letting him do the dunking. Not to be outdone, the sergeant took a wooden pole and whacked the ball out of the sky. It bounced on the roof of the church where it was lost momentarily from view, and both teams jostled for position at its possible landing spot. Tempers flared as the contending groups used increasingly foul tactics. A fistfight finally settled the winner.

Into the brawl stepped Colonel Frederick Funston. He ordered all players confined to quarters. He also banned the sport which was almost as rough as some of their battles in order to avoid unnecessary casualties.

Bailey didn't like the sport at all. Though no less rambunctious than the Kansans as a sailor bearing the scars of a number of bare-knuckled fights, he realized that he was not cut out for the game, being of short stature.

The Filipino spectators, however, thoroughly enjoyed the game. They learned to play the game and took to it like squirrels with a marble. Long after the Americans had left, they would play it as their national sport, more popular than cockfighting – one of the lasting legacies of colonialism.

The inertia of the Army in Malolos began to get into the nerves of Bailey. The weariness of inactivity gave way to the itch of impatience. He couldn't understand what was holding up MacArthur so long in the former headquarters of Aguinaldo. The longer the delay in resuming the campaign the longer it would take him to find Estrella. Drained of spirits and bereft of appetite, he fell ill. He lay on the bamboo floor of his hut with a running fever. There was something more than just psychological causes to his illness, something biological: Yellow Fever or "yellow jack" in soldiers' parlance. He had contracted the virus from the bites of the swarms of mosquitoes that had harassed him relentlessly on the trail, even more dogged than the rebels. They were decidedly more vicious bloodsuckers than the leeches of Wolfgang's stories and they insidiously invaded his body through his bloodstream so that he was reduced into a shivering wreck in his blanket roll moaning and mumbling and whimpering deliriously in the night. In his illness, while his body struggled to cope with the fever and his teeth clattered like castanets, he finally got the attention he craved from his comrades-in-arms. He was not wanting in friends and comforters.

Besides the doctor who regularly visited him to deliver packets of drugs, Wolf and other Kansans took care of him. "You're gonna be all right, kid, I'll stay beside you."

"Is that you, Wolf?" Gatling said weakly. "Ain't you wrastling?"

"No, you're ill! I'm taking care of you. I'm going to stick around until you get well. Then, we'll play basketball together."

Bailey was pleased by the tone of concern in his buddy's voice. "If ever I don't make it, Wolf, in case I kick the bucket, I wish to be dropped in the sea like a sailor, promise to do that for me, Wolf."

"No, never think of that, Gatling, you'll be okay. You'll be up and about and walking soon."

"You gather my cap and my handkerchief and give them to Estrelle, if ever you meet her again, as tokens of my love. My sweet Estrelle."

"You're going to see Estrelle. You're going to marry her, and nobody's going to stop you."

"And tell my old folks back home in Virginia that I died like a soldier, that I lived up to the example of my Dad in fighting the Indians."

Another person who helped restore Bailey's health was Funston. One afternoon, the colonel climbed the bamboo stairs to check on the condition of the soldier confined in the hut. He hovered for a moment over the sick man and brushed his stubbles pensively. "Poor fella. This yellow jack could really knock you down. And I won't be able to look Admiral Dewey in the eye if one of the heroes of Manila Bay died in my hands. I think this sailor ought to be returned to his ship when the next caravan arrives."

Returned to his ship, that was the last thing Bailey wanted. That would end all hopes of his seeing Estrella again. No, he could not be bundled back to his ship. Accordingly, Bailey battled Yellow Fever with all his might and worked his way back to health. He devoured bunches of fresh tropical fruits and ordered exotic medication from the natives. He allowed a local medicine man to wrap his head with balmy bandages of leaves. Even if his head spun like a ship with a broken rudder, he lifted himself by the bootstraps, so to speak, and tried walking around. His single-minded resolve enabled him to rally his body and win its internal war against yellow jack. His fever subsided and his mind cleared. To compensate for his loss of weight, he wolfed down bowls of rice and meat as his appetite returned with a vengeance. He ate native concoctions of vegetables, frogs and mushrooms, prepared by Carlos's wife. He survived all right, just like hundreds of American soldiers in the Eighth Corps afflicted with tropical diseases, which accounted for most of the casualties of war.

"That's right, eat like you've been shipwrecked and never seen land for months," encouraged Wolf. "That's the only way you can be healthy again."

"Have had enough of *camote* leaves, *kangkong* and *ampalaya*," Bailey complained of the staple diet of vegetables being served by the native cooks.

"We've killed all the chickens and pigs we could find hereabouts. How about field rats or iguanas? The natives seem to eat anything that moves."

"Rats? You mean you been feeding me rats!"

"No, that's the rats that live on the rice paddies and eats on rice. No, buddy, no way I'm feeding you that."

Bailey nearly threw up on his plate made of strips of bamboo overlaid by banana leaves. "You been feeding me rubbage. Why, has the Army run out of provisions?"

"We have come so far that it takes weeks for provisions to arrive from Manila. In the meantime, we have to live off the land."

Ironically, as soon as he recovered his health and became his old self again, it was Wolf who made a slow descent into gloom. The German had seen how tropical conditions could break even a seasoned sailor, and it was only a matter of time before he, too, went down with the same yellow fever as his partner and he did not think he had the appetite for the herbal cures that the natives had concocted for Bailey.

In the end it was the imminence of battle and military necessity that returned them to their old fighting mood. General MacArthur could not afford to idle any of his artillerymen at this critical stage in the campaign when victory was at hand. Neither could Funston. When Bailey managed to walk out of the hut like a wraith and renew his contact with the troops, he was pronounced combat-worthy. In fact, he was given a crucial assignment in the campaign for which he was uniquely qualified: being one of the few Americans who knew a smattering of Tagalog, he was tasked to lead a patrol of scouts to reconnoiter the surrounding areas in search of the main body of Aguinaldo's army. It was a temporary assignment that liberated him from the stultifying atmosphere in the camp.

Bailey had little trouble riding a horse even while recuperating from his bout with yellow jack. As a child, he was trained to ride a pony by his Daddy, a veteran Cavalryman of the Indian Wars, and later on, a horse in the farm. His trek to Malolos on the road with a team of horses pulling a three-inch cannon offered him opportunities to go horseback riding. The reconnaissance mission strengthened him further and restored his reflexes. On the third week of April 1899, accompanied by two other scouts, he ranged the hinterlands of Malolos and nearby barrios for signs of Aguinaldo's elusive army. He followed trails and skirted brooks. He talked with the natives in pidgin Tagalog, complemented by sign language, and, surprisingly, he was able to wangle some information from a few Filipinos. They were ready to please the Americans out of plain hospitality, not necessarily out of disloyalty to the revolutionary cause. They told him the day and the time Antonio Luna passed with the main body of rebel troops and tipped him off about some unusual activities going on across the bank of the Rio Grande, at the town of Calumpit, five miles north of Malolos.

He soon found out that the Filipino army was digging in for a major battle.

———————

20

A STORM ACROSS THE RIO GRANDE

General Luna, field commander of the republican army, had not been idle all this time. Working with termite-like industry, he was building defenses along the northern bank of the Rio Grande, where he planned to make a last stand against the U.S. Army. He had tested the mettle of the enemy and found it well nigh invincible; and he was determined to inflict upon it such telling blow, short of destruction, as to make the cost of carrying on the war unacceptable. It was to be a make-or-break engagement that would determine the fate of the independence movement.

Luna's outgunned army fought a running battle with MacArthur's Second Division, withdrawing just a step ahead. He was determined to delay the American advance in order to give El Jefe enough time to evacuate Malolos. Accordingly, he blew up bridges, tore up rail tracks, felled timber for barricades along the way. He fought skirmishes with the advancing troops while the fugitive republic gathered its archives and treasury for an escape to the safety of the mountains.

As fast as the Americans advanced, the rebels retreated and conceded town after town to the former. In a single day alone, March 26, 1899, MacArthur took the towns of Malinta,

Polo, Meycauayan. Three days later, they overran Bocaue, Bigaa and Guiguinto.

While Luna vainly raised obstacles to check the American offensive, Aguinaldo set up a new capital in the town of Cabanatuan, a good 45 miles away from Malolos. He removed himself from military affairs for a while, engrossed in the political as well as propaganda war with the Schurman Commission. He had his hands full waging a war for the hearts and minds of his people.

In the meantime, across the Rio Grande in the town of Calumpit, General Luna dug a twin line of trenches manned by 4,000 troops. He fortified their entire length with earthen breastworks and wooden barricades interspersed with bamboo stakes so as to form a dike 100 meters long on both sides of the main road. The banks of the Rio Grande were 20 feet high, spanned by the remains of a blown-up railway bridge, and the erection of the barriers made the river virtually impassable, a valley of death to an attacking army. At strategic places overlooking the railway bridge, he roofed the trenches with logs and a topping of soil to make two bomb-proof bunkers and beneath the roof, he left gaps in the ramparts wide enough to serve as gun ports. In each bunker he installed a Maxim machinegun, a water-cooled meat grinder more advanced than the Gatling without the hand-driven crank for feeding bullets. Instead, it had an automatic loading mechanism powered by its own recoil so that the explosion of one bullet jolted the next one into the firing chamber. They were the most dangerous weapons in the rebel arsenal, smuggled out of Fort Santiago by departing Spanish soldiers and sold to Aguinaldo at a bargain. Hidden deep in the forest was a battery of smooth-bore Spanish cannons from the galleon era, no more dangerous than Roman catapults.

To deny MacArthur the use of the railway bridge, Luna had the same blown up and the parts collected one girder and one tie at a time. He used the parts to fortify the segments of the trenches close to the road, erecting iron barricades which made the defenses nearly strong enough to withstand artillery bombardment. In the observation of Le Roy in his 1914 history, the Filipino commander had demolished the structure by means of dynamite, followed by well-aimed blasts from a cannon "leaving only the upper girders, seven feet apart, to cross on." Behind such elaborate defenses, Luna's ragtag force, consisting of 4,000 riflemen and bolomen, hunkered down to await the Armageddon, still unbowed despite a series of defeats.

Bailey took note of everything he could see from behind the cover of trees. He was careful not to make a rustle that might betray his position, not wanting to risk capture that might result in his being delivered to the tender mercies of Dr. Joaquin Calderon in chains. He preferred to meet him, and Estrella, for that matter, as part of a conquering army, exuding an aura of authority that would compel submission. He pulled out a pen and sketched the layout of Luna's defenses on the margins of his map, committing the rest of the details to memory. Unquestionably, this was a formidable defense the enemy had cobbled together out of spare materials, stronger than even his fortifications in Caloocan. With his pair of binoculars, he thought he had seen the barrel of a machinegun jutting from a slit in one bunker. Obviously, the three-week respite since the battle for Malolos had given Luna time to regroup and dig in behind new defensive lines.

How did Bailey expect to survive an attack on such a fortified position? In all likelihood, he would be forced to cross the river in the teeth of enemy gunfire from the array of rifles, cannons and, most probably, a machinegun. Funston had such a grip on his men that they would follow his orders unquestioningly for he himself was ready to throw himself into the thick of the fight, not being the kind of leader who fought battles by pushing pawns on a map. If anyone crossing the river ever managed to run the gauntlet, one hack from a bolo of the insurgent would finish him off at the next barrier. For the first time, Bailey began to wonder whether the risks of being killed far outweighed the rewards of seeing his sweet señorita. The best outcome he could imagine was that he would survive the battle with mortal injuries and then die in the arms of Estrella.

His horse snorted as ants climbed up and gnawed at its legs. It began kicking around and lashing against its reins, thus compromising the secrecy of his mission. Its neighing drew the attention of insurgents tending a fire outside the bunkers and they turned their eyes across the river and sniped at the woods with wild abandon. Bailey scampered away as leaves sprayed all around him, impressed by the enemy defenses.

In the last week of April, MacArthur renewed his northern drive against the insurgents and set out with a force of 6,000 men, leaving behind in Malolos a reserve of 4,000. The different volunteer regiments composing his Second Division of the Eighth Corps waved the banners of such states as Montana, Nebraska, Minnesota and, of course, Kansas. Uniting all the state banners was Old Glory which flew prominently at the head of the Kansas vanguard, its stars and stripes now worn and faded. The event that had convinced MacArthur that the time was ripe to prod his division out of its lassitude was the ignominious crime committed by Carlos Calderon, a Filipino of fickle allegiance, against the U.S. Army, an audacious swindle that made his army the laughingstock of the town. Another such incident would undermine American authority in captured territories.

The new objective of the campaign was the capture of the town of Cabanatuan, 45 miles northeast of Malolos, where Aguinaldo had evacuated his headquarters. The American general was determined to shove Aguinaldo out of the inhabited regions of Luzon and into the sea where he could do no harm. He calculated that once Aguinaldo's army was shattered in conventional war and broken into bands, the American colonial government could live with an indefinite guerrilla war in the countryside, which could be contained by continuing police operations. It was in keeping with this theory that MacArthur set out to do battle with Luna's force, the only organized

Filipino army capable of waging a conventional war. Subdue Luna and the insurgency becomes a police problem, he reasoned. Hardly had he gone five miles from Malolos when he ran smack into Luna's army, entrenched across the Rio Grande. The sheer size of the defending army, deduced from the breadth of the fortifications on the bank, pleased him as much as it terrified his troops. This was the decisive battle that he had been waiting for.

At the southern bank of the Rio Grande, MacArthur scanned the enemy position with Montojo's brass binoculars, and he found nothing insurmountable. Luna's position stood exactly as the patrols had described it – the blown up bridge, the bunkers of earth, the reinforced trenches, the breastworks. There was no obstacle that his hard-bitten troops could not breach with the right application of force. With an eye toward immediate engagement, he deployed his troops along the southern bank of the Rio Grande in a line directly facing the enemy fortifications. The exact location of his troops was largely hidden from enemy eyes by the cover of trees that bordered on the river, but their offensive preparations were unmistakable.

Just as MacArthur was about to initiate hostilities, a courier arrived from Manila with a message from the Schurman Commission. The messenger alit from his horse a little out of breath and found the general in his tent pleasantly reading letters from his son whose picture hung from a post. "Oh, must be from Douglas," he sang his constant refrain, then faced the fidgety messenger. He signed the envelope over his name, removed the folded letter inside, then returned the envelope to the messenger as proof of receipt, all in accordance with military procedure practiced since the Civil War. The message from Intramuros soured his otherwise sunny mood: it was from General Otis and he was being ordered to report to Manila to brief the departing Schurman Commission on the status of the war, which meant at least a week's delay in the start of the hostilities. This unwarranted interference by politicians in military affairs annoyed him no end. "I thought Otis was doing a fine job entertaining Mr. Schurman," he remarked dryly of his superior, who wore two hats as commander of the Eighth Corps and governor-general.

Otis needed MacArthur to pour cold water on Schurman's mission. "Mr. Schurman is about to leave for the United States. And he wants to be able to explain the situation to the President in Washington. Are we near to securing the colony to warrant the sending of civilians to man the offices left idle by the Spaniards? Hell, there is not even one teacher in this country. The customs, the post office, the railways, we need civilians to get them running."

MacArthur took the cue. "What we need are more soldiers, not civilians." He then explained that his campaign had proved more difficult than originally planned, that he had not even come close to engaging and destroying the insurgent army, and that Aguinaldo had widespread support in the islands. "We can have civilians running the affairs here once I have Aguinaldo in a cage. Until then, uniformed men will be running the show."

Otis turned to Schurman with an almost disdainful look. Well? That's what I told you, he seemed to say.

The two generals, who had been feuding about war tactics, stood shoulder to shoulder when it came to their opposition to a civilian administration in the colony, especially one with Filipino participation.

Jacob Schurman then said something that illustrated the gulf between the military and civilian attitudes toward the war. "We are prepared to give Aguinaldo a seat in the colonial administration, that's our idea of how to end the war."

The two generals looked at each other, aghast. They muttered something like: "That's nothing short of treason." But their words rang hollow. Chauvinism was the last refuge of the imperialist.

Schurman pressed home his point. "Why is it that when the Confederates surrendered we asked them to vote their own representatives and take back their seats in Congress?"

Otis answered: "Aguinaldo is good only for the gallows. The only good Indian is a dead Indian."

MacArthur put it more pithily: "The Confederates are our blood brothers as Sitting Bull and Crazy Horse are not."

The contrast could not be more manifest: while the civilians in the U.S. government wanted to treat the Filipinos as something closer to brothers entitled to certain inalienable rights, the military men looked at them as little better than the Indians.

The Schurman Commission returned home empty-handed, leaving Otis and MacArthur a free hand to deal with the intransigent Filipinos.

Bailey got word from the grapevine and from Funston himself that MacArthur had arrived from his one-week trip to Manila with peremptory orders to destroy the rebel forces within a month. The news came just as he had fully recovered from his illness, and it served to plunge him into action. In fact, he had sufficiently adapted himself to tropical conditions to deem himself inure to the barbarity of day-to-day life. As a sign of his vitality he dispensed with the rigidities of boot camp and shook off his uniform in favor of less formal wear consisting of wrinkled whites and a native hat to go along with the standard khaki pants and leather boots. This did not camouflage him from the enemy but it sure made him comfortable. The hard-bitten veterans of his army also adopted the same loose dressing style – which was not a sign of deteriorating morale but, on the contrary, of a resurgent army gaining in confidence.

To Bailey's trained eye, the Rio Grande did not provide an ideal terrain for battle. The immediate problem, he saw with his own eyes, was how to cross the river whose currents were so strong that he feared that horses, men and their equipment would simply flounder in the rapids. They would be smashed against the boulders and their broken remains shot at like sitting ducks by the rebels. The demolished railway bridge offered no solution because they could not simply fix it up in the teeth of enemy fire. One idea, brought up to MacArthur during a meeting with the colonels, was to float part of the Army across the river on board rafts which could easily be built from materials in the forest. It would be easier than fording the river in neck-deep waters and enable the Army quickly to establish a bridgehead on the opposite bank. Under the cover of artillery and small-arms fire, the bridgehead could be steadily expanded until enough troops were gathered for a full-scale assault on Luna's fortified position.

This proposal failed to take into account the strong current of the Rio Grande that was likely to drag the rafts downstream and slam them into pieces against the boulders. Funston plugged this hole. He would string ropes between the two banks of the river, he proposed to the colonels during a tactical planning session inside MacArthur's tent. With lines to hold during the crossing, the troops would be able to resist the current and traverse the river on their rafts. They would then avoid the danger of having the goddams drift down the river through a gauntlet of hostile fire. That was easier said than done. Who would take the suicidal job of securing the ropes at either side of the river – especially at the enemy side?

"We'll take care of that," Funston nonchalantly answered. "I'll lead my men across the river."

When Funston asked for ten volunteers from his regiment, 25 raised their hands, amongst them Barton Bailey.

"I'm a sailor. Swimming won't be any problem for me," he said.

"No, we need you with the artillery. Johnson, White, Trembly, De Generes, Clark, Lavalle...." Funston picked the ten men from among the Kansans.

"Well," shrugged Bailey.

"This operation will save a lot of lives, but it may be at the price of those who will bring about its success" were the inspiring words of the colonel. "Remember, you will be crossing the river not for yourselves but for the others because you will be, in effect, carrying the regiment on your backs. If you fail, the entire regiment fails, and that means this country will be our grave for there can be no retreat across the Ocean."

The volunteer cowhands and prairie boys of the 20th Kansas nodded attentively, grimly determined to do what was expected of them in the greatest battle since the Splendid Little War. The Rio Grande was far less challenging than the Arkansas river of their home State.

Bailey listened intently. "My heart goes out to them. It's like the eve of Manila Bay." Only that he never heard the same eloquence from Commodore Dewey or Captain Gridley.

Wolf was not inspired at all by the speech. He kept muttering to himself while they were assembling the wheeled caisson and limber used for dragging the artillery: "Stand on, lean on, hold on, go on..." Nonsensically.

"You'll be all right, Wolf. Our job is much easier than what these guys are being asked to do," Bailey tried to calm down his nerves.

"You mean to say my job ain't dangerous enough –"

"No, it's not that."

"– that it's an easy, old-maidy work?"

"No, Wolf, I mean each one of us is in for a tough fight. But it's the first ones to cross the river who'll draw the most fire, who'll bite the bullet to make way for us. It's a hell of a job and let's acknowledge it."

"I won't have any more of this."

"What do you mean you won't have any more of this or that?"

Wolf lowered over the wheel. "When the opportunity comes, I'll make a run for it."

"What in blazes do you mean by that?"

The German went on with his chore without explaining himself.

Bailey saw something quirky in his behavior. He was again down in the dumps. He was getting cynical about the war. He was different from the scholarly sailor who used to wax heroic about America's Manifest Destiny in the Pacific. His pessimism was relieved only for a short spell of time when Bailey went down with yellow jack, and he had to sing words of inspiration into the sick man's ear.

Bailey insulated himself from Wolf's cynicism by involving himself deeply in the battle preparations. Two days before the showdown, he joined the team of Kansans tasked with the job of twining rope that was crucial to their battle plan. They fashioned the rope out of the abaca hemp that grew wild in the woods, a species of banana plant that bore no fruit but grew stalks made up of tenacious fibers, commonly used by shipbuilders for holding anchors. Five long-haired Macabebe scouts taught them how to twine the rope on whose utility depended their lives. Under their guidance, Bailey cut down one such plant, peeled off the trough-shaped layers of raw hemp that made up the stalk, then combed the hemp into fibers through a strainer. He dried the tresses of fiber in the burning sun until they became tough and stringy, ready to be twisted into rope.

Bailey easily learned the skill and thoroughly enjoyed the work whose tedium irritated others, especially Wolf, and his fingers deftly wove and walked through the fibers as he twisted them into cord, managing to make half a dozen coils 25 yards long. It was a pleasant diversion for him, filled with daydreams about Estrella and their unborn child. With the lengths of rope he had twined, he built himself a raft large enough to buoy his gun and horse. Since it was flat, without a hollow hull, floating solely by reason of the buoyancy of its materials, he needed to find the lightest wood available to cobble together a vessel that could carry a cannon. Again, the longhaired Macabebe tribesmen helped him pick dry logs lying in the forest which suited his purpose just fine. He tested the raft 500 yards downstream, outside the range of enemy fire, but it broke apart in the rapids. After fixing its defects, he was finally able to fashion a sturdy raft for himself.

No sooner had he finished testing it than Funston commandeered it for himself. Rather than feel robbed, Bailey was proud to know that his raft was going to be used by the colonel in his daring mission.

In the early hours of April 26, from behind a thicket, with only the moon to light the way, Bailey and his comrades saw off the eleven Kansan volunteers on their way to put into play the colonel's plan for a stealthy river crossing. They crept toward the southern bank of the Rio Grande with coils of rope slung on their shoulders. They skulked behind bushes and boulders lining the bank of the river. Their bent silhouettes resembled boars looking for an ideal place to drink. Fifty yards upstream where the water ran deep, two Kansan privates named White and Trembly stripped themselves of all gear, except the coils of rope that they carried on their shoulders, and waded into the water until only their heads bobbed on the surface. They swam the rest of the way, paddling and grasping at rocks to resist the currents and at a designated part of the river threw one end of the rope over an overhanging branch of a tree and tied it securely in place. Another Kansan standing on the bank plucked the other end of the rope and lashed it around a boulder. They strung another length of rope in the same manner. With the two lines stretched across the river, Funston launched two rafts at a time, three men to each raft who then dragged themselves across by pulling at the overhanging lengths of rope to keep themselves from being swept away by the current. Some used bamboo poles to poke at the riverbed to steady the craft and steer them to the opposite bank. All the while, they ducked and dodged the hail of bullets raining all around them, unable to fire back with their hands full and their rifles slung behind their backs. They scrambled to the opposite bank and established a bridgehead in the shelter of a fallen tree, within range of machinegun fire.

As the rafts ferried more troops, Funston's intrepid squad made the subsequent crossing safer by clearing a portion of the trenches overlooking the twin lines of rope. They shot their way into the trenches with their Krags and, once inside, fixed their bayonets to fight at close quarters. They soon found out that their bayonets were no match to the bolos of the insurgents. Trapped in the trenches, they stood their ground by clubbing, stabbing and bludgeoning the enemy one by one in the cramped space until the passage was blocked by dead bodies, staving off further attacks. Four Kansans died among the ten who had followed Funston across the river, and their bodies lay inside the trench atop a bigger pile of enemy corpses.

Bailey provided artillery cover for the attacking troops of the Second Division. He was inspired into the action by the epic display of gallantry by Colonel Funston and his indomitable Kansans. He could not afford to look less enthusiastic about killing gooks for the glory of God and country, and as the forest cracked with gunfire, he loaded his three-inch gun, jammed the sliding wedge to close the butt and fired his first shell. The gun kicked back against its wheels but was firmly restrained by a piece of timber extending from the axle, which dug itself into the earth. What the shell left in the gun was a large hollow cartridge of tubular steel, in which the charge was canned, and this he dislodged smoking like burnt bread from the rear. He shoved another projectile into the firing chamber. A dragon of fire spurted from the bore and vanished in a blink, leaving a circle of smoke that was its departed soul. Assisted by other artillerymen, he fed the gun with mechanical speed like a baker putting dough into a furnace, loading ammunition then pulling out burning cartridges. His face turned black with soot and his palms chafed red from the heat. He felt no sense of fatigue.

The shells from his Fletcher gun got ahead of the soldiers. The first shot landed short, crashing on the bridge which, already partly dismantled, shook off a few trusses and, after more shots, weakened by dynamite blasts earlier set off by the rebels, it heaved, sagged and collapsed. Adjusting the range, Bailey started pounding the Filipino defenses at the opposite bank. Branches camouflaging the breastworks broke into splinters to bare the defenses behind. The ramparts of earth lining the trenches caved in and entombed the defenders, then in like manner, the logs covering the bunkers were knocked loose falling down on the heads of the rebels together with the topping of soil. Different types of shells wrought destruction in different ways. The grapeshot, made up of iron kernels packed together, riddled the bodies of the defenders. The armored-piercing, with a solid tip, collapsed ramparts and plowed up the roots of trees. The shrapnel, hollow and easy to rupture, exploded and strew debris in all directions. At the receiving end of the bombardment by the most modern weapons in warfare, the Filipinos did not stand a chance.

Bailey did his job with detachment. Ordinarily friendly toward Filipinos, he did not let personal feelings stand in the way of fulfilling his duty and he therefore dispatched his bombs with no other thought in mind than hitting anonymous targets on the map identified only by their coordinates. Whether they were heads of cabbages or of insurgents did not matter. He had to show to his superiors that he was not wasting ammunition or, worse, was being less than faithful to his oath. The same impersonal attitude he had exhibited during the battle of Manila Bay when he sent Montojo's flagship to the bottom of the sea without regard to the fate of the crewmen trapped below its deck. For if he deliberately missed targets out of regard for human life, he would not be doing the work of a good soldier.

At daybreak, with the front looming into view, the main body of the Kansas and Montana regiments descended the bank of the Rio Grande in force toting their Springfields and Krags. They let out a collective roar that drowned out the noise of the river to conquer their own fears and spur themselves into a headlong stampede into the valley of death. They surged inexorably ahead, their caps folded windward, bandoliers and Web cartridge belts heavy with bullets, their rucksacks bobbing on their backs, doggedly resolute as a herd of wildebeests crossing the Mara River. The slope was quickly eroded by their boots which kicked up pebbles and dirt to color the edge of the water brown. On the bank, they split up into squads to cross the fordable portions of the river that the advance Kansan scouts had marked out for them at a heavy cost in life. Others loaded the rafts with horses, Gatlings and Hotchkiss field guns and propelled themselves across the river with dredging poles and ropes. The movement of men and equipment appeared unstoppable as the raging rapids, with the columns of troops plowing and sloshing their way across the current. They gathered at the opposite banks to regroup themselves into units, then plunged straight into the raging inferno ahead – all along sniped at by the rebels.

After the main body of troops had crossed the river, Bailey followed hard on their heels, accompanied by Wolf and other members of the artillery unit. The nature of their job relegated them to the rear to cover the tracks of the infantry, and while the position was safer, it was wanting in glamour and glory that the Kansans had in spades. They herded their horses toward the bank so that they could be loaded one by one aboard the rafts, separately from the heavy guns which the animals pulled in teams, depending on the gun size.

Bailey searched for a raft large enough to carry his four horses, but he was confounded by the sight of the debris of battle. The water was littered with branches, logs, torn clothing and bleeding chunks of humanity bobbing around to impede further advance. The bridge had collapsed, damming the water with its frame of twisted iron. Across the river, the twin line of trenches had been overrun, clogged with corpses and logs, between which it was hard to distinguish. It appeared that the battle had broken up into skirmishes at scattered places. Faced with a panorama of devastation, Bailey tried to fish a raft, a log or anything from the water that would enable him to transport his gun and animals across the river.

"Let's get ahold of a raft, quick, Wolf. Don't just stand there, come on down!"

"There's one down the river, yonder." Wolf pointed downstream. "And there's another one about to return."

"Okay, get hold of the rope and don't let go of it."

"It's coming ... it's here ... here we go."

Assisted by other troopers eager to cross, the two sailors caught a raft drifting at the end of a loose piece of rope. First, they loaded the three-inch gun and its limber on the raft, which cargo they lashed securely by the wheels, using raw strands of hemp that tore off easily in their hands. Since the tandem of gun and limber was quite heavy, they shipped it across the river first, then came back for the two pairs of horses.

The animals jibbed and neighed in fear. Wolf gave up trying to coax one horse to board the raft. "The hell with it..."

"Lemme do it." Bailey scratched the neck of the balking horse and uttered soothing nonsense – all to no avail.

"Come on, fellas," said the restless troopers flying the Montana banner who were waiting impatiently to board the raft. "Give it a good whack on the behind!"

A scramble for the raft erupted between the troopers and the German who wasn't willing to share it. "This is not a riverboat and it's gonna go under if everybody insists in riding it and we'll all be swept down by the current," he chided them in his most exact manner, then urged his buddy: "Come on, Gatling, move your ass and get on."

Bailey finally succeeded in prodding the horse onto the raft. He jumped aboard, waved his hat and jauntily shouted, "Anchor's aweigh!" – this to the sound of battle.

The Montana boys, managing to get ahold of another raft, also whooped it up and waved their hats in the air. "Right on, steady on the rudder, skipper!"

346

The unique experience of riding a raft in stampeding waters tickled Bailey no end. He tried to balance himself on the pitching platform and jostled with the Montana troopers who tried to jump from one raft to another with boyish glee. They tugged at the length of rope that was tied to the bough of a tree as they struggled to propel themselves across the river.

At the opposite bank, the troops broke up to rejoin their mother units or what remained of them that could be gathered into a cohesive force, with Bailey taking time to assemble his gun carriage from scattered parts. He picked the gun and limber, knocked them together and harnessed them to the team of horses. He got little by way of cooperation from Wolf who was again exhibiting the quirky behavior that made him tough to deal with in the past few days.

"This goddamned horses," said Wolf who had trouble gathering the team of horses by their leashes.

"Just afeard of the water," answered Bailey.

"Better the water buffaloes."

"Wait till I'm finished assembling this, Wolfie, and I'll help you get those animals in harness." Bailey connected the tandem of two box-shaped carriages and hooked the gun to the limber, while Wolf had his hands full restraining the four horses. Having assembled the gun carriage, Bailey helped his partner round up the four horses which he patiently coaxed and leashed together into a mobile team. Then, with humor unspoiled, he mounted the driver's seat, seized the reins and asked the German to jump on board. "Hop in here, Wolfie, we're ready to go!" he rejoiced like an excited cowboy, cracking the reins to send the horses scampering up the slope.

Strangely, Wolf tugged at the reins as they sat side by side on the driver's seat of the gun carriage. "Lemme take the helm, I'll teach these horses how to giddyap," he said. "Full steam ahead."

Bailey yielded the reins. "Okay, just be careful. There are trenches ahead."

"Are they covered?"

"Just follow the tracks."

Wolf broke into a strange grin that did not match his mood. "Ya know what I'm thinking?'"

"Look over there! The trench!"

"Remember what I told you before, Bart – that whenever there's a chance, I'll go for it?"

Bailey held on tightly to his seat, unable to say a word as the wagon rolled over a collapsed trench covered with earth.

"Well, here's that chance!"

Wolf cracked the whip with such force as to drive the horses mad. They dragged the wagon violently over the pitted terrain as though their tails were on fire. The tandem of limber and caisson that formed part of the carriage bucked and pitched over the craters and ruts, sending the gun it was towing behind into wild zigzagging gyrations.

"Where are you driving us, Wolf?" shouted Bailey.

"Where there's no fightin', where there's no marchin', where's there's no shooting!"

"Dammit, Wolf, you're leading us toward enemy lines. Turn around."

Wolf deliberately steered the horses in the direction of danger. Heeding only his own strange impulses, he turned to a quiet trail in the woods unspoiled by the tracks of the marching army – and eerily silent. The seclusion and tranquility of the way were alarming to a trained soldier because it meant that they were leaving the safety of the herd, away from the main body of the army now hidden somewhere behind the woods. Wolf was driving towards the unknown. His quirky behavior was only the latest in a series of bizarre actuations that had puzzled his friends since the march to Malolos, but now it was getting out of hand.

"Wolf, you're trying to get us killed! Turn back!"

The man didn't respond.

"For God's sake, Wolfie, stop!"

He's going bonkers, thought Bailey. In desperation, he tried to seize back the reins but the stronger German shook him away. He gripped the rail in front of him in an effort to keep his balance. If he fell off the wagon, he would either be crushed by its wheels or dragged by the axle of the gun carriage. He attempted to mount one of the horses galloping madly in front of him, hoping to pull them over to a stop, but its sleek hide and rippling muscles resisted firm grip. His action only further scared the horses into a spirited run. Then over the bobbing heads of the animals with their flying manes and jutting ears, Bailey sighted three armed Filipinos standing in the distance. They raised their rifles, aimed straight at the approaching wagon, and fired. Wolf fell on the first volley. He tumbled to the side of the road and disappeared in the bush.

Bailey tugged at the reins with all his might in an effort to pull the horses to a stop while looking over his shoulder in the direction of where his comrade had fallen. A few paces from the Filipinos, he leaped from the limber and rolled to the bush, then picked up himself and sprinted toward his friend, afire with horror. At distance of fifty yards, he found his friend slumped on the side of the road and he gently picked him up and cradled his head in his arms.

"Wolf! My dear Wolf!"

Wolfgang Messner, 23, lifted his head. "Bart..." He had been shot in the chest and crushed by his fall. His speech gurgled as blood poured out of his mouth to drain the life from his body. He slumped back with a fixed look in his eyes. Bailey embraced the limp body, smearing himself with blood. "Oh, my God, oh, my dear Wolfgang." As he expressed his loss in the most primal manner, consisting of sobs and wails, a blow from a rifle butt terminated his sorrow. His face dropped to the bloodied chest of his friend.

21

SUDDENLY, A WEDDING

When he woke up, he found himself lying on a bamboo sledge, a makeshift cart resting on four slanting poles instead of wheels, running on the same principle as its counterpart in the snow. He saw a spindly tail swinging pendulously, to and fro, the rump of a huge animal with cloven hooves and bow-shaped horns, and realized that he was being carried by a beast across a grass field toward a fate that could be worse than death. He was a prisoner. He was being driven toward his doom. Hogtied and bundled on the sledge, he noticed the rustle of persons marching behind and in front of the animal – his captors. There was one other astride the bare back of the pachyderm, talking in a loud voice that elicited occasional laughter from the others.

The swinging tail mesmerized him into a trance. The flickering memories of his friend dying in his arms crossed his mind. *You murdering gooks, you dirty little Injuns...*

He was taken mumbling delirious epithets to a clearing in the woods occupied by a solitary thatched hut, surrounded by a nondescript crowd of refugees. The sight of a white prisoner being brought to the camp caused a commotion among the refugees huddled in the shade. He heard a piercing chant echo in the woods: *"Kano! Kano!"* From the trees rushed a wave of Filipinos – mothers, children, and old men – all of whom were thirsting for blood. The anger smoldering inside him was nothing compared to the hatred that consumed the mob. He was slapped, kicked and spat at by relatives of insurgents killed or missing or wounded in battle. Before they could lynch him, he was whisked away and bundled inside the thatched hut, which turned out to be a hospital crowded by wounded rebels. Again, he was greeted with barely restrained hostility by the accursed patients who despised his presence. The hut shook as the mob outside tried to storm it.

They hate me even more than I hate them, thought Bailey. Whether they had a better right to feel that way, he couldn't say.

A soldier pushed himself past the unruly mob and entered the hut limping from a wound. He unsheathed a bolo and with its flat side turned up Bailey's chin. With a face bloodied by shrapnel cuts, he uttered a string of expletives through his teeth. "I'll kill you!"

For the first time Bailey showed fear. No way he could bail himself out of this fix, he thought. Clutching at straws, he made one last desperate attempt to save his hide. *"Ako kaibig'an* Joaquin Calderon," he spoke in pidgin Tagalog. "I'm a friend of Joaquin Calderon."

"Ano?" What?

"Si Joaquin Calderon, ako kaibigan."

The injured rebels looked each other in amazement as if to say: "He speaks Tagalog."

The strategy backfired. Finding in him a rare breed of a yanqui – one who could be tortured and forced to sing military secrets in an understandable language – they spared his life. Bailey realized his mistake. But given the choice of dying now and dying later, he opted for the second. Who knows what unexpected events might intervene to pluck him out of the valley of death? Events such as the coming of the Americans, thought Bailey. Or Joaquin Calderon who should be in charge of this makeshift hospital. As the staccato sound of gunfire drew near, his captors cut the cord of abaca hemp hobbling his feet then kicked him out of the hut and back to the trail where he was forced him to march barefoot all day, poked and cudgeled by women. The trek took all of three days across an unchanging landscape of forest and rivers such that it looked as though they were just going round and round aimlessly.

In the morning of the third day, he found himself entering a barrio of thatched huts, a remote community set in the shadows of a towering mountain. He espied a company of Filipino soldiers with straw hats and homespun clothes practicing mock battles. What caught his attention in particular was a captured three-inch Fletcher cannon standing along the road with muddy wheels – his own. From the number of curious people examining it as if it had just dropped out from the sky, he surmised that it must have arrived shortly before him, an indication of its value to the rebels. The town was teeming with insurgents as if their ranks had never been decimated by successive defeats. This place must be the headquarters of Aguinaldo, he reckoned.

Then, a strange thing happened. He was told to bath in a nearby spring pouring out the side of a cliff and dropping on a pool of clear water. It was not unusual to find such places in a land visited by heavy rains the whole year round. Bailey was only too happy to take a dip in the cool waters, watched by giggling girls and glowering guards. After refreshing himself in the cool waters, he was led into a stone building that looked like an arsenal from the number of weapons stacked in its courtyard. He expected to see the legendary Aguinaldo in one of its rooms, perhaps to be asked to broker a political settlement, just like Montojo during his days of captivity in Intramuros. History had a way of repeating itself, he mused, and he looked forward to reenacting his heroic role in Manila.

Inside an empty room, he was given a set of homespun clothes, newly pressed by coal-fired iron, which he reluctantly traded for his tattered uniform. The first-class treatment that recalled the latter part of his imprisonment in Intramuros enhanced his feeling of self-importance, and pretty soon he was whistling to himself and cooking up wicked plans at the back of his mind. He'd knock some sense into these people and convince them to surrender, he vowed.

Unknown to him, word of his capture had reached the attention of Joaquin Calderon. Promptly, the doctor, who had an axe to grind, called on General Luna to ask for custody of the prisoner. He whispered his plan in conspiratorial tone which won an approving nod from the general. "Okay, if you need men, I'll send them over. Just remember, after you have redeemed your family honor, we'll finish him off," Luna said mischievously.

It came to pass that even while Bailey was cooling his heels, plotting to bluff rebels into surrender, his fate was already sealed. His good feeling was short-lived. After being made to wait for an hour, he heard the sound of boots and clogs rumbling down the corridor in mounting crescendo. Two burly rebels seized him by the arms and dragged him down the corridor towards a small room, filled with the sound of moaning from unseen people. Doubtless, the torture chamber.

Nudged onto a seat, he came face to face with a plump mestizo with fat hands and upturned moustache: Dr. Joaquin Calderon.

"Whacky!"

"Stop – if you value your hide!" Calderon rebuffed him, pulling out a .35-caliber pistol.

"Whacky, my friend, I know I am a prisoner. But for old times' sake..."

The two guards took their cue from the doctor and cocked their Mauser bolt-action rifles.

The prisoner saw the look of the executioner in Joaquin's countenance, hooded by the expression of hatred. He seemed capable of doing anything.

"Sergeant Barton Bailey, you dishonored my daughter!" Thus, Calderon.

"Doc, my gosh, what's this, I don't know what you're talking about," Bailey laughed nervously.

"We're not here to exchange pleasantries, we're here to make you pay for your crime against my family," said Calderon who followed up with a string of pungent imprecations in Spanish and Filipino that the Yankee didn't quite understand, except for the tone that was suggestive of a very angry man.

"Me, committed a crime, I just don't understand," stammered the prisoner.

"You better do as I say or else you'll be dead within the next hour."

Bailey was close to tears. "But, Whack, do you mean to tell me that I am about to be executed?"

"Do as I say."

"Okay, okay, what do you want me to do? If I am about to die, can I have at least one wish? Can you allow me to see little Estrelle?"

Joaquin pointed the pistol at him as if to shoot. The two guards did the same with their rifles.

Bailey staggered back, mute with terror.

Calderon calmed himself and launched into a speech: "Listen, *yanqui*, the moment I learned who the prisoner was – and the temerity you had to drop my name – I wanted to come to kill you with my bare hands. But I wanted to give you a chance to redeem yourself and erase the stigma you have cast on my family." He stretched himself to his full height. "Bailey, you marry my daughter and you'll live another day. Refuse and you have just said your last words."

Bailey didn't know whether to laugh or cry. He was thoroughly addled by all this fuss. Marry sweet Estrella? But of course! "Where' s Estrelle?"

"Don't ask and don't demand anything. You have forfeited your right to live." Calderon took out a scroll from the drawer and, with trembling hands, laid it open on a table. "Here ... sign."

Bailey stared transfixed at the strange piece of document, filled with sinuous calligraphy in archaic Spanish that was difficult to decipher.

"What are you waiting for? Sign!"

"But where's the pen?"

Calderon put aside his pistol and thrust a quill pen to the prisoner's hand. Scanning the ornate lettering, the American assumed that it was a marriage contract for that was the kind of document a bride and a groom were supposed to sign on their wedding day, although this one was devoid of any ceremony and lacking the bride. His hand was directed to a blank space at the lower left corner where the name of the groom appeared. For all the coercion that forced his shaking hand, the choice between signing and death was completely devoid of the quandary of a dilemma – like being made to choose between wine and poison or between Venus and the Medusa. Of course he'd marry Estrella! He dipped the quill pen in a vial of ink and, with a hand trembling like a tuning fork (more out of excitement than fear), he scrawled his signature. "There..." he said triumphantly, suppressing a smile.

At the sight of him consummating the contract with his signature, Calderon's fair mestizo cheeks flushed red. He closed his plump hands into fists and made an attempt to club him with them, leaning over the table. "Humph!" he fizzled.

One soldier cocked his rifle; the other unsheathed a long bolo.

The groom fell back, quavering. Did he miss something? After all the months he had spent with these people, he could not quite fathom their minds.

Calderon stepped back with a sigh of relief and rolled the document in his hands. He now relaxed, his wish fulfilled. The ceremony might not have been in accordance with church procedure – or the Spanish civil law, for that matter – but it was justified by the abnormal times and, more importantly, suited his ulterior motives: he now had an insurance against being tried for rebellion by the Americans in case of capture. After a minute's silence, he signaled one guard to open a door out of which emerged Estrella, seventeen and pregnant. "I'll allow you to spend an hour with her, then we'll come back for your hide," Calderon declared. He rose and left the room together with the guards.

Estrella stood coyly inside the door, conscious about her appearance. She was on her third month of pregnancy and was beginning to look flabby, though not yet bloated. In an attempt to regain her fresh virginal beauty, she had curled her hair, lacquered her fingernails and powdered her face. To Bailey, she looked as lovable as ever, especially now that she was carrying his child. He had dreamed of her for the last few months and survived grueling marches on her thought alone. He was happy to have finally seen his sweet señorita. "Estrelle."

The girl was undemonstrative with her feelings and just looked at him.

It was Bailey who rushed towards her with all the passion of a man about to die. "Oh, darling, sweet li'l Estrelle. How are you, my dear?"

"Bailey, I miss you, Bailey." Her smattering of English had grown even more rusty with their separation.

"Bart, darling, call me Bart."

"You go home, Bart, you die."

"No, you're mine now, dear. We're going to live together. You're my wife now."

"No, it's papa's do."

He embraced her and murmured in her ear: "How much I have missed you, I have hiked over mountains and crossed rivers looking for you. And when I learned you were heavy with my child, only death could have kept me from finding you..." He smelled her powdered face and buzzed her cheeks and the undersides of her neck, lifting her locks with his nose and burrowing deeper.

"You go, Bart. You die."

"You're going with me."

"No, papa tell no."

Bailey felt his wife's swollen belly with his hand. "This is going to be our child. I can't wait to see him being born."

He embraced her again. "We're going to raise a family. We'll find a way to be together."

Bailey enjoyed married life for barely an hour before Calderon returned to reclaim his daughter. A civil marriage, under Filipino custom, did not confer upon the man the privileges of a husband, which he earned only after a church wedding. The only effect of the shotgun marriage was to legitimize Estrella's child and spare the Calderon family the stigma of siring a bastard line. Furthermore, since Bailey was still an enemy, there was no way he could be allowed to live with her as her husband in the rebel camp.

Quick as a dream, Bailey found himself back behind American lines the following day. He could not believe it. It was as if everything was merely the product of hallucination, induced by the blows delivered to his head by the enemy's rifle butts. But, no, everything was for real. Wolf was dead as a door nail. He had been captured by the enemy. He had seen and touched Estrella. When he looked back, he saw rebels waving at him with their straw hats, one of them astride a carabao. The sense of loss was immense. He had stepped into the door of Paradise only to be thrown back to Earth by the cruel hands of fate. He walked down the beaten trail with a heavy heart, unwilling to step into the field of battle again.

It did not matter to him that the Battle of the Rio Grande would be celebrated back home almost in the same breath as the naval victory in Manila Bay. For their daring, the 20th Kansas Regiment became the darling of the Yellow Press back home, toasted by politicians in the capitol and their home State. Colonel Funston himself was awarded the Congressional Medal of Honor for bravely leading the first assault on the enemy defenses.

All these counted for nothing to Bailey. He wanted this war to end. He wanted to settle down.

22

MANIFEST DESTINY

Washington

On the night of February 15, 1899, a team of carriages left the White House grounds. They were not the kind of carriages that could be seen in the alleys of Manila. They were decidedly more luxurious, with lanterns caged in brass frames, molded handles of bronze, upholstered cushions and curtained windows. Carrying President William McKinley and cabinet officials, the caravan of coaches made their way along frozen streets of the capital covered by a fleece of snow. The winter was unusually harsh that year with snow blanketing the East Coast up to a depth of six feet.

The caravan was on its way to Boston where the Home Market Club was meeting on the eve of the first anniversary of the sinking of the *Maine.* It was to be an extravagant affair, organized not so much for the purpose of commemorating a tragic event as celebrating America's victory over Spain and its coming of age as a world power. The Treaty of Paris had just been ratified by the Congress. American troops were embroiled in a colonial war half a world away against an unknown breed of Asians. But nothing could spoil McKinley's mood that night as he prepared to attend the gala event. He jotted down corrections on the speech he was scheduled to deliver that night – like Lincoln on his way to Gettysburg.

By the account of his biographer Margaret Leech, the Mechanic's Hall of Boston, site of the gala affair, was bedecked with flags, buntings and strings of Edison's incandescent lamps. Behind the stage hung a portrait of McKinley flanked by those of Washington and Lincoln. In the lingering euphoria generated by the victory over Spain, McKinley had acquired a stature equal to that of the great American presidents, being the one credited for realizing America's Manifest Destiny.

The cavernous hail was packed with 1,900 guests. They milled around the tables and behind a 60-piece symphony orchestra, filling the air with a cacophony of voices. So vast was the crowd in fact that, as his biographer put it, wigwag flags had to be employed to coordinate the movements of "an army of Negro waiters" serving food and drinks to the assembly.

Mounting the lectern, McKinley launched to a speech defending his administration's handling of the colonial war then raging in the tropics. "I have no light or knowledge not common to my countrymen," he orated. "I do not prophesy. The present is all-absorbing to me. But I cannot bound my vision by the blood-stained trenches around Manila – where every red drop, whether from the veins of an American soldier or a misguided Filipino, is anguish to my heart – but by the broad range of future years when that people's children and children's children shall for ages hence bless the American republic because it emancipated and redeemed their fatherland, and set them in the pathway of the world' best civilization."

The audience burst into applause. The waiters lost sight of the wigwag flags; and the band played the waltz. McKinley was speaking from the heart. He was a messianically devout Methodist who preached Christianity from the presidential lectern. Few had questioned his sincerity when he told the Methodist ministers two months before that he had no choice but to "educate, civilize and Christianize" the Filipinos "for whom Christ also died."

The sanctimony of the debate on the Philippine question concealed the ignorance of both sides about the colony.

McKinley's knowledge about the Philippines was derived mainly from two Americans who had visited the country before Dewey: namely, Dean C. Worcester, a zoologist who had spent three years in the Visayas islands in the 1880's collecting specimens and Commander R.B. Bradford, chief of the Bureau of Equipment, who had spent time in Manila in the 1860's or more than a quarter of a century before. (Worcester later served as a member of the Schurman and Taft Commissions). From these two advisers McKinley learned that the Filipinos were a "primitive, docile and ignorant race" – except for the "Tagalogs" who were wise in the ways of the world – and that they could be kept under blissful colonial bondage, following the example of Spain, if properly treated. The first impression he got of the country never changed even after an American general who had recently visited the islands described the country differently. General Francis Greene, one of the officers present during the surrender of the Spanish forces in Manila, reported that the Filipinos were no longer docile. They were hell-bent on winning their revolution, even at the cost of so much blood. They hated the Spanish officialdom and, moreso, the friars – "with indescribable virulence," in Greene's words. Greene was the first man to inform McKinley that the Filipinos were already a Christian nation, and had been so for quite some time. In fact, the first Christian missionaries arrived in the islands even before America was settled by the white man. Moreover, they had universities and an educated class that was capable of running a government, given the chance.

American intellectuals sought to frustrate McKinley's well-intentioned plans for the colony. William James, the noted psychologist, said: "We are now openly engaged in crushing out the sacredest things in this great human world –

360

the attempt of a people long enslaved to be free." He was seconded by Henry Adams, the writer and descendant of presidents: "I turn green in bed at midnight if I think of the horror of a year's warfare in the Philippines where we must subjugate a million or two of foolish Malays in order to give them the comforts of flannel petticoats and electric railways."

McKinley found cold comfort in the support he got from European imperialists who also joined the Philippine debate. The British poet Rudyard Kipling published a famous poem in the February 1899 issue of *McClure's* magazine, urging the world's youngest colonial power to take up the "White Man's burden."

> Take up the White Man's burden
> Ye dare not stoop to less –
> Nor call too loud on Freedom
> To cloak your weariness.

The condescending tone of Kipling's poem drew a chorus of rebuke from the American press. Pulitzer's New York *World* retorted:

> We've taken up the White Man's burden
> Of ebony and brown
> Now will you kindly tell us, Rudyard,
> How we may put it down?

The Omaha *World-Herald* also took Kipling to task. "In other words, Mr. Kipling would have Uncle Sam take up John Bull's (London's) burden."

In the run-up to the presidential campaign of 1900, McKinley shed his pious image and hit the road to curry support for the Philippine War. In speeches such as that before the Home Market Club, he drove home the point that maintaining an outpost in the 7,200-island archipelago was vital to America's mercantile interests.

On August 20, 1899, he personally received the homecoming Pennsylvania Regiment at Pittsburgh. He was on hand with a brass band as the troops disembarked from a train on the last leg of their journey home. He led the crowd in giving a rousing welcome to the tanned veterans of the Philippine campaign, sporting fedoras and suntans with striped pants. Popping up next at the Schenley Park, he reviewed a parade of the same troops marching past flag-waving crowds. "You are the heroes of a new age," he praised the troops. "You planted the American flag in the farthest corner of the planet and brought honor and glory to your countrymen. Because of you, America stands today at the pinnacle of its power and the height of its prestige." He extended honors to the 19 State regiments that had agreed to extend their tours of duty in the tropics – among them 1st California, 13th Minnesota, 1st Iowa, 1st Nebraska and 20th Kansas.

At the mention of the Nebraskans and the Kansans, the two most illustrious regiments in the Philippine campaign, the crowd as well as the homecoming troops broke into wild cheering and flag waving.

As hard as McKinley campaigned for public support for the war, his critics were just as indefatigable in their opposition to his war effort. Fanatics of the Anti-Imperialist League – which included a former president, Grover Cleveland, retired Civil War generals and millionaires – flooded government offices with petitions calling a stop to this "hell of a war" and "slaughter of a freedom-loving people" in a conflict that exposed the American soldier to the immediate danger of "tropical diseases." Firebrand Andrew Carnegie continued to write letters to the press, promising to "spread the brains" of sympathetic editors "with my dollars."

League member Edward Atkinson carried the anti-war campaign to extremes. A cotton magnate who invented the so-called Aladdin Oven, he packed bundles of his anti-war pamphlets and readied them for shipment to the Philippines, addressed to such men as Otis, MacArthur and members of the Schurman Commission. Fortunately, they never left the shore. Postmaster-general Charles Emory Smith seized bundles of the mail just as they were about to be shipped from San Francisco.

After this incident, McKinley was constrained to censor all communications to and from the Philippines. He instructed his generals in the islands to edit carefully all dispatches concerning the war in such a way as would avoid stirring controversy at home. General Otis gleefully carried out this order to filter the bad news from the front. He routinely blotted, scissored or spiked the mail of American troops, and soon applied the same treatment to the dispatches of press correspondents until their reports started reading like letters from a summer camp. The wanton censorship raised a howl of protest that soon forced McKinley to rein in Otis.

In an open letter published in various newspapers on July 17, 1899, the correspondents complained: "We believe that owing to official dispatches from Manila made public in Washington, the people of the United States have not received a correct impression of the situation in the Philippines. We have been forced to tell lies. We have been barred from reporting much that we have seen in the field. The stories that Americans read about are different from what we have actually observed with our own eyes. The censorship has compelled us to participate in these misrepresentations." The correspondents went one step further. They spread stories, some of them unfair, dwelling on Otis' incompetence as a general, such as his refusal to leave the confines of Intramuros and his fondness for the siesta. They drew a contrasting picture of MacArthur leading the Second Division in a grueling campaign across the mountains of Luzon, publicity from which MacArthur reaped rich rewards.

McKinley was constrained to dampen the criticisms from the press by clipping the wings of Otis, then firing him altogether in May 1900 and installing MacArthur in his place as governor-general. Unwittingly, the lifting of press controls opened a new phase of the circulation war that gained the Philippines an extended run on the headlines. The papers told glowing stories of American troops at war in exotic battle fields of the Far East, hacking through jungles and crossing rivers in pursuit of a treacherous and savage enemy. As a result, the Philippine War became a cause that was almost to rival the Indian Wars in popular appeal. This time, when the anti-war activists raised their voices, the opinion editors cried "treason" and rattled the bones of Benedict Arnold.

The political consensus on the war, however, did not last long.

The presidential campaign of 1900 loomed into view. Protagonists entered the fray who would make sure that the Philippine War would be one of the principal issues in the election campaign.

The single personality who emerged as McKinley's nemesis in the campaign was William Jennings Bryan. A Nebraskan politician who was the losing Democratic presidential candidate in 1896, Bryan was a man in search of issues. He had nothing to boast about by way of a war record that would set fire to the voters' imagination. During the Splendid Little War, he was drafted as a private but, after pulling political strings, was able to get a promotion to colonel in a matter of days. However, the farthest he got to the front was Tampa, Florida, the jump-off point to the Cuban front, where he sat out the war in a tent swatting gnats. His adoring biographer Louis Koenig managed to wring out drama from this idle episode, pointing out how Bryan promoted the building of platforms inside tents in the soggy Florida camp, thereby beating a plague of typhoid and malaria that had claimed 50 casualties in the Third Nebraska Regiment. Even at this backwater far away from the front and even farther from the political arena, Bryan was already nursing ambitions to run for president. He figured that the best way to spark the public imagination was by riding the debate on the Philippine War at home rather than fighting battles on distant shores. For this reason McKinley tried to ship him out of Tampa, Florida as part of the Nebraskan regiment headed for Manila where he could fight a common enemy and not stand in the way of his reelection for president. For the same reason, Bryan looked for ways to stay grounded.

On the eve of his departure for the Philippines, soldier Bryan found himself on the horns of dilemma that took all his political skills to manage owing to its delicacy. If he boarded a ship bound for Manila, he would be missing his last chance of winning the presidency. If he jumped ship, as it were, he would be leaving himself open to the charges of shirking his patriotic duty which would bury his political career just the same. First, he used the agency of Nebraskan congressman William Stark and governor Silas Holcomb to butter up McKinley into granting him an early release from the draft. Theirs was a sensitive mission intended to protect Bryan from charges that he was dodging duty. McKinley piously answered that he could not "in conscience grant Bryan a release while other Nebraskans were still fighting in the Philippines." Bryan himself left his Florida camp to see the president in September 1899 in the guise of seeking other favors for his beloved Nebraskan constituents. Inside the executive office, he beat around the bush for half an hour while the president listened impassively, equally adamant in avoiding the topic closest to the visitor's heart.

Finally, McKinley said sanctimoniously: "If you made a request that I thought was right I should be pleased to grant it. If you asked one that I thought ought not to be granted my refusal would be based upon good reasons, and with these I should not experience embarrassment."

Bryan walked out of the Cabinet Room in a huff.

Afterwards, in an act of magnanimity, McKinley mustered out the former private to allow him to run for commander-in-chief.

There were two reasons why McKinley wanted to do away with Bryan whom he had beaten in the 1896 election.

Bryan was a political opponent of formidable abilities. First, Bryan was more eloquent than he. If McKinley could deliver paeans about America's Manifest Destiny, Bryan could launch into inflammatory oratory about any topic that stirred public interest. In 1896 he championed the cause of Free Silver with attacks on the gold standard. "You shall not press down upon the brow of labor this crown of thorns. You shall not crucify mankind upon a cross of gold." Second, Bryan was more pious than the president. If McKinley could wax missionary about converting the Filipinos to Christianity, Bryan could embark on a crusade against Darwin's theory of evolution – such as during the Monkey Trial when he prosecuted a public school instructor for teaching the heresy of evolution.

By freeing Bryan, the gentle McKinley took the risk of facing him in another slam-bang campaign. McKinley turned out to be more cunning than magnanimous. He began scouting around for a running mate equally bombastic in speeches who could take on the redoubtable Bryan. He was interested not so much in finding a David who could play the underdog as in picking a Samson who could fight toe-to-toe against the Democratic Goliath. He did discover one such running mate in New York; but early in the 1900 campaign he chose to keep the man's identity secret.

True enough, Bryan threw his hat into the ring. He set the tone for the campaign by seizing a political issue far more controversial than Free Silver: the Philippine War. To a crowd in the Denver Coliseum, he ridiculed the policy of imperialism espoused by McKinley: "It is not a step forward toward a broader destiny, it is a step backward toward the narrow views of kings and emperors." McKinley had every reason to regret not shipping him out to the Philippines.

In his acceptance speech at the 1900 Democratic convention, Bryan chided the Republicans for promoting Big Business – in particular "the army of contractors and shipowners who would carry live soldiers to the Philippines and bring dead soldiers back." He disparaged McKinley's stubborn insistence that the Filipinos needed America's tutelage to bring them into the realm of civilization. "God Himself never made a race of people so low in the scales of civilization or intelligence that it welcomes a foreign master."

At the Indianapolis railroad station, he took exception to the argument that the moral cost of maintaining a colony in Asia would be amply compensated by commercial gains: "Those who say today that the dollar trade is superior to the rights of the Filipinos will be saying ... that money is more important than man."

Answering Sen. Henry Cabot Lodge who in 1898 contended that "where the flag goes up it must never come down," Bryan said: "Who will take down the flag? When the American people want the flag raised, they raise it; when they wanted it hauled down, they haul it down."

McKinley all this time was grooming his Samson, letting him grow hair, as it were. Just as Bryan ran out of steam, he unveiled his running mate: Theodore Roosevelt.

And all that his supporters could say was: "Amen."

Roosevelt was as intimidating a foe as any Bryan could find. Firstly, he was more combative. During the war against Spain, he didn't merely sit in a tent in Tampa, Florida but led a company of "Rough Riders" into the thick of the fight. This was the same Roosevelt who earlier, as assistant secretary of the Navy, overstepped his authority to dispatch Dewey to Hong Kong, fill the army arsenal and fit more ships for war – all in one day. Secondly, Roosevelt was more eloquent than Bryan – stridently so.

He was the Yankee version of General Antonio Luna and it is interesting to speculate how history would have turned out if he had ridden his Rough Riders to the Philippines instead of to Cuba. As the Republican candidate for vice president, Roosevelt took up the cudgels for the courtly, sanctimonious McKinley and fought a bare-knuckled campaign against Bryan. "The bullets that slay our men in Luzon were inspired by the denouncers of America here," he began his campaign.

"The Filipino will stop killing our soldiers very soon after he becomes convinced that he will receive no aid in the effort from the party of which Mr. Bryan is the chief." Before an audience in Saint Louis, he said: "From unimpeachable authority we have heard ... how the friendly natives who have trusted to our good faith are tortured for their friendliness to our flag, how their limbs are broken and their tongues torn out ... because they have been friendly with us in this struggle. Now, shall we abandon them to such a fate as that? Never, never while we keep faith."

Take that, Goliath! Roosevelt had a mouthful to say on every topic that Bryan touched.

On the flag: "We have hoisted our flag, and it is not fashioned of the stuff which can be quickly hauled down."

On imperialism: "Now what is our duty in the Philippines? It is a duty to govern those islands in the interest of the islanders, not less in accordance with our own honor and interest. For peace has come through the last century to large sections of the Earth because the civilized races have spread over the earth's dark places."

On the alleged political maturity of the Filipinos: "The Tagal bandits of Manila are as fit to run a government as robbers are fit to man a bank... The Malay bandit Aguinaldo has to be taught a lesson that he will gain no sympathy for his cause for as long as he lurks in ambush to shoot our men." The prosecution of the military campaign will cause the "Tagal bandits" to respect American might just as the Spaniards "had cause to dread the flag as they saw the great battleships ploughing to and fro through the seas of the Gulf." But Bryan "asks us to dishonor the flag."

He promised, if elected, to give the Filipinos "such liberty as throughout the dark ages of their history they have never known."

The American public thoroughly enjoyed the campaign that was the flipside of the Splendid Little War. They had no trouble making up their minds on their choice of leader on election day. The result: McKinley 292 electoral votes. Bryan: 176.

In an epitaph to the campaign, H.L. Mencken called Bryan a "sedulous flycatcher" for jumping at any issue that would advance his political career.

Despite gaining a new mandate, McKinley gradually lost enthusiasm for the colonial war. Its escalating cost no longer justified its intangible benefits. On the second year of the war, his secretary of war, Elihu Root, recommended legislation that would raise the standing army to 100,000 men, or nearly quadruple its pre-war figure of 28,000. The need was made even more urgent by the outbreak of the Boxer Rebellion in China in the summer of 1900 which required western nations to send troops to rescue their trapped countrymen in Peking. In the Philippines alone, there were already 70,000 men, more than twice the figure that fought Spain, and Otis was asking for more, with no end in sight. The cost of prosecuting the war, in dollars and in human life, could no longer be justified by whatever commercial advantage America stood to gain – of which he could show nothing concrete.

"If old Dewey had just sailed away when he smashed the Spanish fleet," he told H. H. Kohlsaat, a Chicago publisher, in one of his low moments, "what a lot of trouble he would have saved us." To a confidant: "I didn't want the Philippines... and they came to us, as gift from the gods."

23

"*ADIÓS*, GENERAL LUNA"

The war did not defeat the Filipinos but the Filipinos defeated themselves. Centuries of adversity had steeled them to the hardships and cruelties of war, and the American campaign for colonial conquest only marginally worsened their plight. The struggle with the Americans was merely an extension of the revolution against Spain, which in turn was a conflagration stoked by the fires of intermittent rebellions of centuries past against colonial abuse. What the war did was turn the Filipinos against themselves. As if wanting in enemies, they harnessed their excess energy in intramural conflict.

After the Battle of the Rio Grande on April 26, 1899, the rebel ranks were wracked by discord. On the one hand, a pacifist faction wanted to sue for peace to avail itself of the terms of autonomy offered by the Schurman Commission – which were indeed concessions to a victor, if measured against previous settlements with Spain. For their two-year revolution against Spain, all the rebels had won were indemnity and exile for their leaders. On the other hand, a hawkish faction, led by General Antonio Luna, stood pat on its goal of independence – complete sovereignty as that enjoyed by the Latin American nations that had recently won their freedom from Spain. There was no way the gap between the two factions could be bridged, for admittedly there was no middle ground to cover.

Caught between the two factions was Aguinaldo, who wanted to rule both without alienating either. He earnestly wanted to be president of a sovereign country but had not the wherewithal to expel the Yankee conquistador. While holding off intense military pressure from MacArthur, he watched helplessly as the two factions in his government met in a climactic showdown. In the riptide of conflict, one side had to give.

The decisive clash between the two factions occurred in May 1899. The string of defeats suffered by General Luna emboldened the pacifists to press Aguinaldo to accept the Schurman Plan. They criticized Luna's conventional military tactics against a superior force that proved costly in human lives. They felt he wagered too much blood for personal glory. Five weeks after the Battle of the Rio Grande, they met with Aguinaldo in the town of Cabanatuan to discuss the acceptance of the Schurman Plan – and, necessarily, Luna's retirement.

For obvious reasons, the pacifists deliberately sought to keep Luna and his generals out of the meeting. They remembered very well that on May 21, when the pacifists first gathered to float the idea of accepting the Schurman Plan, Luna crashed the meeting and shot down the idea with his pistol, along the way manhandling the foreign minister Felipe Buencamino. They could not this time suffer another humiliation by inviting to the meeting a person who was not amenable to reason. This time, they were determined to press Aguinaldo to approve the Schurman Plan and announce the decision to the public, preempting any opposition from Luna whose voice counted for but a single vote.

Luna, however, could not be kept out of the meeting. As surely as sound traveled in the air, he got wind of the plan and headed for Cabanatuan from his camp seven miles south. Already, he was grumbling treason.

Secretly supporting the pacifists was Joaquin Calderon, the health minister. He considered himself a friend of Luna but his interests lay squarely in achieving peace for his land. For one thing, the only way he could earn from his medical practice was to maintain a clinic in Manila where he could cater to the hypochondria of the upper class. An American colonial presence would provide him a rich source of clientele. In addition, he had to allow Estrella to live a normal life with her American husband, a family responsibility that he had to discharge in his emerging role as a patriarch.

In the crucial cabinet meeting in Cabanatuan, held on May 30, 1899, Calderon deliberately stayed out of Aguinaldo's headquarters, housed in the old town hall. He did not want to partake of the responsibility for the pacifist coup and, more importantly, did not want to place himself on the opposite side of the table from Luna during the inevitable confrontation. That ran counter to his peaceful nature. This was not a family affair in which he could speak his mind out and command obedience, as in the row with Bailey.

As soon as the rumble of hooves sounded outside Aguinaldo's office, he felt himself quaking in his boots. He saw Luna dismounting from his horse, followed by two aides. When Luna strode into the door of the town hall, Calderon promptly accosted him to urge him to rein in his temper, whispering words of restraint, but the general merely brushed him aside without a word.

From beneath the stairs, he tried to eavesdrop on the conference going on at the second floor of the town hall, but not a sound leaked out of the room where the cabinet was confined. The silence was encouraging to Calderon because it meant that Luna was behaving himself. The silence was short-lived. Pretty soon, the hall resounded with the unmistakable baritone of the mercurial general. It rose above a rumble of a chorus of voices that trailed away, leaving Luna's voice echoing in the hall. He was again berating the cabinet members in vulgar Spanish, the context of which Calderon had trouble comprehending.

A man of cultivated manners, the doctor was deeply offended by the general's attitude. How could he do that to his colleagues in the cabinet – all perfectly respectable people?

How could he persist in conducting himself like a rogue ilustrado? Humiliating his peers in front of El Presidente? Not even Aguinaldo raised his voice during cabinet meetings because he held his ministers in high regard as illustrious people in their own right with superior education. Regrettably, Calderon could not bring himself to straighten up so irascible a colleague as Luna for he did not have the courage to match. It was a far more ticklish problem than breaking in his son-in-law with the aid of a pistol and two burly riflemen. This one was a tough nut to crack.

At the end of Luna's tirade, a cabinet member went out of the room in a huff, his curled moustache twisted in an expression of helpless rage, his cane beating the floor with his every step. Calderon recognized the minister as Felipe Buencamino whom Luna had slapped at their last cabinet meeting. The man seized a calesa and disappeared. To the rumble of boots, Luna appeared equally distraught, his nostrils flaring, his eyes scanning the distance for somebody. The wild look on his face discouraged Calderon from making another attempt to calm him down, for the doctor knew he risked burning himself on a hot rod. He just watched the man as he stood on the porch of the town hall, arms akimbo, his body stiff with tension. Then, after a while, the general also mounted his horse and trotted away, followed by his two aides.

There was something ominous in the aftermath of the whole affair. The cabinet did not break up with the departure of Luna, unlike before. It continued meeting in cloistered silence, the gravity of its deliberations weighing heavily in the air.

Then, a company of troops marched from the nearby field and positioned itself around the town hall, as if to guard the meeting from further disturbance. Two officers with stars on their straw hats straddled the entrance to the town hall where Luna had stood a few moments before. Somebody had tipped them off about the commotion caused by Luna – perhaps Buencamino.

Calderon recognized the troops as Aguinaldo's loyalists from his hometown of Kawit, well-armed with Mauser rifles and long bolos. He became apprehensive. The cabinet was closing its ranks against a rogue colleague. No, Luna was not a renegade, thought Calderon. He was just a man driven by primal instincts, passionate in his patriotism and mad in his desire for freedom. Five days later, or on June 4, 1899, Calderon mustered enough courage to see the general. By this time, Luna must have quieted down considerably to welcome a serious, heart-to-heart talk with a friend.

He found the general in his field command at a bivouac located five miles south of Cabanatuan. Gingerly, he spurred his old horse toward a shade and tied it to the wheel of a gun carriage. Luna was flicking the loading mechanisms of a captured Fletcher cannon when he noticed the doctor loom into view. He broke into a smile.

"Yo tengo una visita. My dear, Joaquin, it's you!" Luna was in a sunny mood. He walked on a plank of wood that spanned the muddy ground and led the doctor toward his tent flying the republican colors. "So, how is your daughter now? *Como esta su hija?* Did the two soldiers I sent you do their job?"

"Yes, yes, compadre. I got them married."

"Now that you have redeemed your family's honor, we can finish him off!" Luna grinned, his moustache stretching. "I'll arrange a firing squad tomorrow."

"No, Antonio. I'm here to talk to you about some serious business."

"Que noticias tenemos? Any news?" Luna's expression turned grave.

"It's about the mess you left at the headquarters. Tell me, Antonio, why did you do it? Why do you treat our colleagues that way? Why do you have to shout at them in front of El Jefe?"

Luna looked down. "Oh, them," he shrugged.

"Please, my friend. *Antes de hablar si tienes ira.* Learn to control your temper. You have caused our colleagues to lose face in front of El Jefe. They feel that you can't work with them as part of a team and that you want to have things your way." Sensing that the general was receptive to criticism, Calderon pursued further. "They feel threatened. They are going to take action against you, with El Jefe's support."

Luna thought for a long time. He became solemn, almost contrite. "Look, compadre, I respect my colleagues," he explained. "But they have to give equal consideration to the people here who fight their battles. We sleep on a plank of wood in the mud, we hike day by day delirious from hunger, yet behind our backs there are people who are working to make all the sacrifices we have made count for nothing."

Calderon was not impressed. "Listen, my friend. I understand how my colleagues feel. They see no point in sacrificing more lives when the Schurman Commission has conceded them everything that we have fought for against the Spaniards. *Everything* short of independence. And that's what they wanted all along."

"Nothing short of independence. We have declared to the world the birth of our republic, now we must fight to keep it alive."

"Compadre, look at it from my point of view. I am a doctor. I have treated hundreds of wounded men and seen hundreds more die. Another round of fighting and the blood will be in our hands."

"To die is not to fail. The dead are the ones remembered, not the living. And if I am the only one left willing to die...."

"All these losses, all these lives: you will never succeed. You have not won one victory to assuage the grief of widows," Calderon disparaged the general's achievements.

Luna bristled. "Yes, I may have lost some battles, but they were not in vain. Success is just a series of failures. If you try hard enough and fail often enough, then you will succeed."

"End this insurrection, and we can live to fight another day in the political front."

"Insurrection?" laughed Luna. "A people of one country cannot commit insurrection against the people of another country."

Calderon cut short the spat. He was finally emboldened to declare his opposition to his friend's policy of all-out war. "Antonio, you are my friend and will always be. But on the matter of politics, I'll have to part ways with you. I'll support whatever my colleagues in the cabinet decide from here on."

Luna rose to the challenge. "Joaquin, I do not run my affairs as field commander of this army on the basis of personal ties. If the home or country asks..." He shook his head. "It matters not."

"Well..."

"I can have you arrested right now for talking surrender. But since you're my compadre and you're also a doctor and my troops need you, I shall spare you. But as for those perfumed traitors..." Luna fumed. "I will ask that they be exiled."

Calderon muttered something, at a loss for words.

"I will have to take decisive action. I will go see Aguinaldo tomorrow alone. From now on the government will be run without the cabinet. He will make the decision as president and I as head of the army," Luna declared. "The do-nothing ministers will be exiled. Military men will run the government as wartime conditions demand. If the president decides that we must surrender because that is what the military situation calls for, I will abide. But I don't want the suggestion to come from perfumed ilustrados who have not spent one day at the front!"

Calderon took affront at being lumped together with the "perfumed ilustrados." He had spent time at the front and dirtied his hands with the gore of the injured and the dying. He was too intimidated, however, by Luna's threat of arrest to answer back.

The doctor turned around, saddened. *"Adiós,* General Luna," he said. Their friendship was at an end.

On June 5, Luna reappeared in Cabanatuan. He had only two escorts with him to show his peaceful intentions – officers named Colonel Francisco Roman and Captain Eduardo Rusca of the professional Republican Army who had borne the attacks of MacArthur's Second Division but whose defeats had broken the spirits of the civilians in the cabinet.

The capital was practically deserted. Upon hearing Calderon's tidings that Luna was coming to arrange the formation of a military dictatorship, the courtly intellectuals of the cabinet made themselves scarce, afraid of being caught at the wrong end of Luna's temper. They had taken Calderon's sketchy news to mean that Luna was preparing to overthrow the government and install himself as a dictator. Since the doctor could add little more information on Luna's exact plans, the ministers thought that prudence was the better part of valor and fled town. In their hurry, four of them bundled themselves aboard a carabao-drawn cart, with their top hats and canes, a singular sight that drew the curiosity of the barrio folk.

Aguinaldo himself expected the worst. In an interview with Calderon years later, he said that he had feared a coup. He fled to the town of San Isidro, 30 miles away, and left his praetorian guards to deal with Luna. He had always been wary of the ilustrado general who so differed from the dapper intellectuals of his cabinet. In him, he found a greater threat to his authority than in Andres Bonifacio. Luna was educated as Bonifacio was unlettered. The one was a military tactician while the other was a simple proletarian who fought at the head of a mob. The moment Luna threw a challenge to Aguinaldo's authority, the power struggle was bound to be titanic.

The cabinet was misled by Calderon's dire warnings of Luna's approach. For all his authoritarian leanings, Luna had no intention of deposing Aguinaldo and installing himself as a dictator. He believed that El Jefe was a revolutionary at heart, a son of the earth, reared in the simple virtues of the province, where violations of honor and justice fueled the rebellions against Spanish rule. His judgment had only been clouded lately by the addled advice he had been getting from the intellectuals who could not quite agree among themselves.

The habitually sluggish Calderon failed to take the last calesa out of the town. He was fussing about packing his surgical tools inside Aguinaldo's headquarters when Luna entered the town with his two aides, all on horseback. He paced about the deserted town hall, afraid of confronting the general. "*Hijo*, tell General Luna that nobody's inside," he told a young Kawit soldier assisting him. "Aguinaldo's out. Got it? Everybody's out!"

"He's got two men with him."

"Don't let him come in. By all means, don't," Calderon panicked.

The Kawit guards in town, 25 of them, were in no mood to fight Luna in the absence of their leader. Most of them had retired to their quarters because there was no high official left to guard inside the town hall, except one plump doctor who was quite harmless. The two remaining guards in the town hall played checkers in the balcony.

Tying his horse to a flagpole, Luna strode to the town hall and pounded on the main door. "Open the door! Is there anybody inside? Open the goddamned door!"

One of the two guards looked down the balcony. "They are all gone, sir."

Luna stepped out of the porch and looked up, squinting from under his scrambled-egg cap. "Didn't Señor Calderon tell your chief that I was coming?"

"He *is* here."

Upon hearing the guard's indiscretion, Calderon winced behind the window, out of the general's sight.

"Let me see him! Joaquin!" Luna called at the top of his voice.

Calderon prodded the rear end of the soldier with his cane.

"I mean, sir, he left with them also. There's nobody here."

Luna stood outside the porch, his arms locked behind him in a Napoleonic stance. Just then, the bells of a nearby church tolled to signal the hour of ten o'clock and the holding of a baptismal ceremony. Luna was moved into piety and doffed his cap. With deliberate steps, he proceeded toward the church to pray but found its heavy timber doors closed, guarded by two mean-looking soldiers who seemed to have had one drink too many.

"What the hell are you doing here loafing in a house of worship? Can't you find some other place to grow beard?"

"Don't talk to us that way, Señor Luna, you are not our chief," answered the older of the two men.

Insulted at being addressed as a mere "Señor," Luna flushed. "So, you think you're not answerable to anybody but your boss Aguinaldo? That you don't have to treat me with respect? Let me tell show something, *hijo de –*"

The elder soldier made a move towards him. As Luna was about to reach for his swagger stick to emphasize his anger with a flourish, the two soldiers, threatened, pulled out daggers. They began stabbing Luna in various parts of his muscle-packed body. He staggered back while his escorts froze in shock. He parried the daggers with his bare hands, withstanding all the cuts that would have felled a smaller man, then turned around to escape. Calderon, watching from the window of the nearby town hall, could see in the man's eyes the glare of terror. This was perhaps the only time in his life that he had fled a fight. As he carried himself across the square toward his horse that he had tied to the flagpole, spilling his blood with each heavy step, one of the guards raised his Mauser rifle and fired. The general tumbled in a heap at the feet of his horse. His aide Colonel Roman was also shot and fell at his side. Both bodies lay still on the cobblestoned pavement as Luna's terrified horse neighed and jumped around in an effort to free itself from its leash, almost hitting the bodies with its hooves and kicking up sprays of blood where blotches of it pooled.

From the town hall a hundred yards away, Calderon ran, walked and ran toward the sprawled bodies for he was much too heavy to jog the distance all the way. It was obvious from afar that the wounds of his friend were mortal: all his learning was inadequate to bring back a life irretrievably lost. For some reason, the scene of Jose Rizal being shot down at the Luneta flashed before his eyes, and the contrast could not be more glaring: in a little over two years, the halo of righteousness that Rizal's glorious death had lent to the revolutionary cause had given way to the ignominy of fratricide as exemplified by the sight of Luna being slain by his own men. As he knelt down beside the body, he touched his friend, not to take his pulse, but to comfort him in his repose. "Antonio. Compadre. Antonio," was all he could say.

He recalled the second stanza of Rizal's *Mi Último Adiós*:

> *En campos de batalla, luchando con delirio*
> *Otros te dan sus vidas sin dudas, sin pesar;*
> *El sitio nada importa, ciprés, laurel ó lirio,*
> *Cadalso ó campo abierto, combate ó cruel martirio,*
> *Lo mismo es si lo piden la patria y el hogar.*

> *In fields of battle, deliriously fighting,*
> *Others give you their lives, without doubt, without regret;*
> *Where there's cypress, laurel or lily,*
> *On a plank or open field, in combat or cruel martyrdom,*
> *If the home or country asks, it's all the same — it matters not.*

380

24

JOAQUIN'S CHOICE

Three months later, on September 21, 1899, Joaquin Calderon appeared at the Parian Gate of Intramuros on board a calesa. The sight of the Walled City, after more than a year on the run, evoked a tide of emotions from him: it was a symbol of sovereignty, a fixture in every Filipino's dream, a bastion of privilege as well as a shrine of worship. It was the heart and soul of the colony, straddling the course of its 300-year history. Let the Filipino reign supreme within its walls, and he holds the entire country in his grip. It drew the same feelings from a Filipino as Rome would from a Roman or Jerusalem would from a Jew.

He stepped off the calesa and scanned the walls. Their ancient stones seemed to have been scrubbed to bonelike baldness, completely stripped of lichens and grass, the bas-relief and statuary on the gate revivified from centuries of neglect, burnished to a rocklike finish. He sought to be recognized.

"Papa, where are you going?" Estrella asked, seven months heavy with child.

"Just wait there, *hija.*"

The war situation had become desperate, though not yet lost, but for Calderon there was no point in resisting further. With Luna out of the way – a tragedy that turned out to be a blessing in disguise – Calderon found a pretext to cut off all ties with the rebel movement, declaring himself disgusted over the killing, although he had had an unwitting hand in setting it up. He wanted to get away from the madness of internecine conflict and to seek refuge in the welcoming arms of the Americans.

The war had driven down his living standards to a level which stripped him of self-respect, being no longer able to garnish himself with the frills of a fop. The only garments he had with him were homespun clothes that frayed out quickly in the unforgiving weather. His most precious personal belongings were irredeemably lost: the leather boots in his clinic, the monocle in the Pasig River, a trunk full of the finest apparel, souvenirs from a friar, his house in Malolos. Whatever he had salvaged eventually wore out during the repeated flights away from the pursuing Yankee army – e.g., his heavy overcoat of cashmere, his bowler hat, his cravat and woolen pants. The war had taken a heavy toll on his resources. His clinic was closed, his farm abandoned and his practice profitless. Before he could be bankrupted by the war, he had to make accommodations with the conquering master.

In fact, he had already started the process of wooing the Americans. He belatedly realized that by marrying his daughter to a Yankee soldier he could open doors in the colonial offices that were closed to natives, exactly as during the Spanish times. So was his thought. He did not like the uncouth sailor one bit; however, it was Bailey's influence (or the perception of it) that mattered.

As a doctor, he was temperamentally against Luna's conventional tactics of massed confrontations in set-piece battles. Against a superior force with devastating firepower, Luna's orthodox warfare exacted a horrifying toll in lives. Calderon had had a first-hand look at the casualties of war at the front as almost daily he treated various kinds of injuries – to the eye, limbs and internal organs – inflicted on Filipino troops. He had sewn up wounds with fibers of hemp, amputated dozens of legs with a knife and a saw, wrapped a hectare of burns with leaves. In discharging his duties, Calderon felt more like an undertaker than a doctor. Since he was in constant touch with death, he was more likely to meet the relatives of the dead than Luna. And the hardest part of practice was having to face the anger or grief of widows. He was more likely to be blamed for every death than Luna's military tactics. Consequently, he felt disgust at Luna's callous attitude toward human casualties which ran counter to his mindset as a physician. It was these conflicting interests in the war that broke their friendship.

"Papa, don't leave me here..."

"I'm going to talk to some Americans." Calderon put a piece of paper into his pocket and walked across the bridge.

"Come back, pa, they'll pick you up," cried Estrella. Fragile of health, she was already more rotund than the doctor.

"Don't worry, *hija*. I told you, they won't harm me." As he walked deliberately along the wooden bridge lined with parapets of crossed bars, he was stopped by a sentry.

"Halt! Who goes there?" said the trooper wearing the uniform of the Pennsylvania regiment. "Halt! Or I'll blow your head off!"

Calderon doffed his straw hat which he wore awkwardly in place of his lost bowler hat. "Good morning, sir, I'm looking for General Otis," Calderon said in his accented English. He wouldn't surrender to a lesser man.

"The general? Ha-ha! Why, do you have an appointment with him? I never seen him myself."

"Excuse me, *yo soy ministro de la campamento de general Emilio Aguinaldo*," he identified himself as a member of the insurgent cabinet.

The soldier, red-haired and freckled, gaped in shock at what he understood of the introduction. "You're *what?*"

Calderon explained in a roundabout way, aided by gesticulation.

"So, you're a reb and you're turning yourself in?"

"That is correct."

The soldier turned around and hollered across the moat. "Hey, boys. Come over here. I've landed a big fish!"

As three soldiers ran out of the gate to arrest Calderon, Estrella alit from the calesa and, touching her swollen tummy, bounded her way toward her father. "Papa, papa."

"The guy's got his missus with him. What are we gonna do?"

"Take her along with him."

"If you please, she's my daughter and she's heavy with child."

The red-haired guard assured Calderon: "Don't worry, mister, you'll be safe and we won't touch a hair on your head. We treat rebels who turn themselves in a whole of a lot better than others. I dare say, you're going to be well-treated."

Calderon held on to something in his pocket that was his insurance against imprisonment. From the tenor of the Yankee propaganda, he had no reason to fear that he would be thrown into the dungeon as the Spaniards did with captured revolutionaries. But it was better to hold on to his precious document. Removing his hand from his pocket, he held his daughter protectively as they were led inside the Parian Gate which opened up the forbidden capital to view. The Americans had not altered, but merely primped up, the citadel. Flowering hedges lined the cobblestoned alleys which segregated the complex of palaces and churches. The mahogany trees that grew tall and hirsute were now cropped to form rounded crowns and lush foliage. They were almost as perfectly shaped as the domes of the numerous churches that hogged the skyline, along with the gabled roofs of palaces housing public ministries. Without need of guidance from the guards, Calderon turned toward the sprawling monastery of San Agustin, which occupied a whole block, with one side lining the entire length of a street, forming an unbroken wall of sculptures, framed windows and fluted columns. This was the headquarters of the Army Eighth Corps where General MacArthur held office.

Calderon fully expected to be introduced to Otis whom he thought still ruled as military governor of the islands. He stood for some time at the entrance of the monastery in the company of gargoyles and hydras spouting water on a nearby fountain. His escorts stayed only long enough to get their instructions from an officer in the building. Instead of bringing the captives to the opulent chambers of the military governor, the two guards led Calderon and his daughter toward the more austere bastion of Fort Santiago, the corner of the Walled City guarding the mouth of the Pasig River.

The sight of the Spartan camp, with functional barracks and darkened stables, dismayed Calderon. He found himself being taken alarmingly close to the Baluarte de Santa Barbara, the elevated gun emplacement overlooking the river which stood on the infamous dungeon that once held captured rebels and Barton Bailey. Its forbidding appearance made Calderon's hair stand on end. He balked.

"Wait, wait, there must be a mistake," he quavered.

"We're taking you to the general. Just cool it, the general's mild as goose milk."

"You're not taking me to the dungeon?"

"No, unless you consider the general's office a dungeon."

"But...um, may I ask one more thing?"

"Go ahead, shoot."

"Isn't General Otis holding office at San Agustin?"

"General Otis is no longer the military governor. It's General MacArthur you're gonna see."

Calderon saw the prospect of seeing MacArthur equally daunting. He was the mighty field commander of the U.S. Army which had repeatedly dealt General Luna crushing blows. "MacArthur....the new governor?"

"Yeah, and I tell you, he's mild. Just keep cool and not let on," the red-haired trooper raised his spirits.

Calderon braced himself for the meeting with Aguinaldo's nemesis who had acquired a near supernatural status among Filipino rebels. He wasn't at all comforted by the guard's assurances that he was safe in MacArthur's hands – a captured minister of the rebel government.

The new military governor had the hard-bitten look of a seasoned soldier. His skin was tanned and nearly sunburned, the arms blistered by mosquito bites. The fat that padded his jaws was concealed by a sparse growth of whiskers, flanking his dense moustache. News of Luna's death had eased the sense of crisis at the front and enabled him to concentrate on the civil administration of the colony. Though newly promoted to governor, he declined to transfer his command to Otis's posh quarters in the San Agustin monastery but contented himself with living in the soldier's barracks of Fort Santiago.

Calderon fidgeted in the presence of the great commander. He was overcome by the majesty of the general's presence as if facing a plumed Spanish magistrate. Asked about his name and position, he rattled off his gilt-edged credentials, from his degree earned at the University of Santo Tomas to his office as minister of health in the Aguinaldo cabinet. He reserved his proudest qualification for last. From his left pocket he pulled out a piece of folded parchment lined with frilly borders and filled with sinuous lettering – the marriage contract between Estrella and Bailey.

"You see, señor field marshal, I have a son-in-law who is a soldier in your army, Sergeant Barton Bailey." He nodded toward Estrella. "And my daughter here is his wife."

MacArthur was taken aback. "One of my soldiers? Her husband? How could that be?"

"If you remember, during the battle of the Rio Grande, where you pulled off the greatest victory of American arms in Philippine soil," Calderon tried to butter up the general, "one of your soldiers strayed to our lines and was captured. But I took him under my wings and made sure he was well treated like a special guest in our house. And he turned out to be my daughter's sweetheart from way back..."

"How did they get to know each other?" interrupted MacArthur.

"Well, it seems, in Manila, before this war broke out, they were already acquainted," beamed Calderon.

Just as the proud father-in-law thought he had racked up big points with MacArthur, the latter sighed and lamented: "That is the problem with discipline." He turned to an aide. "Be sure you get that Bailey's name and unit."

Calderon was confused. He could not read the general's reaction.

"I'm very generous with rebels who surrender," MacArthur patted the captives down to a comfortable talk, "especially those holding high-ranking positions like yourself. You can rest assured, Señor Calderon, that our quarrel ends with your voluntary submission to our authority and with your swearing allegiance to the American flag. We intend to work with you, live in peace with you, as brothers in one house. We will offer you a seat in the colonial government which we are right now in the process of organizing, just as we promised you in the Schurman Declaration. Specifically what position we will offer you, that can be discussed later, but with your kind of credentials, a doctor and all, we certainly can put you to good use. Now, are you willing to swear allegiance to the American flag?"

MacArthur seemed to have mellowed overnight. His promotion to governor-general from fighting general instilled him with pragmatic ideas that would ease his civil administration of the colony.

The transformation was lost on Calderon. "Swear my allegiance?... whatever you say, señor Field Marshal," he said fawningly.

An aide led Calderon to a corner where the American flag was displayed on a staff. With MacArthur observing on his feet, the aide asked Calderon to raise his right hand, face the Stars and Stripes and recite the following Oath of Allegiance:

> "I pledge allegiance to the Flag
> of the United States of America and
> to the Republic for which it stands,
> one Nation, indivisible, with liberty
> and justice for all."

The oath of loyalty rolled off Calderon's lips all in one breath, without a pause of hesitation or a tremor of regret. It sounded so like a prayer that the ilustrado doctor punctuated himself by saying "Amen" and began to make the sign of the cross – until interrupted by MacArthur. After reciting the oath, Calderon felt a huge burden roll off his shoulders as if he had purged himself of a terrible sin against God and country. He embraced his daughter who understood nothing of the ceremony and whispered to her: "Let us go, *hija*. They're letting us go."

"Papa, what will become of us?" she asked as they were being led back to the Parian Gate.

"We can now go home as free persons and attend to our problems, especially the birth of your child."

"How about Bart, did you ask them about him?"

"Yes, I even mentioned you were his wife, and I overheard MacArthur ordering his assistant to look for Barton. He was very urgent about it. I'm sure that in a few day he'll come looking for us."

"Let's look for him now. He's here, he's here."

"No, *hija,* we can't be too familiar with them, we just escaped prison by the grace of the field marshal. You stay at home and let the Americans do the work for you."

"Look, there are so many soldiers, he might be among them. Let's go ask them."

Calderon let the driver of the calesa speed on. He said to himself in a voice that sounded like a murmur: "I wasn't wrong in coming down from the mountains. I should have done this a long time ago."

Estrella kept looking at every soldier she encountered around the perimeter of Intramuros and she scrutinized every face under the dented fedora. Once or twice, she thought she had spotted Bailey whom she had last seen riding a carabao cart on the day after their shotgun marriage, but the sightings turned out to be of other soldiers wearing the same uniforms, walking around the secure premises of the conquered city.

Estrella finally gave up and slumped down in her seat. She touched her distended belly wistfully. "I want him present when I give birth to my baby."

"Don't worry, my surrender will be big news to all the city, and Bailey is sure to pick it up and see us."

"And when he sees us, are you going to quarrel him?"

"We'll live as one family. When the Americans give me a job in the colony, we'll work together as partners under a new dispensation," he said pompously.

Calderon was the first minister of the Aguinaldo cabinet to take the Oath of Allegiance to the Yankee flag. In less than a week, news of his surrender reached the rebel headquarters in Cabanatuan, 100 miles from Manila. True to Filipino culture, the news did not elicit cries of treason or betrayal from among the ranks of revolutionaries but induced serious soul-searching among his former colleagues. They tried to understand and justify his motives. Perhaps, he was simply demoralized by the killing of his compadre General Luna, which he had seen with his own eyes. Or, more likely, he was drawn to the American camp by the ties of affinity that bound him to his son-in-law, Barton Bailey. Either of the two reasons was sufficient to undermine his relations with the rebel movement and, particularly, his loyalty to Aguinaldo. They wished him well.

In the next few months, other ilustrado ministers trekked to Manila to follow the example of Calderon – e.g., Paterno, Buencamino, Agoncillo and Arellano. They all pronounced themselves disgusted at the killing of Luna by Aguinaldo's henchmen, a crime that ranked with the execution of

Andres Bonifacio as the darkest blot on Aguinaldo's career, and condemned their president to high heavens. For all of Luna's faults, he was still an ilustrado, and the manner of his liquidation was revolting to their sense of decency as enlightened men. All of which criticisms were mere pretexts for breaking with their patriotic oath. They followed Calderon because they knew that their cause was lost and that the Americans had come to stay – and rule. Most importantly, they didn't want to be shut out of the colonial government that the Americans were forming, with native representation. In the mad scramble for prominent seats, the aristocracy of the learned could not afford to be mere bystanders.

The defections left Aguinaldo alone, virtually without an educated adviser. This did not hamper Aguinaldo's ability to wage war. On the contrary, it consolidated all power in his hands, such that the republic he had inaugurated in Malolos with much fanfare, one governed by a constitution, was now without most of its officials, reduced to a mere guerrilla band in the mountains. In short, he was now just an outlaw on the run. The prestige he lost with the defection of his illustrious ministers stripped away his pretensions to democratic leadership. With the loss of his cabinet, he scaled down his objective from governing a country to killing Yankees.

Contrary to the claims of his detractors, Aguinaldo did not instigate Luna's murder. It was an ordinary if not random crime, which just happened to be committed by his bodyguards with insufficient provocation. Aguinaldo shared Luna's dream of an ultimately free and sovereign Philippines. Only their tactics differed. He was not party to Luna's quarrel with the members of the cabinet, because he stood above the fray. He had not made a decision whether or not to accept the

Schurman Declaration. Neither did he consider Luna a rival to the leadership of the republican movement because, for all of his authoritarian ways, Luna was not a politician. He did not hold the love and loyalty of the Filipino troops, but commanded only their fears. On the other hand, Aguinaldo held the affection of a vast number of Filipinos, starting with the inhabitants of his home province of Cavite and other Tagalog provinces who were impressed by his successes against the Spaniards. Luna was more of a soldier than a politician, unlike Aguinaldo who was both.

As proof that he had no quarrel with Luna, Aguinaldo pressed ahead with the war following the news of his death. The mass surrender of his enlightened advisers did not give him pause but instead rallied his resolve – exactly the same reaction as it would have drawn from Luna. In a way, he felt liberated from the endless bickering around the cabinet table and he preferred to settle the issue at the battle front. In tactics, however, he did not follow Luna's trench warfare and set-piece methods, lifted from the Clausewitz school of military science. He was more at home with the instinctive, unpredictable tactics of guerrilla warfare, which was the preferred method of fighting by Filipino rebels since time immemorial. The method proved effective.

While the conventional phase of the war lasted all of six months, the guerrilla warfare which Aguinaldo inaugurated with fresh energy lasted years. It confounded American strategists and exasperated politicians in the mainland. Aguinaldo divided his army into small bands of guerrillas, often composed of as few as a dozen men, and deployed them all over the provinces to prey on American camps and supply lines. They laid ambush to passing columns and patrols, then, after a brief skirmish, faded back to the forest. They did not fight to hold a position, unlike Luna, but fought to inflict casualties. As a result, Aguinaldo was able to engage the American forces in sporadic battles in several places at the same time. His mosquito warfare across an amorphous front that dissolved into footprints drove MacArthur into a tizzy the way Luna's orthodox tactics never did. When he pushed his forces into Cabanatuan, he found that the enemy leader was gone. In fact, Aguinaldo had decided to disappear completely from the map, abandoning the practice of holding town after town as he retreated. His whereabouts became a mystery to all except a handful of select officers. In time, he was rumored to have stolen away with the wind to the north, across several mountains ranges. The location of his guerrilla camp was traced as far away as the mountains of Palanan, Isabela, near the coast of the Pacific, which was a good 200 miles from Manila by the South China Sea. Equally remote was the end of the war.

Aguinaldo's most notable achievement as a guerrilla leader was his reversal of the disproportion in casualties that the war inflicted among combatants in both camps. Under Luna's generalship, ten Filipinos died for every American killed. With Aguinaldo in command, the ratio was about even at worst, or lopsided in the guerrilla's favor at best. At the end of May 1899, Otis was sacked. Washington was going to reexamine its military policy in the Philippines.

———————

Two months after Calderon's surrender, or on November 15, 1899, another person entered his life: a grandchild. Estrella gave birth to a bouncing baby boy of complex genealogy. He was one-half American, one-eight Spanish, one-sixteenth Chinese and of indeterminate fraction *indio*. His skin was pink and his hair brownish. Even his cry sounded a little exotic, halfway between a sing and a bawl. Though he was fully qualified to midwife the delivery, Calderon modestly opted out of the operation and allowed a barrio lady *comadrona* to do the job herself in accordance with native tradition.

"Look how very pretty she is," he gushed.

"It's a he," corrected the old lady.

"Oh-ho-ho, so cute, look at his cheeks, so like a pair of apples." Calderon was tickled pink by the sight of the squirming baby. Barely in his middle age at 41, he was already a grandfather like so many other Filipinos who had married early. "It feels so good to be a Lolo," he said. "It's like being born to a new life."

Estrella was asleep in a room at the upper floor of his Escolta clinic, and when she woke up, pale and dizzy from her travails, Calderon cheered her up. "Look at your kid, Ella, isn't he so plump? So like an apple?"

She groped for her child which was lying beside her, wrapped in a cocoon of linen. "Bart?"

"Oh, I'm sorry but he is still not around. But I left a message at his camp. The last time we spoke, about a week ago, I told him you were going to give birth this week. He must be back right now."

She sank back to sleep, then, half an hour later, woke up to caress her son. "He'll be happy to see him," she smiled, referring to Bailey.

"Yes, yes, just as I am."

"Soon?"

"Once he reads my letter, he'll come running. And don't worry, *hija,* we're getting along. I don't have any problems with him anymore."

Calderon doted on the infant in his Escolta clinic. This one is a little mestizo like me, he gushed. With the father away on war duty and the mother recuperating from the labors of childbirth, he took care of the baby with the same solicitude that he showed his patients. The child's wrinkled face was wont to break up into a scream, and its limbs to flail and wriggle in its linen. It slavered milk, pissed a clear liquid and extruded dung. For all these, it was a bundle of joy and blessing. The doctor took delight in his parental chores, which recalled the best moments of his youth. His most pleasant routine was giving the child a ritual bath early in the morning. This he did by floating the baby in a vat of water at the backyard, steering it like a boat, then, with one hand underwater to support its keel of a spine, he slopped water all over its body with his other hand. How cute, how sweet little thing it was, he kept cooing. He countered its frequent bawling with songs of his own – Spanish lullabies, church hymns, Tagalog ballads. When Estrella gained enough strength to take up the motherly chores herself, he yielded the child reluctantly and resumed the drudgery of medical practice.

Then, one day, Bart Bailey appeared on the doorstep of the clinic. He was wearing his weather-beaten Army uniform with a faded cap and frayed suntan, with some buttons missing. He knocked gently on the door which on his last visit he had half-demolished with his rifle butt.

It was Estrella who answered the knock carrying their child. They exchanged glances in silence. The sight of the baby yawning in her arms followed by the sound of it burping moved Bailey almost by reflex to cradle it in his arms.

Bailey looked at the mother. He chuckled. He yelped. "Our baby?"

"Bart."

"His name?"

"No name. We were waiting for you."

He smelt and tickled the baby with his nose, prattling a string of nonsense. Its warmth and softness aroused in him for the first time the instincts of fatherhood.

From the stairs rumbled the footsteps of Joaquin Calderon. "I'm sure it was just in the *aparador* somewhere." He seemed to be looking for something. "I was just looking..."

"Papa."

"Uh."

"Sir..."

Calderon looked over the stairwell landing at the man who, five months before, he had wanted to kill with his bare hands.

Bailey stayed in the clinic only for a few hours. Army regulations made it impossible for him to cohabit with his wife. Home for him was the barracks and it was there that he returned later that day and every day thereafter. U.S. servicemen were prohibited from fraternizing with natives and his marriage to Estrella was a transgression of a serious kind. His double-life didn't escape notice by the Army for long, courtesy of the boastful if unwitting admission made by Calderon to MacArthur during his surrender. His continued stay in the Army became untenable and so, toward the end of 1899 at the close of the century, he opted to be discharged honorably from the military. He became one of the first American colonists to settle in the islands, which saw an influx of teachers, engineers, Protestant missionaries, prospectors and traders, different from the carpetbaggers who invaded and picked on the bones of the downtrodden South after the Civil War because the colonists were motivated by good intentions, being idealists and men of visible means out to make contributions to the land.

Bailey walked out of the Army barracks in Fort Santiago with only a duffel bag containing his meager belongings and $175 in his pocket. He had only vague plans ahead of him – which included applying for a post in the fledgling civil service as a tugboat captain in the Manila harbor or a locomotive operator in the Luzon railway, jobs where his sailor's skills could come in handy (e.g., steering a boat or stoking coal). There was absolutely no doubt in his mind that he could put down stakes in the islands.

He showed up at the clinic with his duffel bag to inaugurate a new life as husband and father. While Estrella was only too happy to have him, he soon got under the skin of Joaquin for his lack enthusiasm in finding a job. He seemed content to help in the household work and play with his son. It appeared that he was intent in burning through all his savings before even considering the imperative of finding a means of living.

Calderon soon discovered that he had overestimated Bailey's usefulness to the advancement of his career: it was utterly irrelevant since his ilustrado credentials alone qualified him to the top of the totem pole. He was able to get an appointment right away as chief of the Manila public hospital in Paco, which used to be headed by a Spaniard and which for the first time allowed him to earn a decent salary. But this was no more than a stepping stone for him – he was angling for one of the positions in the colonial cabinet which the civil administration had reserved for Filipinos. It was while warming his seat that he learned that the U.S. military frowned upon marriages between soldiers and local señoritas. The reason had to do less with racial prejudice than with the morale of troops whose fighting ability suffered as a result. It was therefore the bitterest of ironies that Calderon ended up supporting Bailey.

As to what his Yankee son-in-law intended to do with his life after his discharge, Calderon had not the faintest idea. He did not share Estrella's happiness in simply seeing Bailey at home doing nothing. He wanted Bailey to join the rush to take advantage of the job opportunities that suddenly opened up for both colonists and locals – such as positions in the Insular Police or the Customs, for examples. Instead, Bailey played the bum. When he did go out of the Escolta neighborhood, it was to paint the town red with his former Army and Navy buddies and, as Calderon later learned to his disgust, to bet on cockfighting. He was extremely disappointed that the young man exhibited none of his ambitious drive.

"And by the way, Barton, instead of loafing around the house, start thinking of a civilian job. The Customs is a good place to start."

"I have several plans, but I have not settled on one just yet."

Such nonchalance about one's own future irked Calderon no end. He wanted to see more of himself in Bailey, the young man who spent a family fortune to get an education in

Spain. "I would be glad if you start writing letters to the governor's office now."

Bailey did not even bother to answer the doctor. He had his own way of doing things.

"So, where do you plan to go after you've spent all your savings?"

"Fix up the house. Do some carpentry work."

Calderon reddened. "What do you mean carpentry work? That's not the kind of livelihood I expect of my son-in-law! Find something respectable to do!"

"I'm gonna find a job, sir, that's for sure. But I just can't say what now."

"Well, *hijo,* better do so now," Calderon tried to control himself. *"El tiempo perdino no se recupera jamás.* Lost time can never be recovered. And I say now because all the choice jobs are bound to be filled up in a short time. There's the Customs, there's the police."

Bailey was unperturbed. "Don't worry, papa, I can very well find something respectable to do. Don't get hung up over it."

When the family debated the name to give the child, Bailey did not even assert his own choice. Joaquin wanted an Anglo-Saxon name in keeping with the times, whereas Estrella insisted on a Spanish name in accordance with tradition.

"Let's call him Stephen," he proposed aloud. "Well, Robert is okay. And why not William?"

"That's Bart's first name."

"So much the better."

"If we give him a peculiar name different like no others, all the boys will kid him and laugh at him," she demurred. "Let's not make growing up hard for him." She made a run-down of acceptable names, such as Diego, Simeon, Jaime, Sebastian and Tadeo. The last name appealed most to her ears.

"It's Tadeo." She bounced the baby in her arms and cooed: "Hello, Tadeo."

Bailey only laughed at the debate.

Calderon whined: "But aren't you the wife of an American?"

"It's perfectly okay with me, papa," Bailey seconded his wife – which did not please the patriarch at all.

After grumbling for a few minutes, the doctor cheered up. "If I remember it right, Abraham Lincoln had a son named Tad. Very well, you call him Tadeo, I call him Tad."

"Tad, Teddy, sounds good," the father shrugged.

Bailey did not impose himself on his family. He subordinated himself to a minor role in family affairs, deferring to the wishes of the patriarch Calderon and the whims of his wife, Estrella. Motherhood had transformed Estrella from an innocent teenage girl with juvenile impulses to a domineering, headstrong woman. She ceaselessly pecked on Bailey for stealing weekdays away to carouse around with his buddies. Her increasing fluency with the English language gave her enough confidence and facility to nag him to death whenever she got wrought up over her marital woes.

Therefore, the aristocratic Calderon took it upon himself to build the family a foundation on the rock of the new colonial order. If Barton Bailey could not be relied upon to raise the family's social stature, Joaquin now knew how to do it. He announced plans for holding an extravagant baptism of his grandchild at the San Agustin monastery. To the ceremony he invited Bailey's Navy and Army colleagues, among them, Scott Preston, Lt. Cocker and five Kansan volunteers (Preston and Cocker having been discharged earlier from the Navy to found a successful trading company in Binondo). On the mother's side, Estrella allowed his proud father to invite a gaggle of ilustrado guests, all surrendered members of the Aguinaldo Cabinet: Paterno, Agoncillo, Buencamino and Arellano. All of them stood as godfathers to the infant Tadeo.

Exactly as Calderon had predicted the grand baptism kicked up a fuss in the enclave of Intramuros, now the bastion of American rule. He was able to gather in one place the former warring protagonists of a colonial conflict. On one side of the church stood the Yankee godfathers mostly clad in starched khakis and dented fedoras, and on the other side crowded the well-heeled ilustrado godfathers garbed in tail-coats, bowler hats and polished canes. They occupied separate columns of the church pews but after the ceremony they hob-nobbed together as if they had never been at war. A crowd of curious people gathered outside the church to witness the odd assembly. They were attracted by the sight of the Yankee con-quistador and ilustrado caste joining hands to bless the birth of an American *mestizo*.

His choice of the baroque church of San Agustin was inspired for it was the erstwhile haven of the Spanish aristo-cracy. Apart from being one of the oldest churches in the Phil-ippines, it contained one relic that attracted both the pious and the curious: the bones of Miguel Lopez de Legazpi who con-quered the archipelago for the Spanish crown in the 1570's. His remains lay interred in a tomb at one side of the altar, with his finned bronze helmet set on top.

Under the vaulted ceilings of San Agustin church, an Augustinian priest with a shaven pate subjected the infant Ta-deo to the Catholic rite of baptism. He uttered a string of Latin verses that were intended to instill the articles of faith into its tender soul. He fed the infant with salt and sprinkled its red hair with holy water while the wisp of a being squirmed in the arms of the mother. Amidst the echoes of prayer, the father and godfathers surrounded the infant holding lighted candles which wafted black fumes to the paintings of angels and saints above them, seemingly afloat in the air, riding billows of clouds.

After the rite, they filed out of the chapel to attend a photographic session. Calderon insisted on taking a memento of the event that he could show off to visitors as proof of his mighty connections. "This will take only a few minutes," Cal-deron explained. "Let's get ready, keep the boy quiet, *hija*."

The guests didn't need prodding. The Yankee godfa-thers, all sunburned and ramrod straight, stood at one wing.

The ilustrados, mustachioed and monocled, gathered at the other wing. At the center of the assembly clustered the parents and Calderon in all his rotundity. "Ho-ho, only my second time here," he smirked.

"Okay, hold on there, look at the camera," said the photographer who was hiding under the skirt of a tripod topped by a camera. "Move a little closer ... there."

The two wings huddled closer.

"Ready..."

Calderon's smirk was getting strained.

The photographer stooped into the skirt like an ostrich and signaled with his arm. "The tall guys, a little closer, no moving now. Okay, ready, one-two-beautiful."

The photograph that Calderon got from the ceremony survived long in his household, a treasured memento in his living room which grew in sentimental value over the decades even as the paper itself yellowed with age. It evidenced the sterling bloodline of the family and illustrated the essential role of the mestizo in the colony's history.

Calderon's prospects brightened even more with the arrival of a group of civilians from the United States. On June 3, 1900, a steamer carrying the Taft Commission dropped anchor at Manila Bay to pave the way for the disbandment of the military rule of MacArthur.

At the head of the party was William Howard Taft. His arrival made a mark on the islands which was not just symbolic but real as his footprints. As soon as he stepped off the ramp of the *Hancock,* the steamer seemed to bob an inch up in the water, because this passenger was a 300-pound behemoth, nearly twice the size of Calderon. Rolled up in his coat was a document signed by McKinley appointing him civil governor with the requisite authority to organize a civilian administration in the islands. Part of his mandate was to give the Filipinos "such representation in the civil government as to give them the opportunity to manage their own local affairs to the fullest extent."

Taft's arrival buoyed Calderon's hopes. He was becoming unhappy with his job as director of the Paco hospital, which was a hurried appointment to get him off the rebel ranks but which did not quite suit his high opinion of himself. He was angling for a higher position befitting his ilustrado credentials.

Ever since he swore allegiance to America, he had written dozens of letters to MacArthur whom he obsequiously addressed as "His Grand Excellency the Honorable Governor-General" seeking appointment to the cabinet, which the Schurman Plan promised to open up to the Filipinos. All went unanswered. Unknown to him, the governor-general preferred to govern by martial law while playing lip service to the intendments of the Schurman Plan. He put a glass ceiling on all appointments beyond which no Filipino could rise. Positions in the police, the Customs and the public schools were all right but not higher. The arrival of William Howard Taft changed all that. A former Ohio judge and later U.S. President, he was toting a more authoritative "McKinley Plan" that MacArthur could not merely fiddle with. The plan relegated the position of military governor to a transitory figure who would warm the seat of power until a civilian administrator was deemed fit to take over the reins of government. Martial rule was to give way to full civilian rule in a year's time. Under the scheme, the military governor was to serve as "the chief executive head of the government of the island" only "until the complete transfer of control" of the insular administration to a civilian body headed by Taft. Therein lay the seeds of discord between the two governors that redounded to the benefit of Joaquin Calderon.

The lumbering Taft was not one to mince his steps in the presence of a battle-scarred general. He took the reins of power right away. He governed the colony as if MacArthur had only ceremonial duties. With full confidence in the support of McKinley, the portly lawyer began appointing former insurgents to high positions in the government over the objections of the general. MacArthur "looks at his task as one of conquering eight million recalcitrant, treacherous and sullen people," Taft wearily wrote to secretary of war Elihu Root. He was determined to govern differently.

On September 10, 1900, Calderon found a letter tucked in the shutter of his window, bearing the heading of Malacañang Palace and the signature of William Howard Taft, now known by the unofficial title of civil governor. It was the first time Calderon learned of the ascendancy of a civilian in the land. In his message Taft offered him a position as administrator of the mountainous Cordillera region. "I have taken notice of your position in the Aguinaldo government and wish to avail ourselves of your able services. The Filipinos have gone through difficult times during the past years and doubtless would benefit from the services of educated men like yourself. I need a qualified man to act as the deputy chief of the Bureau of Non-Christian Tribes, one of the most important offices of my Commission. He will be the administrator of the Cordillera region, tasked with the duty of civilizing the Igorot tribes of the North. Of all the educated natives qualified for the job, I have found you best suited for the position. If you're interested, my office will make the proper arrangements."

The courtesy of Taft's message was music to Calderon's ears, contrasting to MacArthur's snobbery. Although the office was not the kind he had sought, being alien to his qualifications as a doctor, the significance of the offer slowly dawned on him. Calderon was being made a chieftain of the mountain tribes, particularly the head-hunting Igorots of the north. Under Spanish rule, the authority to "civilize" the natives included the power of life and death over the subject people, a power that had been wielded by Spanish magistrates assigned to remote positions in the interior. That Taft appointed a physician to a top post in the bureau, instead of a surrendered general, spoke of the Americans' enlightened style of colonial administration. He felt good about himself that his outstanding merits had been recognized and he took a deep breath of satisfaction. At the same time, he felt pity for his colleagues in the revolution who were still out in the mountains. Here he was, being installed in an office that Filipinos could only dream about under Spanish rule, and there they were, still holding out in the forest, fighting for a lost cause. They should all come out of the cold now and join hands with him in administering the colony.

Unknown to Calderon, his appointment as Cordillera administrator strained the relations between the two American governors to a breaking point. MacArthur was adamantly opposed to giving former insurgents major positions in the insular government: the practice mocked his bloody campaign to bring down the local insurgency, he said, for it enabled the rebels to rise from defeat to positions of power in the American Raj. "It is not all too strong an expression to say that he is sore at my appointments," Taft wrote to secretary of war Root. "His nerves are so tense on the subject that the slightest inadvertence on the part of any of the Commission leads to correspondence which shows it only too clearly."

By way of relief from the heated dispatches he was getting from MacArthur, Taft kept up a lively correspondence with secretary Root in Washington. In response to a query from Root about how he was "adjusting to the weather in the islands," the 300-pound Taft related that he was doing fine in his Malacañang retreat and, in fact, he had "just finished a 25-mile horseback ride along the Pasig River," thank you. Root inquired: "How's horse?"

Governor Taft's closeness to the Washington bigwigs enabled him to override MacArthur's vetoes on his appointments. Thus, he was able to dispatch Calderon to the Cordilleras.

Before departing for Baguio, capital of the Cordillera highlands, Calderon agonized over the prospect of leaving his daughter and grandson in Manila. To be torn away from his family again by the call of duty was heart-rending to a man who thrived on the affection of his family. But duty took precedence over sentimentality. Besides, he was getting fed up with the growing bad habits of Bailey who, together with other discharged American soldiers, had taken a liking to the bloody sport of cockfighting, which appealed to their taste for combat. Giddy with excitement after a visit to the arena, they would unwind on whisky and song at a corner *carenderia* where they frittered away the rest of day. So taken was Bailey by the national pastime that he tried his hand at raising fighting cocks in Caloy's abandoned workshop, a vice that annoyed his aristocratic father-in-law who looked down on the depraved sport. This was not the way Calderon had wanted the marriage to turn out. Maybe, if he cut the umbilical cord, he thought, his dissolute son-in-law would shape up and learn to provide for his family.

"I am going up to Baguio, Ella," he bade farewell to his daughter. "Learn some English, I will see to it that you get a job in my bureau."

"She gets enough English in the house every day," drawled his bum of a son-in-law in the living room. "No reason for her to leave."

"And you, I've been telling you to see MacArthur in his office so you'll land a job at Customs. You won't listen. What will you do after you spend all your back pay?"

"Pops, there're a hundred ways to earn a living. Don't you worry. I'm planning to start a fishing business with Scott Preston. Or a tobacco farm. What the hell. We've seen carpetbaggers become rich men with nothing but the shirts on their backs."

"My daughter and grandson, I am leaving them in your hands..."

"Go, now, pa, don't worry about us." Estrella led the doctor out of the door. "We'll manage. Bart, help him out with his bags, he's leaving for the mountains alone."

"Okay, okay, darling. Let me carry this one for you, pop."

Together, the two men loaded boxes and chests full of clothing and medical equipment aboard a pair of calesas. Calderon planned to ride the urban conveyance only up to the northern border of Manila, where a caravan of ox-drawn carriages was waiting to take him and a group of U.S. Army engineers to the highlands of the Cordilleras. He edged his daughter aside and reached into his wallet tucked in the inside of his coat to pull out a roll of bills. "This will take care of your needs for the next two months," he handed the money to the barefoot Estrella who had followed him to the street. "I hope by then your husband will have already received a call from MacArthur."

Estrella looked around to make sure Bailey was not watching, then pulled her father aside. "Pa," she said in a hushed voice. "Will you be the one to write Señor Taft a letter? Barton is much too proud to do such a thing."

"Yo he escrito la carta. I have written the letter already. Knowing him, I don't want him to think he got his job because of me." He never expected that he would end up helping his own son-in-law get a job in the colonial government.

Estrella was pleased and stood on her bare toes to kiss her father. "Bye, pa."

"Okay, now." Calderon mounted the calesa and waved. *"Me voy ahora mismo."*

———————

25

BACK FROM THE SIERRA MADRE

Carlos let the scene play out before him before taking action that would redeem the reputation of his family. In a remote barrio in Tayabas at the foot of the Sierra Madre mountain range, he allowed a cockfighting match to engage the attention of five members of the Tenth Pennsylvania Regiment before giving the signal to attack. He was as much engrossed in the spectacle as the Yankee soldiers who were drawn to the native sport in the way it spilled blood and guts. The two roosters faced each other, their eyes flaring, hackles raised, straining at their handlers who held them back by their tails to inflame them with impatience and make them more willing to kill. They were armed with iron spurs called gaffs lashed to their legs by a band of cloth. Released, they blew into each other in a frenzy of hacking and flailing that took all but a few seconds but appeared to take an eternity to a trained eye such as Caloy's. He saw every bit of action in the whirlwind of motions, of the gaffs ripping into the breasts and slashing at the wings, of the dominant bird flying higher than the other and fighting from a height and riding down the blows all the way back to the ground, where they continued to duel with dwindling strength, thrashing and kicking until one collapsed and became a ball of feathers and tattered flesh. It was every bit as gory as hand-to-hand combat between samurai swordsmen or soldiers with bayonets, a fight to the death in its most barbarous but purest form. The action took place in a clearing in the barrio bordering on a bamboo grove, with a thatch hut on the other side and children playing naked in the sidelines.

The Yankee volunteers stumbled upon the game in which they had taken a perverse interest while on jungle patrol in the mountains of Tayabas where Aguinaldo was thought to have fled with his elusive army. Distinguished by their dented fedoras and thin band of cloth running down the length of their trousers, they let down their guard to lay their bets, leaving their Springfields propped up on the wall of a nearby hut in the care of a native scout. They cheered as the barefoot *sentenciador* or umpire raised the winning cock with one hand and let the losing one dangle from the other. They cashed their bets laughing at each other. At which time, Carlos gave the order to attack.

From behind the bushes and a covered cart, a dozen rebels brandishing bolos far bigger than the roosters' bladed spurs swarmed upon the five Yankees as the crowd broke up. Carlos stabbed one on the back with a dagger that he had hidden in his shirt, then let his comrades finish the others off while he helped himself to the dollars bills flying around. The ground, already sprinkled with blood and feathers of the fighting roosters, became slick with the blood and guts of the surprised Americans who fell into each other without a fight. In the stark silence of the aftermath, the band picked the wallets of the Americans, their watches and rings, their boots, canteens and Web-cartridge belts. Most importantly, they carried away their rifles which the native scout abandoned to flee with the rest of the villagers. They also made off with the two carcasses of the chickens that had been dropped by the panicky sentenciador (the winning one having also expired from its wounds) to feed their empty stomachs in the long trip back to the mountains.

As they retired, one of the soldiers stirred and with a revolver which the rebels had missed fired off all of its six bullets into the bushes before expiring.

One of the shots hit Carlos on the buttocks and he dropped down screaming, "I'm hit." He felt the blood running down the back of his thigh. "Son of a...." He cursed. "Kulas, I thought you made sure everyone was dead."

"There could be other soldiers," Kulas answered. "Hurry."

"Pick me up. I can't run. Let's go!" Carlos urged, scared by the thought of the enemy giving chase.

They carried him alternately on their backs until, at a safe distance in the jungle, they were able to fashion a makeshift hammock out of tent canvas and a bamboo pole.

"We have to catch up with El Jefe," urged Carlos. "We have to tell him we have just won a battle."

"Don't you want to be taken to Tayabas where a doctor can take care of you?" said the co-leader of the band named Kulas, a man in his fifties.

"Don't tell me you are tired of carrying me around?" Carlos said bitterly.

"It's not that."

"You can't take me to the town. I will be arrested there."

"You will be safe in Tayabas. Your brother has already joined the *yanquis*, they won't give you trouble there," followed another comrade with a touch of sarcasm.

"I want you to bring me to General Aguinaldo so he will give me proper credit for killing five Americans. Don't you understand?"

That he would talk nakedly of grabbing credit for the bloody ambush before they could even catch their collective breath spoke of how far his reputation had fallen in the organization. Carlos Calderon was the most unpopular officer in the guerrilla band. His double-dealing with the Americans had nullified whatever credit he gained for killing Esteban Zaragoza. Coupled with Joaquin's surrender to the Americans, his record of duplicity had marginalized him in the rebel army so that his rank of captain meant nothing. He was looked down upon with barely concealed contempt even by the ordinary soldiers who were left to pick up the pieces after the elite ilustrados had deserted the cause. Until now, he had escaped punishment because his ambiguous actions always fell short of patent treachery; but his perceived disloyalty alienated the unlettered soldiers so as to leave him virtually friendless. After the war shifted to guerrilla warfare, without a front and organized resistance, he drifted from one guerrilla band to another until he chanced upon the idea of luring a band of Americans to an ambush in order to prove his loyalty to the movement with the blood of the enemy in his hands.

After days of continuous hiking, they finally caught up with the remnants of Aguinaldo's army which had abandoned Luna's conventional warfare in favor of hit-and-run tactics.

"El Jefe, you know what we just did?" he reported to the chief.

"So, I heard. Four *yanquis*, not bad," said Aguinaldo exhibiting surprising foreknowledge.

"Five."

"The last one lived long enough to shoot you."

Carlos smirked, then slumped down in disappointment in his hammock. The fact that the chief knew of the incident in advance showed that someone else had reported the feat to Aguinaldo – and claimed credit for it while minimizing his participation. That could only be his co-leader Kulas who had rushed ahead of his hammock as they approached Aguinaldo's bivouac and whose figure he saw slinking away from behind the leader as Carlos narrated the incident.

In addition, the tone of El Jefe's voice was cold, subtly disparaging, opposed to the triumphant nature of the news. The unwelcoming mood of his comrades further alienated him and he spent the next days sulking in his litter. It all had something to do with the defection of his brother, he thought, yet no one brought up the matter as if it were an infectious subject that had to be declared taboo for its capacity to corrupt everyone's mind.

On a ridge atop the Sierra Madre Mountains, overlooking the Pacific Ocean, 300 miles from Manila, the wounded Carlos felt that he could go no farther. He felt he was dying of his injury, made worse by neglect and compounded psychologically by ostracism. Moreover, the changing climate was retarding his body's ability to fight off infection. From his hammock, he could sense that they were high up in the mountains where the biting cold turned his breath into fog and the mist into frigid rain. He could tell the remoteness of their location from the sight of monkey-eating eagles gliding in the skies with wings spread like sails to carry them long distances, surfing the wind streams that were roiled by the mercurial weather of the mountain range. He was impatient. He was miserable. And he had to go home.

When El Jefe next passed by his way in an inspection of the troops who had joined him in his grueling retreat to the north, he brought up the courage to plead: "I don't want to be a burden to you, sir, please, allow me to go home. Let me live my last days in the company of my family, El Jefe."

"You mean you want to *join* your brother."

"Just go home to Bulacan. Join my family, I'll get by without *Kuya*."

"We'll bring you all the way to Manila. So your *Kuya* can give you the proper treatment at the hospital in Intramuros where he's now treating the American wounded."

There it was. The gentle sarcasm. The backhanded retort. "No, too dangerous, General. I will be happy to get home to Malolos."

Upon Aguinaldo's orders, Carlos Calderon was sent home, carried by two pairs of soldiers who took turns supporting the hammock on their shoulders while they wended their way along trails and river banks. After a week's journey across the Sierra Madre mountains, the party caught a stray carabao

410

and fashioned a sledge out of bamboo with two reclining stilts which carried Carlos leisurely the rest of the way home. It took the party more than a month to reach Malolos, Bulacan, a good 300-mile journey from the Sierra Madre mountains.

When his family saw his frail, emaciated figure, they first cheered at his miraculous return, then later broke down in tears at his condition, seeing in him the plight of their other relatives and townsmen who had joined Aguinaldo in his long march. "How about Jose? How about Tomas? How are they doing?" they wept.

Carlos, however, enjoyed peace for only a few days. He knew the long arm of the American authorities would soon reach him. He didn't wait for long.

At midnight on April 5, 1901, he was awakened by the rumble of hoof beats, followed by persistent knocks on the door. This was it. They had come to get him. Having gained some mobility, he hobbled toward the door himself to meet his fate, guided only by the faint glow of a lamp; but even his uncanny instincts for danger did not prepare him for what he saw.

"Caloy." In strode Joaquin, accompanied by two figures who stayed behind. "I'm so glad to see you."

"*Kuya*," Carlos could only address his elder brother.

"God, how you look."

Their year-long separation, spanning seasons of adversity and peril, heightened the emotion of their reunion. They hugged each other, Carlos exerting a limp embrace and Joaquin a robust clutch. Only the year before, it was not difficult to tell which was the stronger brother. Tears snagged the words before they left their lips and they broke down into sobbing. Carlos noticed the two men outside the door bearing torches: they were American soldiers.

"You've come to take me, *Kuya*?"

"I'll take care of you. Just come with me. Nothing's going to happen to you."

"Where are we going?"

"I'm taking you to Manila. Don't talk about it now. I'll nurse you back to health there."

As quietly as he had arrived, Carlos mysteriously disappeared from Malolos, his fate unknown even to his other relatives in the small community. The following day, American troops made the motion of conducting a house-to-house search for the fugitive blacksmith, but no trace could be found of him. It was rumored that he had fled back to the mountains to rejoin Aguinaldo. The rumors were to prove right.

———

A courtyard full of horses and oiled cannons was the sight that got Caloy's attention in the first light of day. It was here where the endless columns of soldiers and their armaments started out on their trek to the mountains in the hunt for Aguinaldo's army. Surrounding the courtyard was an arcade of barracks made of concrete and brick, each arched cell containing quarters for a dozen soldiers. Lining the courtyard were six rows of modern cannons, detached from their gun carriages and resting on pairs of wooden wheels, their barrels glistening from a thick coat of oil. Along the rambling alleys of stone marched a constant parade of officers, smartly dressed in starched tunics and bulbous pants with a single stripe running along the length of their legs. This was Fort Santiago, the center of operations of the U.S. Army.

He was brought in chains inside a brick building where a three-man military tribunal sat ready to try him on one charge of swindling the U.S. Army and another charge of rebellion. In contrast to the rap on the knuckle he had received for the killing of Esteban Zaragoza two years before, he faced the maximum penalty of death. He was subjected to a mock trial heard by an American magistrate, attended by an American prosecutor who lined up American witnesses to prove the

412

charges so that, in all of one day, he was tried and convicted, pursuant to the Spanish Penal Code that the Americans continued to enforce.

The head magistrate was 36-year old General Frederick Funston, now commissioned officer of the regular army, which absorbed him after the disbandment of the Kansan volunteer regiment. He was now commanding general of the 3rd Infantry Brigade. He gave the accused a cold, penetrating look as soon as he was ready to read the sentence. For a country which prided itself on its devotion to the ideals of fair play and free enterprise, the act of swindling Uncle Sam of money through the pretense of hard work was an odious crime. This was especially so for the military judge, who lived by the simple virtues of his farming state of Kansas.

"On the count of *estafa* or swindling committed by false pretenses or fraudulent acts, by falsely pretending to possess power, influence, qualification, property, credit, agency, business or other imaginary transactions, to the prejudice of the United States of America in the amount of $200 received by you in part payment of 1,000 bolos which you did not deliver or did not intend to deliver, this tribunal hereby sentences you to ten years in prison at hard labor. On the count of rebellion committed by rising publicly and taking up arms against the government, this tribunal sentences you to … death by firing squad. Let this be an example to all. Post notices of the date of execution at prominent places around the City of Manila." The hardscrabble Kansan banged the gavel, satisfied that justice had been served.

Carlos was stunned, then outraged. He thought he was going to be taken cared of by his brother Joaquin. He thought he was going to be given an appointment of some kind. Instead, he had been set up for arrest. He had been sold down the river by his own kin – something far more dishonorable than swindling. He was dragged screaming Tagalog epithets at his guards and at the panel of judges.

When the man was safely out of sight, Funston relaxed and broke into a grin. It was all a charade – or so it seemed. He turned to a pair of officers who stealthily appeared from behind a curtain. "Well...?"

The two officers clapped their hands. "Bravo. Bravo. It was better than real. You can make a living on the stage, sir."

They were cooking up something fishy, conditioning the mind of Carlos Calderon. Instead of torturing him, such as by beating him black and blue or putting him through the rigors of the water cure, they delivered him to the tender mercies of a mind warrior.

Taken to a bare cell within the fort, Carlos was visited by Joaquin. "*Kuya*, why did you do this to me?"

"No, Caloy, there was a misunderstanding."

"You told me when you picked me up that nothing's going happen to me! That I'm going to be quickly released!"

"Yes, and that was the way I wanted it to be, but the Americans have something else in mind. I'm going to see General Funston to straighten things out."

Carlos wept. "You sold me," he sobbed uncontrollably. "You, Judas."

The fat doctor shook to his bones, staggered by the bitterness of Caloy's feelings.

The Americans were secretive about their plan. They seemed intent on standing up Carlos against the wall, and the thought drove the prisoner to the edge of despair. As if by design, his cell overlooked a barren yard abutting on a thick wall riddled by bullet holes and smeared with blood – not merely a place for target practice but a real place for execution by musketry. Or he might have just been paranoid. The ominous rolling of drums, the volleys of gunfire reverberating in the vicinity, the sight of a squad of riflemen marching in circles around the grounds – all these conspired to bring him to the brink of madness. The feeling of approaching death, untimely as it was undeserved, broke his mind and body. For all these, Carlos had his faithless elder brother to blame.

Details of the plan slowly fell into place. The day following his sentencing, a bearded American civilian paid him a visit to inveigle him to cooperate with the plan. He painted a happy picture of Manila at peace and a dark image of the countryside at war. He was part of the plot to poison the prisoner's mind in small doses.

The visitor grinned at him through the mat of hirsute beard. "Carlos, do you recognize me?"

Carlos was too preoccupied by thoughts of death to pay any attention.

"It's me, your brother's son-in-law."

Brother's son-in-law. The introduction shook him up, requiring him to connect the dots in his family tree to divine the meaning, and he recognized the visitor only when he made out the outline of Bailey's face under the beard. "So, it's you."

"Carlos, I'm here to help you."

"I've had enough help from relatives – that's what got me into trouble in the first place."

"Carlos, listen to me, I can get you out of this fix," Bailey continued excitedly, shaking the bars of the cell. "I have it on good authority that if we can get your cooperation on one matter, you're going to get a pardon... That's straight from MacArthur's mouth. Clemency, they call it."

"What cooperation? What clemency?"

"Freedom. As in you walk. Scot free. Home." Bailey flailed his arms for emphasis, then continued: "It's this. Listen carefully. We understand that until the day you were captured, you were in the company of Emilio Aguinaldo and you know where he can be found, his hiding place. Very well. In other words ... if you can guide a company of troops to his camp – help us capture him – you're out of this calaboose. Got it? The Army will erase your conviction. And to top it all, the insular government will give you 50 hectares of land wherever you might choose to live. You have my word for it – and Godawful MacArthur's, too."

Carlos grumbled: "What good is their word – I can't even trust my own brother."

"Carlos, papa has got nothing to do with your problem. He is merely being used by the Army for its own ends, unwittingly. He's exerting every effort to get you out of here. And I'm pitching in for the sake of Estrella and the peace of mind of papa who's been without appetite for the past few days. This is a family problem, and we're all working together to solve it."

Far from being relieved by the news that his family was working for his release, Carlos was saddened: he couldn't believe that his elder brother would stoop so low in his bid to win his release by, in effect, trading him for the hide of Aguinaldo. The plan lacked any subtlety. Using his brother to work on his emotions, the Americans were pressuring him to guide a contingent of U.S. Army troops to the hideout of the elusive Aguinaldo. It was far worse a crime than stealing $200 from the pocket of Uncle Sam because this involved the betrayal of El Jefe, the light and soul of the revolution. "May I please speak to my *Kuya?*"

Joaquin met with him alone in the cell after pleading with his guards for privacy. He had taken an extended leave from his duties as Cordillera administrator to attend to the problem of his brother whom he had handed over to the Americans on the expectation that he, Carlos, was going to get the same treatment accorded him: a warm welcome and an appointment to the insular government. It turned out that his superiors had other ideas.

"Is this what you want me to do, *Kuya?*" he asked dejectedly.

"No, I don't know, it's going to be your decision. Do what you think is right."

"But why did you turn me in?"

"I was asked by General MacArthur himself. I was in the Cordilleras when I received a letter from the general asking me to report to Intramuros immediately. Then, somehow, they

416

managed to convince me to bring you in. All along I was thinking you were going to given an appointment."

"Barton, he told me –"

"I never proposed such a thing to the Americans – asking you to betray El Jefe. That's beyond the pale."

"What do you want me to do then?"

"Do what you think is right."

"Barton is asking me to do it."

"My son-in-law still has his loyalty to the U.S. Army. He doesn't speak for the family."

"Tomorrow, they're going to stand me up against the wall."

Calderon dabbed his eyes with a silken handkerchief. "I'm sorry, dear Caloy. I can't do anything about it. I'm just a civil servant. My influence with my superiors is limited."

"If I had to take Barton's advice, I should sell El Jefe down the river so I can escape the firing squad."

"That's his idea. When I told him that I turned you over to the Americans, he immediately went running to his former superiors. I think he was the one who cooked up this whole idea."

"This is terrible. We got an enemy within the family. We married Ella to a wolf in sheep's clothing."

"I don't want to hear of it, Caloy," Joaquin said wearily, caught in a web of conflicting emotions.

As Carlos remained intransigent, the Americans proceeded to carry out his execution on a Sunday morning. They fed him his last meal, summoned a priest to give him his last rites, bound his arms, and led him to the firing range at the back of his prison cell. With drums rolling in the background, he was marched against a wall, escorted by a priest mumbling incantations every step of the way, a parody of that infamous execution at the Luneta five years before. So, this was how Rizal must have felt when he was being marched to the Luneta which was just a short distance away. However, his was an execution without a redeeming cause, without a last farewell in poetry, without a mourning crowd. He caught sight of two drummers marching into the courtyard to the melancholy percussion of their drums, followed by a squad of riflemen with stony faces and rigid steps.

As the squad arrayed itself in a line twelve paces from the wall, Carlos felt the blood deserting his flesh so that his face turned pale and cold as his palms. His knees buckled under the weight of realization that he was at the threshold of death and as the squad leader put a blindfold on his eyes, darkness sealed all hope of salvation. I don't deserve this, I can't die like this, the thought kept throbbing with his heartbeat. He had to do something now to reverse this fate. Suspended in eternity, he heard the priest switch from chanting Latin verses to small talk. "If I were you, son," he whispered, "I will take the 50 hectares."

Carlos then felt hands lifting his blindfold slightly while groping to secure it in place, thereby enabling him to catch a glimpse of the squad of riflemen.

"You can say your last words now," said the squad leader.

Carlos said nothing.

"Listos! Apunten!"

"Wait!" shouted Carlos. "I want to confess…"

26

A HUNT IN THE JUNGLE

Past midnight, on March 10, 1901, a gunboat rode the waves of a stormy sea off a distant coast. It was the farthest one could go from Manila if one had to cross the whole breadth of Luzon Island because the gunboat was now skirting the waters of the Pacific. The sea was much rougher here than in the South China Sea which lay on the opposite side of the island off Manila Bay. Aboard the boat was a party on a head-hunting mission with no less than Aguinaldo's head as the trophy. An odd collection of troops and irregulars, the band consisted of 80 Macabebe tribesmen, 2 Tagalog guides and 5 white men.

Viewed from the vessel in the wee hours of the morning, the coast was just a blot of darkness. There were no bonfires on the palm-fringed shore and no moonlight in the overcast skies to light the landing place. The captain steered the ship along the coast by dead reckoning, calculating the distance to the shore and the landing place by time elapsed and occasional glimpses of stars in the sky. The gunboat *Vicksburg* was a three-masted steamer with an elongated prow that stuck out like a fishing rod and a row of portholes lining its hull. Its naked masts stood uselessly in the wind, with its bundle of cables and halyards whipping in the wind.

As the gunboat skirted the Pacific coast of Luzon powered by its steam engine, the waves rolling unbroken from the high seas slammed down hard on its starboard, curling over the deck to thrash the bulkheads, whip the masts and wash the portholes. The waves were a lot stronger than most of the passengers could take. The repeated pounding of the waves sickened most of the soldiers packed in its holds and cabins like slaves of old. But one man was unfazed by it all: Barton Bailey.

He was ensconced in a gondola hung 30 feet up in the mainmast. Equipped with binoculars, he peered through the wind in search of telltale lights around the inlet of Casiguran, 150 miles east of Manila. If they were lucky, a 17th century Spanish lighthouse should guide their way, situated on a promontory overlooking the Pacific. In reaching the secluded bay, the party had to take a roundabout course around the serpentine coast of Luzon, from west to east, a journey that stretched hundreds of miles over a period of three days. It was the fastest route towards their destination, considering that the alternative was to hike over steep mountain ranges and lush tropical rainforests that covered much of Luzon Island. A sailor, Bailey preferred this route, and after being out of commission for almost a year, he was glad to be back in action as part of an audacious mission organized by General Funston.

It began to rain, cold drops from the sky that the wind spattered on his face – but he remained on his post. When rammed by a big wave, the boat would tip over along with the mast, and Bailey would cling precariously to the gondola, a wicker basket wrapped around the post. The slightest tip of the ship was exaggerated into a sweeping motion of the mast at his height, so that he kept teetering on his perch like a caterpillar on the tip of a blade of grass. In the rain everything he touched became slippery. He could slip on the stand, lose grip of the mast and tip over the gondola.

The driving rain was not altogether a bad sign. It minimized the chances of their landing being seen by unwanted eyes, for surely it would have driven almost everyone into taking shelter to sit out the inclement weather. This was a secret operation, borne of unconventional thinking by weary officers intent on defeating the offbeat tactics of an enemy who had managed to stretch out the war to an inconclusive mess.

The wind died down to a breeze. The rain eased to a trickle. Correspondingly, in an example of the harmony of nature, the waves slowed down to a crawl and lapped at the sides of the ship. All these were signs that the gunboat was now deep inside Casiguran sound, a carrot-shaped inlet protected from the Pacific by a sliver of land and flanked on the mainland by the spine of the Sierra Madre mountain range, which was topped with knuckles of rock running the whole length of its crest. He smelt land. He smelt jungle. The first rays of the sun broke past the hills that lined the strip of land on the east. The horizon glistened and opened the morning hours on the eastern coast of Luzon. It was indeed Casiguran sound, pristine and crystalline as Manila Bay was not. He became restless in the gondola and he sloshed the water that pooled at his feet.

"It's land, ahoy," he shouted playfully, like a South Sea explorer. "Land, land everywhere."

His drenched shirt sticking to his flesh, he climbed down the mainmast by gripping a series of holds.

From the bridge, newly promoted Brig. Gen. Frederick Funston emerged wrapped in a woolen sweater. He assessed the situation with the skipper, an elderly officer who used to captain the gunboat *Petrel*, and decided they must throw down the whaleboats and paddle the rest of the way to the shore a mile away. The captain was not familiar with the conditions of the coast which had no natural harbor or obvious mooring place.

"Roll over one of the boats, Bailey," ordered Funston.

"The whaleboat, sir? The outrigger?"

"Anything that will float, unless you can walk on water. You're a sailor, you should know what to do!"

This man really gets my dander up, Bailey muttered good-naturedly. He held the Kansan in the highest regard, although he still had difficulty calling him "general." In his mind, Funston was as much a hero as old Dewey, although the two couldn't have been more different.

Helped by the Filipino crewmen, Bailey dropped four boats from the portside, including two native outrigger boats called the "banca." He took command of the landing because he was conversant with the Filipinos who composed the bulk of the raiding party. He herded them ten at a time aboard the whaleboats, which were repeatedly dashed to the hull of the mother ship by waves. As the first whaleboat rolled on the water, the Filipino soldiers boarded it gingerly one at a time, already seasick from the three-day journey. The outrigger boats could take only seven persons each, being no bigger than the canoes of the Indians, and they looked so fragile that their seaworthiness was suspect.

The air buzzed with Tagalog talk as the first batch of soldiers filled the four boats. Among the Filipino soldiers, Carlos was the most seasick, not having ridden a ship across the seas before and he spent the whole journey retching on a rug on the floor, so that, by the time Bailey led him onto an outrigger boat, he was already walking on water. Bailey paddled the outrigger boat expertly together with a Filipino crewman of the *Vicksburg,* using his oar to steer and propel the boat like a flipper. The outriggers of bamboo rode the waves like wings in the wind and performed the function of a keel in steadying the boats as they climbed the crests and dove into the troughs. Light and agile, the rigged-out canoes left the whaleboats lagging at their wake and reached the shore ahead.

It took six trips of the four boats to bring all members of the raiding party onto the beach together with their meager provisions, a task that took the whole morning to complete.

They gathered at a rocky stretch of beach of Casiguran sound, shaded by palm trees that grew wild by the sea. By a stroke of good fortune the landing was undetected. As soon as the assembly was complete, they took their lunch of dried fish and rice, supplemented by coconut meat taken from the wild palm trees. With only five white men among 87, the party did not look like an American force. It was not meant to be. Wearing the rugged uniforms of insurgents topped by straw hats, the party of mostly Macabebe tribesmen was dressed to look like a guerrilla company marching towards El Jefe's secret headquarters in the jungle. The five white men – General Funston, Bailey, two lieutenants and a Kansan private – were made to appear as captured Gringo soldiers, unarmed and unkempt. Accordingly, they traveled light in the manner of half-starved Filipino troopers, without rucksacks and wagons of provisions. The success of the plan depended solely on the loyalty of the Macabebe tribesmen, the only armed members of the contingent, and on the reliability of the two Tagalog guides. Absent either, the five Americans were up for slaughter.

The objective of the mission was the capture of Aguinaldo. The plan was hatched in the fertile mind of General Funston, now commander of the Third Infantry Brigade of the regular Army, to which he was commissioned after the 20th Kansas Regiment was sent home. In planning his masterstroke, two events coincided to fire up his imagination. The first event was the capture of a Filipino courier named Seguismundo who was found carrying a packet of letters written in a cryptic language. Funston put his best men to work deciphering the message scrawled in a jumble of words neither Tagalog nor Spanish. Over pots of tea and boxes of cigars, they discovered that the letters were written in reverse in an obscure Igorot dialect – instructions to different guerrilla commanders to commence certain kinds of operations, signed variously "Colon Magdalo," "Capitan Emilio" and "Dictator." The cryptographers concluded that the letters had only a single author: Emilio Aguinaldo himself.

The counterpart incident that gave birth to the plan was the arrest of Carlos Calderon, a rebel craftsman who knew the way to Aguinaldo's headquarters across the Sierra Madre mountains. The information provided by the two Filipinos landed the Americans a windfall of intelligence that formed the necessary ingredients to the plan. Funston laid down before the brass the rough details of his plan: He would lead a band of about a hundred Macabebe scouts and five American volunteers to the Sierra Madre mountains. The natives would pose as guerrillas and the Americans their captives. In every village they passed, the "guerrillas" would subject the "captives" to indignities in order to bolster their credibility and spread the word around. Once they had gained access to Aguinaldo's lair, the Macabebe tribesmen, headed by the Tagalog guides Seguismundo and Carlos, would present Aguinaldo with a gift of five American captives. Then, at the drop of a hat, the Macabebes would overpower the guards in the camp and secure the premises while the five Americans would turn on Aguinaldo himself. They would then spirit away the prized captive to the nearest American outpost. Outlandish and impractical, the idea was shot down by the brass.

Funston, true to his swashbuckling reputation, was determined to carry out his plan even without the blessings of the Army. He'd recruit the hundred Macabebe tribesmen himself and pick the four Americans from the disbanded Kansan regiment. "If the Army finds the plan too risky to put its official stamp of approval, I'll organize a band of volunteers myself," the grizzled Kansan passionately made his case before a meeting of the general staff presided over by military governor MacArthur. "The hundred long-hairs, I have them and the four American volunteers I can easily find among the discharged Sunflowers. Two years into this morass, anything is worth trying."

In his *Memories of Two Wars,* Funston recalled that the brass received his plan with considerable skepticism. "It was said that the Army brass cannot survive public criticism at home if the plan failed," he said. "So, I offered to organize a band of volunteers outside the chain of command... I realized perfectly well that according to the rules of the game a general should not accompany a detachment smaller than a company in size, but I initiated this enterprise and felt that I must see it through. Otherwise, I would be damned in my home State all the rest of my life and held up to scorn by all the corner-grocery tacticians in the country."

MacArthur, a tactician of the classic mold, refused to give the plan his blessings. "If General Custer couldn't get Sitting Bull with 600 men, I don't see how five Americans can get Aguinaldo, considering how the bastard has been running circles around our Army the past two years," he said, pacing around his map room. "It's the perfect plot for an adventure story, gentlemen, but the Army operates in the real world and this is not Arabian Nights." So high was the prestige of General Funston, the winner of a Medal of Honor for his heroics in the Luzon campaign, that the military governor finally allowed him to go off the reservation with a bunch of irregulars. The Army had nothing to lose and a war to win.

Funston set himself to the task of organizing his private militia. He sent a Tagalog scout to the province of Pampanga to recruit a hundred Macabebe "long-hairs" from among the veterans of the campaign against Luna but managed to gather only 80, at wages of 50 cents a day. For hundreds of years, the Macabebe tribe was a prolific supplier of mercenary troops to the Spanish government which used them to quell the periodic rebellions by the Tagalogs and the Ilocanos. They proved true to their colors with the switch of sovereignty to the Americans.

A more ticklish task was getting the two Tagalog scouts to cooperate with the hated Gringos. The captured courier Seguismundo was a tough nut to crack. He had already been through the wringer after being beaten to a pulp, dunked in water and fed to the ants by his captors who had learned to fight by the laws of the jungle, but the man was grudging in his cooperation. Even if Funston were able to bend him to his will, he might later turn against the Americans once in the safety of the rebel camp. Accordingly, after breaking Seguismundo's resistance, Funston sought to recruit one more Tagalog scout with close access to Aguinaldo who was more pliant and reliable. He found one in Carlos Calderon, a former supplier of the U.S. Army and brother of a high-ranking Filipino civil servant.

Funston had a far easier time finding four American volunteers. He immediately recruited two from among his officers in the Third Infantry Brigade who stepped forward to join his adventure without being asked. The two others answered his call – a Kansan veteran of the Battle of Rio Grande and Barton Bailey. Of the four Yankee recruits, Bailey proved indispensable to the task of coaxing the cooperation of Carlos Calderon. Informed during a visit to the camp that Carlos was under detention, the discharged gunner immediately rushed to Fort Santiago to volunteer his help.

"I'll be damned," said the officer who received him. "You're the man General Funston wants."

"The colonel. Of course, Funston."

"He is now general."

Bailey saw Funston at his barracks near the Baluarte de Santa Barbara in time to save Carlos Calderon from the water cure.

"I'll talk to Carlos myself," he offered to the general. "He's one tough, bull-headed numskull, but he's scared of his elder brother, the doctor. I'll give it a try."

"Try to convince him," Funston readily accepted his help, knowing Bailey's facility with Tagalog. "It's either his cooperation or the firing squad."

"I'll lay it on thick on him, sir. Like this is what your brother wants you to do. You want him fired from his job?"

With not-so-gentle persuasion, Bailey was able to get Carlos on board. He had no trouble convincing his wife to allow him to perform one last service for the U.S. Army, telling her that it would make it easier for him to wangle an appointment to the Customs by way of reward. His termagant of a wife was only too happy to get him off the cockfighting arena and back in uniform.

With all the men that counted on board, Funston embarked on his dangerous enterprise on the *Vicksburg*. MacArthur was at the harbor on Manila Bay to see the party off at sundown, March 6, 1901. Despite his reservations, the military governor could offer no alternative plan for ending the war, having emptied his bag of tricks, from the conventional tactics of the Civil War to the ruthless scorched-earth methods of the Indian Wars. "Take care. This is a desperate undertaking, I fear that I shall never see you again," MacArthur is quoted as saying in Funston's memoirs. The Kansan snapped to a salute, clicking his boots together. "Whatever happens, sir, we shall make the U.S. Army proud." He turned around, then walked up the gangplank as the gunboat prepared to weigh anchor. On the other hand, filled with pessimism, MacArthur waved the party goodbye with a languid flick of his hand, his tired eyes shaded by his dented fedora, his body stooped by the crushing responsibilities of a colonial master.

The *Vicksburg* sailed into the sunset of Manila Bay with its improbable contingent of adventurers. With its three masts standing naked and its elongated prow leading the way, the gunboat began an odyssey along the sinuous coastline of Luzon toward the south, skirting the South China Sea, then slowly turning east into the interior seas of the archipelago. It passed between islands of Mindoro and Romblon and nameless islets that littered the sea lanes, barged through schools of sailfish fleeing colleges of shark and chased fishing boats on their way to fertile fishing grounds. The steamship followed the twists and turns of the tail of the Luzon Island which stretched interminably south, searching for the exit to the Pacific Ocean. To reach the eastern high seas, the vessel had to thread the narrow San Bernardino strait, the gateway to the soft underbelly of the archipelago, then push against the strong currents that flowed through the strait like floodwaters at high tide. Finally, the ship had to battle the headwinds from the Pacific and the giant waves that thundered down uninterrupted from the stretch of water whence Magellan came.

Palanan, the destination of the party, lay just five miles west from the Pacific coast of Luzon. Funston could have landed on the nearest beach and marched to the jungle camp of Aguinaldo, said to be 13 miles from the open sea. For secrecy's sake, however, he decided to land at a secluded beach of Casiguran sound 60 miles to the south, intending to hike on a roundabout route to Palanan, a grueling 11-day trek along rough terrain. Accordingly, early in the morning of March 10, the party disembarked from the *Vicksburg* at the remote cove, unobserved by native informants.

They had two weeks to find Aguinaldo and return to the coast. On the 25th of March, pursuant to the plan, the *Vicksburg* would reappear at Palanan Bay to fetch them. If none of them showed up, part of the crew of the ship would make a forced march to the nearest barrio to gather information about the fate of the mission. The crew was under strict instruction not to initiate hostile actions and to set sail for Manila on the 27th, with or without Funston's raiders.

The sun burst through the clouds and beat down on the heads of the assembled raiders on the beach. At two o'clock in the afternoon, Funston issued orders to commence the 11-day march to Palanan. They would keep close to the coastline of Luzon, within sight of the sea, to avoid losing direction. Still dazed from seasickness, the Macabebe troops lugged their straw bags on their backs, secured by rattan loops around the shoulders, then they made a beeline for the distance uncomplainingly. The less hardy Tagalog scouts, Carlos and Seguismundo walked in their midst together with the five American "captives." It was the first time the two scouts were reunited since the assassination of Esteban Zaragoza, and the sight of each other filled them with mutual shame. They had once worked together to carry out El Jefe's orders but now they were collaborating to bring about his downfall. But after convincing themselves that their mission served a higher patriotic cause, i.e., the end of pointless bloodshed as only the perfumed ilustrados who had surrendered before them could articulate, they threw themselves into the mission with a firm sense of purpose. It was "Segui" who had led Carlos to Captain Zaragoza and it was the same man who would take the Americans to the doorstep of Aguinaldo. They left a trail of trampled sand that the waves swept and smoothened at their wake. The sun baked their heads for hours so that their ears felt like shriveled mushrooms sticking off their scalp.

For his part, Bailey walked in deep thought. The only thing that held the party together was Funston's faith in the mission. Everybody else in his party, including Bailey, went along out of loyalty to the Kansan who had led them through the toughest trials and battles in the war and who for sharing the same risks as ordinary foot soldiers had earned their abiding respect. Neither the prospect of loot nor glory motivated them. They walked toward the heart of darkness in answer to Funston's call to join one more campaign to extricate the U.S. Army from its quagmire.

Still, Bailey began entertaining bouts of skepticism. What if the insurgents blew the cover off the Macabebes and engage them in a firefight in the middle of the jungle? How were they going to fare in a battle without sufficient arms inside rebel territory? Even assuming that they managed to infiltrate Aguinaldo's headquarters, how long would they be able to keep up the charade before the wily revolutionary chief woke up to the trick and turned the trap on them? Assuming, furthermore, that by the most optimistic scenario they were able to seize El Jefe, how far could they flee before other insurgents learned of the raid and swooped down on them in a bid to rescue their leader? Such imponderables troubled Bailey as he plodded along on the sand.

Then, there was the problem of the reliability of the two Tagalog scouts. Carlos and Seguismundo were both traitors to Aguinaldo. They could sell the Yankees down the river, too.

"Carlos, how far are we to the camp?" he asked his in-law in broken Tagalog.

"I hate to think about it. At the rate we're walking, following the length of the coast, a low of ten days, I think, and a high of fifteen," said Carlos. He had sufficiently recovered from his seasickness and his wound to keep pace with everybody else. "We could have landed right on Palanan Bay and it would have taken us just three days. But I understand we guerrillas are not supposed to have a navy to ferry us around." He laughed.

"Is he still there, Aguinaldo? You seen him yourself?"

"I never reached his camp because I got wounded and had to turn back. But we're on the right track, just follow the coastline and we're bound to reach the town."

"And how about you, Segui?"

"I've seen him, señor. So starved and so tiny. I could wring his neck with my bare hands," replied the messenger, a squat chubby fellow with a wry sense of humor.

"And what is he doin' now?" Bailey pursued further.

"He has this big map in his room, full of pen marks. He meets with his commanders every month and keeps in constant touch with them through messengers like me."

"Does he ever leave his camp?"

"Seldom nowadays, señor, if ever. He has found what he thinks is a perfect hideout, deep in the jungle."

Funston sidled towards Bailey whose command of Tagalog allowed him to wring out information from the scouts. "What are the gooks saying?" Told of the details of their talk, the general nudged him. "Okay, keep an eye on them. If you smell a rat, just give the sign and we'll finish them off."

"Aye-aye, sir."

Late in the afternoon, their way was blocked by a river delta that opened into the Casiguran sound. The coast turned into a marshy, impassable basin covered by a mangrove forest. Here grew masses of the nipa plant, dwarf palm trees that grew in tight bunches and hedged the banks of the rivers, crowding the view with their frilly foliage. From their leaves were made the straw hats that the rebels sported, along with their sleeping mats, bags, the roofs and walls of their shelters that served as tents, among countless other applications. The Tagalog scouts led the party along a murky river that offered the only passage through the mangroves wherein they warded off fronds of the nipa plants that thrived in the briny water, with pliant ribs lined with thorns and sharp leaves capable of cutting a man's skin. Bailey blazed the way for Funston so that the general could slip through the passage cleared by him. He would push a palm leaf out of the way, and long enough to clear his leader, but as soon as he freed the frond, it would whip the face of the next man and riddle him with thorns. There was nothing he could do to protect the general from the stink of rotten plants, the stifling humidity and the delirium of indirection.

The mangrove basin bubbled with pools of swamps screened by the crowd of nipa. The party balked at crossing so forbidding a barrier that seemed capable of sucking a whole company of troops without a trace, save for spitting out their boots that floated. Fortunately, they came upon a decayed mahogany log conveniently spanning the breadth of the quagmire, its branches sticking to the air to act as holds, and they fumbled their way slowly to the other side.

At night they found themselves back on the coast and smack against the churning waves, and they pitched their camp under a line of coconut trees. In the moonlit night, Bailey had the feeling that they had come full circle. Why, the landscape looked unchanging. It was indistinguishable from the place where they made their landfall, with the same onrushing waves, the same flora and fauna and the same wavy patterns on the sand. The only sight that looked new to him was of a naked Funston doing some laundry work under the stars in waist-deep waters where he scrubbed the mud off his pants and the grime from his tunic. He was joined by two other American officers who started a prank by stealing Funston's pants from under the water, triggering a good-natured fracas broken by shouts and laughter. It was a pleasure to see the stern disciplinarian stark naked, romping like a little boy for a change. By and by, Bailey was lulled to sleep under the stars by the soothing swish of the palm leaves.

"Okay, everybody up!" the drillmaster's voice of Funston roused him from his sleep. "Gather your kits, bury your trash and get moving! We have a long way to go."

"Are we not eating breakfast first?" Carlos wondered.

"We eat on the go. The Macabebes are done cooking."

And so it was another dreary march in tropical heat past a monotonous landscape.

Later in the day, the party met its first test. They filed into the fishing town of Casiguran, ten miles from their landing place which lay directly in their path. In his memoirs, Funston took pleasure in relating how they pulled off the charade of having the five Americans play prisoners while the Tagalog and Macabebe scouts paraded them as their captors. In the town plaza, the mayor even greeted them with a marching band and then launched into a long-winded speech praising the bravery of the captors. The irony of the speech was not lost on Funston and Bailey who soaked it up with a straight face. They observed with satisfaction that their Filipino companions played their roles to the hilt, thereby proving their loyalty to the mission. Noting this episode, Funston further wrote that he rather "felt bad" about how he had taken the mayor for a ride but he hoped the man "had a sense of humor."

Bailey became a victim of his own trickery when Carlos took advantage of the situation to pick on him. On their way out of town, the mayor gifted them with a sack of rice which Carlos, playing the mean captor, ordered Bailey to carry without any help until he almost collapsed.

Outside town, Funston retook control of the troops whom he congratulated for their exemplary conduct in the town. "Everybody did his role very well, the folks really fell for it. If we can keep this up until the end, I have no doubt about the success of our mission."

"Too well," Bailey frowned at Carlos. "You played your role too damn well."

Carlos shrugged. "You've done worse things to us."

432

"What do you mean?"

"You treat prisoners worse than animals."

"Hell, you were wined and dined out there."

"The others, I mean. When I was in the mountains, my comrades complained of water cure, beating, being fed to the ants..."

"I never done that thing!" protested Bailey. "I never saw anybody doing that thing."

"Carrying rice, that's nothing to get upset about, that's what we do on the march all the time."

There was hardly any talking when they began the second leg of their journey, a 50-mile headlong assault on the jungle. They had to turn inland because the coastal route had become impassable as the sand turned to rocks then to soaring cliffs. The jungle was more accessible by virtue of its ability to entice men with the promise of food and water, which could be wrung out with great difficulty. It was a ten-day journey that proved the usefulness of the bolo manufactured by Carlos and which served finally to vindicate his skills and worth as a man, without which victory for the Americans would not have been possible. Without the bolo, the Americans could not hack through the thickets that choked the undergrowth of the forest. Without the bolo, they could not slash the stem of the bamboo tree to drink the water that filled its segments, or hack open the coconut shell to devour its meat or kill the occasional snakes that were disguised by the roots of trees, or cut the vines to serve as ropes or sharpen the stakes to hold down their tents. The man who operated a humble foundry in Manila at the beginning of the war became the instrument of the Yankees' success in the last stages of the conflict. When their Krags and Fletcher cannons proved useless, the Americans picked his bolo to cut them a route through the jungle and sunder the insurgents' last line of defense.

Within a day's march of Palanan, Funston dispatched "Segui" to the rebel headquarters with a letter from one Tomas Claudio, the purported "leader" of the Macabebe band, informing Aguinaldo that he was approaching camp with a company of guerrillas and five prized Yankee prisoners. As Funston explained it in his memoirs, he didn't want the rebel chief to turn suspicious about the approach of a large body of armed men into his lair. In his choice of Segui, Funston considered the advice of Bailey that Carlos could not be trusted with the job, having proven faithless in the past. It was better to keep the dog on short leash, as it were. Besides, the wily Aguinaldo would never believe the story that the sneaky Carlos had suddenly raised a rebel army to return to the fight after abandoning the march in the Sierra Madre mountains. At the mere mention of the man's name Aguinaldo would likely smell a rat.

"Just be cool about it and not let on," Funston told Segui. "Tell Aguinaldo you have taken five Yankee prisoners during an operation in the south."

"And also that you have intercepted their payroll," butted in Bailey. "That will get him excited."

"That's right," seconded Funston.

"Or if you wish, I'll shoot him between the eyes already," said Segui exuberantly.

"Don't do any such thing!" Funston restrained the courier. "We want him alive."

"If you will allow me to go, I'll help explain it to El Jefe," volunteered Carlos.

"Stay with us," said Bailey curtly.

Segui's relaxed jocularity and guileless ways had earned the Yankees' trust. He disappeared for one day, then came back with tantalizing details of the conditions in the enemy camp. So well did he play out his role that he was able to bring back a bagful of salted meat, courtesy of El Jefe.

"Is he there?" Bailey asked, hungry for news.

"He's there, playing checkers all the time. And he sent this wild boar meat as a gift," Segui said, glancing at Carlos.

"Anyone else?" Funston was all ears.

"About fifty men. And double the number of civilians, mostly women and children."

"No other camps nearby?"

"None that I could see."

The report that only fifty rebels were in the camp relieved the Americans. One would expect the headquarters to be teeming with hundreds of guerrillas on leave from their hit-and-run attacks on American camps.

"You're a beaut, Segui." Bailey pinched the fat Tagalog on the cheek.

"But there's a problem," the scout continued. "He doesn't want to see all the Americans, just their leader brought before him. The rest will have to be kept in a stockade across the river."

"What does he mean by that?" asked Funston, puzzled.

"Maybe he thinks it's not safe for him to see all of you at the same time or there's not enough space in the house."

"We can't do that."

Funston was not about to go along with Aguinaldo's wishes even at the risk of the plan being compromised. He was going to enter the insurgent camp with all four Americans in tow to make sure he had enough officers to direct a firefight if one broke out. The plan was for two of them to enter Aguinaldo's house, including Funston, while the remaining three would wait outside, all surrounded by their Macabebe escorts. Upon the signal from Funston, delivered by means of a furtive scratch of his beard with his hand, five of them would jump on Aguinaldo while the rest would raise their firearms to secure the house and repel any resistance from the outside. With the plan explained and understood, they followed Segui to the rebel camp located at the edge of the jungle 13 miles from the sea where Bailey found himself in a familiar location that recalled the town in the mountains where he was married to Estrella. Like the typical Filipino barrio, it was set in the middle of a clearing, with two rows of huts lining both sides of the main road of hard-packed earth, plied by a traffic of carabaos dragging wheeled wagons or spindly sleds. Women sat on the bamboo steps of the houses, winnowing rice grains or weeding out lice from their daughters' hairs. There was no visible military activity in the place and nary a soul around carrying a weapon. In the middle of the village stood a huge building of wood and thatch without walls which served as the barracks of the rebel soldiers, filled with empty cots laid side by side on the dirt floor and with sagging hammocks festooned between posts. A lone cannon was positioned like a battering ram at its entrance, where one had an unrestricted view of the interior filled with about 20 men tinkering with metal parts. Beside the huge shelter, separated by a fence, stood a two-story house made of hardwood, with a balcony extending from upper floor – apparently the residence of a rich landowner. There, inside the imposing dwelling hid the target of the largest manhunt ever conducted by the U.S. Army since the Indian Wars, Emilio Aguinaldo, president of the first Philippine republic.

His transformation into a warlord began with the killing of Luna. Without his ablest commander, Aguinaldo took a step down from his political role and assumed direct command of Luna's conventional army – which he promptly led in a disastrous campaign against MacArthur's Eighth Corps. The result was the loss of Cabanatuan, his second capital, and every other town where he made his stand. From October 1899 onward he went into a headlong northeasterly retreat across the wilderness of Luzon, past the Cordillera highlands, over the Sierra Madre mountain range, and on to the remotest jungle of Isabela at the typhoon belt of the Pacific coast.

It was while smarting from the drubbing he got from MacArthur that Aguinaldo got an epiphany. Why fight the Americans on their own terms when he could very well resort to the unconventional tactics practiced by his forefathers that turned his weaknesses into strengths? On November 12, 1899

436

he disbanded his army and dissolved the front. He saw that he could better use his inferior weapons in hit-and-run attacks by small bands of rebels operating by surprise against random targets at unguarded moments, night and day, such as by ambushing patrols and burning isolated camps. He divided the country into sectors comprising towns or entire provinces, each headed by a guerrilla chieftain who waged a campaign of attrition in his territory. From his headquarters deep in the mountains of Isabela, he maintained contact with his commanders through a network of couriers such as Seguismundo traveling by horse or carabao or on foot.

In his own words proclaimed to all his commanders in secret dispatches, Aguinaldo's strategy was to "harass the Yankees in the barrios where they had camps, to cut off their convoys, to cause all possible harm to their patrols, their spies and their scouts, to surprise their detachments. The guerrillas shall make up for their small number by their ceaseless activity and their daring."

MacArthur took note of the insurgents' change of strategy in his 1900 Annual Report to the War Department: "Wherever throughout the Archipelago there is a group of the insurgent army, it is a fact beyond dispute that all the contiguous towns contribute to the maintenance thereof. We have ceased to meet fixed Filipino resistance and have lost contact with their organized army. Indeed, it is now the most important maxim of the Filipino tactics to disband when closely pressed and seek safety in the nearest barrio... The success of this unique system of war depends on complete unity of the entire native population."

An American soldier, quoted by historian Le Roy, put it more earthily: "Since the insurgents have adopted their guerrilla methods of attacking weak parties of Americans and boloing men who get outside our lines, a feeling of intense bitterness has sprung up among our soldiers. It is the old cry: 'The only good Indian is a dead one.' Some of the most atrocious butcheries have been committed by the Filipinos, cases where a dozen or more natives have killed a single American and hacked the body frightfully. The news reached the nearest post, and a scouting party goes out to the scene of the killing. It can be imagined that the comrades of the murdered man do not feel in a merciful mood, and they moved to burn the village and kill every native who looks as if he had a bolo or a rifle."

The toll on American morale, much more than on lives, was horrendous. Cases of barbarities committed by crazed American troops abounded, from torture to wholesale massacre. The U.S. Army found itself at a loss for tactics for combating the brush fires that erupted indiscriminately in unforeseen places in the countryside. The most infamous atrocity of the war occurred on the island of Samar on September 28, 1901. Then, a band of guerrillas surprised the members of Company C of the 9th U.S. Infantry who were attending the mass in the town of Balangiga. In an orgy of hacking and stabbing lasting less than an hour, 48 Americans were slaughtered, leaving 28 survivors to drag themselves back to their camp to tell a tale of horror. Their commander, General Jake "Hell-Roaring" Smith, vowed to turn the island into a "howling wilderness." He issued orders to his men "to kill and burn. The more you kill and burn the better you will please me. I want all persons killed who are capable of bearing arms against the United States." His men did as they were told until the interior towns of Samar flowed blood. For ordering the massacre of countless civilians, General Smith was tried by court martial, convicted and forced to retire in disgrace.

Bailey knew nothing of the atrocities, having left the Army during the conventional phase of the war to raise a family in Manila where he boondoggled the time away in blissful ignorance of what was going on in the countryside. What he knew of the horror stories came from second-hand tales of former comrades spread in the bars and cockpit arenas of the city. Whatever the truth of the matter seemed irrelevant to him now. He had his own compelling motive in taking part in the capture of Aguinaldo, the most dangerous man in the country.

The arrival of his group of five Yankees in the hideout surrounded by disguised troops did not arouse much curiosity among the villagers unlike their passage through the town of Casiguran. As the band neared the thatched barracks on one side of the road, idle guerrillas stood to ogle at the five American prisoners without taunting or saying a word. They were used to seeing large numbers of guerrillas pass by town. None of them seemed to recognize Carlos Calderon who deliberately hid himself in the middle of the marching troops, his usefulness having ended. Someone must have informed the occupants of the adjacent building of their arrival because a figure appeared at the balcony under the loft to take a peek at the company, then quickly vanished from view.

Bailey caught a fleeting glimpse of the figure on the balcony. It was a slight, frail-looking officer with closely cropped hair. Was it Aguinaldo? Why did he disappear so fast? Did he notice something suspicious in the approach of a hundred armed strangers?

Segui cheerfully towed two of the Americans toward the wooden house together with the Macabebe leader Tomas Claudio and his "escorts." The Tagalog scout did not even bother to knock. With an air of familiarity, he herded the group into the door, talking aloud to herald their approach to the people upstairs.

The wooden floor rumbled with the sound of boots and clogs. The staircase shook under the weight of nine men climbing toward fates unknown. Laughter echoed in the stairwell as the Macabebe troopers continued to exchange banters to relieve the air of tension.

Bailey tried to calm his nerves. He seemed to float in the air as he climbed the stairs one step at a time. He fixed his eyes on the heels of the boots rising on the steps above him while absently brushing the pistol tucked deep in his pants. His head bobbed over the floor to bring him level with the host then face to face with three rebel officers with holstered pistols and bandoliers. He stared in awe as each of the officers gave Segui and Tomas a warm pat of welcome. With a flourish of his cap, the Macabebe leader showed his two Yankee prisoners, Funston and Bailey, to the hosts.

The leader Aguinaldo stepped forward. He was wearing a khaki uniform bare of ornamentation and was almost overshadowed by his officers. He took a good look at the prisoners who tried to appear forlorn. *"Los gringos estan cansados.* The Gringos look tired," he remarked.

"Sí, sí, El Jefe," laughed Segui. "We made them hike for two weeks."

"Where did you catch these poor fellas?"

"We were on our way to burn their camp in Cabanatuan at night," Segui related proudly, "when we came across a patrol crossing a stream just outside the town. We fell on them and killed six. We then gave chase and caught seven of them but two got away."

"I'm very proud of you. I'm glad that even after I have retreated to this faraway camp, my people have not lost their ardor for the revolution. They continue to fight for freedom, with vigor and honor and desire to win."

Bailey found it difficult to associate the spare, ungainly figure, whom he had first spotted at the balcony, with the legendary warrior who had tied up the 70,000-man strong U.S. Army in the tropics. He seemed older than his 32 years, displaying bristles of gray on his head, folds of weariness on his Mongoloid eyelids and furrows on his mahogany-brown face. Foregoing his fondness for gaudy military dress, he was decidedly unimposing and his voice was soft and polite, without the slightest hint of peremptoriness.

"It's regrettable that I could no longer lead my army in the field. But tell me, comrades, you've been to the big towns, what do the people think of me? Do they still remember me?"

"They do, señor presidente! They all consider you their leader," Segui assured the chief. "They know that every engagement is done upon your command. You are everywhere.

They haven't forgotten you at all."

"I hope they understand why I preferred to stay out of public view. You can't tell your enemies from your friends nowadays, with many of my colleagues gone over to the other side."

"You can be sure the ordinary Filipino remains loyal to you," the sweet-talking Tagalog cooed. "Forget the ilustrados and the mestizos. It's the vast number of *indios* that matter."

Go ahead, work him up to a lather, Bailey silently urged while stealing sidelong glances at Funston to prompt him to scratch his beard. The man's hands drip with the blood of hundreds of American soldiers hacked in cold blood, he thought. Through the window Bailey could see the straw hats of the Macabebe tribesmen gathered outside the building, with the three dented caps of the other Yankee officers mingling with them.

Sensing nothing, Aguinaldo ushered them to a larger room dominated by a display of his rack of swords, a Moro warrior's shield, a conquistador's finned helmet and other war artifacts.

"By the way, how long did it take you to get here from Cabanatuan?" he asked casually.

"Two weeks."

"Two weeks! It took me two months. You must have ridden something fast."

Segui found himself groping for an explanation. The deception was starting to unravel. "Well, we rode..."

"A ship?" wondered Aguinaldo.

Bailey began to get alarmed. If the Tagalog were allowed to continue talking, thought he, he would soon blow their cover to the skies. He glanced at Funston who, for the first time in the war, seemed suspended in indecision. Come on, cut the crap, scratch your beard! Bailey itched.

Suddenly, the sound of commotion in the street distracted Aguinaldo's attention from the conversation. Shots rang outside the building – a sign of trouble. Aguinaldo rushed to the balcony and shouted over the balusters: "Stop that shooting, there's nothing to celebrate, five captured *yanquis* are nothing to get excited about!"

With his back turned, Bailey and Funston stared at each other, the look of panic drawn on their faces. A punch to the chin by the Kansan set off the bedlam.

Bailey lunged at Aguinaldo as the latter turned from the balcony to face the visitors. He wrestled the man to the floor and covered his body while Segui caught the flailing limbs.

For his part, Funston, seeing that Bailey had beaten him to the draw, threw himself at the two other rebel officers, assisted by the five Macabebe tribesmen, but the two rebels were put on guard in the split second that Funston hesitated. They fell back on a rack of swords on the wall and were able to draw their pistols as their assailants rushed to disarm them. They managed to discharge a couple of rounds before being overpowered by the six men.

Bailey did not mind the commotion behind him and kept Aguinaldo pinned to the floor under his body. He gripped the man's neck with one hand and his left forearm with the other while the others sat on his thighs and pressed on various parts of his body. As if that were not enough, Carlos Calderon came running up the stairs to lend a hand.

The excess of force almost crushed the rebel chief. He lay on the floor helpless as an overturned tortoise on the sand, lying on his back under the weight of three men.

In the meantime, gunfire resounded in the street, followed by a stampede. The shouts of Macabebe tribesmen holding up the entire neighborhood and shooting down resistance with their Mausers sent a message of urgency to the men inside the house.

Sprawled over the rebel chief, Bailey locked himself in position like a wrestler pinning down an opponent as the floor shook under him to the rumble of men scuffling, the screech of furniture toppling and clatter of swords spilling from their rack. He heard the voice of Funston announce over the din:

442

"Señor Aguinaldo, we are the United States Army! We are putting you under" – pant – "arrest."

Bailey relaxed his hold on Aguinaldo but the two scouts held their grip like terriers. He tried to rise but felt his strength deserting his body.

"I'm General Frederick Funston, commander of the Third Brigade, United States Army. By virtue of the authority vested in me by the governor-general, I'm arresting you on charges of insurrection against the United States government. Tell your men not to resist. We have 200 hundred men deployed around your camp, ready to cut down any resistance. Follow us, if you value your life and the lives of your men."

Bailey rolled to his side to allow Aguinaldo to rear his head and face Funston, but the move took effort. He felt a creeping wetness on his backside that spread to wreak paralysis on his body. He had been hit on the back with a pistol shot, the bullet barely missing his spine to lodge in a vertebra. With a groan, he slipped free. "I'm hit, kernel," he said before collapsing.

Aguinaldo rose to a sitting position and faced the bores of Mauser rifles. He glanced at the Macabebe scouts, then fixed his eyes on Carlos Calderon whom he recognized hovering over him. "Traitors," he spat.

Funston moved to wind up the mission. "Okay now, on your feet. Get moving." He ordered a march back to the sea.

Barton Bailey woke up to find himself lying on a bunk inside a cabin of the *Vicksburg*. He was rocked by the constant pitching of the ship in the choppy waters roiled up by the wind that carried torrential rains. He could see the water washing over the portholes to becloud his view of the sea and he could hear the waves drumming at the bulkheads – an onslaught that added seasickness to his many maladies.

"Get me a doctor," he cried deliriously in the night. "My father-in-law, where is he?"

"Bear with us a few more days," said Carlos, who was attending to him. "The captain said we're heading home full steam."

"Where's Colonel Funston?"

"He's with Aguinaldo."

"Call him, please call him..."

The feverish Bailey desperately sought the attention of General Funston who was responsible for his recovery from the yellow jack. He was a demanding patient, constantly whining and blabbering. He was tormented by fever inside while rocked by the storm outside. Several times the skipper came down to say that Funston was equally indisposed, that he was fighting off seasickness and a bum stomach, and that, in any case, he could not leave an interview with Aguinaldo. In truth, Funston had no taste for nursing chores and no interest in seeing Bailey in the middle of a storm.

"Carlos, I'm gonna die."

"Stop thinking of it, brother. You're going to make it! Manila is only two days away and Joaquin is going to take care of you immediately upon our arrival."

Swimming at the fringe of unconsciousness, where he could see the image of the Grim Reaper behind a shroud of smoke, he dictated his will to Carlos. "I'm going to leave all my belongings with my family. But since I'm broke, ain't got much to give. All my back pay goes to my wife, Estrelle, so she could buy a farm and provide for my kid. My cap and uniform I give to Tad so that he will remember me as a soldier and share my love of country. And I give all my thanks to my father-in-law Whacky Doc Calderon for giving the hand of his lovely daughter to me, a simple man that I am, and for tolerating all my faults and my monkey business, and I now beg for his pardon with all my heart, that I may rest at peace with my conscience."

With those words – which Carlos had trouble committing to memory – he went to deep sleep, broken by intermittent snoring.

27

AGUINALDO... AT LAST

There is a picture of Aguinaldo standing aboard the *Vicksburg* as it was about to weigh anchor off the coast of Palanan. He is wearing a safari helmet and carrying a leather bag by the sling. He is unattended by the American crewmen who are busy going about their business on the deck.

The capture of Aguinaldo precipitated the end of the Insurrection. Just as they followed his lead into every battle, his officers followed him into detention at Intramuros – and eventual amnesty. It was noteworthy that the last officers to surrender were all of the unlettered stock, the ilustrados having made the trek long before the imminence of defeat.

The Calderon family rose back to prominence by the good graces of Governor-General Taft, and they were taken back by their town folks in Malolos without a stain of stigma as a consequence of their role in the capture of Aguinaldo. The rewards that Joaquin in particular reaped put him back near the top of the totem pole of Filipino society, right back to where he was during Spanish times, even perhaps higher, given that he now had official title as minister in addition to the honorifics of his profession.

News of Funston's arrival reached military governor MacArthur at Malacañang Palace by the Pasig River to which he had transferred residence after the ouster of Otis, only in turn to face eviction by Taft. It was the bleakest day in his career. He had been relegated to ceremonial duties in the capital by a civilian governor-general. His superiors in Washington was blaming him for the stubborn insurgency, fighting which was a thankless duty conceded him by the clever Taft. Roused from his sleep in the early morning of April 1, 1901, he hurried out of his palatial residence to meet an important visitor. He tied his robe and shuffled to the veranda, where Funston was waiting.

MacArthur was incredulous to see the Kansan whom he had dispatched on a dangerous mission at the Manila harbor.

"Well, how did it go?" he asked the Kansan.

"He's right here, in the other room!"

The military chief stood petrified as he digested so astounding a news, then rushed to the visitor's room to find Emilio Aguinaldo seated on a sofa, guarded by two soldiers. There, he tried to strike up a conversation with the prisoner but the latter was cold and reticent, besides understanding no English.

The news of Aguinaldo's capture equally buoyed up William McKinley in Washington who was struggling with the growing unpopularity of his colonial policy. However, he didn't live long enough to see the good tidings from the Pacific restore faith in his quest for America's Manifest Destiny. On September 6, 1901, while attending the Pan-American Exposition in Buffalo, New York, he met his end. He was shaking the hands of a line of well-wishers when he reached to shake a hand wrapped in a handkerchief. Flames shot through the handkerchief which hid a .32-caliber Iver-Johnson revolver. The first bullet crushed a button on his vest and glanced off his breastbone. But the second bullet hit him below the ribs, pierced his stomach and burst his kidney, thereafter lodging in his pancreas. As he lay in the arms of a Secret Service agent, he called out to the crowd who had pounced upon the gunman, later identified as Leon F. Czolgosz, 28: "Don't let them hurt him."

McKinley underwent two operations that for a time appeared to put him on the way to recovery. On the seventh day, he abruptly went downhill. Digitalis, a drug ground out of the seeds and leaves of the herb foxglove, was injected to stimulate his heart, to no avail. On September 14, he died after uttering his last words: "It is God's way. His will, not ours, be done."

The immediate cause of his death was gangrene which wasted the tissues around his wound and along the track of the bullet. His killing had nothing to do with the war. Czolgosz was an ardent anarchist who wanted the world rid of imperialist leaders, from the Tsar right down to McKinley.

Theodore Roosevelt mounted the presidency and the bully pulpit to carry on McKinley's imperial policy in the Far East. On him, the most virile of presidents and the youngest at 43, fell the task of completing America's conquest of the Philippines.

On the Fourth of July, 1902, amidst the firework displays that marked independence day celebrations, President Theodore Roosevelt appeared before a cheering crowd to declare that the Philippine Insurrection was over and that the Stars and Stripes flew unchallenged over the islands.

Mi Último Adiós

[Composed by Jose Rizal on the eve of his execution]

¡Adiós, Patria adorada, región del sol querida,
Perla del mar de oriente, nuestro perdido Edén!
A darte voy alegre la triste mustia vida,
Y fuera más brillante, más fresca, más florida,
También por ti la diera, la diera por tu bien.

En campos de batalla, luchando con delirio,
Otros te dan sus vidas sin dudas, sin pesar;
El sitio nada importa, ciprés, laurel o lirio,
Cadalso o campo abierto, combate o cruel martirio,
Lo mismo es si lo piden la patria y el hogar.

Yo muero cuando veo que el cielo se colora
Y al fin anuncia el día tras lóbrego capuz;
si grana necesitas para teñir tu aurora,
Vierte la sangre mía, derrámala en buen hora
Y dórela un reflejo de su naciente luz.

Mis sueños cuando apenas muchacho adolescente,
Mis sueños cuando joven ya lleno de vigor,
Fueron el verte un día, joya del mar de oriente,
Secos los negros ojos, alta la tersa frente,
Sin ceño, sin arrugas, sin manchas de rubor

Ensueño de mi vida, mi ardiente vivo anhelo,
¡Salud te grita el alma que pronto va a partir!
¡Salud! Ah, que es hermoso caer por darte vuelo,
Morir por darte vida, morir bajo tu cielo,
Y en tu encantada tierra la eternidad dormir.

Si sobre mi sepulcro vieres brotar un día
Entre la espesa yerba sencilla, humilde flor,
Acércala a tus labios y besa al alma mía,
Y sienta yo en mi frente bajo la tumba fría,
De tu ternura el soplo, de tu hálito el calor.

Deja a la luna verme con luz tranquila y suave,
Deja que el alba envíe su resplandor fugaz,
Deja gemir al viento con su murmullo grave,
Y si desciende y posa sobre mi cruz un ave,

Deja que el ave entone su cántico de paz.

Deja que el sol, ardiendo, las lluvias evapore
Y al cielo tornen puras, con mi clamor en pos;
Deja que un ser amigo mi fin temprano llore
Y en las serenas tardes cuando por mí alguien ore,
¡Ora también, oh Patria, por mi descanso a Dios!

Ora por todos cuantos murieron sin ventura,
Por cuantos padecieron tormentos sin igual,
Por nuestras pobres madres que gimen su amargura;
Por huérfanos y viudas, por presos en tortura
Y ora por ti que veas tu redención final.

Y cuando en noche oscura se envuelva el cementerio
Y solos sólo muertos queden velando allí,
No turbes su reposo, no turbes el misterio,
Tal vez acordes oigas de cítara o salterio,
Soy yo, querida Patria, yo que te canto a ti.

Y cuando ya mi tumba de todos olvidada
No tenga cruz ni piedra que marquen su lugar,
Deja que la are el hombre, la esparza con la azada,
Y mis cenizas, antes que vuelvan a la nada,
El polvo de tu alfombra que vayan a formar.

Entonces nada importa me pongas en olvido.
Tu atmósfera, tu espacio, tus valles cruzaré.
Vibrante y limpia nota seré para tu oído,
Aroma, luz, colores, rumor, canto, gemido,
Constante repitiendo la esencia de mi fe.

Mi patria idolatrada, dolor de mis dolores,
Querida Filipinas, oye el postrer adiós.
Ahí te dejo todo, mis padres, mis amores.
Voy donde no hay esclavos, verdugos ni opresores,
Donde la fe no mata, donde el que reina es Dios.

Adiós, padres y hermanos, trozos del alma mía,
Amigos de la infancia en el perdido hogar,
Dad gracias que descanso del fatigoso día;
Adiós, dulce extranjera, mi amiga, mi alegría,
Adiós, queridos seres, morir es descansar.

ACKNOWLEDGMENT

The English translation of part of Jose Rizal's *Mi Último Adíos* is by Edwin Agustin Lozada. Accounts of Felipe Agoncillo's visit to the White House on October 1, 1898, and President William McKinley's speech before Boston's Home Market Club on February 15, 1899, among others, are based on Margaret Leech's *In the Days of McKinley*.

I took copious notes from the Thomas Jefferson Library of the U.S. Information Agency in Sen. Gil Puyat Avenue while researching the book in 1985-1986.

I thank my brother Ferdinand for his critique of an early draft and valuable help with editing.

Finally, may I thank the National Library of the Philippines for the original accounts of Commodore George Dewey and his captains concerning their individual actions in the Battle of Manila Bay of May 1, 1898.

WMG

THE AUTHOR

Wilfredo Garrido is a lawyer dabbling in literature. He hails from Jaro, Leyte, the Philippines. He graduated from the University of the Philippines College of Law in 1991 and since then has been practicing law in Makati City. He is also the author of *Stolia* (1984), *The Trail of the Chop-Chop Lady* (2008) and *Wild Roosters* (2008).

www.ingramcontent.com/pod-product-compliance
Lightning Source LLC
Chambersburg PA
CBHW031246170626
46807CB00001B/3